Se
Vow

BOOKS BY NATALIE MEG EVANS

The Dress Thief
The Milliner's Secret
A Gown of Thorns
The Wardrobe Mistress

the Secret Vow

NATALIE MEG EVANS

bookouture

Published by Bookouture in 2018

An imprint of StoryFire Ltd.

Carmelite House
50 Victoria Embankment
London EC4Y 0DZ

www.bookouture.com

Copyright © Natalie Meg Evans, 2018

Natalie Meg Evans has asserted her right to be identified
as the author of this work.

All rights reserved. No part of this publication may be reproduced,
stored in any retrieval system, or transmitted, in any form or by
any means, electronic, mechanical, photocopying, recording or
otherwise, without the prior written permission of the publishers.

ISBN: 978-1-78681-760-0
eBook ISBN: 978-1-78681-759-4

This book is a work of fiction. Names, characters, businesses,
organizations, places and events other than those clearly in the
public domain, are either the product of the author's imagination
or are used fictitiously. Any resemblance to actual persons, living or
dead, events or locales is entirely coincidental.

For Mel Hayman, the light at the end of the tunnel

Thanks also to my wonderful agent, Laura Longrigg, for helping me arrive at the point where *The Secret Vow* became reality and not simply an idea, and to Kathryn Taussig, my talented editor at Bookouture.

Part One

Chapter One

Winter 1918

The train from Stockholm to Gothenburg was on time, thundering through the dark towards the first light of morning. Harry Morten dropped his cigarette case into his coat pocket, where it clunked against penknives, fish hooks and assorted, vital, travelling kit. He'd been going to allow himself a cigarette, until he spotted the woman in the otherwise empty carriage. She was rocking a baby in time to the bludgeoning sway of the train, staring through the door window where rags of steam mixed with the dawn.

Harry had left his sleeper compartment to see the sunrise. Swedish skies in winter were capable of an intense smelting of reds and oranges. He fancied a dawn like a Viking boat-burial on a sea of snow. A memory to carry away with him. But he'd take this woman's company instead. Young, dressed all in black. He sensed she needed help and would not ask for it.

He leaned his shoulder against the carriage wall, his fur *ushanka* hat absorbing the vibrations. He'd noticed her with her family, waiting to board at Stockholm. Three shrouded women, a babe in arms and a fourth woman with a red kerchief knotted under her broad chin. Two sisters, their mother, a baby and their maid was his guess. He'd listened to them whispering in Russian.

From Gothenburg, ships sailed to Britain, France and America, which gave a clue to their possible final destination. Paris was a favourite bolthole of refugee Russians. If that's where they were going they were in for a shock, as Paris was scarred by war, shaken by guns.

The train hit a smooth section of track, and he heard the young woman singing to the baby in her own language:

'There was once a beautiful princess and all the princes sought her, yet—'

The train bucked and the rest was lost to him.

Harry silently filled in the missing line. *All the princes sought her, yet she loved a humble woodcutter.* Something like that, or why make a song out of it? A moment later, he heard her singing again. She never went beyond *yet*, always returning to the start, over and over. It was mesmeric, like a Gregorian chant. It was certainly working on the baby.

She was a riddle in her black floor-sweeper coat, a morose shawl swathing her head and shoulders. But her eyes, which he'd glimpsed once, were sapphires under ice. As she pushed the shawl off her face, he discovered that her hair was fair, like his, and thickly plaited. He also noted a delicately moulded chin, a fragile neck. Fragility could be deceptive. As they boarded the train that morning, he'd tried to take a heavy-looking holdall from her, the same yellow bag that was at her feet now. She'd looked so weary. *Well!* She'd reacted as if he'd attempted some violation. He'd spread his hands in apology.

'*Izvinite.*' Sorry.

The lady he assumed to be her mother had pushed past him and waved him away. *Enough of you.*

Perhaps she had a point. He'd caught his reflection in the washroom mirror earlier and seen the coarse hair growth on his jaw. He was unkempt, remnants of outdoor living clinging to his skin, his clothes. They'd reach Gothenburg in an hour or so and once he'd collected any waiting messages from the telegraph office, he'd travel on to his father's house. In that haven of expensive soap and hot water, he would mend his appearance. As the train flew through a deserted station, sounding its whistle, the young woman sang more loudly. Harry moved towards her, pulled by her wretchedness.

'There was once a beautiful princess and all the damned princes sought her, yet…' This time, she finished, 'they threw her into the Lubyanka.'

A chill struck him. The woodsmen and herders he'd lived among these last weeks had spoken of the Lubyanka prison. Fleeing Russian nobles had brought tales of it into Finland and Sweden. The Lubyanka was headquarters of the Cheka, the secret police who carried out executions on behalf of the Bolshevik revolutionary government.

Harry watched, confused, as the girl laid her baby down on the floor. She swaddled the infant in its blanket and dropped tender kisses on the tiny face. He couldn't imagine why a mother would think the floor the safest place for her child, unless… *She couldn't… she wouldn't…* Yet he saw her take two steps back, then reach behind herself for the door handle.

He knew beyond doubt what she meant to do. Step out of the moving train backwards so she didn't have to see the flash of wheels or the blurred steel of the track.

'*No!*' He wasn't sure if he shouted it or thought it before he launched himself at her.

*

Eleven days earlier, Moscow

Katya Vytenis wound a stole around her shoulders, pushed her feet into slippers and went to her bedroom window. What kind of day lay ahead? The frost-ferns on the glass were too thick to see past so she opened the window, breaking the ice seal on the frame. She discovered that 1 November 1918 had arrived with a sunrise as pink as raspberry sorbet.

Katya drew her stole across her mouth. Nobody sensible stood at an open window in winter, but she needed to impress this view on her heart; trees and shrubs dredged in crystal. The motionless garden of their beautiful house, where icicles clicked and snapped as the sun rose. Downstairs in the front hall, steamer trunks stood waiting for the horse-drawn cabs that would transport them to the railway station. Katya and her family would leave with them. Since the Bolsheviks had seized power a year ago, life in Russia had become a gamble for survival. Her family belonged to the class the new regime had vowed to annihilate. The class that a million soldiers, brutalised by war, were impatient to butcher. Last July had seen the murder of the Imperial family. A week ago, friends of her mother's had been shot, their home set on fire. So, one last breakfast in the house where she'd been born and then to Paris, the safest city in the world. Katya would see tomorrow's sunrise through a train window.

By the time the family were breakfasting, the sunlight through the glass was blinding. Uncomfortable in a heavy skirt and a high-neck blouse, Katya refused the maid's offer of more tea and helped herself to water. With visions of elegant Frenchwomen in her head, she'd laced herself tightly that morning and was regretting it. Her breakfast of buckwheat porridge lay heavy inside her.

Katya was enjoying the water's freshness on her tongue when an elderly manservant shuffled in and presented a sheet of paper to her father.

'Wages due to myself and the cook, *comrade* Vytenis.' Ignoring the sarcastic, 'Thank *you*, comrade,' from Katya's father, the old man folded his arms. 'I trust you'll pay us before you leave here?'

'I'm sure you do, Konstantin.'

Grumbling, the old man moved to the sideboard where the maid was refilling the teapot from the steaming samovar.

'Enjoying your last day in your homeland, Yana Borisovna?'

'No.' The maid, a sturdy figure in a pinafore dress, blouse and apron, gave way to the sobs she'd been suppressing all through breakfast. Yana was most reluctantly coming with them to Paris as she had nowhere else to go. When Katya and her sisters had shown her France on the globe, and the route they would take through Scandinavia and around the North Sea, she had turned pale.

Katya's father glanced over Konstantin's bill and called the man back to him. He said, 'Your figures seem fair but unfortunately I can't pay you as I need every ruble for our journey.' Behind his neat, red-grey beard, Prince Ulian Vytenis's mouth kept its placid line but Katya knew what this moment was costing him. 'Fear not…' the prince gave a short smile as old Konstantin's face turned mutinous – 'Once we're gone, you may remove everything of value from this house and sell it. Pictures, furnishings, silverware.'

'Husband, no!' Katya's mother dropped her bread and reached for a salt-and-pepper set embellished with the Vytenis crest. 'What would he do with a piece like this?'

'Sell it at an outdoor market.' Ulian Vytenis shrugged bleakly. 'I've explained, my dearest, we can take only what we can carry. In Paris, we'll acquire what we need.'

His wife said bitterly, 'A family's past cannot be "acquired".'

'No, but it can be destroyed, which is why we leave in twenty minutes.' The prince addressed Konstantin again. 'Move nothing until our train has left. After that, it's all yours. I hope that in the joyous dawn of your new-found freedom, you won't forget to pay the cook.' Prince Vytenis reached for his wife's hand. She was crying too now, though more elegantly than her maid.

Katya did not like the way Konstantin was sizing up the massive silver-gilt samovar, the jugs and salvers on the sideboard, his eyes full of rubles. 'You haven't told anyone our plans, I hope?' she asked.

The old man looked offended at the question. 'Indeed no, Princess.'

But Katya heard a clear hesitation. As Konstantin left, slamming the door behind him, she turned to her father. 'Why don't we leave for the station right now, Papa, and have the trunks follow? I won't breathe freely until we're on the train. Mama, you agree, don't you?'

But her mother only became more distraught. 'I don't know… the snow will be over our ankles, surely?' She turned her tear-stained face to her husband. 'Could I walk to the station, dearest?'

'Katya, be patient.' This was Vera, the eldest of the three Vytenis sisters. She was still picking at her food. A new mother, Vera ate only to be able to breastfeed her baby. She'd taken no pleasure in anything since her husband's arrest last Christmas. 'I certainly couldn't trudge through the snow, holding up a coat-hem and carrying a baby at the same time.'

'Nor I,' Katya's younger sister, Tatiana, pitched in. 'I don't want to go anywhere on a train. There's a hideous disease killing everyone outside Russia. Polish influenza, they call it.'

'Spanish,' her father corrected.

'Wherever it comes from, I shan't dare breathe until we reach Paris.'

'You won't reach Paris at all in that outfit,' Katya pointed out. Tatiana had rejected all advice on what to wear for the journey, choosing a button-fronted dress whose green colour suited her coppery hair and made her eyes gleam emerald. But as Katya pointed out, unless their train carriage was hung with charcoal braziers as in the time of the old Tsars, Tatiana would freeze between Moscow and St Petersburg.

Petrograd. They had to remember to call it Petrograd. Katya said, 'We have to go. Right away. I feel it.'

Her father raised his hand. 'We'll await the cabs. It hardly makes a difference now and as your mother says, it's dangerous on foot.' He asked Katya to fetch the object under the silver stag-head candlestick on the sideboard.

She frowned. 'I thought we were leaving heavy luxuries behind, Papa.'

'I said *'under* the candlestick'.'

She found a parchment-coloured envelope and took it to him. He opened it.

'Our train tickets, Katya, and the letter from my cousin Count Lasunskoy, with his address in Paris, where we'll stay until we establish ourselves. See this?' Her father briefly exposed the head of a document, waiting for her nod before pushing it back out of sight. 'That humble sheet is our future. I put you in charge of it, Ekaterina Ulianova.' His formality solemnised the moment. 'Whatever else you forget or mislay, keep hold of that.' He rose, to take his final walk in the garden.

At Vera's request, the maid went to fetch the baby. When at last she returned – Yana was incapable of speed – she laid a wicker bassinet next to Vera's chair, saying, 'I wouldn't feed her yet, Vera Ulianova. Never wake a sleeping child.'

With a smile that dismissed the advice without offending, Vera picked up her daughter, dropping kisses on the baby's cheeks while her free hand loosened the drawstring neck of her blouse. With hair so fair it was the colour of beaten egg white and arresting, pale eyes, Vera Vytenis had been the belle of St Petersburg as one of the Tsarina's retinue during the season of 1913-14. Marriage proposals had poured in and she'd seemed destined for an enchanted future. Though they were not rich compared to other aristocratic families, owning only the Moscow house and a small manor and estate in the countryside, the Vytenis name was descended from ancient Lithuanian nobility. In the end, it was an up-and-coming architect, Mikhail Starov, who had won Vera. A story of love hacked heartbreakingly short. Within a fortnight of their wedding, Russia was at war with Germany and the army had owned Mikhail for the next three years. He had limped home at the cessation of hostilities and barely a week later Cheka fists had hammered on the door. Fifteen years in one of the new labour camps, for what? 'Subversive activities'. Twelve weeks ago, Vera had given birth to their only child, a premature daughter she had named Anoushka. She often spoke of setting out to find her husband. Though she adored her frail baby, Mikhail filled her mind, her heart.

'You aren't going to feed the infant here at the table?' Their mother looked scandalised at the sight of Vera's engorged breast.

Katya rolled her eyes. 'Mama, we're all women.'

Vera smiled. 'Feeding my baby myself, how revolutionary.'

Katya watched her tiny niece latch on. She also noticed that her sister's fingers under the baby's head were inky. Vera wrote every day to Mikhail, leaving letters on the hall stand to be posted to God only knew where. *It's why I'm so jumpy*, Katya realised. *I'm scared Vera will refuse to come at the last moment.*

A door shut in the depths of the house. At the same moment, a sound like spades biting into grit started up outside the window. Katya rose to see what was going on and stumbled over the baby's basket. Detaching her foot from one of its handles took several seconds, so that when bullets shattered the window glass and blew plaster from the walls, she was bloodied but not blinded.

Chapter Two

They all screamed. Vera curled her body around her baby while their mother gaped in horror at the blood trickling into Katya's collar. Yana whimpered prayers. Tatiana ran towards the window, only to be hauled back by Katya.

'Fool! D'you think they have no more bullets?'

Into this racket lurched Katya's father, cheeks ashen behind a slick of sweat. He stopped when he saw Katya's collar, but she assured him she was unhurt.

'What's happening, Papa?'

'Cheka thugs. The gates… locks cut. I don't know—' His ragged breathing suggested a hard sprint to beat the policemen into the house. 'I've bolted the front door but it won't hold long.' Hardly were his words out before there came a splintering crash. He went to his wife. 'Irina, rouse yourself. Let's not be caught like fish in a bowl.' Irina Vytenis simply stared up at her husband so he tried Vera. Vera also seemed deaf. A heavy-booted invasion was on its way.

'Katya,' the prince looked back towards the door, 'get everyone to the cellar. I'll draw them away. That envelope – quick, hide it.'

Katya made a tube of it and pushed it far down into the neck of her dress.

Ulian Vytenis tilted her face and kissed her brow. 'If anything should separate us, take shelter with my friend Emil Zasyekin. Yes?'

'With Dr Zasyekin. Yes.'

'You know where he lives?'

'Yes, Papa.'

'And if we are separated forever, take your mother and sisters to Paris. Remember who and what you are, my lioness.' He stroked her corn-yellow braids. 'A Vytenis, descendent of the warrior duke. Even if you run from here wearing one of Yana's old head-shawls, never forget it.'

'I will never forget.'

'Promise you will protect your mother, your sisters, your little niece with every drop of your blood.'

'And every fragment of bone. I swear it, Papa.'

'I believe you.' Ulian Vytenis walked from the breakfast room calling, 'I am coming. I am unarmed.'

Katya had never heard fear in her father's voice, but she heard it now as he confronted the men who had broken into his house. She prayed as Vera soothed her baby, who was filling the room with screams. Tatiana had disappeared and Yana had made a dash towards the kitchen. Her mother and Vera were immovable. Katya couldn't leave them, even as the doorway filled with men whose black leather coats bore red ribbons to mark the revolution's anniversary. They carried pistols and one held a rifle aloft, its barrel lengthened by a glinting bayonet blade. Her father stumbled into the room, goaded on the point of a second bayonet. His shirt collar had been ripped off and his nose was bleeding.

A waft of eau-de-cologne reached Katya along with the reek of unwashed flesh. It was so unexpected, she looked for a gentlemen among the mob until she realised that the fragrance was no compliment to the Lubyanka's bathing facilities. Eau-de-cologne was a vodka surrogate, swallowed when the real stuff was unobtainable. These men were drunk. It explained why, when her father put up his hands and asked for his family to be treated with respect, a man with a shaven head and razor-nicks above his ears kicked him violently. Ulian Vytenis crashed into the chair where he'd sat to eat his breakfast.

'Please, comrade,' Katya stepped between her father and the shaven man who seemed to be the leader. 'You saw those trunks in the hall? We're leaving everything. All this—' a sweep of her hand offered the sideboard and its contents, the portraits on the wall, the brocade window drapes. She saw toes poking beneath the curtains. So that's where Tatiana had hidden. Quickly, she drew the policeman's attention to the tableware. 'Solid silver. Take it all – oh!'

An open-palm slap whipped her neck sideways. 'Good try,' the officer jeered. 'We saw the trunks. Off somewhere nice, you filth?' Katya felt him looking her up and down and her flesh crawled. He demanded, 'Is it you?'

She stared dumbly back.

The policeman put the same question to Konstantin who had slunk in behind the last of the rabble. Whether to gloat or keep his booty from being plundered, Katya had no idea. Konstantin didn't understand the question either, so it was put again.

'Which of these bitches is the enemy of the revolution?'

'They're all enemies of the people, Comrade Captain.' Konstantin's fawning manner left Katya in no doubt who had cut the locks on the gates. 'And he,' Konstantin jabbed a finger at Katya's father, 'won't pay us. Arrest them all.'

'We've come for one traitor, not a wagonload,' the officer snarled. 'So let's help you remember.' At a nod, two square-jawed subordinates hauled Konstantin up by the underarms until he kicked. At a second nod, they dropped him in a heap. 'Memory improved, old man?'

'It's her.' Konstantin's wavering finger went past Katya, past Katya's mother. Seven pairs of drunken eyes swung to Vera who stood against the wall, a petrified Madonna cradling her baby. 'She's the counter-revolutionary.'

Vera shook her head numbly. 'I haven't been out of the house since my baby was born. How can I be anything but a mother?'

The officer recited, 'Vera Vytenis, you are under arrest for sedition and attempts to overthrow the people's revolution.'

'I am Vera Starova. Starova, not Vytenis.'

The officer shrugged. Two of his men tried to seize Vera's arms but they couldn't loosen her clasp on the child. When one tried to rip the screaming baby from her, Vera screamed too.

Katya ran forward, reaching through her sister's terror. 'Give the baby to me. Vera, to me.' She was pulled back, thrown down. From the corner of her eye, Katya saw her father struggle to his feet. Saw him limp to the sideboard and pick up the silver candle tree. Before she could call out, 'Don't, Papa!' he swung it in an arc and one of the policemen dragging at Vera dropped unconscious.

Like starving wolves, the men leapt on Ulian Vytenis, who fought like the devil. When they had finished with him, they took Vera and her baby.

Katya's retching sobs mixed with Tatiana's, with Yana's prayers and with their mother's crazed wailing. Smashed crockery and splintered chairs littered the floor. The carpet, a rare Caucasian rug, was a welter of blood. Blood everywhere, even on the curtains, the light fittings.

Why didn't we go when we could? Katya couldn't shut out the question, nor its tailpiece – *You should have forced Papa to listen. Now he's dead and it's your fault.*

Taking care not to look at Papa's broken body, she got to her feet. 'Tatiana?' Her sister was a trembling blur. 'Can you hear me?'

Tatiana gaped at Katya's blouse, red-daubed from cradling their father. 'What – can – we – do?'

'We're going to Dr Zasyekin's house,' Katya replied. 'Those men will be back.' She went to her mother. Princess Irina Vytenis still sat where she'd taken her breakfast, clutching her abdomen as if grief was ripping her apart from the inside.

'Mama, stop your noise.' Respect and daughterly obedience must be set aside. Papa had extracted a solemn promise. The envelope containing tickets and other documents inside her clothing reminded her of it. Giving up on her mother, Katya instructed the maid to go and find smelling salts. When Yana hesitated, Katya found a lethal fragment of a china flower bowl and tossed it to her. 'If you meet Konstantin on the way, you have my permission to stab him.'

The horse-drawn cabs came but Katya sent them away, bar the one they needed to take them to Dr Zasyekin's where they'd stay until Ulian was buried. They couldn't now leave accompanied by six enormous steamer trunks. That would only advertise their status as wealthy, unprotected women. They must disappear from Moscow like melting snow.

'Pack overnight bags,' Katya ordered her mother and sister.

But her mother clutched at her husband's hands as if her grief might spark life in him. Only after Katya, with Yana's help, had cleaned and dressed Ulian in his old white cavalry uniform and laid him out on a draped table with candles and icons around him, did Irina Vytenis consider the next hours of her life. She insisted they would be spent there, in her home, saying prayers for her husband's murdered soul, and waiting for Vera. 'Imagine if she came home and we'd gone?'

They won't release her that quickly, Katya thought grimly. Though they might, in compassion, hand over the baby. 'Papa trusted Dr Zasyekin more than any other man in Moscow, so obey his wishes and go there. I will organise a funeral, then enquire after Vera.'

Their cook came up from the kitchen to pay her respects to her master. Katya took the woman to one side and asked her to pack a bag with napkins, towels and baby clothes. 'And then, I want you to ride with my mother and sister in the cab, see they're safe. Oh, and see if you can buy some goat's milk on the way. It's on Komsomolskaya Square—'

'Goat's milk?' Cook looked baffled.

'—The doctor's place. Opposite the railway terminus. But please don't tell anyone it's where we've gone.' In any case, their stay there could only be a brief one. Like most educated Russians, Dr Zasyekin was of noble birth and it was possible that he too was under surveillance. 'Don't forget the milk. My niece will be returned to us, I'm sure of it, and she'll need to be fed.' After which, the authorities would surely accept that the charges against Vera were ludicrous.

Yana, standing by, grunted that the baby would most likely die. 'And you won't get her mother back.'

Katya bid the maid hold her tongue.

Yana bid her hold *hers*. 'I don't work for you, Ekaterina Ulianova.'

'My father paid you up to Christmas, so theoretically, you do.' Katya had never before had to deal with servants who argued back but she couldn't afford to antagonise the maid. So she tried to adopt her father's laconic, patient manner. 'No doom-mongering, Yana. Be helpful or say nothing.'

'I'm saying what is true,' Yana came back sulkily.

Patience be damned. 'I'll tell you what's true: my sister Vera will be free, her little one will thrive and you will end up on the streets. There.'

The noon bells were ringing by the time she waved off her mother and sister. Putting on her warmest boots and coat and a fur hat, Katya walked to the church to request an immediate funeral for her father. The priest-in-charge, who had seen so much violence over recent months, registered little surprise and quietly offered tomorrow morning. 'Can you pay extra, as it is such short notice?'

Grimly, she handed over half the money her father had saved for their journey. Returning home took courage but everything seemed quiet. She got to work, opening up trunks that had been so carefully packed a few days ago. Out came dresses, coats, furs, shoes and slippers. No time for sentimentality, for thinking about art galleries or the couture houses she'd imagined visiting once they'd arrived in Paris. Two trunks could be managed between them. They would take a hand-valise apiece so that if needs must, they could abandon the trunks and run. Yana edged into the hall, inspecting the piles Katya had made. Taking off the red headscarf she always wore – red was the colour of beauty as well as the worker's emblem – Yana gave Katya a sidelong glance, then tried on one of Irina Vytenis's hats.

'Every Russian should have one hat, but only one. To have more is decadent.'

Her mind elsewhere, Katya murmured, 'In Paris, I shall have a milliner make me twenty hats.'

'Like your father, you are a capitalist oppressor.'

Katya looked up, spurred to anger. 'My father was a badly paid museum curator who never oppressed anyone in his life. Now go, just go.'

Yana did not go.

'Stand by the door, then,' Katya ordered, 'and listen in case those thugs come back.'

Somebody had packed books inside a mustard-yellow carpetbag whose lining smelled of mothballs. Katya emptied it out on the floor. 'We'll hide our jewellery in this. That weasel Konstantin will have told the Cheka that we're loaded with treasure, so we need to be clever. See what you can do.' She pushed the bag over to Yana and set about repacking the reduced piles of clothing. Yana, at first grudgingly, unpicked the carpetbag's base. Into the space she created, she shoved rings, gold chains, religious artefacts, brooches and earrings, then re-stitched it using the sewing kit that hung at her waist.

'Is this good?' She showed the bag to Katya who tried it out. It felt weighty, but no one would guess what was hidden unless they picked the bag up and shook it.

'Yes. You've done well.' Katya took the precious envelope from inside her bodice, warm from her flesh. She extracted the document and most of the money, and making another small cut in the bag's lining, hid them deep inside. *Had Papa foreseen today's horror?* Fresh tears welling, she said to Yana, 'I'm glad you're coming with us. Papa knew we'd need help.'

'I am not coming.'

'But you must!' Katya pictured herself travelling with a mother half out of her mind with anguish, yet still needing help to dress and manage her hair. Irina Vytenis had never lifted a valise or travelled anything but first class in her life. No use relying on Tatiana, also on the edge of a nervous collapse. Or Vera if… *when*… they rescued her. And what would it be like, travelling for days or weeks with a tiny baby? She pleaded with Yana. 'After all, where else will you go?'

'I will get myself a husband.'

'You're thirty-four.' Katya could have added, '*with a downturned mouth and a bean-shaped face,*' but limited herself to asking, 'Who? A bearded Bolshevik who will punish you for being our servant, or will you lie down for Konstantin? Is that the plan, a life where you never run out of silver egg spoons and monogrammed salt pots? Fool. He's cruel and sly.'

Yana's cheeks crimsoned. 'I know that, but I understand men like him. We are the same, he and I. Same dreams.'

'I doubt it.'

'We eat the same dirt.'

'But you don't have to eat dirt! Did you know, in Paris, they bake wheaten bread that creaks when you break it and…' Katya's knowledge of French cuisine was limited to the restaurant dinners described by her parents, regular visitors to Paris during its lavish pre-war epoch. 'Duck in wine sauce, with truffles and the best dumplings.'

'Dumplings?'

'Mm. With every meal. Frenchmen treat their wives like queens.' *Or was it their mistresses?* Vera had whispered something about that. 'Anyway, they're awfully romantic.'

'They don't speak Russian and I won't speak French. A stupid, weak language.'

'There are Russians in Paris, so many, there's an enclave called 'Little Moscow' with an Orthodox cathedral as beautiful as any. There'll be plenty of men ready to appreciate a nice Muscovite wife.

And our cousins, Count and Countess Lasunskoy, will welcome us. You remember them?'

'Yes. They were rude to us servants, clicking their fingers.'

'There'll be no more of that.' Katya threw in everything she thought that Yana must surely want to hear. A fine house overlooking a park. A kitchen with a coal range that never went out. 'We'll keep other maids for the heavy work so you can saunter in the park each morning.'

Yana's eye went to the yellow bag. 'I need better wages. I will not be your serf. Nobody will shout at me again.'

Katya assented readily. 'Would you prefer a room that faces the street or the gardens?'

Yana sniffed. 'All I know is that war still goes on in France and to be murdered by those devils, the Germans, is no better with a nice view than without it.'

'France and her allies are winning, Yana. There'll be peace over there soon. Papa was sure of it.'

That earned a sceptical grunt. 'How do I know you will keep your promise?'

Katya reached behind her neck. She'd discarded her blood-stained clothes before going to the church and underneath the fresh blouse she'd taken out, she'd found a box stamped with the family crest. Inside, her string of Murmansk pearls. Perfectly matched stones with a teardrop pendant displaying the Vytenis Hart: a stag's head with fiery antlers. 'If I break my pledge, you may keep these.'

The maid held the string to the light before finally saying, 'Very well, I will come. But no more "Yana do this, Yana do that".'

'Understood. In return, no talk of Vera or her baby dying. Let's finish packing. I have to find out where Vera is before dark.' Within an hour, they were gone. Katya did not glance back at the home she was leaving forever.

Katya travelled the short distance from Dr Zasyekin's house to Lubyanka Square in a horse-drawn cab. Whirling snow was consuming the last of the daylight and soon, street lamps would be lit. Dr Zasyekin had been adamant she should not walk, pressing money on her after she'd explained her need to eke out every last ruble and kopek. 'Until we reach Paris, we have to live like paupers.'

'But not in my house,' he'd replied, fetching a bag of coins from a drawer.

She'd entrusted the yellow carpetbag to him and watched him lock it in his dining-room cabinet. For the first time in hours, she'd felt calm. Or was 'numb' a better word? In flat boots borrowed from the doctor's housekeeper, a plain scarf over her rich hair and a makeshift red ribbon on her breast, she looked more like a friend to the revolution than a Vytenis princess. It would be different when she reached the prison and had to give her name.

The Lubyanka was not an ugly building, but it was titanic in size. Which of those uncountable windows was Vera's view on the world? By the time the building sucked her in, Katya was perished with cold. She stammered as she answered barked questions at the front desk, certain she'd say something wrong and the guards would be called over. But somehow, she passed inspection and was sent to join the 'prisoner queue'. Subdued people bundled in scarves and fur hats. Nearly all of them carried parcels or baskets of food for the inmates. Katya hadn't realised she could bring anything for Vera, but she couldn't give up her place now. They shuffled forward an inch every ten minutes. Dead on five o'clock, a disembodied voice ordered everyone to leave. 'We are now closed.'

Back at Dr Zasyekin's she found her mother and sister sleeping side-by-side in the guest bedroom. Their heavy breathing sounded like the in-and-out of the tide and Katya eyed them enviously. A fire smouldered in the grate, making her toes and fingers tingle painfully. There was no second bed, just a sofa from which she removed a pile of baggage and Yana's threadbare cape. Where was the maid?

Unable to find her in any of the upper rooms, Katya went down to the basement kitchen and found Yana fast asleep on a camp bed beside the coal-burning range. The aroma of onions and garlic braising in a skillet made Katya's stomach growl. How long since she'd eaten?

The doctor's housekeeper, a solemn, older woman who had introduced herself as Olga Kirillova, looked up from her chopping board at the same moment as Yana issued a stupendous snore. 'It saves making up another bedroom and lighting a fire. Please, warm yourself, Princess. May I ask, do you bring news?'

'Not really.' Pulling a chair up to the range, Katya described her frustrating errand. 'Though at least I know Vera's in the Lubyanka. Her name is on a manifest, or whatever you call it. "Starova and infant". Have my mother and Tatiana emerged from the bedroom at all since they arrived?'

'No. Dr Zasyekin administered a sleeping aid. Would you like some?'

Katya shook her head, though she longed for oblivion. 'I'm scared to sleep. They don't heat the prisoners' rooms, do they? How many days will Vera survive, and the baby?'

'As long as the mother keeps making milk, the baby will be all right.'

They spoke Russian, though Katya had heard the housekeeper using French with the doctor, in an undertone. French, the language of the elite, was not safe to speak these days. 'It's good of you to take us in. I'm so grateful.'

The housekeeper wiped a hand across her eye which was watering from the vapours of the horseradish she was chopping. She was making *hron*, a relish with grated beetroot. A handsome woman for her age, unassuming in black, she seemed to embody two roles. Well-bred housekeeper upstairs, busy cook below. There were no other servants in the house.

'I was most sorry to hear about your father,' Olga Kirillova said. 'I enjoyed his visits. They argued about politics, he and the doctor, and sometimes they allowed me to join in. Usually, after the brandy was poured.' She looked uneasy all at once. 'You'll not stay longer than necessary? Please don't misunderstand me but one never knows… there are traitors everywhere. Sometimes, it is the most unexpected people. The doctor works so hard for his patients but he's not a well man, you must have noticed.'

Katya hadn't, to her shame. 'We won't outstay our welcome, I promise. It's good to meet someone so loyal. Dr Zasyekin is lucky to have somebody in his household who hasn't fallen under the Bolshevik spell.' She glanced at Yana who lay mouth-open on her pallet.

The housekeeper smiled, sadness trapped in her expression. 'I fell under a different spell, long ago.'

*

The following day, Ulian Vytenis was buried, unmarked, in a public cemetery far from the monastery where his forebears lay in their mausoleum. Katya attended, as did the doctor, Yana and their cook. Her mother and sister, floating on barbitone, slept in their borrowed bed. It was 2 November but to Katya, a century had crawled by since she'd looked out at a raspberry-ice dawn.

Coming down to an early breakfast the day after the funeral, she heard voices in the dining room. Expecting to find the doctor and his housekeeper, she was surprised to discover Yana serving tea. The maid gave a conscious start. Katya saw why at once. Yana was wearing her pearls.

Katya strode over and bid the maid stand still while she undid the clasp. Hot tea in her hand, Yana couldn't stop her, but she didn't hold back her opinion.

'You said they were mine.'

'I said nothing of the sort. When did you take them?'

Yana shrugged. 'At the house. I knew you would cheat me.'

Biting back a retort, Katya coldly asked, 'Will you please take tea up to my mother?'

When Yana had gone, she explained how she'd bribed Yana, telling Dr Zasyekin, 'I will do what I can for her in France, but I won't give up those pearls. They were my twenty-first-birthday gift from Papa.'

'Beware of promises, my dear.' The doctor got up to pull out a chair for her. 'Dreams are dangerous when fuelled by revolution. What have they gained, the peasants and the workers? Having broken our world, they are not a mite better off.' The news of his old friend's violent end, and the arrest of Vera whom he'd cared for so tenderly, had hit Dr Zasyekin hard. But it hadn't shocked him. He had told Katya that of ten university friends who used to meet to smoke cigars and put the world to rights, only he and two others survived. Of them, one had 'gone over' to the Bolsheviks and the other, a chemistry teacher who had worked at Moscow's best-known boys' school, had fled to Paris. 'They were both wise, in their way.'

Katya slipped into her place at the table. 'I understand you've been ill? Please forgive me. I should have seen it at once.' In all the years she'd known him, Dr Zasyekin had boasted a head of thick, black hair and a beard as full as an Orthodox priest's. No longer. Olga Kirillova had told her why. A few weeks ago, a patient had come to him with a burning fever, following a trip to Poland where influenza was rife. The doctor had tried to help, only to succumb himself. Olga had shaved him as he sweated and tended him. His beard and hair were now in the early stages of regrowth, giving his head an all-over bluish stipple. Katya told him he looked like a blackbird's egg.

He smiled at her impudence. 'As for you, you don't look like a girl who has just buried her father.'

'What does that kind of girl look like?'

'Like your mother or Tatiana. Drunk with grief, sleeping hard.'

Katya knuckled her eyes. 'I daren't weaken until I have Vera and baby Anoushka home.'

The doctor held her gaze then sighed. 'Make fresh tea, *pchelka*, save me the pain of getting up again.'

Katya removed the teapot from the top of the samovar that steamed on its bed of coal. She diluted the brew, pouring it into glass beakers, diluting hers further. The doctor stirred a generous spoonful of red jam into his tea. Katya looked for lemon, but seeing none, nor sugar, she too added jam. Cloyingly sweet and tangy, the tea coursed through her veins. She filled up on black rye bread spread with more jam before asking the doctor if she might show him a document that her father had consigned to her care. 'I don't quite understand it.'

Dr Zasyekin studied the certificate that Katya fished out of the yellow bag. He held his glasses close to it to read the flourishing script. 'It looks to be a fixed-term bank deposit, made in Paris, which at maturity pays the bearer 500,000 French francs.'

'That feels like an awful lot.'

The doctor grinned. His teeth were bad, she noticed. All that jam. 'It will keep you comfortable.'

'And what is "maturity"? You say it pays out "at maturity".'

The doctor pointed to a date next to a signature. 'The money is eligible to be paid out in two months' time. I recall your father sold some mining stock before the outbreak of war. Perhaps he invested the cash while he was in Paris. He made a trip there, d'you remember?'

'Yes, early in 1914. Mama and Vera went with him to buy wedding clothes.' Katya read, '"Franco-Russe Bank, rue de la Paix, 2e". Will they honour the bond, now Papa cannot cash it himself?'

'If your mother presents her credentials. Do you have identity documents?'

'In here.' Katya patted the close-fitting woollen jacket she had on. 'The Lubyanka queues form early. If you could lend me enough for another cab?' The high-denomination ruble notes hidden in the yellow bag could not be spent on the street without rousing suspicion. 'I can walk, I don't mind.'

The doctor stared into his tea for so long, Katya feared she'd overstepped the mark. But, looking up, he said gravely, 'I will give you money, but take my advice. Leave Moscow today. Get your family to Paris. Interceding for your sister Vera will be fruitless. The Lubyanka swallows its prisoners and the Cheka is everywhere.'

Katya sat down, stunned by the cold logic. 'I won't abandon Vera.'

'If it is the price of your family's survival?'

Katya could think of no answer, other than to put on her coat and shawl and leave again for Lubyanka Square.

'Not on my list,' she was informed by a desk clerk who blinked at her from behind thick spectacles. Katya had repeated 'Vytenis. Vera Ulianova Vytenis' three times. Dread owned every inch of her. What if Vera had succumbed to cold? Or if the Cheka had used their gun butts on her? Or violated her and thrown her from their car? The bodies of women were often found, frozen, in parks, on river shores… 'Please look again,' she begged. 'She arrived with a tiny baby.'

The clerk was adamant. 'There is no Vytenis.'

'Starova!' Katya exclaimed. She'd pulled out the wrong name. Her brain was like a bowl of fog. 'Vera Starova.'

A corner of the clerk's mouth lifted. 'Oh, her. In the lower section, but you can't see her. Traitors awaiting interrogation get no visitors.'

Katya's hand stirred in her pocket. Dr Zasyekin had given her all his available cash for a horse-drawn cab and something else from his cabinet. Something which, if offered at a carefully calibrated moment, might unlock a door for Vera. Scratching up a smile, for the clerk must surely have a heart of some description beneath his waistcoat, she said, 'I'd be grateful if you'd take me to whoever's in charge of her case.' She drew from her pocket a bottle of pre-war vodka, showing enough of its neck for the clerk to realise what he was seeing. 'So very grateful.'

The clerk leaned forward. 'Is that real?'

'As real as I am.'

'No fraternising!' The gunshot command came from a uniformed figure scrutinising the visitor line. Katya's clerk abruptly sat back. She was told to move away, to give the next person their turn.

She left the building. Snowflakes coating her lashes, she paced the square's slippery paviours until the urge to scream had passed. *What now?* She must either go back and join the rear of the line, or return to Dr Zasyekin's. She chose the Lubyanka and this time, she found her way unchallenged to a stairwell. She went down several flights and when she emerged – she could never say how much later – she carried two treasures: Vera's wedding ring and Vera's baby.

At the house on Komsomolskaya Square, she found a desolate scene: her mother propped on pillows in bed; Yana on the sofa, asleep under a mess of coats and scarves; while Tatiana cut a lonely figure at the window.

As Katya closed the door, Tatiana swung round, her eyes filling with question. 'Did you…?' Seeing Katya unbutton her coat to reveal a baby, naked and inert, she put her hand to her mouth. 'And our sister?'

'No. Wake Yana,' Katya said tonelessly. 'Anoushka needs to be warmed and fed. Somehow. Then we have to leave.' After waking Yana and transferring the baby into the maid's clumsy embrace, bidding her go down and seek the doctor's help, Katya pulled their travel bags off the top of the wardrobe where she'd put them the night before. 'Mama?' She found a strident tone. 'Get up and dress. We're catching the next Petrograd train.'

Her mother lifted her head, then sank back. 'Not without Vera.'

'Not without Vera,' echoed Tatiana.

Katya looked from one to the other. Did they not understand what the last hours had cost her? Of all the images quarrelling for dominance in her mind, her last sight of Vera was the most horrific.

'Vera is dead.' Katya displayed the wedding ring on her middle finger. 'I took this from her ice-cold hand.'

'You're lying.' Her mother turned her face to the pillow.

'Am I? Shall I tell you what they threatened to do with the baby?' Katya shook her head. 'No, I'll spare you. Vera is gone, and now we have to save her child.'

She followed Yana down to the kitchen where the housekeeper was chafing warmth into the limp little body. Later, the doctor showed them how to coax Anoushka to take drips of condensed milk from a pot with a spout.

'For ladies whose milk has dried too soon.'

Vera's milk had not dried, it had pooled out of her and frozen on her clothes. Katya concentrated on the drip and on the tiny, sucking mouth. Two hours later, they were on a train, steaming away from Moscow, towards a different life.

Nothing goes away from wishing. Eight days later, hurtling towards the coast of Sweden as dawn rose over the deaf, white countryside, Katya found her memories too much. Days of trains, boats and hard hotel beds, eking out the sleeping grains her mother had come to rely on. Buoying up Tatiana, mopping up Yana's mistrust. Keeping Anoushka alive, no space to grieve. The moment came when she couldn't be strong any longer and decided her family would be better off without her. All it needed was the train door to swing open and for her to lean back...

Chapter Three

Katya was knocked cleanly sideways. As her cheek burned against the carpet, she felt the inrush of wind, the clatter of wheels on the track, the summoning mewl of a terrified baby.

'Anoushka.' She was pinned down. Then dragged like a sack, down the middle of the carriage and, finally, hauled on to a seat. White birds were swooping – how could that be? Until she realised they were linen squares, blown off the headrests. Where she'd been standing moments before was a gaping rectangle, full of whirling steam and snow.

'Anoushka! Where is she?' She used Russian, the language of passion. An answer came in the same language, over the roaring air.

'I have her. A little late to think of that, no?'

A man she had exchanged a glance with on the platform at Stockholm had Anoushka clamped against his coat. A coat of thick, khaki cloth reinforced with leather. Grey-green eyes stared coldly down at her. She made out a strongly bridged nose and fair brows beneath a grey *ushanka*. The leather, the military colour, screamed *Cheka*! She lunged for the baby, but he kept Anoushka from her.

'What kind of mother throws herself from a train, leaving her child on the floor? She could have been sucked out.'

'Give her to me, you animal.' She found a patch of unguarded flesh between his cuff and his watch strap and sank her teeth in. He swore violently and she tasted blood.

'Animal? You're the one who bites.' Unexpectedly, he laid the baby in her arms. 'Don't move.' He strode back up the carriage, and Katya suddenly understood why.

A long whistle from the engine meant a tunnel, or another train coming from the opposite direction. *If the open door flew off its anchors…* it didn't bear thinking about. Katya buried her face in Anoushka's blanket. 'Forgive me,' she whispered. 'I'll never weaken again, I swear.'

The man – who had saved her life, she couldn't deny it – was reaching up towards the ceiling. His coat skirts cracked in the rush of air. He'd pulled off his hat, revealing hair fairer than hers. She'd already noticed his strong physique, but even he was struggling in the slipstream. If she'd fallen through that door, there'd have been little left of her by now. How could she have been so wicked? Her poor, poor niece, the tiny baby that needed her…

He found the communication cord and pulled it.

Did that mean arrest at the next station? Almost at once, she felt the train braking. *This is neutral Sweden*, she reminded herself. The man came back, carrying the yellow bag she'd abandoned in the chaos of the moment. As she snatched it from him, he asked, 'Have you left a husband somewhere? I know you're not travelling alone.'

His glance fell to her left hand. She'd put Vera's ring on her wedding finger, because it fitted and because it was convenient to let the world think her a widow with a baby.

'I have no husband.'

'Ah. I see.'

'No you don't. This is my sister's child.'

'Is that why you don't look after her?'

She lifted her head, lashed by the comment. 'That isn't fair.'

'No? Come on.' He held out his hand to her.

'Am I in trouble?' Her gaze swung to his belt, searching for a pistol. He didn't seem to be armed. Unless he had a hidden firearm in his pocket.

'Not from me,' he told her. 'I'm thinking the restaurant car might be open, for *fika*. You would like to join me? We've time, I think, before Gothenburg. Fine, stay,' he said as she shook her head, 'only, the guard will be along in a moment and you might not like explaining the open door.'

'*Fika*' meant coffee and pastries, whose smell made Katya shake with hunger. She sat with Anoushka wrapped tightly on her lap as her rescuer discussed something at length with the waiter. The men spoke Swedish. When they were alone again her companion explained, 'I asked why the train had stopped. Apparently a door opened by itself. It has never happened before and now the guard is having to check every one.'

'Oh.' She looked away, seeing their spectral reflections in the window. Her plaits were coming loose, her cheeks hollow, while he was somewhat bedraggled too, his hair falling in a hank over his brow. Without the *ushanka*, he looked younger than she'd first thought. About the same age as Vera's Mikhail. Twenty-eight, a year or two more? He'd undone the top buttons of his coat, revealing a tight-fitting jumper such as fishermen wear. No wonder she'd gone flying when he'd landed on her. He was built of solid muscle. This was the moment to introduce herself. To admit that he had saved her from a cowardly, despairing action. But his irises were a feral shade, as if he'd had wolves for grandparents. A tiny flicker disturbed a nerve above his left eye every minute or so and he was unshaven, his beard at the stubbly, impolite stage. His mouth ceded only occasional smiles. In every detail, he was an unsuitable recipient of confidences.

He raised an eyebrow. 'Which bit of me intrigues you?'

'You are Swedish?'

'Half,' he answered. 'Through my father. My mother was English.'

'She has passed away?'

'Several years ago.'

As the train began to pull away again, Katya forced out tepid words of gratitude. 'How fortunate you came into the carriage just as… well, never mind. Were you following me?'

'Don't flatter yourself. I came out to smoke.'

Anoushka kicked to escape her blanket and when Katya refused to free her, she began grizzling. Wordlessly, the man unstrapped his wristwatch, swinging it side to side. Anoushka screwed up her face and cried harder.

'Now look what you've done,' Katya snapped.

'Look what *you've* done.' He showed her the underside of his wrist, where her teeth had gone in. 'Do all Russians have fangs?'

'I've never bitten anyone before.'

'No? You're very good at it.' Anoushka had stopped crying, and was reaching in an unfocused way for the watch. He let her tiny fingers wrap around the strap. 'What is her name?'

'Anna Mikhailovna. Anoushka to us.'

'"Anna, daughter of Mikhail." Where is… Mikhail?' His Russian was competent, but staccato as if he didn't practise enough.

She pretended not to hear the question. 'Will you tell me your name?'

'Only if you tell me yours.'

She hesitated. One did not give first names to strangers, but she could hardly give her title either. He wouldn't believe her, the way she looked. Before this journey, she'd never realised how much of her identity was vested in her hair, clothes, posture. How much unearned approval her looks had brought her. Her treacherous inner eye gave her Vera in prison-stained clothes, hair matted from lying on a wood-plank bed. Gripping hard to the present, Katya gave her name as Ekaterina Ulianova.

'Russian, obviously. Are you ever "Katya" or "Katyushka"?'

'Only with family and those I trust.'

He took the frosty put-down. 'I am Harald Dagnar Morten, but most people call me Harry. You'll have noticed that I'm a poor Russian speaker. Do you have any French?'

She shook her head, though she spoke and read French fluently. With the revolution, they'd reverted to Russian, struggling to lose their Gallic inflection, covering up their lapses. Mama had been the worst, tagging every Russian phrase with, '*pas vrai?*' or '*n'est-ce pas?*' Katya wouldn't dare speak a word of it until she knew she was safe.

Their coffee arrived and a plate of cinnamon buns with almond-paste filling. Katya forced herself to delicately take the smallest of them. 'Thank you.' *Ha-rry.* She tried the name out in her head. She would not use it, of course.

'What is in that?' Harry Morten pointed to the yellow bag, which was lodged against her hip. 'You hang on to it like an albatross guarding her precious, single egg.'

'Anoushka's things mostly. Towels and clothes, tins of condensed milk, a few books. That's all.'

'It weighs a ton. *Tack.*' The waiter had placed a newspaper down beside Harry who, having thanked him, passed over a tip. He explained to Katya, 'I want to see how the war is going. Not that the Swedish press talks much about it. Tell me, why were you standing alone in an empty carriage?'

Because I dare not close my eyes. 'I am afraid of the baby catching Spanish influenza. You've heard of it? It's out of control. At one of our stops in Finland, there were coffins on the platform. The town had run out of places to bury their dead. Fresh air has to be good.'

'Maybe. Luck helps, too.' He glanced at the paper's front page, shaking his head at what he saw. 'No mention of war, nothing about the epidemic either. Did Anoushka's mother die that way?'

'No.'

'Her mother is dead, though? I'm guessing she was imprisoned?'

You guess too much. Hear too much. She drew in a breath. 'Yes, dead.'

'And her father?'

'He was taken to the Butyrka, a prison in Moscow, then sent somewhere else but we don't know where.'

'What did he do?'

'Remained loyal to the Tsar.' She shrugged. 'Mikhail believed vows to be sacred, and he took an oath of loyalty to the Imperial family. Like Vera, my sister, he never understood that sometimes you have to turn your face away…' Katya broke off.

Harry Morten responded thoughtfully, 'You speak as though you blame him, but could he have hidden his feelings for a lifetime? Truth usually makes itself known.'

The way he looked at her made her long for the journey's end. His features were as hard as any Cheka policeman's, yet he brought a flame to her belly, a dangerous urge to unload her mind. She hitched up her coat, intending to take her leave but the train sounded its whistle and before she could gather herself, a tunnel had swallowed them. The lights in the dining car weren't working and for maybe fifty heartbeats they sat in utter blackness. Katya waited for her new acquaintance to take advantage. Waited for the trespassing fingers, the nudge of a foot under the table. Nothing. When they shot out from the tunnel, he was sitting back, looking out at the ice-blue landscape.

'Not long now. Please, take what's left on the plate.'

'I couldn't—'

'Your family might enjoy them.'

Reddening because he was absolutely right, Katya found a clean cloth and wrapped up the last of the almond-paste buns. Harry, meanwhile, leaned into the aisle and signalled to the waiter. Digging into his pocket, he produced more coins, depositing them on the cloth along with wood shavings, some twine and a short metal implement with a lethal beak. 'Tin opener,' he said, noticing her sudden tension. 'Army issue, cuts through anything. Want one for those condensed milk tins?'

She accepted the gift. 'Which army? Not the Swedish.'

'The British army. I grew up in the north of England.'

Katya had to ask, 'You are not in uniform?'

Harry Morten folded his arms. 'How do you know what I'm wearing under my coat?'

'If you were a soldier, you would be at the front. Perhaps you're a deserter?' That evened the balance. He had called her a bad guardian to Anoushka, which she had been, but no longer. Hitching the baby on to her shoulder, she rose and left the dining car, her nose high in an attempt to stave off tears. She was a few strides from her own carriage when she heard footsteps behind her. Swinging round, she hissed, 'Why are you following me?'

He held up the yellow bag. The second time she had lost it today. 'Your servant, Ekaterina Ulianova.' He said it with a satirical tilt of the head.

Katya watched him walk back to his own compartment and noticed a stiffness in his gait. *He's been injured.* She told herself she didn't care. A few more leagues of track, another slice of daylight, and she'd never see him again.

Chapter Four

Katya woke Tatiana as the train nosed into Gothenburg station. 'Come on, look lively.'

'Are we going straight to the docks?' Tatiana asked, her voice all gravelly.

'No. We'll rest here a night. There's bound to be a respectable hotel near the station.'

Her mother was harder to wake. In the end, Katya had Yana wave smelling salts. 'Stand up, Mama. We've arrived.'

'In Paris?'

Heaven help them. 'No, it's still Sweden, but we've reached the sea.'

'We've already crossed the sea.'

'I'm talking about the North Sea.'

But Irina was slapping away the smelling salts. Then she slapped at Yana, who persisted in holding them under her nose, and her wedding ring caught the maid's face.

Yana's mouth crumpled. A scarlet stripe shone on her cheek.

Katya quickly found a handkerchief and dabbed the wound. 'I'm so sorry. Mother is not herself.'

'Your mother is very much herself,' Yana retorted.

Borrowing Dr Zasyekin's terminology, Katya explained, 'She is in shock. Would you please get her bags down? I'll get the baby into her basket and Tatiana can bring—'

'Stop ordering me about.' Tatiana's green eyes flashed rebellion. Copper-haired from her father's side of the family, she had all his fire and none of his prudence. At nineteen, Tatiana was impatient of restraint and knew only one way: her own. Only Vera had been able to smooth down those bristling spikes. 'I have two bags and two arms,' she informed Katya. 'You, I seem to notice, have two arms and only one bag. *You* bring Mother's things. You're in charge, after all. The eldest sister now Vera's dead. I wish to God it was the other way round.'

'Tatiana Ulianova!' Their mother came to life like a sparking flint. 'Ask your sister's forgiveness. Ask mine. Ask God's.'

'All at once?' Tatiana snipped.

'Let's just get going.' Fatigue was eating Katya from the inside. Anoushka wouldn't settle in her basket, and cried like a siren until Katya put her on her hip. A voice from the corridor asked if she needed help.

'Oh. Thank you. Would you help get our trunks from the guard's van?' Picking up the yellow bag along with Anoushka's basket, she blundered past Harry Morten and out on to the platform. Porters with trolleys clustered about her, and one tried to persuade Katya to relinquish her precious bag, but she handed it to Yana instead. She couldn't carry it, the baby *and* a wicker basket. When they reached the guard's van, Yana sidled up.

'You must give me your pearls now. Your mother struck me.'

'It was an accident.'

'You swore, no more "Yana do this, Yana do that". You have broken your promise, so the pearls are mine.'

'For pity's sake.' Katya's back ached wretchedly. If she didn't lie down soon... 'Stop pestering, Yana. You make me feel as though I'm feeding breadcrumbs to crows.'

Tatiana arrived and joined the quarrel, commenting ominously, 'Remember the old proverb? "You may feed the crow but she will still peck out your eyes".'

Harry, who had overtaken them by now, called from the guard's van, wanting to know what name was on their trunks. This time, he spoke French, which, to Katya's astonishment, was more fluent even than her own. She cleared her throat. 'Our name is—'

'Vytenis.' Eager to display her accomplishments along with her rank, Tatiana said in her most courtly French, 'We are the prin... Ouch, that hurt!'

Katya had trodden hard on her foot. 'Don't bandy titles. You don't know who is listening.'

'You said Sweden was safe. Why are you blushing? Him?' Tatiana looked narrowly at Harry who was now helping the guard lower a trunk onto the platform. 'Strong as well as handsome. If one is to bother at all with men, they might as well have muscle. Wait until he has bathed and shaved.'

Their mother, overhearing, slowly shook her head. 'Do not be vulgar, Tatiana. He is hardly one of us.'

Katya agreed, 'Quite so, Mama.' And felt bitterly ashamed.

With a single look, Harry showed that he had heard them too. He helped bring their second trunk off the van, then disappeared inside, jumping down a moment later with a bullet-shaped kitbag over his shoulder. Katya saw him hand krona notes to the guard. She ought to offer to pay him back, but Yana had the purse full of change, and most of the rest of their money was sewn up in the yellow bag. She looked around for Yana and saw her standing a little way off, refusing to catch her eye. If she saw a suitable shop, she'd buy something for their maid, ribbons perhaps, or a cake.

Harry walked alongside as they made their way past the ticket gate and asked, very formally, if they had a hotel reservation. 'If not, I recommend the Gustavus, on Drottninggaten. Shall I have the porter send your trunks there?'

'Are you staying there?' Tatiana asked.

'What does it matter where he's staying?' Katya intervened. 'This is where our ways part.' She'd become indebted to this man. It wasn't like taking help from Dr Zasyekin. Harald Dagnar Morten… Harry… kept sawdust in his pocket. He wasn't in uniform and had no reasonable explanation. And their mother was right. He was simply not of their class. Yet as Katya pulled her eyes from his profile, almost beautiful in spite of that persistent tic, she felt the shattering of something private and dear.

Harry answered Tatiana in a neutral voice. 'I don't need to use Gothenburg hotels as my father lives in the city. In fact, the only hotel I ever stay at is the Ritz in Paris.'

Tatiana gave a patronising smile. 'I'm sure you do.'

'Your sister is right,' he continued coolly, 'this is where our paths divide. So good to have met you.' With an ironic bow for Katya and her mother, he was gone.

The Gustavus lay on the other side of the river. Not a long walk, but tiring with snow underfoot. They plodded up and down Drottninggaten twice before realising that the building with cracked stonework, whose front steps were swimming with salty slush, was their destination. Perhaps Gothenburg's citizens were feeling the effects of the European war. They were stamping their boots on the lobby mat when their trunks arrived. There was nobody at the reception desk, so Katya paid off the porters with the last money in her pocket and smacked her palm down on the bell. Through an arch, a stove cast a flickering grin at a semicircle of armchairs. Katya settled her mother in one of them and put Tatiana in charge of the baby. 'Take off your headscarves,' she whispered as she unwound hers. 'Look regal. I wonder where the staff are. That man, Morten, seemed to think this was a good place.'

'No doubt it is, to him,' her mother sniffed. 'He looked like a wild tribesman, the kind that used to hunt our forests, who now visit our houses with kerosene and matches.'

'Yana?' Katya looked about but Yana wasn't there. The entrance lobby was also empty. She returned to Tatiana who was tickling the baby's chin with the fringe of her discarded scarf. 'Did Yana come in with us?'

Tatiana glanced up. 'Probably. She was behind me when I was knocking snow off my boots.'

'You're sure?' Katya was appalled by the tremor in her voice.

'She was fiddling with her stockings, leaning down.'

'The yellow bag, did she...' Katya swallowed, 'have it with her?'

'I think so. Is she playing games?'

'No. No, it's fine.' Panic at her heels, Katya left the hotel. Drottninggaten was a long street of stone buildings, with shops whose awnings sagged under the weight of snow. Yana might have been drawn by the window displays. Russian eyes were so used to poverty, they were easily dazzled. Katya chose a direction, walking as fast as she could on frozen slush. At the end of the street, she crossed over and returned the way she'd come. Once she'd exhausted Drottninggaten, she struck out towards the station. Yana might have doubled back, though Katya couldn't think why. Crossing the river with an icy wind blowing had been a miserable experience.

The platform they'd arrived on was empty. All right. Yana will be at the Gustavus, she told herself. We'll have passed each other, ships in the snow. The maid would offer no apology for scaring her, but Katya needed none. She just needed to feel the weight of her precious bag and smell its musty, mothball odour.

This time, she left the station by a side entrance. Walking under a brick arch, she caught a whiff of horseflesh that told her she'd come out by the cab stand. There they were, a line of motley hansoms and 'retired' quality carriages with family crests painted out. Cloaked cabbies sat up on boxes, horses with snow-covered backs breathing out white vapour. Something snagged Katya's eye. A tin, discarded in the snow. Condensed milk. 'Yana?'

A woman in a cherry-red headscarf was stepping into a cab whose driver sat behind a grey horse. Even if Katya hadn't recognised the scarf and the sand-coloured plait trailing down below, she knew the yellow bag in the woman's hand. Stretching her voice to its limit, she yelled, 'Yana – Yana, stop!'

With a nimbleness Katya had never seen from her before, Yana whipped the bag into the cab and slammed the door. The driver sent his horse forward. Katya pursued them to the bridge where she fell down in a spasm of coughing brought on by the freezing air. Picking herself up, she continued her pursuit until she came to a thoroughfare that was busy with cabs and coaches. *Wait – was that Yana's vehicle, turning in the road?*

Katya blundered towards it, still holding the tin of milk in her hand. The cab's wheels had hit a rut, giving her time to run alongside, to get its door open, a foot on the step. But as the vehicle jolted away, she felt herself falling backwards, pulled by the weight of her coat. The life force that had burned so low that morning flared hot, and she screamed. Hands grabbed her around the waist and hauled her inside, head first.

'Damn you, woman,' she spluttered. Her face was mashed against a dusty bag that took up most of the cab's floor. 'I don't understand.' She knew she resembled a donkey getting up from a roll in the mud but the cab was swaying and she couldn't find her balance. 'You'd leave us stranded in a foreign place, take food from a baby's mouth?' She shoved the tin of milk hard into the lap of the person sitting on the seat, hoping it hurt. From the ensuing in-breath, she gathered it had. 'Serves you right.'

'Have you jumped into the wrong vehicle?'

Katya recognised Harry Morten's voice a moment before she realised she was sitting on his kitbag. His eyes were filled with something far, far from amusement.

She gasped, 'Heaven help me, my maid's run off. I don't know what to do.'

'Learn to brush your own hair and polish your own shoes.'

'You don't understand, she's taken all our money.'

Harry Morten glanced at the frost-rimed cab window. 'I can't see her surviving long. Has she ever lived outside Russia?'

'She's never lived outside Moscow. Or outside our house.' Katya moaned. 'It's my fault. I gave her the bag.'

'Ah.' *Fatal lapse*, his utterance implied. 'What about your documents? Passports, identity papers, that sort of thing?'

'In here.' Katya patted her coat. 'I made a pocket inside the lining, thank God. At least I got something right. That treacherous woman! I should have let her have the damn pearls. I expect she'll go back home and marry Konstantin.'

'Home to Russia? She'd have to be stupid.' There was no sympathy in his tone, none in his eyes either. When Katya hoisted herself on to the shallow seat opposite him, he looked away. Katya cupped her frozen ears. She'd probably catch pneumonia now, or starve. Who needs to take their own life, when fate is so eager to do it for you?

Harry Morten rapped on the carriage ceiling and the vehicle immediately slowed down. *He's going to order me out*, Katya thought. *I won't get out. Not until he's told me where the nearest Russian church is.* In the old days, a stranded foreigner would go to their country's embassy. She wouldn't set foot in any place run by the current Russian government. She needed assistance from somebody who would grasp her plight, help her locate a bank that might in turn contact the Parisian one that held her father's money. And then it hit her. Papa's certificate of deposit was in the yellow bag. Yana hadn't only stolen their present means of survival, she'd taken their future as well. Lowering her chin, she began to sob.

That one tin of milk, which Harry had put on the seat next to him, would not last long. The feeder was in the bag too, along with baby clothes and linen nappies. 'The devil take Yana Borisovna.' She leaned forward to touch Harry's hand, but the carriage lurched to a halt and she ended up prodding his knee. 'I need help and you're the only person I know here.'

He still wasn't looking at her. He'd let down the door window and was listening to something. After a moment, Katya heard it too. Bells, pealing as if every belfry in the city was shouting a message.

'What is it?' She wiped her eyes. It wasn't the dignified knelling her own church went in for. *Invasion? Or had Spanish influenza swept in?* Dread stole over her. 'Tell me!'

Bells, endless bells, a clamour of sound poured in around her.

Harry called a question to a passer-by. There followed a fast exchange in Swedish, to which Katya blocked her ears. She needed the world to behave predictably, not disintegrate into a fresh catastrophe.

When Harry turned back to her, she could have clicked her fingers in front of his eyes, he looked so blank. Somebody important had died, perhaps. The King? Or had the Germans marched in, defying Swedish neutrality?

He extended his arm and shot back his cuff, showing her the luminous dial of his wrist watch. 'Fifteen minutes ago – it's all over.' His voice gave out.

'I'm sorry?'

'Don't you understand? As you were running after your bag and I was telling the cab to take a different direction, the last bullet flew in France. The last man died and the trumpets sounded. Peace, on the stroke of eleven. Peace, Ekaterina. But too late.'

Slowly, she caught his meaning. 'The war—?'

'Is over. Germany has capitulated.'

So that was the reason for the rioting bells. Eighteen months ago, the same joy had come to Russia. She and her sisters had danced a wild circle until they'd fallen, dizzy and laughing. The memory caught in her throat. All she could muster was, 'I am glad.'

He didn't hear her. He spoke to himself. 'I thought I'd never see Paris again.'

Katya leant forward, gripping his knee in a way that would have horrified her mother. 'You know Paris?'

He glanced at her gloved fingers, then took her hand in his. 'It's where I live.'

'Then help us get there and I will pay you back double. Whatever you want.'

He made no answer, his mind seemingly lost in the clamour of bells. When he looked at her again, Katya saw an echo of her own raw vulnerability.

She tried again. 'Tell me what you want in return for helping.'

'What I want,' he said slowly, his gaze drilling into hers, 'is to live through this moment in a way that I can bear. Because as it stands, I can't.' Emotion was gathering behind his eyes. He was close to the edge.

Something in his expression shook her. She reached for the door handle. He stopped her.

'I need to remember this moment, Ekaterina, not simply endure it. And not be crucified by it for the rest of my life.' He opened the cab door on to a paralysed world, though he made no move to step down. People had stopped on the pavement, on the road. Drivers had got down from their boxes and were staring into the sky as if 'Peace!' was branded on the clouds.

She said, 'You'll remember this tableau. So will I.'

'No, like this…' Harry leaned forward and pulled her onto the seat beside him. Cupping her chin with a purposeful hand, he put his lips on hers. A moment of hesitation and then he was kissing her in a way that dimmed the city's bells.

*

On 20 December 1918, Katya's ship came into port at Brest on France's west coast. As she stepped on to dry land, an embittered man who hoped to profit from the Vytenis family's misfortune, disembarked at the Normandy port of Le Havre. He had taken the shorter, riskier, sea route to France via the Straits of Dover, where remnants of the defeated German fleet waited for their orders. Travelling with him was the former servant, Yana Borisovna Egorieva. He'd come across Yana at Gothenburg railway station, begging for coins, clutching a bag full of jewellery she didn't know how to sell. 'You didn't get far,' he'd jibed. She'd tried to keep possession of the yellow bag, but not for long.

He would enjoy profiting from Vytenis treasure – he had long resented Ulian Vytenis's comfortable life, the unassuming wealth that had always been denied to *him*, no matter how hard he laboured.

He had another woman with him, whom he called 'Cook' with dry simplicity. He and Cook had been locked in a liaison for years, a dependency he could not seem to break. He, Cook and Yana boarded a train for Paris, arriving before Christmas, well ahead of Katya and her family.

Part Two

Chapter Five

That kiss had followed her every sea mile. Nine days on a Swedish freighter, rounding the northernmost tip of Scotland, down the Atlantic coast of Britain to France's western seaboard, it had kept her company. They were held up in Brest for two weeks while Irina recovered from a painful bout of shingles, brought on after Katya finally confessed that all their jewels had disappeared with Yana. The kiss invaded Katya's dreams each night.

It was a memory on her lips as they steamed through the Paris suburbs a week after New Year, 1919. That morning's sunrise arrived without panache, filling the train windows already looking exhausted. On the trackside, snow lay in dirty crests. The countryside was peaceful. Though as the houses became more densely packed, Katya saw strong hints of war. Barbed wire tracked between buildings like bad stitching. Masts strung with cables disfigured parks and gardens. As her stomach cramped in anticipation of breakfast, she made out the ghostly outline of a city.

Tatiana pointed. 'The Eiffel Tower, isn't it?'

'I think so.' The airy pillar brought to life postcards sent from Paris. 'I'm sure it is. We'll be with our cousins by lunchtime. I hope they have hot water.'

'They will,' Tatiana said confidently. 'Count Lasunskoy had the best bathroom in Moscow, Papa used to say. I wonder how high it is.'

'Their bathroom?'

'The Eiffel Tower, silly.'

'Look, Anoushka.' Katya held the baby to the window. 'Your grandmamma climbed it once and was sick.'

Irina Vytenis joined the conversation. 'You have no idea how high it is until you're rising up,' she said drowsily. Irina had not entirely shaken off her illness and, having used up Dr Zasyekin's barbital during the voyage, had found sleep impossible until she was prescribed morphine by a doctor in Brest. 'When I saw people leaning out at the top, I was terrified it would fall over. Ulian laughed at me.' Tears pearled her cheeks. 'I never thought I'd see this city again without my husband.'

Katya sought to distract her. 'Our cousins' home is in the shadow of the Orthodox cathedral, isn't that right? In the eighth?'

'You wrote to them, Katya, to say we were coming?' her mother fretted.

'Twice. Cousin Sonya answered the first letter, though not my second.' Katya wasn't anxious, having been told by more than one person that the French post was sluggish. Still recovering from war.

At a little after nine, they pulled in at Montparnasse station and stepped stiffly down onto the platform. Journey's end. She had kept the first part of the vow laid on her by her father. Katya had got her family to Paris.

As Katya looked around the cavernous station, she sent quiet thanks to Harry Morten. He'd withdrawn enough from his bank in Gothenburg for them to complete this journey, including the unexpected stay in Brest and her mother's medical costs. Katya had been anxious about accepting so much, but her enigmatic champion had waved the matter away, more interested in knowing where her cousins lived. 'Left or Right Bank?'

She'd answered vaguely, 'Right, I think.' Her mental picture of Harry's home in Paris was of a room with a sloping ceiling and no running water whereas her Lasunskoy cousins had a house of some size with a courtyard garden. Or so the countess had told Irina in a letter sent last summer. Sonya Lasunskaya had described their street, rue Brazy, as '*a shady walk fringed with horse chestnuts near a park laid out in the English style*'. Harry Morten would never be invited across the threshold.

As she oversaw the unloading of their trunks from the guard's van, she touched her lips, symbolically brushing away the kiss. She would see Harry Morten one more time, when she repaid him. And that would be that.

As she led the way towards the barrier, her eye singled out a patch of crimson among the soberly dressed crowd in front of the arrivals board. *Yana?* Had she not been carrying Anoushka, she'd have run forward. A moment later, she saw a child in a red jumper being carried on a man's shoulders. Her mind was playing tricks. She'd seen numerous mirages of Yana since Gothenburg. She dreamed of the woman too, and of that grinning fiend Konstantin. She didn't care if Yana was tucked up in that old man's bed. All she wanted was the stolen bag, the one containing her life.

As their porter took them out on to Boulevard Montparnasse, Katya drank in her first unobstructed view of Paris. What she saw was wrapped in a curtain of sound; the whirr of tram engines and the warning 'ding' of their bells; the grind of motor-buses; hooting taxis and the hacking of shovels. A band of female labourers was clearing ice from the tram tracks. Horse-drawn vehicles, bicycles and cars seemed to roll by soundlessly, overwhelmed by the foreground noise. She had forgotten what a city felt like.

'Let's take a tram! That one's got "Louvre" on the front.' Tatiana pulled out her pocket map. 'Isn't that sort of where we're going? Hi, there!' She waved to attract the driver who remained sublimely unaware in his cab, though passengers getting off sent curious glances. Tatiana forged ahead, forcing Katya to follow. The baby's basket collided with several pairs of knees before she caught up with her sister. Anoushka began to wail.

'You can't get on a tram without a ticket, idiot. And who will unload our trunks when we get off?'

'The boy. The porter,' Tatiana said carelessly. Wand-slim in her travelling coat, her bright hair streaming loose beneath her headscarf, she was attracting considerable male attention. And playing up to it. 'Some kind gentleman will help us with our baggage.'

'Don't count on it,' Katya said flatly. 'You and I will end up carrying it.'

'You should have engaged the man who helped us before. What was his name?'

'I don't think I ever knew,' Katya said untruthfully, eager to change the subject before their mother joined them. She'd said not a word about borrowing money, pretending instead that she'd secured an advance on her father's French deposits. Irina and Tatiana were happy to believe that funds flowed from banks like water from a drinking fountain.

'I'm telling Katya that we should have kept that man with us,' Tatiana said as their mother arrived, offended at being abandoned. 'You remember, Mama? The wild tribesman.'

'Of course Mama won't remember,' Katya cut in.

'But *you* do.' Tatiana's eye gained a gleam. 'You always touch your face when you mention him, and he looked at you like this...' The unswerving gaze her sister imitated was so accurate, Katya flinched.

'Honestly, my girl, you've regressed. I know it's your way of... Holy Mother, look at that!' Fate dealt Katya a shatterproof change of subject. A green tram was gliding to a stop beside them. The figure in the forward cabin wore a tunic and a peaked cap perched on neatly curled hair. 'The driver – it's a *woman*. Isn't that wonderful?'

'Heaven help us, what has become of this city?' Irina moaned. 'Now I shall not ride on a tram. Not ever.'

As they followed their porter to the taxi rank, Katya's fascinated eyes recorded another female driver and several conductors, as well as women pushing goods-barrows. Not entirely a joyous scene. Katya had imagined Paris as a perpetual fashion parade, but the only colour was on the trams. No rich fabrics, no wonderful hats. Just headscarves and straight skirts revealing practical boots and an inch of heavy stocking. Shapeless coats and everywhere, black. *We slot right in.* The Paris of her dreams was a reflection of Moscow. Women, old men and boys everywhere, but few young men. A legless beggar in an army tunic hunkered by a station pier, a bowl between his stumps. More beggars lined the station wall. A final shock awaited her: taxi-cabs were horse-less. Chauffeurs sat at the steering wheels of open-fronted Renault cars.

She glanced at her mother who looked as bewildered as she felt.

Katya was about to claim the first car in line when a tall young man in a button-front coat hailed her.

'This way, Madame.' He indicated the car fourth in line, which had yellow wheels, the paintwork badly chipped.

'Shouldn't we take the front car?'

'*Mais oui*, Madame, if you like men with tobacco-stained whiskers who belch garlic.'

'I don't, though in Moscow it's a rule—' but their porter had begun loading their trunks on to a flat-bedded dray pulled by a sturdy horse. It wouldn't do for their luggage to arrive before they did, so she nodded. 'All right. Rue Brazy, by the Russian cathedral.'

'I know it.' Instead of rushing to open doors for them, the cab driver stood looking at Katya. Under his peaked cap, his eyes were heavily lashed, with a slight up-tilt. Pale in colour, like glass washed up on a sea shore. A dramatic contrast to the black hair that fell to his collar. He was tall, taller even than Harry Morten, but slimmer built. Add to that a square chin and sharp cheekbones, she had to wonder, were all Frenchmen this handsome? He was about her age, twenty-three, and Katya's next thought was, *Why isn't he in the army?* Men were being released from the forces, but with so many to be processed, most still waited in holding centres. Perhaps he was some kind of runaway, as she suspected Harry Morten was. 'Would you like me to put our bags into the car?' she asked pointedly, and the driver broke his gaze.

'Pardon. Allow me.'

Katya dashed off to make sure the haulier knew where he was taking their trunks. She tipped the porter, giving him extra coins. 'For the soldier without legs.'

'Which one, Madame?' the boy asked. 'There are three such invalids on this side of the station alone.'

Deflated, Katya climbed into the taxi alongside the driver. Her mother and Tatiana were ensconced in the back with the baby. As the driver fired the ignition, she checked the time by the station clock. Too late for breakfast, but hopefully her cousins' staff could rustle something from the kitchen. Eggs, she hoped, and white bread.

There'd been no white bread in Brest, just a greyish product similar to the loaves Moscow bakers churned out. But that was the provinces, not the Promised Land. She grasped the safety strap as they accelerated away into the flow of traffic. Pungent smoke coughed from under the Renault's hood. 'Will it get us there?' she asked dubiously.

'Of course. Are you afraid of motor cars?' The driver slipped her a sidelong glance.

'Not at all. My father used to drive a Russo-Baltique, until the army took it, and he'd let me get up beside him. He once let me take the wheel.'

'He should not have. I do not approve of woman drivers.' Their driver spoke French with a precision that made Katya look harder at his profile.

'I was a competent driver,' she told him.

'We will shortly cross the river,' he answered in a unilateral change of subject. 'Rue Brazy is *Rive Droite.*'

'I know,' she said, nettled by this assumption that she was an ignorant newcomer, incapable of reading a map. To prove herself mistress of the situation, she mused out loud, 'Why does the Seine have a right and left bank, I wonder? It should be 'north' and 'south'.'

'It is always assumed you are on a boat, travelling downstream. The Right Bank is then to your right. It is where the best people live. The Left is for students and artists of the wilder kind.'

Was he teasing, or giving a sermon? She couldn't tell. Harry Morten had been stern with her, but she'd never had the impression he'd thought her lacking in brains. Her father had always respected her mind too. So when the driver told her he was intending to cross at Pont Royal and take them past the Louvre and the Tuileries Gardens, she expressed the wish to cross the river by Pont Alexandre.

'You'll put more on the clock.'

'Pont Alexandre,' Katya repeated and the handsome profile tightened.

Until he smiled and said in Russian, 'Naturally, your first crossing of the Seine must be by the bridge that celebrates—'

'The Franco-Russian alliance of 1892,' Katya finished. 'I am beginning to suppose you're not French.'

'You are correct. Aleksey Pavlovich Provolsky at your service. Welcome to the City of Light, Madame. Your French is good but not excellent.'

'I beg your pardon?'

'Parisians tut-tut at lazy pronunciation and incorrect idiom. Is the baby yours?'

'My sister's.' An automatic reply. Katya was bristling. She'd been taught by the very best French-speaking governesses.

'That young lady is your sister?' He made a backwards nod at Tatiana. 'She is young to be married – to be a widow.'

Katya stared straight ahead. Some subjects she would not discuss with a stranger. However, it wasn't long before she burst out, 'There is nothing incorrect about my French.'

'*Ah, non? Pardonnez-moi.*'

They ignored each other until, waiting at a junction for a tram to rattle by, Aleksey Provolsky gave Katya's headscarf a critical inspection. 'You should visit a milliner. A few have stayed open for business, in spite of the war.' Giving her no time to ask who the devil he thought he was, he gunned the engine. As they rocketed out on to another broad boulevard, he shouted, 'The address you've given me on rue Brazy is the Council for Russian Émigrés. It looks after new arrivals, lends money, finds accommodation. You are sure it's the right place?'

'I don't know what you're talking about. You are taking us to the home of Count Lasunskoy.'

'Is this why they let you out of Russia – you are too stubborn to keep?'

Katya turned her face away. This impudent young man had kept her from the view for too long. She must record her first journey through Paris. She touched her mouth. Some moments were to be remembered, and others firmly forgotten.

Nobody who had grown up in Moscow with its state buildings, palaces and basilicas could be awed by the architecture of Paris. It was the symmetry of the boulevards and the biscuit-blonde terraces that stamped themselves into Katya's consciousness. So instantly did she fall in love, when they passed a row of gutted houses with fire-ravaged interiors, she burst out furiously, 'Who did that?'

'Zeppelins,' Aleksey Provolsky informed her. 'German airships delivering gifts.' Over the grind of his engine, he imitated a string of rumbling detonations. 'That or shell blast. You know the enemy got within firing distance of Paris? They built a great cannon, powerful enough to fire into the heart of the city.'

'Did people die?'

'Of course.' He sounded contemptuous. 'And hundreds of thousands of young men. Millions, perhaps.' He salvaged a newspaper from under his seat. Its masthead featured the Imperial Eagle and a silhouette of the Tsar. Its title, printed in Russian, made Katya flinch. It was called *Vera*: 'Faith'. 'This is the journal of "Little Moscow",' he told her, adding proudly, 'I help produce it, though it is hard to get the newsprint. Sometimes we can only publish a single sheet. You must subscribe.'

'I'll see.' The paper's coarse texture had made the printing ink bleed. It would leave smears on her hands and cuffs.

'It will tell you the truth about war, here and in Russia. You sound as if you know very little.'

'I know what took place in Russia.' *Slaughter, revolution and hunger.* Of course she must learn what had happened here, too, but in her own time. 'Did you fight?'

'For Russia? Need you ask?' He did not speak again until they reached an embankment, hemmed one side by stately buildings and on the other by a line of silvery trees. Behind the trees flowed the sage-green river, its surface agitated by falling snow. 'Pont Alexandre,' came the curt announcement.

Thanks to the flurries of white, Katya's first Seine crossing was a mere Impressionist hint. Their progress along the Right Bank into the elite heart of Paris was equally vague. Here, the architecture was more embellished, the roads wider, but detail would have to wait for another day. She turned to see how her mother and Tatiana were enjoying the journey. They were both asleep. Anoushka stared up from the basket on Tatiana's knee.

'I wonder if we should put the baby down for a girls' academy rather than a convent school?'

'For that you need money,' Aleksey Provolsky said, though Katya's question had been addressed to herself. 'The good things of Paris are for the rich.'

'One can dream.' Katya took out her map, to follow the final stretch of the journey. 'Don't worry, I can afford to pay your fare.'

They travelled on for fifteen minutes and then swung off a gracious thoroughfare, which Katya reckoned was Boulevard de Courcelles, into a narrower, though no-less-impressive street. Rue Pierre le Grand: '*Peter the Great*'. This must be the Russian enclave.

Aleksey Provolsky pulled over and woke the sleepers by shouting into the speaking tube, '*Mesdames*! Step out, so you never forget your first sight of our cathedral, Saint Alexander Nevsky.' Katya did as he suggested. A bemused Irina and Tatiana joined her in the road. Katya hastily took the handles of the baby basket from her sister. Their driver restarted his engine, telling them that they were a stone's throw from their destination.

'I will leave your bags outside Dedushka's Café which belongs to one of your fellow Muscovites, who also makes the best *golubtsi* in Paris.'

Katya hadn't recalled telling this driver that they had come from Moscow. 'Wait— '

'Don't fret, your bags will be safe. Here, we respect and help each other. Goodbye – I have to find more passengers. More people, more dreams.' He said it cynically.

'Your fare,' Katya cried as he pulled away.

'Your first journey is my pleasure,' came the reply in Russian. Then, confusingly, he added, 'I'm sorry.'

They watched him go, then took in the sight he had left them to enjoy. At the street's end, on a bank of steps, the cathedral reared above every neighbouring building. Gold onion domes and black crosses pierced the leaden sky. Irina gasped, 'It's a miracle.'

'Stones, blood and sweat,' Katya huffed. Her faith in God had weakened because He had certainly not been in Moscow last November. 'That and a slice of the congregation's wages.'

'You are turning into a Bolshevik.'

'No, but I think our driver is secretly one. This is a strange place, where taxi drivers make you get out and walk.' Katya lifted Anoushka's basket and began walking up rue Pierre le Grand, golden domes filling her vision. Irina wanted to go into the cathedral and light candles for her husband and Vera but Katya dissuaded her. 'Anoushka needs feeding and besides, I don't share our driver's confidence. Somebody's bound to wonder why there are six bags sitting on the pavement.' They were now directly in front of the cathedral, on a street marked 'rue Daru'. Katya recognised the name from the Countess's directions. She pointed. 'Is that the place our driver mentioned?'

Dedushka's Café took up the corner of rue Daru and rue Brazy. It was flanked by a courtyard whose open gates revealed numerous doors with peeling paintwork and a row of dustbins. A snow-furred washing line stretched from one side of the court to the other.

Tatiana frowned. 'Perhaps this is where the servants live.'

They found their bags outside the café next to a chalkboard announcing, 'In Paris, best *golubtsi*.' *Golubtsi* was stuffed cabbage and its hearty smell mixed with that of coffee and fresh pancakes. 'Little Moscow' indeed. Rue Brazy was a narrow stub leading back down to Boulevard de Courcelles. Its houses were six floors tall, counting the dormered attics under the eaves, with half-size balconies and brown-shuttered windows. Wet cobbles made an uninspiring seam down the middle.

A shady walk, fringed by chestnuts. Katya muttered, 'This can't be the right place.'

Tatiana pointed at the street sign. 'It's what it says. What number is our cousins' house?'

'Number 6, but I don't know…' Correspondence over many months had led Katya to imagine an old family mansion with a carriage arch and tall windows.

Their mother doubted they'd even been brought to the right district. 'If as you say, the driver is a Bolshevik, he will have stranded us somewhere dangerous. Whenever we came to Paris, your father and I, we never strayed from the first, second or eighth *arrondissements*. Occasionally the sixteenth, the diplomatic quarter.'

Katya consulted her map. 'This is the eighth.' And there was only one rue Brazy. The arrival of the dray with their trunks sealed the matter. The driver hauled his horse to a stand outside No. 6 whose door plaque announced it to indeed be the headquarters of the Cou ncil for Russian Émigrés. Katya extracted some of the currency she'd exchanged for Harry Morten's krona, thinking she'd waste no time in asking her cousin to escort her to Papa's bank. Paying the driver, adding an exact tip, she rapped the door knocker of No. 6.

Chapter Six

'I regret to tell you, Count Lasunskoy died a week ago, as did his wife. From influenza.'

Katya stared at the middle-aged woman who had invited her into the entrance foyer, introducing herself as the manager of the building.

Katya shook her head. *This couldn't be.* Indeed, the woman looked a little crazy to her, in her shin-length skirt and mannish green tunic belted high above the waist. The clothes reminded Katya of the Lubyanka wardress who had tried to stop her as she'd run from the prison that final time. 'Why are you lying to me?'

'I'm afraid it is true. I can take you to where their deaths were registered, if you'd like?'

Katya felt faint. The woman and the walls behind her dissolved like a chalk-portrait in the rain. 'But our cousins urged us to come here.' *So they must be here*, roared Katya's logic.

'When did they write?'

'To invite us? Five months ago.' Katya was able to be precise. The letter had come on 1 August, the day Anoushka was born. Oh, why hadn't they left then and not delayed? Five months of dithering, when a few hours could change everything? Grasping the handkerchief the woman offered, Katya stammered, 'I thought they lived here.'

'They did. Two floors above me.'

'But that's impossible. My cousin Sonya described living in grandeur.'

'If you call a single room in a shared house "grandeur" then I dare say they did. Though, pardon my saying it, the countess was given to flights of invention. My dear…' The woman placed long fingers on Katya's arm. She was shorter than Katya, though not by much, with white hair coiled in braids across her brow. Something in the shape of her eyes set Katya's instincts racing. 'We're all proud,' the woman was saying. 'We all like to think we're a little better than fate makes us… I'm sorry, did you give me your name?'

'Ekaterina Ulianova, Princess Vytenis.'

'Of course, you are the Moscow cousins! The countess mentioned you to me. This is a terrible shock for you but one that, I'm sorry to say, is replicated across the city. Homecoming soldiers, widows, children; influenza has wielded a ruthless scythe. Indeed, they're saying more have died in this epidemic than on the battlefields. Would you like to know where your cousins are buried?'

'No.' The woman recoiled but Katya couldn't explain the bludgeoning sense of betrayal in this latest blow. 'I can't face any more death.' Yet, she had to know. 'When did they fall ill?'

'New Year's Day. The countess collapsed at a little soiree here and her husband succumbed a few hours later. Our own doctor looked after them and did his best. I hope you understand why I couldn't nurse them myself. For reasons nobody understands, this horrible disease takes young lives more readily than old ones and I have a son.'

Yes, Katya thought. *And he drives a taxi*. Noises took her to the door. The scene outside was not inspiring. Anoushka was wailing. Hungry, needing to be changed. Her mother hadn't budged from the pavement. Still telling herself that they were in the wrong part of Paris, no doubt.

Tatiana stood like a striking worker, arms folded. In desperation, Katya asked the woman, 'Did my cousins perhaps own a property elsewhere?' It had suddenly struck her that they were homeless in a snow-locked city.

The woman's look of pity said it all. 'Nothing to my knowledge. Your cousins rented their room through me and it is still available, if you are interested?'

Katya wondered what this woman had been before coming to Paris. A teacher, a governess? Her mode of dress suggested something artistic – perhaps that was why she didn't grasp the polite realities. 'My mother could not sleep in a room with me, my sister and a baby. Nor could she tolerate noise day and night.' Somewhere above their heads, a scale was being laboriously repeated on a piano. 'I'm finding this hard to understand. Our cousins had a house in Moscow, on the river, and estates in the country. They travelled in luxury. How can they have existed here in such—' Katya couldn't think of an acceptable word.

'Poverty?' The woman displayed a signet ring whose band was worn to the thinness of wire. 'I am Ludmilla Yakovna, Princess Provolskaya, and once, I too had great wealth. My son, Prince Aleksey Provolsky, who brought you here, was heir to thousands of acres.'

'You knew we were coming?'

'No.' Princess Provolskaya laughed. 'His vehicle has a very particular rattle. I keep telling him he must get it fixed, but he can never quite make enough to do the repair.'

'So... a prince drives a taxi?'

'Several do so, and three others are hotel doorkeepers. My sister-in-law is a ladies' cloakroom attendant at the Crillon Hotel. I volunteer for the welcoming council, helping to settle refugees in return for reduced rent and being allowed to give music lessons. Piano, as you can no doubt hear. Do I need to tell you what the revolution in our mother country did to fortunes such as mine and your cousins'? I will help you, Ekaterina Ulianova, but please abandon all expectations of luxury. Take the room. It is not damp and there are no mice. I can give you vouchers for food while you find work. What can you do?'

'Work?' Katya suspected her gaze had gone blank.

'Type? Teach languages? Which do you speak?'

'I – Russian. A little English. German. French, of course.'

'That's no use. We Russians speak French already and the French don't want to learn Russian. As for German... hardly. Good English would have been a string to your bow. Can you be charming?'

'I'm sorry?'

'Humble enough to work in a shop.'

Katya shook her head. 'Patience isn't my leading virtue. I can't work, anyway. Anoushka, my sister's baby... my late sister... is five months old. She can't be left.'

'But you're not alone. I heard other voices.'

'My mother and younger sister. That's why we'd need three bedrooms, oh, and an attic for a nursemaid.'

The princess rolled her eyes. 'I came to Paris when war was at its height, not realising how quickly it would devour the nest egg I smuggled out with me.' She held up her hand, showing off her frail ring. 'This is all I have left. Your sister – how old is she?'

'Tatiana is nineteen.'

'You can both work in that case. Your mother can look after the baby.'

'Mama's not strong.'

The princess cocked an eyebrow. 'Anoushka is a baby elephant? No? Then how "strong" does "Mama" have to be?'

Katya was tempted to outline the rigours they'd endured, the brutality of their last days in Moscow, but this dry-eyed princess would then ask questions she could not, would not, answer. 'My mother's set her heart on regaining the life she's lost. What she's been through has made her ill.'

'Then I will be happy to introduce her to our own Dr Shepkin,' smiled Princess Provolskaya. 'Never fear, we like our titles here in "Little Moscow". Serene Highnesses all, so long as in the daytime, we are wage earners. Do you like fashion?'

'Very much.' *Unlike you*; a thrust of silent revenge. 'I can't wait to visit the House of Worth. It's my mother's favourite couturier. My sister's wedding dress came from there...' Katya's voice tailed off.

'Not what I meant.' Princess Provolskaya clucked. 'Can you sew?'

'Naturally. My governesses taught me.'

'Good.' The princess took Katya's hands. 'These are an asset. Soft, no callouses to catch threads. They may get you work in an atelier.'

'A sewing workshop?' A flickering picture-reel came to life in Katya's imagination: herself in a busy studio, wax figurines draped in half-made clothes. Sketches pinned to every wall. 'Princess Katya Vytenis, dress designer.' The picture-reel snapped. Where did one start as an outsider in a city bursting with established talent? And besides, 'We have money here. We don't need to work.'

Princess Provolskaya went towards the stairs, no doubt to return to her pupil. She casually threw out, 'In the Franco-Russe bank?'

'How did you know?'

'It's where we all put our money when we had it. Rue de la Paix, at the Opéra end. Your first port of call?'

Katya nodded.

'Then good luck. Would you like to store your trunks here? I can ask Georgy Filatov from the café to bring them in.'

Katya accepted with gratitude.

Chapter Seven

It wasn't pettishness that impelled Katya to take them all to the Hôtel Ritz on Place Vendôme but the conviction that a few days of ease would benefit her mother's health and Tatiana's state of mind. She calculated she had enough money left for one last splash. After that, it would be frugality and iron rations until her father's investment came through. Meanwhile, she couldn't delay the news of their cousins' fate. She came straight out with it.

Her mother at once began to weep while Tatiana rounded on her.

'Did you know that when you brought us here?'

'Dear God, Tatya. It was as much a shock to me.'

Tatiana raked at her hair, pulling out strands. 'What's to stop us catching Spanish influenza and dying as well?'

'Because we'd have caught it by now on one of our trains, or on the ship. And life goes on. For Vera's memory, for Anoushka's sake, it goes on.'

Place Vendôme lay serene under feathery snowfall. The cab they'd picked up on Boulevard de Courcelles stopped outside No. 15. Getting out, Katya saw a row of arches and the famous name inscribed in curly ironwork. Discretion incarnate. If she'd come on foot, she'd have walked past.

'Has it closed?' Irina Vytenis screwed up her eyes against the glare, her gaze dismissing a pair of Renault taxis, parked with their flags lowered to imply they were for hire. 'One should not be able to see the hotel door for the horse-drawn vehicles.'

'It's open,' Katya assured her. Their elderly driver had told her on the way that the army had requisitioned most private cars, and almost all the horses. 'Even fashionable people walk these days.'

To prove it, a lady emerged from the hotel, attended by a doorman who handed her an umbrella. Katya watched her amble towards the square's central column whose base was walled around with sandbags, a remnant of civil defence. She wore a skirt cut short to reveal slender calves clad in silk stockings. Ankles at the Ritz? Her coat whispered 'high price-tag' for all it was an ugly, tubular shape. Her hat, a soft thing with a bow at the back, carried the stamp of a good milliner. Katya looked down at the spoon-shaped toes of her own boots. The last time she'd shown an ankle in daylight had been the day before her fifteenth birthday, when she'd graduated to long skirts.

The next person through the door was a man, who struck off along the sand-sprinkled pavement giving the impression he had to be somewhere urgently. He walked with a slight hesitation, as if he carried an injury. Katya's heart jumped even as she told herself it couldn't be Harry Morten. This man wore a tailored coat with a velvet collar, and a brimmed hat and gloves. A well-to-do officer most likely, wounded on active service.

'Everyone in Paris is better dressed than us.' Tatiana tugged her cuffs to hide the ragged tops of her gloves. 'I don't want to go inside. It'll be embarrassing.'

Katya was inclined to agree. They should ask the driver to take them somewhere affordable. Perhaps that room in rue Brazy—

'Katya, Anoushka's going blue with cold.' Her mother sounded really alarmed.

'Let's do it.' Katya ushered her family through the canopied entrance, settling with herself that she'd go to the Franco-Russe bank as soon as she'd secured a suite and swallowed some hot tea.

Just as Princess Provolskaya had described it, the Franco-Russe bank stood at the junction of rue de la Paix and place de l'Opéra. The couture house, Worth, was its near neighbour and Katya promised herself a longer look after she'd completed her business. The bank's solid columns and stone swags suggested a temple to money, though less reassuring was the criss-cross tape on the windows, a reminder that artillery attacks had spread terror until a very few months ago. Inside, at a marble counter, she explained her business. One clerk consulted with another before escorting her to an office, where a gentleman wearing the stiffest of starched collars glanced over the family's identity documents which Katya laid before him.

'You are claiming a deposit held at this establishment, Madame?'

'Yes. Money invested by my father. Five hundred thousand francs, to be precise.'

The man's expression did not change as he shook his head. '*Non.*'

'What do you mean, 'No'?'

He jabbed a finger at the papers. 'These are written in Cyrillic. Everything must be translated and certified by a notary as genuine. Only then, will I look at them.'

'But you're the Franco-Russe bank. There must be somebody on your staff who reads Russian. *Please.* My father bought a bond from you and it has matured. His family needs it.'

'Why does your father not come?'

She explained. 'We fled, we had no choice.'

'I see.' The official gathered up the papers, using the top of his table to bang them into an even shape. 'You'll find translators around rue Daru. I believe there's a fellow, sits on the cathedral steps, who works for a few centimes per line. Good day, Madame.'

As she left the bank, two female customers tittered at her hat. It was the only hat she'd packed, a black velvet plate laden with magenta gauze roses. So cast down, she walked right past Worth without even looking up.

'Mama, I thought you could wear this.' Katya held up a black satin gown for her mother to see. Worth, from the spring season of 1914, and still ravishing. 'I didn't pack mourning colours for myself or Tatiana. It didn't seem an efficient use of space.'

Katya was surprised when her mother replied, 'Your father hated to see young women in black. I shall wear it forever but you and your sister must wear white.'

'I didn't pack any of that, either. White always needs special care.' They were dressing to go down to the restaurant. On her return from the bank, a steward had asked if 'their Serene Highnesses' wished to reserve a table and Katya had stumbled into another expensive decision. 'Yes, for eight o'clock.'

Having foreseen the need for evening gowns, she'd earlier taken one each from their trunks. The one of honey-coloured silk with a gold satin sash was her all-time favourite. Holding it against herself at the mirror, she knew it was still pretty in spite of being several years old.

Two unknown women sneering at her hat had sunk her confidence but what did they know?

'It needs pressing,' Tatiana informed Katya's reflection. 'Where were you earlier?'

'Just strolling,' Katya lied.

Tatiana took up a hairbrush, brushing her tresses until they crackled over her shoulders. 'Shame Yana ran away. Ironing was her job.'

'I know.' Yana had liked touching fine things, a little too much. 'Will you wear this?' Katya meant the honey silk. 'Or the pink?'

'Neither. My ivory,' Tatiana answered.

Katya put a hand to her head, dreading what was coming. 'It's in Moscow. I'm sorry.'

Tatiana absorbed the information silently, then with a power that woke Anoushka, she shrieked, 'My ivory gown is the one grown-up thing I have and you left it behind! Why?'

Because on that blood-soaked November afternoon, it had slipped her mind that she ought to pack the gown made for Tatiana in honour of Vera's wedding. 'I'm truly sorry. Oh, darling, don't take it so badly, listen, you can wear the pink. It should fit—'

'Pink with *my* hair?' Tatiana hurled the hairbrush. 'I'm not going down to dinner.'

'Of course you must. Take my gold dress. I don't mind which I wear.'

'It's old and ugly.'

'Try it on.'

Keeping her anger alive like a flame in a draught, Tatiana grudgingly held the honey silk against herself. It was a perfect shade for her and she saw it. 'I suppose. All right.'

'Keep it. A gift.' Katya gratefully escaped to find a housekeeper, taking Anoushka with her. All their gowns needed pressing and somebody must watch the baby while they dined. She'd hoped for a relaxing dinner, but she'd be scanning every price on the menu. Would there be written prices? *What if I can't pay?* She had no answer to that.

By the time she returned to their suite, Tatiana had pinned her hair in a sophisticated roll and was being cinched into her corset by their mother.

'Nineteen inches,' Tatiana said proudly, clasping her hands around her middle. 'An inch for every year of my age. How about you, Katya?'

'I hope you won't swoon into your soup.' Retiring to the beautifully appointed bathroom, Katya spent private minutes discovering the novelty of running hot water and a china sink wide enough for Anoushka to swim in. The hotel had central heating; you could walk comfortably about in a shift. After this, how could they sink to one rented room? Tomorrow, she'd seek out the man on the cathedral steps, as advised. She was capable of translating their passports and baptismal certificates into French herself, but a professional would be a safer option. What had one of her governesses liked to say? 'Do it badly, do it twice.' When she emerged in a bathrobe, her skin flushed, the bronze drawing-room clock showed half past seven. Their gowns were ready and somebody else had come in to light their fire and side-table lamps. Tatiana posed before the mirror, a human flame.

Irina laced Katya into the rose-pink silk, cut low on the bosom. 'Twenty-one inches. Well done. In Moscow, it was twenty-three.'

Katya drew on her gloves then helped button up her mother's full-length ones. All in black, falls of jet lace around her shoulders, Irina Vytenis took her breath away. How like Vera she looked, pearl-blonde hair masking the encroaching white. A living ghost. Katya became busy all at once, putting handkerchiefs, smelling salts and a scent bottle into an evening bag. A brisk knock at the door brought a nursemaid into the room and Katya passed Anoushka into her care, repeating every instruction four times. As the clock struck eight, she took her mother's arm. Irina flinched.

'My darling, I don't need an iron grip. I will come quietly. Tatya?'

Tatiana was at the mirror still, fluffing out the lace on her bodice. Katya told her to leave it. 'What isn't right now will not become so from fussing.'

A sweeping staircase led down to a gallery. The buzz of laughter and chatter mixed with the clink of glass. By the time she was halfway down, Katya was aware of a gradual quietening. Faces turning towards them. People twisting to look. This staircase was designed for making a grand entrance, she reassured herself. One person looks up, they all look up.

A moment later, silence. The kind of silence that has no good in it.

'Why are people staring?' Tatiana faltered at the last fantail curve of the stairs.

'I don't know.' They entered a gallery where guests sat at small, drum tables. Heavy drapes were closed against the night.

'It's our dresses,' Tatiana hissed. 'Nobody else is wearing colour. Why didn't you bring black for us? That woman is glaring, the one in snuff-brown. I want to go.'

'It isn't a crime to wear colour.'

'I think it is, Katya.'

'Smile and look straight ahead.' Their dresses were drawing amusement and in one or two cases, outright hostility.

Honey and pink, when every other woman in Paris was in black or one of the mossy shades that are first cousin to black. The Vytenis girls were dressed as if they didn't know there had been a war, or didn't care. Katya spent intense seconds realigning her ideas of fashion. The baggy outlines she'd dismissed as eccentric and unfeminine were, it seemed, the pervading mode. Nineteen-inch waists were out. Ankles were in.

'I can't bear this.' Tatiana's hectic breathing warned of an approaching storm while her mother simply looked sad and lost. Katya suggested they find the dining room but her mother refused to move until somebody came to escort them.

'Imagine if we entered the bar by mistake.'

'I'll fetch somebody.' Nothing could be worse than providing a silent cabaret show. Or so Katya thought until, walking as fast as the swish of her skirts allowed, she smacked into a man in conversation with the maître d'hôtel. As they both recovered from the collision, he exclaimed, 'Ekaterina. Is it you?'

Harry Morten.

Chapter Eight

No mistaking the only man who had ever kissed her – and lent her a substantial amount of money. The well-cut evening clothes had blinded her, as had a light sheen of oil that neatened and darkened his hair. The tic above his left eye ended all doubt. It flickered, fast as a bee's wing.

Katya asked pardon for walking into him and turned to the maître d'. 'Would you please show us to the dining room?'

'Allow me,' Harry interposed.

The maître d' sought her permission. 'Your Serene Highness?'

Harry repeated 'Serene Highness?' and raised an eyebrow. 'You are... what? A princess?'

'Well, yes,' Katya faltered. 'My grandfather left Lithuania to serve the late Tsar's father who raised him to the rank of prince.' Katya asked the maître d' to *please* take her mother and sister to their table. 'Say I'll join them in a moment.' As the man left, she turned to Harry, but he spoke first.

'You hid that very well.'

'I couldn't confide in you. It was dangerous.'

'You could have trusted me.'

She hadn't at any point trusted him, not even when he'd extended the hand of friendship. She didn't want to insult him, but his presence pushed her back towards the very thing she was running away from. 'I'm always afraid.'

'Of the Cheka? I'm sure the Russian police have a long reach, but not all the way to the tip of Sweden. Certainly not as far as Paris.' He shrugged. 'It's your business… though you deemed it safe enough to tell the staff here.'

Caught out, she flew back with, 'I suppose you think we shouldn't be in the Ritz at all?'

'I don't criticise anybody for coming here. I haunt this place when the heating in my apartment feels inadequate.'

'You're wondering how we can afford it.'

'Princess,' on his tongue, her title was ironic, 'I wouldn't stoop to anything so vulgar. Shall we?' He offered his arm, while Katya considered the social consequences of slapping his face: *dire, most likely, with little advantage to her.* As she laid her gloved hand on his sleeve, a yearning voice spoke his name.

'There you are, Harry-my-heart. Stay and tell me how you are. Poor, poor darling.'

Harry put up a hand, a definite veto. 'Una, please. Don't.'

'Yes, I know all about the stiff upper lip but you cannot hold in the ocean. You will drown…' The new arrival took in Katya. Blinked. Then, bizarrely, turned her thumbs and index fingers into make-believe spectacles and scrutinised Katya like a myopic dowager. 'Who is this, Harry? Do I know her?'

Katya shied back. Considering that the woman before her could be no older than Tatiana, this approach was presumptuous. A Parisian eccentric, wearing a dress made of the soft material used for gentlemen's undergarments. A printed sash tied a fraction under her bosom ended in pompoms, reminiscent of a bell pull. Was she what Katya's mother would term 'a theatrical'? Odder still, her light brown hair was cut radically short. Perhaps the poor thing was recently released from a sanatorium? Spanish flu? Even this was not the most unsettling part of the picture. Preening at the ends of their leashes, a pair of creatures Katya at first thought were satin-black dogs… until one of them pulled back its lip and fixed her with unblinking topaz eyes. Cats. And not the fireside variety.

A vision of Anoushka sleeping innocently in her cot leapt to Katya's mind. 'I cannot believe that wild cats are let in here.'

'Oh, Lola and Leo aren't wild,' the girl assured her. 'Not until they're hungry, anyway. Forgive me, they're not "cats", they're jaguars. Felines, but so much more intelligent. Chérie, do you mind me asking,' – she inspected Katya's dress with great concentration – 'you are so pretty and your figure's the bee's roller skates. So why, I ask?'

'Why what, mademoiselle?' was Katya's stony response.

'*Why* are you dressed in a style that died the moment the guns began firing and the men marched away?'

Harry cut in then. 'Una, you are not at a party, entertaining your crowd. What you call "modern manners" is plain rude to the rest of us.'

Marvellously undeterred, the girl demanded, 'But who is she, Harry? Not French, with that colouring. Most assuredly not English, with those cheekbones. Why have I never seen her before?'

Harry sighed. 'Allow me to introduce her Serene Highness…' A dry smile flitted across his lips. 'Come to think of it, I don't know who you are either.'

'Princess Ekaterina Vytenis.'

'Then Princess Ekaterina Vytenis, allow me to present Mademoiselle Una McBride.'

'Russian,' the girl said triumphantly, as if she'd been pipped at the point of guessing. 'From the snow-scoured east, the cruel-hearted steppe.'

'No, from Moscow.'

'But your people came from the steppe.'

'Not at all. Originally—'

'Oh, but they did. It's in the eyes, like slanting sapphires. Is that what you wear in Russia now?' She poked Katya's tightly corseted waist. 'Can you breathe?'

'Perfectly,' Katya said untruthfully. 'You… have been unwell? Is this why you've cut off your hair and wear only your shift?'

Harry's snort of laughter earned him a glare from Katya, and a delighted chuckle from the girl.

'This is my newest thing. I designed it myself. You like it?'

Katya sought a tactful reply. 'It's very clever to design your own things. Most resourceful.'

'Thing is, I could never afford Mademoiselle Chanel's models – this is based on one of hers. You know Coco? No? Where have you been? She was the height of *chic* in Deauville when the fighting started, and all the rich dames flocked there to escape Paris. She made them throw off their girdles and dress as nature intended. Now she's back, she's doing the same thing, but she's got so pricey. Only…' – the girl leaned in to deliver something Harry must not hear – 'there's a woman on rue Duphot, a hop from here, who'll run off a Chanel or a Paquin, a Vionnet or a Callot Soeurs if you take her a drawing. Say, would you like an introduction?'

Katya shook her head violently. *Pay to look like this child-woman? As likely as cutting off her own hair.* 'I prefer to find my own dressmaker.'

'Oh, sure. No skin off my nose.'

'No skin? I'm sorry?' The girl was incomprehensible.

With a shrug that implied, 'You work it out,' the girl mewed to get her cats' attention and blew Harry a kiss. 'We will talk.' She placed her hand on her heart. 'For now, toodle-pip, Harry-of-my-dreams, unless you're also going to the bar?'

'Not tonight, Una. I'm dining with a business contact.'

'Male? Can I join you?'

'Female.'

'Brush-off received and understood. *A bientôt.*'

'*A bientôt, chérie.*'

When she'd gone, carving an easy path as people moved when they saw the cats, Katya let out her irritation. 'I understood hardly a thing she said. Who is she?'

'I told you, Una McBride. She's American. Though she's fluent in French, she translates literally from the American which is why you found her hard to follow.'

'What is "toodle-pip"?'

'English for "goodbye". My brother…' The flickering muscle made a sudden return. 'A bit of slang from British officers she came into contact with.'

Katya opened her eyes. 'What kind of female is she?' The sort who strolled unescorted into the male preserve of a hotel bar, it would seem, dressed in next to nothing. Harry drew his brows together.

'You really are a gem from a vanished age. Una left New York to join those of her countrymen who came to fight for our freedom. She did a fine job of being a nurse. I met her in a field hospital when I was an involuntary guest.'

Katya reddened. 'Oh. I see. I wanted to nurse in Moscow, when I saw the wounded soldiers pouring back from the front. But Papa refused. He felt it would be indecent for me to touch men brutalised by combat. Not to mention blood and other… other realities of nursing.'

'Quite so. Too much reality is a most uncomfortable thing.'

How easily he mocked her. She could hand him a real example of irony – that in fact the reek of fresh blood was embedded in her mind. 'How does this Una make her living now?'

'Una has wealthy lovers. One recently returned home, so she is actively seeking another.'

'So she is—'

'She is *not*,' he thrust back in a tone that dared her to contradict. 'This is Paris. If a woman wants a position, she marries well or becomes the mistress of a man with power and money. Nobody minds, or gets hot under the collar about it.'

'Except the wife of the man with the mistress. She would care.'

'Not if she takes a lover of her own. You've heard of a "virtuous circle"? Paris enjoys virtuous triangles.'

'They sound anything but virtuous. If my husband took a mistress, I would kill him *and* the whore.'

Harry whistled. Eyelash shadows fell across his cheeks as he gazed down at her and she sensed him digging into her mind. Perhaps he was intrigued by her hair, its sweep and the tendrils lying against her throat. He said, 'There is a third way for a woman to make something of herself.'

'I'm not sure I wish to know.'

'With her mind.'

'Employment, I suppose,' she said despondently.

'Not employment. No woman makes her way working for somebody else. She uses her skills. Starts her own business and rises, like champagne bubbles.'

'Is that possible?'

'I have personally met five women who have done it, and all but one work in the couture industry. Take the Callot Sisters as your example.'

That girl, Una, had mentioned 'Callot Soeurs' so it was no recommendation to Katya. Besides, how could she start a business with no experience of anything? 'Take me to the dining room. Mama will think I've fallen asleep.'

As they walked, she asked the question that had buzzed like a persistent fly since she'd walked into him. 'In Sweden you looked like a ruffian and now you don't.'

That's harsh, his look implied.

'Like the opposite of a gentleman, then.'

'Why did you look like the opposite of a princess?'

'I was a fugitive.'

'And I was venturing through harsh terrain, dressed so as not to freeze to death. How is the baby? Anoushka, am I right?'

'She's well enough.'

'And you. How are you?'

She knew what he was asking. 'I am often anxious, frequently confused but no longer – no longer wishing for death.'

'I'm glad. Any word of your fly-by-night maid?'

'None.'

He'd evaded her question, Katya realised. As they were now in the dining room, their conversation was over.

Irina Vytenis was gracious, unaware that she'd met this well-groomed man in very different circumstances. Tatiana, however, offered an arch look.

'I know you. You've mislaid your beard.'

Harry stroked his jaw. 'I dismissed it. It had served its purpose.'

'Which was?'

'To keep my chin warm.'

'I'm certain you were on a mission to overthrow the Bolsheviks.'

He clicked his finger. 'Dash, you've found me out. I had a try, but apparently revolutions can't be reversed, only re-run and you never know what the new result will be.'

Tatiana gave a slightly frantic giggle. 'What was in your kitbag? It looked so heavy.'

'Is that your business, Tatiana?' Katya feared that at any moment, Harry might mention the loan. Specifically, when he might expect repayment. More worryingly, her mother was eyeing him in a way that suggested the morphine curtains in her head were drawing back.

Sure enough, Princess Vytenis frowned. 'I'm certain I know you too.'

Harry bowed. 'In which sense of the word "know", Princess? When last you saw me, I was a ragamuffin, unfit to venture into your presence.' Belatedly, he answered Tatiana. 'It was sawdust in the bag.'

'Not diamonds?' Tatiana deployed her dimples and Katya felt a little push of jealousy. Meanwhile, her mother's expression had hardened. She had finally worked out who he was.

'We have detained you too long, Monsieur—'

'Morten, Mama,' Katya supplied. Her look urged Harry to go. Harry did not move.

'It was my privilege to help your daughter…' He glanced at Katya, who fed him a pleading look. 'To find the dining room.'

Irina Vytenis inclined her head so slightly that it was a crafted insult. 'We are obliged to you for this last service, Monsieur Morten, but please do not trouble yourself further. As you have already discovered, I am careful with whom my daughters associate.'

'What exactly is your objection, Madame?'

'A man who trades in sawdust is not one I wish my girls to know.'

'Mama, please,' Katya begged.

'That's your only objection? That I earn my living through trade?'

'Since you ask, it is not.' Princess Vytenis gave Harry a fresh glance, a flick of the aristocratic whip. 'What nationality are you?'

'I am Anglo-Swedish.'

'Then that is my point. A man who rides the railways while his countrymen fight and die is not worthy of the name. When we encountered you in Sweden, you were not in uniform.'

'Madame, how do you know?'

It was the answer he'd given Katya, but whereas then he'd been teasing, now he was deadly serious. Katya saw her mother turn a glacial cheek which meant '*conversation over*'. Taking Harry's arm, drawing him away, Katya tried to explain.

'My mother has been through so much.'

'But not enough, since her arrogance remains intact. Will it hold up when she discovers that war has torn up her right to wipe the floor with the rest of humanity?' His pride was wounded, evidenced by the jumping nerve beneath his temple. 'A spell of hardship will show her that Russian princesses, countesses and grand duchesses have little social worth here. There are too many in Paris. Too many of anything, the price drops, like table wine in a glut year.'

Katya reared back. 'You have no idea what it cost us to get here.'

He removed her hand from his arm. 'I believe it cost a very great deal. Your soul, perhaps?'

'What do you mean?' she whispered.

He looked around. 'The beautiful princess in the Lubyanka might wish she was here with you.'

He caught the hand that came so close to striking him. Raised it to his lips in a way that was almost an insult. He whispered, 'Dare you bite me again. No? Not very "Ritz" behaviour. I can help you find your feet in Paris, but not until you climb down from your ivory tower and tell the truth. You didn't try to kill yourself because you were cold, or depressed, but because you could not bear to inhabit your skin a moment longer, Ekaterina.'

'Serene Highness to you.' A crude snub, falling flat when she heard his derisive laugh.

Through dinner, though she tried to stop herself, she couldn't resist looking to see which table he was given. A good one. And his guest? A woman around her own age, with reddish, curly hair. Clearly enjoying herself and the champagne that Harry bought.

The following morning, she waited nervously as the front-desk clerk tallied their bill. She'd passed a broken night, alternately fretting about the cost of this stay, and dreaming weirdly that her Lasunskoy cousins were still alive, living in America. 'Come to us here,' they'd urged from the top of a towering building. She'd woken with the feeling of an egg whisk in her stomach, whipping up a froth.

'All is taken care of, Serene Highness.'

'Taken care... What do you mean?'

The clerk re-consulted his book, as if he might have made a mistake. 'Your account was added to that of Monsieur Harald Morten and has been paid.' The clerk presented her with a receipt. 'Do you wish for a taxi?'

'Taxi? No, thank you.' Her head reeled. *All paid? After the things she'd said?* 'Is Monsieur Morten here still?'

'No, Madame. He did not stay the night.'

What now? Leave, of course. She deferred the moment, however, taking the elevator to collect the documents to be translated, and calling to Tatiana that she was 'stepping out on business'. She left the hotel and walked through spiralling snow to rue Daru, to Saint Alexander Nevsky.

Hardly a surprise to find the cathedral steps deserted. No translator, however desperate for business, would sit outside in this weather. There was nobody inside either except a pair of women polishing the candlesticks. The sight of their flat shoes and shapeless smocks made Katya think of Princess Provolskaya.

A smart, chauffeured car was waiting outside No. 6 rue Brazy and Katya hesitated before knocking, uncertain how the princess might receive her on this second call. Snow settling on her head and shoulders eventually persuaded her to lift the knocker and give three raps. The door was answered after a short delay. Princess Provolskaya greeted Katya with pleasure.

'My dear, you are quite the ice maiden.' She stood back to allow Katya in. 'Let me send my little pupil on her way and then I am at your service.' Ludmilla Provolskaya lifted her hand, signalling to the waiting chauffeur that he might collect his passenger. 'Tread carefully, Clémentine,' she told the small girl standing shyly behind her. 'The pavements are slippery.'

The child, who was clutching sheets of piano music, bobbed a solemn curtsey. 'Thank you, Madame la Princesse.'

'Thank *you*, Clémentine, for being such an adept and charming pupil. I will see you next week. Remember to practise the Brahms piece especially.'

'*Oui, Madame.*'

'And what else must you remember, *petite*?'

The little girl bit her lip. 'To enjoy myself, Madame la Princesse.'

'Exactly!' As the chauffeur took his charge away, Princess Provolskaya shut the door and sighed. 'So tragic, a child living life as though it were a heavy overcoat. She lost her father to the war, though not the family fortune. Aleksey would cut off an arm to drive a car like theirs. Now tell me, did you find a place to stay?'

Katya dissembled, not daring to say, 'yes, the Ritz'. Instead she explained the bank's intransigence. 'Is it true, there's a translator who touts for business on the cathedral steps?'

'Indeed, though I haven't seen him recently. He was once a university professor, I believe. A little slow these days – what is it you need translated?'

Katya showed the princess her documents.

'And you need it done in the correct legal language. Of course.'

'Where does he live, this man?'

'Oh, here and there. I tell you what,' Princess Provolskaya took the parcel of documents out of Katya's hand. 'Leave these with me and Aleksey will find him. Aleksey can find anyone in the Russian quarter.'

Katya reluctantly agreed, telling herself she had to trust somebody, some time.

'Ah, excuse me.' Princess Provolskaya turned to respond to a knock at the door. 'My next pupil.'

Left to herself for a moment, Katya surveyed her surroundings. The lobby looked clean, as did the stairs, even if the decor was basic. No signs of damp, at any rate. When the princess returned and held out her hand to say goodbye, Katya heard herself saying, 'That room you mentioned before. The one my poor cousins had? I don't suppose it is still available?'

Chapter Nine

They moved in on Saturday, 11 January, two days after first setting foot in Paris. With money remaining out of reach, Katya knew she had to find work. With the single-mindedness that had got them across a continent, she took a job in Dedushka's Café, starting immediately.

At five each morning she walked to the courtyard with its dustbins and washing line, and in through a side door. For two hours, she'd stand at a bench preparing a day's worth of *golubtsi*, stuffing the wilted leaves with rice, pork or chicken. At first, she made a terrible mess, her little parcels disintegrating in the pan, but her employer, Georgy Filatov, was patient and soon she got the hang of it. And of making another of his specialities, buckwheat blinis, served with smoked fish and soured cream, or jam, when fresh foods were in short supply. From seven to twelve, she waited tables, dashing in and out of the kitchen. To her surprise, once she grew used to being on her feet, she enjoyed the work. Earning her first money felt liberating and Georgy allowed her to take home any leftovers. It also afforded her an escape from her mother and sister. Finding themselves walled-in six floors up, Tatiana became even more contrary while Irina discovered the sleeping aid veronal. That was courtesy of Dr Shepkin, Princess Provolskaya's friend who practiced on rue Brazy.

In this patchy fashion, January 1919 passed. Katya paid the rent, though she knew her job couldn't last – she was filling in for Georgy's wife who had recently given birth. Whenever she saw Princess Provols-kaya or the princess's son, she would ask about her documents and was advised each time to be patient. Better the work was done correctly than in a rush. 'The bank would be sure to notice discrepancies.'

Patience, Katya was discovering, was the child of necessity. Still, life wasn't all gloom. Having her afternoons free meant she was able to explore. Katya quickly grew to love the unpretentious eighth, its tall terraces with balcony railings as lacy as stocking tops. Elegant and rational but with a dash of illicit champagne. Wrapped up against the weather, she discovered Parc Monceau with its architectural surprises and hidden corners; seemingly endless Boulevard Malesherbes, neighbour to Boulevard Courcelles, with its fashion boutiques, milliners and drapers. Soon she knew every shop window in the neighbourhood as well as all the Morris columns: spherical advertising boards that promoted upcoming plays and recitals, headache pills and shoe polish.

She became familiar with Kaminsky's, a second-hand jeweller's on the corner of rue Daru and rue de Courcelles, where a permanent queue of cash-strapped Russians sold their treasures. One afternoon, she was peering through its window when a pair of cufflinks on a tray with a heap of others snagged her eye. She rubbed the glass, faint with apprehension. They were her father's, bearing the family arms! Katya rattled the door but it was locked. Lunchtime closing. By the time she returned, they'd been sold. 'A regular purchaser bought the whole tray,' the jeweller explained. 'He sells cufflinks table-to-table in cabaret clubs.' Nor could the proprietor, Monsieur Kaminsky, recall who had originally brought them in, though he was certain it had been a woman…

'Russian?' Katya asked breathlessly.

'I think so. Yes, Russian.'

Could Yana have got herself to Paris? 'Red headscarf?'

He was unsure. 'I get so much stuff.' But he let her draw him a sketch of the Vytenis Hart and promised that if anything came in with that emblem, he would contact her. Katya kept the mystery to herself and tried not to scan every face she saw in the hope that one of them would be Yana's.

Katya discovered the métro and her first trip underground was from Monceau to Place de l'Étoile, where she emerged into the light with knees shaking and a massive smile. In rue Saint-Honoré and rue de Rivoli, she found the more exclusive boutiques. These, and Galleries Lafayette, the luxury store on Boulevard Haussmann, gave her the opportunity to digest the story of Parisian fashion and completed the re-education of her eye. Since 1914, when Irina and Vera had shopped in blissful ignorance of the cataclysm to come, every established rule had been rewritten. No wonder people had stared at them at the Ritz! Modern fashion reflected women's new-found freedom, their burgeoning sense of what they could do and be.

Katya tried to explain this to her mother. 'I see women jumping on and off buses. They don't need men to hand them in and out. Yesterday, I watched a girl leap off a bus while it was still moving.'

'Then she deserved to slip on the ice and break her leg.'

Coco Chanel. Jeanne Paquin. Vionnet. Callot Soeurs. '*Take the Callot Sisters as your example*,' Katya recalled Harry advising her. But it wasn't until she heard their name for a third time that Katya felt the shoulder-tap of destiny.

*

It happened on a dank bruise of a day in early February. The café was packed, Katya serving bowl after bowl of the lunchtime special, potato soup, and stacks of blinis. Enough tea was being poured to float a small ship. Princess Provolskaya, seated with her son, touched Katya's hip as she sidled by, saying, 'Well done.' When Katya passed again with a tray of dirty crocks, she asked, 'Your sister working yet?'

'Not yet.'

The princess observed that, 'Those who did not work, did not eat. Not so, Aleksey?'

Her son muttered something. He was wolfing down his food, eager to get back to work. A national fuel shortage put a cap on how much driving he could do on any one day. He made most of his money either very late at night or at dawn, hours the older drivers were not so keen on. Katya had heard him complain that he could waste half a day at the railway station, which explained the way he'd ambushed them as they arrived, though it made his subsequent refusal of a fare harder to explain. Today, he wasn't making eye contact so Katya refrained from asking him if her documents were ready yet and instead asked his mother.

'A day or two more,' Princess Provolskaya assured her. 'The old man has been unwell, but he is doing the work as we speak.'

'Could I go to see him, check how he's doing?'

The princess quickly shook her head. 'He has a condition of the lungs, doctors suspect tuberculosis. It's why he's no longer to be seen on the cathedral steps. Living with a baby as you do, it might not be wise…' She left the rest unsaid and pointed to the top she was wearing, a striped blouson with a sailor collar. 'This is new. Modern, isn't it? I had a girl make it for me.'

'Very chic.' Katya had stolen that word from Una McBride.

The princess frowned at Katya's work dress, which was grey wool, second-hand and too big for her. 'All I did was cut out a picture from a fashion journal, the girl took measurements and a week later… This is based on something from Callot Soeurs.'

Katya had heard their name three times now. *They must be doing something exciting.*

'In the old days,' Princess Provolskaya said, 'whenever I was in Paris for the collections I would take a cab to the ninth, where Callot Soeurs started out. They're in better premises now, on Avenue Matignon, but I loved their old shop. Such energy!' Sighing, she explained how she never visited them now, for the same reason she wouldn't let a shop girl dab perfume on her. 'If one can't afford the bottle, one would rather not be tantalised by the smell, don't you agree?'

Katya thought such ideas heresy and to prove she didn't share the princess's defeatism, she ripped off her apron the moment her shift was over and hurried home.

'Soup for you,' she told Tatiana, pouring it from a canister into a pan, lighting the stove. She'd run all the way upstairs. 'Don't let it scorch.'

'Hey!' Her sister was huddled in a blanket, reading a book bought from a seller on Quai de Montebello, by the Seine. 'Where are you going?' Tatiana watched as Katya put on her rose-trimmed hat.

'To start my life.' The picture-reel was running through Katya's head again. She didn't visualise herself in an atelier this time, but as a version of Princess Provolskaya's 'girl': sewing dresses for private clients. She could do it; she had the hands, after all. She only needed to polish up her ideas. Polish herself.

'Don't let Mama doze all afternoon.' Katya checked on Anoushka, who was fast asleep in the dresser drawer they used for a crib. Picking dirty nappies from the floor, she went down to the courtyard wash house and put them to soak. She lingered, warming herself at the stove that heated the water, and which still contained a few red embers.

Her gaze fell on a pile of scrap paper on the hearth. There were out-of-date café menus, along with bundles of used prescription forms that must have been thrown out by Dr Shepkin, who held his surgery above the café. Katya leafed through in the hope of finding a sheet or two of clean writing paper. One re-used everything these days, old envelopes, packaging. She thought she'd found something, until she turned it over and saw a hand-written note on the back.

Somebody had listed step-by-step instructions on how to deal with a patient suffering from a heart attack. The writing was not Dr Shepkin's, which Katya knew well from scrutinising her mother's prescriptions. It was neat writing. A woman's hand? The idea reinforced Katya's suspicion that their Russian doctor was not all he claimed to be. 'I hope none of us is ever seriously ill,' she muttered, returning the paper to the pile.

She quit the wash house and struck out for rue de Courcelles, walking its length to the junction of one of her favourite streets. The perfect place to begin this new chapter of her life.

Parfums de Rosine at No. 107 rue du Faubourg Saint-Honoré boasted hanging glass shelves that had entranced Katya since she first discovered the shop. She always paused to look, but today she walked in.

'I'd like to try a fragrance.'

'Which, Madame?' The saleswoman stayed behind the counter, arms crossed. As a *vendeuse*, her salary was almost certainly built around commission. Katya evidently didn't inspire much hope.

Katya's eyes sped over crystal bottles and rows of perfumes in more primitive stone and metal vessels. This was the great couturier Paul Poiret's perfume shop and she admired his taste for the exotic. 'That one?' She indicated a squat onyx bottle that the *vendeuse* passed over with some reluctance. It was a tiny work of art. Its delicious prettiness transformed a measure of fragrant water into an object of deep desire. Katya wanted it so badly, she came out in goosebumps.

'It comes with its own travelling box, see?' The *vendeuse* showed her a dainty case with Chinese silk lining. 'To keep the bottle safe on long journeys.'

Perfect for ocean-liner voyages she was never likely to make. Katya put the perfume back on the counter and flashed a painful smile. This adventure would end in humiliation. She ought to go home and mimic her mother and Tatiana. Read a book, go to bed. Wait for things to get better on their own. 'I can't afford it. I simply wanted to know what something so beautiful smells like. I'll go.'

'Wait.' The *vendeuse* reached under her counter and brought out a silver tube. 'Monsieur hasn't released this yet, it is called "Aladin". I am allowed to offer special customers a drop or two. To tease, you know?'

Special customer? The girl must need her eyesight checked. But as Katya dragged off a glove and presented her wrist, her sense of adventure returned. The *vendeuse* drew a trail of amber tincture across Katya's flesh. Musky scents rose up. *Church, incense, old wood.*

'It diminishes with wear, Madame. With a fine perfume, a little goes a long way.'

Katya put her glove back on. 'One day, I shall come back and buy a bottle. You've been generous.'

The *vendeuse* inclined her head. 'When I first started here, a customer, a very old lady, told me, "Always be kind to young girls.

You do not know who they may become." She was a duchesse, so I
accepted the lesson.'

From the rue du Faubourg Saint-Honoré Katya headed to Avenue
Matignon, where she found Callot Soeurs' salon conveniently close to
the corner. For a while, she watched a stream of mainly female visitors
entering the coolly unremarkable building. Some were staff, judging
by their sober clothes. Others were certainly clients, marked by the
indefinable stamp of money. These women wore *de rigueur* black hats,
but not hats like hers. She wished she'd left hers at home, it was not
the kind you could take off and slip under your arm. Blowing on her
fingers, Katya paced up and down to keep the blood flowing. She
needed to see behind the doors.

*'No woman makes her way working for somebody else. She starts her
own business and rises, like champagne bubbles.'*

Or sinks like a stone, the more likely scenario. But what else could
she do? Of the five self-made women Harry Morten knew, only one
worked outside couture. He hadn't said what she did, and Katya sensed
it wasn't respectable. As the short day faded, she made repeated forays
toward 9–11 Avenue Matignon, veering away at the last moment.
In the end, chance came to her aid. A taxi drew up, disgorging an
immense lady in furs, with ankles so thick she waddled. The woman
became entangled in the doorway and Katya bounded forward to
help. After thanking her, the lady barked, 'Well, are you coming in?'

It felt like permission.

She trailed the woman into a large salon furnished like a town
mansion and lit with gilded lamps. A buttoned-up assistant stepped
forward to intercept Katya. 'Madame?'

'I – I'd like to see your current stock. The parade, I mean.' *Stock, for goodness' sake. She wasn't at a horse sale!*

'Have we had the pleasure of welcoming Madame before?'

Katya raised her wrist, sharing a reassuring note of Aladin. 'I am new in Paris. I am Princess Vytenis.'

That was her passport. Though the assistant's gaze lingered on the rose-smothered hat and on Katya's scuffed leather purse, she gestured towards an arch that divided the room. 'Go through. The parade begins in a few minutes, *Princesse*. Perhaps you would be more comfortable at the rear.'

Katya noticed a dish of marshmallows placed enticingly on a side table. One straight in the mouth, two more in the pocket. As she lowered herself onto a spindly, gilded chair furthest from the front, a clock struck three. Other ladies took their places and clouds of gently competing perfume enveloped the rows. Katya took a good look at Callot Soeurs' clientele. They'd all kept their hats on. Whereas hers sat on her head like a chicken on its eggs, theirs sat low. The large lady who had ushered her in, and who was seated directly in front of her, was wearing a black velvet hat that made Katya think of a soldier's helmet poking over the side of a battlefield trench. She recalled the early years of the century when her mother's friends would visit in their carriages. Back then it had struck her, young as she was, that it was the gowns and hats that had come to call. The women beneath had been merely the means of propulsion for expensive textiles. Vera had hated the excess more than she had.

'They're like roses, these ladies. Beautiful heads, feet in manure.' Vera had been alluding to the unwashed hair beneath the false curls, the whiff of perspiration behind the drenching violet water.

'I wish you were with me now, Vera,' Katya murmured. 'You'd like what you see.'

The large lady creaked in her seat. 'Did you address me?'

'No, Madame. I was thinking of my sister – she was lost.'

'How sad.' Older than Katya by at least three decades, the woman spoke through a handkerchief. A powerful odour of balsam seeped from it, which Katya associated with childhood chest infections. Though she'd discarded her furs, the woman was clearly struggling in the salon's heat. Her cheeks were rosy under her face powder. She beetled at Katya over the handkerchief. 'Aren't you a little young?'

'To lose my sister?'

'To be sitting here. This herd is twice your age.' She gestured to the other women with a flick of her hand. 'Where is your mother?'

'At home, Madame.'

'Ah-ha?' The lady pushed up the front of her hat to see Katya better. Her brows were plucked clean away, redrawn with kohl. Small eyes, deep like currents pressed into a bun.

'Shopping for a new wardrobe?' She took stock of Katya's coat collar, trimmed with nail scissors to disguise the fraying. Her interest moved to Katya's purse. 'Let me guess, you have a little notepad and pencil in there. Are you a journalist? Accredited?' She toyed with the idea. 'Seems more likely.'

'I'm here to see the collection. I want to know – I mean, I'm trying to learn—'

'What's your perfume?' The question cut through Katya's shambling explanation in a manner that bordered on rudeness.

'It's called Aladin,' Katya offered her wrist. 'It's a *Rosine* perfume, available only to special customers.' She let that sink in. 'Tell me what you think.'

'Poiret always puts in too much of the Eastern bazaar. You were saying why you were here?'

Katya answered defiantly, 'I want to work in fashion so I need to know what fashion is.'

'Keep that to yourself, or you'll have Madame Gerber after you.'

'Who is Madame Gerber?'

'Marie Callot Gerber, the senior of the sisters. She *is* Callot Soeurs and she doesn't take kindly to copyists.'

'I'm not—'

'Ah, there's the *directrice*. She runs the show. It's about to start.' The woman turned her back as long-necked girls with classic profiles filed in. Unhurried and faintly bored, they posed one after the other in front of a voile-draped window. Katya had a hindered view, but it was enough. Enough to be awed and confused at the same time.

Wealthy Paris would continue to wear black, if this collection was indicative of the spring trends, but flourishes of red, peacock and metallics suggested a creeping subversion. The blousy tunics and roomy skirts she'd assumed were the latest mode were nowhere. For spring 1919, Callot Soeurs served up a pencil-straight silhouette. Filmy fabrics obscured waistlines. Hems were jagged or asymmetric, falling to mid-calf. For evening wear, trains gave the impression of length but legs were exposed every time. Bare shoulders too, covered only with chiffon or fringing… *I must record this*, Katya thought, and dug inside her bag for her address book. It had a few empty pages and a slender pencil. She'd been taught to draw and confidently dashed off an outline. A hand descended on her shoulder. Her pencil was taken from her.

A voice whispered into her ear, '*Absolument défendu.*'

Absolutely forbidden. She looked up in shock. Somebody stood so close behind her, his cuff brushed the side of her face. She recognised the fingers, scattered with fair hair. Recognised the hand that had hefted her steamer trunks off a railway car. She hissed, 'Monsieur Morten, give me back my pencil.'

'I thought it was you. Tell me you're not snooping.'

She wouldn't dignify that with a reply. 'Are you selling sawdust to the Callot sisters? Oh no, I forgot. You habitually breathe down strange women's necks.'

'I don't think you're a strange woman. Angry and fierce, and often ill-mannered.' He touched a crescent curl that had worked loose from under her hat. 'Your hair gives you away. Ochre, corn, a hint of umber... I haven't settled on the shade.'

'I am not a tube of artist's oil paint,' Katya said through clenched teeth and swiped her pencil back, dropping it into her purse along with the address book. She'd felt strangely alive for a few moments. She'd remember enough detail to entertain Tatiana later, at any rate. *Poor caged Tatiana.*

It wasn't going to be easy to slip away without creating a fuss. Harry Morten had not moved and a new fragrance was invading her senses, a darkly masculine scent of frankincense and orange oil. Church again, with summer picnics rolled in. Four chimes of the clock was her excuse to stand up. Night had arrived behind the voile drapes and gas lamps illuminated the ceiling. As she got to her feet, so did the intimidating woman in front, who, turning, exclaimed, 'Why, Monsieur Morten!'

'Madame Claudine.' He reached over chair backs to shake her hand. 'How are you?'

'Oh, you know.' She still had her handkerchief over her mouth. *Had she sat like that the whole time?* 'I heard about poor Christian. What a miserable pity. My condolences.'

Who, Katya wondered, *is Christian?*

Harry accepted the kind words but turned the subject. 'Did you like the collection, Claudine?'

'I'd have liked it a lot more if they turned their heating down.' The woman pounced on Katya, waving her pungent handkerchief. 'What did you think, hm?'

'Glorious. Sumptuous. Only, confusing because—'

'It's not Callot Soeurs' best, though I don't doubt it will fill the coffers very nicely. What about you, Monsieur Morten? Will it take?'

Katya slipped away, glad to escape the oppressive stink of balsam. She paused to steal another marshmallow for Tatiana who would rage at being left alone so long. She allowed herself a last glance at a mannequin in a coat of grey-tone shark's tooth. The girl posed, letting the coat shoulder fall to her mid-arm. The garment was big enough for a Russian coachman, and the girl inside it reminded Katya of a sausage inside a split bun. That was the trouble with long-term hunger: everything became food.

Outside, a taxi waited, its wheels lipping the kerb. *One day, perhaps, but not today.* She hadn't gone far towards the métro when a voice hailed her, offering her a lift. She walked on, pretending she hadn't heard. Suddenly Harry Morten was alongside her. Wearing a velvet-collared coat, a hat pulled down over his brow, he was armoured against the cold.

'Before you say it, it will be no trouble sharing a taxi and you're shivering.'

She was, after the cosseting salon. 'It'll take you out of your way.' Actually, it wouldn't, or not by much. She knew he lived on rue Goya in the eighth, on the smarter side of Parc Monceau. She'd made him give her his address when they were in Gothenburg, and had assumed then that rue Goya must be a down-at-heel location. A stroll past a few days ago had proved her wrong. She said, 'Very well. Take me as far as Boulevard Malesherbes and I'll walk the rest.'

'Am I not allowed to see where you live?'

'For your information, my home is on rue Brazy, by Saint Alexander Nevsky. When the organ plays, our windows shake.' *Window* – they had only one. She wouldn't tell him that she and Tatiana took turns in traipsing downstairs each morning to fetch water. Or that they cooked using a single saucepan and folded away their camp beds each day so they could move about without colliding. Once, she'd thought herself so very far above this man and the reversal was hard to swallow. 'Boulevard Malesherbes will be fine.'

They spoke little on the journey until Harry asked after Anoushka. Katya was happy to catalogue her niece's achievements; her precocious ability to almost grasp objects and to make sounds that sometimes sounded like real words. 'A neighbour is teaching her to play scales on the piano.'

'You mean, someone holds her finger and plays for her.'

'You can never start learning music too young.'

'Do you like to dance?'

Katya was jolted into an honest answer. 'I love it. I used to adore balls, my dance card filling up. Then there were no balls, no receptions. I haven't danced with a boy in more than five years.'

'Dancing with boys is overrated. Try dancing with a man.'

She reared up at that. 'Perhaps you imagine no one has ever flirted with me? Well, I am a profoundly good flirt and Russian boys – *men* – are good at it too. You suppose that when you kissed me it was the first time?'

'The question didn't occur to me, Princess.' Street lights chequered the cab's interior, glossing Harry's face. His lips curved in a smile.

What was he thinking? Planning? Her pulse stirred. He'd kissed her that one time so he'd never forget where he was when the Armistice came. It hadn't been for passion. She would keep telling herself that. 'What took you to Callot Soeurs?' she asked. 'Escorting a woman-friend?'

'Why do you ask questions, then answer yourself?'

Vera had often commented on this habit, saying, *'Darling, tennis is much more fun played with two.'*

'To save time,' Katya informed him. She sat bolt upright, every sinew fighting the taxi's motion. Imagine, being thrown against a man who traded sawdust and was looking at her as if he were about to prise open a dubious oyster.

'How can it save time,' he asked, 'to repeatedly lurch to the wrong conclusion?'

'Why else would a red-blooded man be at a ladies' dressmakers, unless on escort duty?'

'There are many reasons a red-blooded man might want to watch beautiful girls drifting around in silk. Show me your drawing.'

'The one you stopped me finishing?'

'Yes. I'm curious.'

'All right.' It was too dark for him to make anything of it – until he flicked the cigarette lighter concealed in his hand, casting a halo on the page. Katya found herself unaccountably nervous. 'A stupid little drawing,' she said.

'Actually, quite adept. You've caught something… the swing. Who taught you?'

'A woman my father employed to paint our portraits who stayed on, teaching us. We lost touch. Who was Christian?'

'My brother.' Harry didn't look up from her sketch, his features a broken mask in the flickering light. 'He died a week before the end of hostilities, in northern France, at the Sambre Canal.'

From the way he extinguished his lighter and closed her diary Katya understood that commentary wasn't welcome. He'd parried that girl Una's sympathy and Madame Claudine's condolences in the same fashion.

When he spoke again, the last few moments might not have happened. 'Don't ever sketch at a couture show unless you want to be put out on to the street and blacklisted. Copyists are the bane of couturiers' lives.'

'I only wanted to record what I'd seen. Sitting in that little chair I felt I'd arrived where I've wanted to be all my life.'

'Well, I respect you for wanting something. All the more for wanting something so—'

'Impossible?'

'Demanding. But what are you if not demanding? I can help you, but don't make it harder.'

'You said before you'd help me.' *But what do you want in return?* There were many ways a woman could be trapped. Intimidation; prison walls; gratitude; desire, even. 'How do you imagine we'd work together, Monsieur Morten? I grant, you've improved your appearance since Gothenburg, but we still occupy very different spheres.'

'Radically different, Princess. The greatest difference being that mine still exists.'

The driver swung into Boulevard Malesherbes, taking the corner too wide and Katya slid across the hard leather seat, hat-first into Harry. Gauze roses and millinery wire buckled against his hard skull while her nose filled with the fragrance of orange and frankincense. He shifted, and she fell across him. In her urgent desire to get away, she put out a hand to push herself up, and discovered his thigh. 'My God, sorry.'

'No need to be. But how awful for you, to lose your dignity.'

Scrambling back to her side of the seat, she leaned forward to use the speaking tube. 'Pull up, please,' she instructed the driver. 'I want to get out.'

With a sigh, Harry rapped on the glass and the cab pulled in. 'No,' he insisted as Katya reached for the door handle. 'My place is a few strides away. You travel on to your princess castle.'

She tried to argue – in truth, she didn't have the fare. But Harry was already passing notes to the driver. As the taxi pulled away, Katya half-expected him to gaze after her. But he hadn't a glance to spare. She saw him approach a huddled figure in a doorway. A vagrant whose pale arm reached out from under a ragged cape for money. 'Deeds make the gentleman,' had been one of her father's sayings. Harry was kind. *But not a gentleman.* Come to think of it, she still had no idea why he'd been at Callot Soeurs.

Something knocked against her hip and she felt for it in the darkness. Metal, with a spring-clip. A cigarette case. It must have fallen out of his pocket when they tussled. Instead of passing it over to the driver, she put it in her bag. She'd have to return it to him... some time.

Chapter Ten

As Katya closed the door of their room behind her, she saw Tatiana standing up against the fireplace, tears bright on her cheeks. Anoushka kicked and cried in her arms.

'Do you know how long I've been pacing this floor? "I'm going to start my life" you said. What about mine?'

Katya held out her arms for the baby. 'I'm so sorry. Darling, make us both a cup of tea.' She put her nose to the baby's bottom. 'Ooh. Needs changing.'

'We're out of tea. No more clean nappies, either.'

Katya remembered putting them to soak several hours ago. 'One of my underskirts, then? Cut it into squares.' She glanced across the room and made a noise of exasperation. 'Astonishing. Mother's fast asleep.'

'She woke for lunch and criticised the seasoning in the soup before taking to her bed again.' Tatiana flourished a small brown bottle. 'Doctor's Special Mixture did the trick. It's the worst thing you've ever done, sending her to Princess Provolskaya's quack.'

'Ludmilla Provolskaya brought the doctor into our lives, not I. Veronal is strong, I admit, but Mama doesn't seem to sleep without it.'

Dr Shepkin's surgery was accessed from the courtyard behind Dedushka's Café, so perhaps it was too easy for their mother to pop over whenever she felt ill or anxious. To the Russian community, Vasily Shepkin was a lifeline. He had pills for every ailment. He never lectured and he knew their language. Patients who could not manage the stairs might have their consultations in the café instead. Katya shared Tatiana's dismay at their mother's growing dependence, but the alternative was also exhausting. She soothed the baby who was pedalling her little legs. 'Do we have milk?'

'I used it in a rice pudding,' Tatiana muttered. 'I'll warm some up.'

'Dill water is what we need.'

'Mama put the bottle down, then kicked it over. Katya, when will we get our money? This place – it's sending me mad.'

'Soon, when our identity papers have been translated.'

'What does "soon" actually mean?'

Unable to answer, Katya evaded the question by nipping across to Dedushka's. Maria, Georgy's wife, was resting, but Georgy found gripe water and decanted some into Katya's bottle. Katya asked after their newborn, named after her mother and known as Masha.

'A little butterball,' Georgy said proudly. 'And we've found a girl to take care of her, a neighbour's daughter, so my wife can come back to work.' He spoke as if this were a triumph. Perhaps it was for him, but it spelled the immediate end of Katya's job and the generous leftovers. Swallowing the blow, she asked to borrow some tea leaves. Back in their room, she found Tatiana holding something up to the ceiling light. 'Is that my address book?' Katya noticed her shoulder bag open on the table. 'Who are you looking for?'

'Nobody. When did you draw this? It's quite good.' Tatiana turned the book round, showing Katya the sketch she'd made at Callot Soeurs.

Katya told Tatiana how she'd barged into the salon, describing the scene until her sister reverted to her tireless theme.

'When will we get our money? I want to go to fashion parades too. I want clothes I'm not ashamed to be seen in. When? Or does "soon" actually mean "never"?'

Katya explained the need to have their documents presented in French, not Cyrillic.

'Why is it all taking so long?'

Repeating what Princess Provolskaya had told her, Katya said, 'They can't be translated word for word, they have to be presented in legal language. The man doing it is unwell, but he'll do a good job in the end, I'm assured of it.'

'What if he dies first? Get somebody else.'

'That would offend the princess, who is only trying to help.'

Tatiana made a sound of disgust and went to bed.

Midnight saw Katya at the window with Anoushka in her arms, worries chipping away at her. Tatiana was right, the translation should be ready by now. She would call on the princess in the morning. She didn't like the suspicions percolating her thoughts: perhaps there was no elderly, ailing translator at all… Or even if there was, maybe he was an irrelevance and the princess was playing some kind of game with her? But why?

Locked in the stance she'd perfected on the train journey from Moscow, she stared out at a moonlit sky, sipping tea sweetened with the gluey jam the grocer sold. The gripe water had worked, Anoushka was quiet but it was a challenge to put her down. Mama often expressed incredulity that her granddaughter was so allergic to sleep – 'None of you were like that.'

How would Mama know? A trio of nursemaids had been employed throughout their childhoods. Katya sang the song ingrained on her tongue: 'There was once a beautiful princess and all the princes sought her, yet they—' The creak of a mattress and the sound of slippered feet brought Tatiana to her side.

'I'm hungry.'

'What about the potato soup I brought home?'

'Katya, that was *hours* ago. And I gave Anoushka most of mine. She gobbled it up like a little greedy old man.'

'That explains the colic. Tomorrow, one of us needs to queue for bread. Eggs too. Anoushka should be having one every day now.' Eggs were expensive. Bread was still rationed, as the government had not yet released the grain it had stored to feed its army. Katya wondered if they would be married to hunger forever.

Tatiana interrupted her thoughts again. 'This room is so cold.'

'It'll warm up by Easter.'

'At least in Moscow we had proper stoves instead of a smoking hole in the wall.' Tatiana glanced bitterly at the fireplace of pitch-painted brick. 'And the snow in Russia stays white. Here, the streets look as if a coal cart has been dragged through them.'

'The parks are like crystal forests.'

Tatiana snorted. 'Full of boys throwing snowballs.'

'And in Moscow, anarchists throw hand grenades. Anything else wrong with Paris?'

'Plenty. The shelves are empty. Prices are rising, nobody has any money. Half the women are widows. The single girls scrap over the few men who've hobbled home with limbs intact. As for all those poor, maimed creatures on the pavements... they say we're taking their jobs.'

You aren't taking anybody's job, Katya thought. 'Things will get better.'

'You're parroting Princess Provolskaya. "God willing, our ship will come in." She's convinced that one day her son will own a fleet of luxury cars instead of one farting rust bucket.'

Laughing, Katya remembered the marshmallows she'd filched at Callot Soeurs. They probably had fluff on them, but it was too dark to see. 'Two for you, one for me.' Before Tatiana could complain any more, Katya began describing the Callot Soeurs' parade.

Tatiana nibbled her sweets but could not stay silent for long. 'How many dresses? What style?' Questions flowed. 'Who was in charge? Who was in the audience?'

Katya described everything she'd seen, including larger-than-life Madame Claudine. She didn't mention meeting Harry Morten, however.

'Were there flowers? Did they serve drinks?'

'Baskets of ivy and snowdrops, no drinks.'

'Show me how a mannequin moves.'

Katya did an approximation of the floating walk, the turn, the pose. Not easy with a baby in her arms. 'I didn't have the best view, but now I know what we should do. Become couturiers. Well, dressmakers to start with, but in time, the new Callot Soeurs.'

'Vytenis Soeurs sounds good,' Tatiana agreed.

Later, lying in their side-by-side camp beds, the sisters whispered a dream into existence – a boutique with deep carpets and gilded seats, Venetian mirrors and sculpted light fittings. Flowers and a perfume counter selling their own fragrance. It was the most enthusiasm Tatiana had showed for anything in weeks.

Katya suggested naming the perfume "*Bienvenue à Paris*".' Welcome to Paris.

Tatiana reminded her of their welcome. Beggars, snow shovels and their cousins' deaths. 'Let's call it "Tatiana".'

'For that matter, why not "Ekaterina"?'

'We'll call it "Vera". Vera means "Faith" in Russian and "Truth" in Latin. *Parfum Véra.* The bottle can have a dome top, like the cathedral.'

'Then it'll look like a jar of pickled gherkins.'

'Not if it's gold.' Tatiana took over the fantasy again. Their salon would be near Place Vendôme, convenient for the Ritz. It would have a 'Vytenis Soeurs' sign painted over the door in script that looked like woven tresses of hair. 'You can design, and I'll be the house mannequin. People will flood to see the ravishing Tatiana. I need only one name.'

Katya muttered into her pillow, 'Maybe I'll do some designs and show them to someone who understands what they're looking at.'

'Who do you know in Paris, except that Monsieur Morten? D'you think we'll ever see him again?'

'Shh, I need my rest.' As Katya slipped towards sleep, the recent memory of a thin, white arm reaching out for charity took her mind on a new path. She had no defences as memories of Moscow overwhelmed her dreams.

*

She paces outside the Lubyanka until the urge to scream has passed. She must either go back inside, or return to Dr Zasyekin's home. She chooses the Lubyanka and this time, she is in luck, finding her way unchallenged to the lower section. This is where the prisoner Starova is being kept. Katya knows that if she's caught, she's doomed. Dr Zasyekin has given her his last bottle of vodka to offer as a bribe in exchange for her sister's freedom. The bottle weighs heavily in her coat. The deeper she penetrates into the building, the more her lungs tighten from the ice-cold air. Only the thought of Vera alone here with her baby drives her down into the dark...

Katya, dreaming, reached a corridor lit by unshaded bulbs.

'You – what are you doing?' The question came from behind her. Katya spun round and at the sight of military black leather, began gabbling incoherently. It was the Cheka officer who had led the assault on their home, who had stood aside as her father was murdered. His shaven skull had an oily gleam under the low-wattage lights.

'I asked what you were doing.' He strode towards her.

No way out and anyway, her legs were almost spent.

She dragged up a travesty of a smile. 'I'm only looking for my sister. I've brought her a present.'

Recognition chimed. 'Oh, you're the bossy one, aren't you? Well, she's down one whole other level. Your father knocked one of my men to the floor, so—'

'He was defending us.'

'So... somebody pays. How it works.'

Katya showed him the vodka, and his tongue darted like a toad's while his eyes caressed the bottle. 'I thought,' she said in a coy voice, 'we could drink this together.' Walking up to him, she pressed her lips to his, steeling herself not to recoil at the greasy stubble of his upper lip, the onion smell of his breath. 'You, me and Vera. They say three is the perfect number for sharing a bottle of vodka.'

'Let's see, shall we?' He took her down one more flight, then along a narrow walkway lined with cells constructed from welded iron mesh. Dog kennels occupied by men and a few women. Each cell contained a most basic bed and a metal bucket. Ragged heads lifted as they passed, the silence more disturbing than any shouting.

At the end of the corridor, the officer rapped against metal. 'Starova, stand up.'

A crumpled bundle stirred. A face lifted blindly to the direction of the command. Holy Mother, her sister had come to this so quickly? Katya clasped the bars, which were burning cold. 'Vera? It's me, Katya. Where's the baby? Where's Anoushka?'

Slowly, Vera swung her feet off her couch of planks and straightened up painfully. Her hair hung lank and the drawstring neck of her blouse gaped. She'd knotted her underskirt around her shoulders in a bid for modesty. She came to stand at the bars and Katya saw a glittery sheen on her front. A moment's confusion before she realised it was ice, where breast milk had leaked, then frozen. Katya gripped the bars harder, not caring about the searing chill through her gloves. 'I'll pay for a hearing. I'll tell them you're the mother of a tiny baby.'

Vera shook her head. 'It's too late. They have my letters.'

'What letters?'

'Those I wrote to Mikhail. Love letters.'

'Why should you not write to your husband?'

'And others, condemning the revolution. Wishing the Tsar's killers would rot in hell.'

'Oh, Vera.'

'My interrogator read them out to me. They never reached Mikhail, never even left Moscow. So I confessed.'

'Konstantin.' Hatred had a taste, Katya discovered. It had been Konstantin's job to handle the household mail. Katya flinched as Vera grasped one of her hands, pulled off the glove and gripped her fingers in her own deathly cold ones. Katya felt Vera's wedding ring pressing into her palm.

'Take it,' Vera said. 'I keep losing it, I've grown so thin.'

'I'll keep it safe. But where is Anoushka?' No mewling cries, no little lump in the bed. *'What have they done with her?'*

A cackle came from the adjoining cell. 'The baby was crying, on and on. It was driving us mad.'

Katya recoiled at the grinning, emaciated figure staring through the bars from the other side of the narrow walkway. Shaven-headed; gender impossible to guess. 'It's no place for babies down here,' the toothless mouth intoned.

Pulling her eyes away, Katya gripped Vera's arms through the bars. 'Tell me! Where is Anoushka?'

'Katya, wake up. Wake up!'

Her own name was bouncing off her eardrum. She was being shaken. The pin-sharp reality of a subterranean vault dissolved, though the cold did not. Her blankets had slipped, her limbs were rigid.

'Vera?'

'It's Tatiana. You were shouting about Anoushka, as though you thought Vera—'

'Stop, please. It was a nightmare.' The real-life baby was wailing and though her body groaned with resistance, Katya went to her. Picking her up, she took her to the window and rocked her. She sang, filling her head with her own voice to block out Tatiana's question:

'Katya, when you were at the Lubyanka, what exactly did you see?'

*

Some days after this, Harry Morten dropped by the Ritz on his way home and glanced in at the ladies-only bar. Two feline profiles trapped his attention and he hesitated, fatally.

A slender figure jumped up. 'Harry-my-heart, you can't come in here.'

'That's why I'm hovering in the doorway.'

'Wait, I shall come out.'

No choice then but to invite Una McBride, plus cats, to join him for a drink. There was nothing irksome in her company – though he'd happily have dispensed with the jaguars. He just wasn't up to discussing the subject she was feverishly eager to bring up.

'Champagne?' he enquired.

'Why yes, but will you excuse me? I ordered a bottle earlier, so I'd better—'

'Put it on my tab. Drinking alone?'

'Not entirely. I had a meeting but she – *he* – has gone.' Una looked sweet when she blushed. Today, she was captivating in a beige-and-black jersey ensemble that could have been Chanel, but which Harry was damn sure wasn't. He also had a good idea whom she'd been meeting. He'd seen Katya Vytenis leaving the hotel as he crossed the square, going in the direction of rue de la Paix. He hadn't attempted to waylay her. Their every meeting ended with her insulting him, and he had begun the process of eliminating her from his thoughts. He and Una retired to the gallery, where he ordered Pol Roger, *rosé vintage*, before asking her about her meeting.

'Oh, somebody brought me some little drawings, is all.'

'May I see?'

The 'little drawings' turned out to be fashion sketches, evening and daywear. Golf was becoming an increasingly popular sport with women. No proof these drawings were from Katya's hand, though there were a few clues. With one exception, the sketches could have been done by Callot Soeurs' principal designer, Madame Gerber, herself. The exception was an evening dress based on a Russian peasant costume. The model, who on closer inspection looked remarkably like Katya, wore a *kokochnik*, a traditional Russian headdress. The full, black-silk skirt had horizontal stripes of gold tissue. A note to that effect was written in the margin and in spite of himself, Harry was amused. You'd be lucky to get gold cloth in these restricted times, without robbing a Masonic lodge, but he liked the designer's ambition. He liked the camisole too, with its filmy over-blouse. *Would Katya wear something so revealing?*

'You've been silent a whole five minutes.' Una dropped an olive into her mouth. 'I'm starting to wish they were my drawings.'

'So whose are they?' Harry never expected a straight answer from Una, and tonight was no different.

'A friend who wants an honest opinion, though I told her – *him* – that those are the worst kind. Give me insincere flattery any time.'

Harry looked again at the work. The paper was the poorest quality, but wasn't poverty a stimulant to talent? Coco Chanel had stormed into couture making dresses from underwear grade jersey-knit, such as Una was wearing tonight. 'For what it's worth, I think they're very decent. They're also very Callot Soeurs.'

'Really?' Una opened her eyes innocently.

'You hadn't noticed? Perhaps you haven't had a chance to get to Avenue Matignon. I saw your friend Madame Claudine there the other day, by the way.' He took an unhurried mouthful of champagne, noting that Una was suddenly anxious to straighten the cats' collars.

'My stars, never.'

'One could hardly miss her. I'd been discussing next season's textiles with Madame Gerber and stayed on. How Claudine got past the door, I'll never know. She'll have memorised every stitch of their spring–summer collection. As I'm sure she's memorised Chanel's too. She made this?' He indicated Una's ensemble.

'Well, yes.'

'Who got hold of the original, you or one of Claudine's minions?'

'Heavens, what an inquisition. Harry, you haven't given me a chance yet to say how desperately sorry I was when I heard about Christian.'

Truly, she had no shame. 'I'm not ready to talk about it,' he replied.

'No, of course. It's unbearable that he died when he did.'

'Seven days before the Armistice? I'm alive to the brutish irony. Not least the fact that I was elsewhere at the time.'

'When did you get the news?'

'In Gothenburg. A wire was waiting for me. At least I was able to tell my father in person. Let's talk about something else. Isn't it time you took those damn cats back to the zoo?'

'But they're sweet.'

'They're the opposite and admit it, they've done their job. Paris has rebounded in awe at your outré antics and now you're one miaow away from tedium.'

Una appraised the cats stretched at her feet, batting each other's paws. 'I look after them now and then as favour to the Countess Simeonescu.' She lowered her voice. 'She pays me to take them for walkies.'

'Walkies to the Ritz. Sometimes I'm so glad we fought a war.'

'Now, Harry, don't grow crabbed and cynical. Why don't we go find dinner on the fun side of the river? Montparnasse, Café du Dôme? Get drunk with a tableful of starving artists. Hmm?'

He'd drifted. It took so little to push his inner eye backwards in time. At the smallest prompt he was back on the battlefield and his face would start to flicker. He tried to control the jumping nerve, and, of course, others had it far worse. Some men jerked as if spiteful schoolboys had control of their strings. Others couldn't speak at all. He caught a waiter's eye and asked if someone could bring him the cigarette case in the pocket of his coat. Lighting up and inhaling sometimes helped.

When the waiter left, he smiled at Una. 'I'll give you dinner here, but if you're sold on Montparnasse, you're on your own. I find riotous noise hard to bear these days.' He arranged the sketches in a neat pile. 'Tell your friend that her ideas have merit, but they sail too close to piracy.'

His voice dropped a pitch. 'Una, I know of your arrangement with Claudine Saumon. She was my first customer in Paris and I think well of her, but even so, if she uses fabric supplied by me for illegal copying, I'll revoke her credit and close her account. Don't push me to it.'

'Why are you such a purist?'

'Why did Paul Cézanne paint pretty apples and not potatoes?'

'Because the man didn't know a good potato when he saw one.'

'Wrong. Because he refused to waste his talent on anything second-rate.'

'Harry-my-heart, everyone copies.'

'Then why would you want to?'

The waiter returned, apologising – there appeared to be no cigarette case in Monsieur Morten's coat pocket. 'I will have some brought to the table.'

'Don't bother. Una?'

'Not I. You may pour me another glass of champagne to repair my feelings.'

He filled their glasses, puzzling over the missing cigarettes. He could go a week or more without reaching for his case and tried to remember where he'd last taken it out. Shrugging, he gave up and made a toast. 'To art, the pure variety.'

They clinked glasses. Una said, 'Let me pay for my half.'

'All right.'

She laughed when she realised he was joking and took his free hand. 'Oh, Harry. It's good to have a friend.'

He raised her knuckles and kissed them, and their eyes collided. Hers were honey brown and something deep within him seemed to melt. One word, one flick of an eyebrow and he knew they would end the night in his apartment. He kept his face so still, the moment passed.

Harry's bid to eject Katya Vytenis from his mind was in trouble. Before they parted that evening, he asked Una if he could take the sketch of the black-and-gold evening dress.

'I promised Ka… I mean, my friend, um, Bill – not to let them out of my sight,' Una hedged.

'You don't have to.' He asked their waiter for paper and made a quick copy. An idea was growing, a way to help Katya. And himself. Aiding her was a sublimation of everything else he wanted from her. He'd probably get a tongue-lashing for his trouble, but at worst it would take his mind off Christian and the void his brother's death had left in his soul.

'You've been drinking. I can smell it on you. Why are you not at home, with your family?'

'Answer my question first.' Katya had flagged down Aleksey Provolsky's taxi on rue de la Paix, recognising it by its chipped yellow wheels and the rattling bumper. It wasn't just to spare herself the walk home: here was a chance to chase him up about her documents. Twice, she'd knocked at his apartment, hoping to catch him or his mother in, but nobody had come to the door on either occasion. Yesterday, she'd caught sight of Ludmilla Provolskaya drinking coffee in Dedushka's Café but by the time she'd got across the road, there was no sign of the princess. Having hopped up into the open cab beside Aleksey, she was freezing. Unlike him, she wasn't dressed for it, which didn't help her temper.

As he roared towards the intersection of rue de Monceau and Boulevard Malesherbes, she raised her voice over the noise. 'Has your translator-friend done my work or not?'

'Friend? He's an acquaintance and you are changing the subject, Ekaterina Ulianova. Why were you in that hotel? Who did you drink with?' Aleksey bumped the kerb as he swung left into rue de Monceau. He ought to have continued straight on, up Malesherbes. She hoped he wasn't attempting to extract a larger fare from her.

'If you must know,' Katya yielded, 'I met a woman, a business contact. I'm turning my hand to fashion and as she is an eminently chic individual, I presented some ideas to her.'

'But you should not drink in public. You, a lady of good family.'

'My father never minded us having the odd glass of champagne. In fact, Papa seized any excuse to have a bottle brought up from the cellar. Aleksey, where are my papers? You've had them long enough.'

Taking one hand off the wheel, Aleksey reached under his seat and retrieved a package. 'All here, translated into legal wordage as the bank requires. It was not a five-minute job.'

'You're telling me.'

'There is a bill inside, to pay at your convenience. A small bill, as Igor Tolbanov is a modest man as well as an invalid. He works hard to help his fellow Russians. I had planned to bring them to you tonight.'

Point taken. 'I beg pardon. I have an impetuous soul.' She felt thoroughly ashamed of having suspected Aleksey and his mother of deliberate delay.

'Yes.' He finally showed her a smile. 'A Muscovite soul.'

'That reminds me, I have a bone to pick with you, Aleksey. The day you picked us up at Montparnasse station, you were expecting us. True?'

'Of course.' He shrugged, as far as he could with both hands on the wheel. 'We knew you were coming, Mother and I.'

'From my cousins? Yes. I wrote some days before we set out for Paris, giving the day of our arrival but they must have been too ill by then to read the letter.'

'My mother had permission to open their post.'

'But how did you recognise us?'

'Three tall women, a family resemblance… Call it good fortune I was there that day, to conduct you safely to your destination.'

Since he drove as if brakes were a minor inconvenience, presumably Aleksey was trying to be funny. Katya didn't smile.

'You knew our cousins were dead, yet you said nothing.'

Aleksey didn't speak until he'd turned into Pierre le Grand, the cathedral in their sights. 'It was not my place to tell you.'

'It's why you turfed us out of the car and left it to your mother to break the news.'

He denied and then admitted it. 'I wanted to give you a memory that would live in your hearts, alongside the sorrow that was waiting. It may not seem so, but I think of your welfare. You know that, Katya?'

'Yes, all right.' She said it caustically, to discourage any further appeals to the heart. Handing those drawings to Una earlier had felt like a trainee trapeze artist's first leap into the void. If the American returned them with mere polite comments, or worse, with humour or disdain, Katya's embryo ambitions would be dashed.

Drawing up outside No. 6, Aleksey shut off the engine. 'You can take those translations to the bank now.'

'First to a notary, to get them stamped as genuine. Then to the bank. What I really need,' Katya said with feeling, 'is the original deposit certificate. That was worth a fortune to us.' Inside the house, she went quickly upstairs, regretting the impulsive confidence. Aleksey was no gossip, as far as she knew, but he was human. She didn't want every neighbour knowing that the Vytenis ladies had money locked up, just out of reach. Aleksey followed her up to the next landing and she prepared once more to rebuff him, but again, he surprised her.

'What did you mean before, about turning your hand to fashion?'

'Exactly that. I mean to become a dress designer.'

'Until you marry.' 'Marry' sounded like a heavy book falling shut. 'Then you will take care of home and husband.'

'Will I? Thank you. Goodnight.'

The following day, the Vytenis family visited a notary on Boulevard Malesherbes where they swore oaths as to their identities and had their translated documents stamped as authentic. Suddenly, Irina and Tatiana were brimming with ideas of how to spend money that was surely as good as in their pockets. Leaving them to window-shop and dream, Katya went on to the bank where she handed the papers over to a deputy-deputy clerk.

She was told to expect the bank's decision in due course.

'How long might that be?' she asked.

The answer: As long as is it took.

Katya launched her fashion venture within hours of Dedushka's Café's Georgy Filatov giving her notice for the end of the month.

'I'm sorry I cannot employ you alongside Maria, but…' he shrugged. Prices, taxes, inflation. However, he invited her to canvas his female customers for commissions. 'Since Maria tells me that dressmaking is how you mean to earn money now.'

Katya hadn't told Maria of her intentions. Clearly, news moved fast in "Little Moscow".

She secured three orders in as many days, but the weakness in her plan showed at once. She'd been taught to sew and embroider prettily, but was not by any stretch a professional. Of her new customers, two gave her a picture cut from a magazine with the instruction, 'Like that, only in my size'. Princess Provolskaya produced a worn-out summer frock and a newspaper image of the silent film star Mary Pickford, asking Katya to remake the dress to match.

'Only shorter, and perhaps with a slightly higher neck?'

With no idea how to draft patterns from pictures, Katya unpicked the princess's dress and spread the segments on the floor. Their room was too small for a proper table. She drew around the pieces with a crayon, on newspaper, and her mother kept walking on them. Anoushka crawled over them, mixing the pieces up. When Tatiana pointed out that she'd cut two left sleeves, Katya gave up in despair. However, a trip to Galleries Lafayette brought the welcome discovery that *Vogue* magazine had started producing paper patterns. A week's wages went on three dress patterns and squared paper for scaling them to fit her customers' dimensions. That was when it struck Katya that she hadn't measured her clients.

Every night after work, she hand-sewed into the early hours, until her fingers thickened and her eyes dried. She persisted and, at last, she completed the work. Washed and ironed, the finished results were better than she'd hoped. Except she hadn't factored in the disappointment of clients who, finding they did not look like the ladies in their pictures, cavilled about payment. Only Princess Provolskaya paid in full, but Katya was badly out of pocket. With the end of paid employment only a few days away, she trudged through Parc Monceau. Harry Morten's conditional promise walked with her: '*I can help you, but don't make it harder.*' Dressmaking *was* hard. Dreams were painful.

On the last day of February, she collected her final wage packet and a wedge of poppy-seed cake. Georgy Filatov added a bonus, which she thought she might justifiably spend on a book on sewing techniques. Instead, she found a doctor's bill waiting at home. Six consultations for Princess Irina Vytenis with Dr Shepkin, and an on-going prescription of veronal.

'How many bottles, Mama?'

'I only take a tablet when I need it,' Irina insisted. Though it was after two in the afternoon, she was huddled under her blankets. 'Take them from me, you might as well push me into the river.'

'In a wheelbarrow or an invalid chair?'

Her mother didn't smile.

'You'd sleep better if you got some fresh air and exercise.'

'The doctor says I must rest.'

Knowing better than to pit her opinion against the revered Dr Shepkin, Katya pursued her point by other means. She took the baby on a motorbus ride to the flea market at Porte de Clichy, in the neigh-bouring district. Anoushka loved the motion of the bus, squealing and charming the other passengers who all assumed Katya to be 'Maman', thanks to Vera's ring. At the market, Katya spent her bonus payment on a second-hand baby carriage with silver wheels and sprung suspension, and a cabriolet hood to keep off the rain. The man who sold it to her said it was English-made. 'Over there, it is called a "perambulator" or a "pram".'

Katya added the words to her vocabulary. For some reason, they made her smile. At home, she called Tatiana down to help her lug the carriage into a niche under the stairs, and even her sister smiled.

'Let's take an afternoon stroll,' Tatiana said, bouncing it to test the springs.

'Let's. The daffodils are poking through in the park.'

'Not Parc Monceau, it's full of ancient gardeners and English nannies. Bois de Boulogne is the place to be seen.'

'Perhaps so, but I never want to haul this contraption on or off a bus again.'

Parc Monceau it was. For an hour, they walked and chatted and regained a spark of the friendship they'd enjoyed before tragedy had distanced them. Katya acknowledged the crash of her dressmaking dream, and broached something that needed saying. 'You and I have to find work.'

'Why, when we'll be rich in a matter of weeks?'

'It could take months.'

'But we can't leave Anoushka alone with Mama,' Tatiana said.

'I know, I know, but Mama has to do her bit too. Papa wouldn't have let her sleep her life away.'

'You aren't Papa.'

'No, but I'm his representative in Paris.'

*

Katya found them both a job in a tearoom on rue Cambon, a smart street behind the Hôtel Ritz. Irina, who had hated the indignity of her daughter slaving over saucepans at Dedushka's, expressed relief at the change. Everything about the English Tea Parlour was genteel. Waitresses wore spotless aprons and fingernails were manicured.

With a few days free before starting the job, Katya persuaded her mother to step out with her to the park. Tatiana had disappeared off on her own somewhere, and Katya needed to raise the subject of childcare with her mother. 'You can push the pram,' she said as she humped it over the door sill.

'All the way up rue Brazy, you trust me?' Irina asked with a scathing edge.

As they approached the café, Katya saw Aleksey crossing the courtyard behind, passing through the door to Dr Shepkin's surgery, which was always propped open with a rusty horseshoe. Her mother saw him too and sighed, 'I hope he is not unwell. Such a fine figure of a young man. He would suit you, Katya.'

'No matchmaking, if you please.'

'Don't you wish to marry?'

Katya thought of Vera and Mikhail. 'Marriage means heartbreak. So, no, I don't.'

They walked on for fifteen minutes, Anoushka's babbling the only conversation. On leafy Avenue Van Dyck, leading into the park, Katya finally said her piece. 'You will have to take over caring for Anoushka while we're at work, Mama.'

No response.

'Mama? You have to share household burdens. Please say you understand.'

Irina gave an annoyed gasp. 'Vera would never have spoken to me as you do.' She grasped Katya's hand, making Vera's ring dig in. 'I don't want to walk any further. Take me to Saint Alexander Nevsky. Vera's soul is restless today. I feel her with me.'

'You feel the memory of her. Anyway, the incense in the cathedral makes Anoushka sneeze.'

With an angry snort, Irina grasped the perambulator's metal push-bar and strode on. Katya hurried to catch up and perversely, Irina stopped. Seeing her mother staring down at her granddaughter as if looking at a changeling, Katya felt a chill.

'How is it you brought the little one out of the Lubyanka but not Vera?' Irina asked. 'Tatiana says you shout in your sleep, accusing Vera of terrible things.'

'I'm not responsible for my dreams, Mama. Let's walk on. It's too fresh to stand about.' It was only the 3 March, and patches of snow lingered under shrubs at the park's margins.

'You took that ring from her ice-cold finger, you said. How?'

*

'Take it,' Vera sighs. 'I've grown so thin, it falls off me. Wear it in Paris and forget me.'

'Where is Anoushka, Vera?' Katya cannot see the baby anywhere in the cell.

Vera turns around, showing her back. The underskirt Katya assumed was a modesty piece is in fact a makeshift sling for a baby. A tiny arm hangs limply from it. A lolling head is half-hidden by Vera's hair.

'Oh, Vera. She's – dead?'

'She died this morning. I need you to take her and bury her with Papa, or they will throw her in a drain.' Vera fumbles over the knots of the sling. She holds up the baby who is naked and magnolia pale.

The sisters make a bridge of their hands and angle the little body between the bars. Anoushka feels like a wax doll left outside overnight.

'That's your lot, bitches.' The Cheka captain cares only about the vodka in Katya's pocket. Knowing he's about to rip it from her, Katya thrusts the bottle towards Vera. 'Quick, take it.' It's their only bargaining chip. Dr Zasyekin urged her to leave Vera to her fate, but what kind of sister would do that? The Cheka captain roars as he realises the bottle has been passed beyond his reach.

'Hand it back, Starova. It's forbidden for prisoners to have liquor.'

*

Katya pulled Vera's ring off her finger. 'Here, Mama. You should have this.'

Irina Vytenis looked at it dumbly. 'I need to understand, Katya, how it was my daughter died and *her* daughter lived. Until you tell me, I will not be whole.'

Tatiana was Katya's unwitting saviour, coming upon them on the gravelled allée. 'Goodness, you two look like the twin pillars of Hades.' She'd been walking by the river, she said, calling their attention to the spray of violets in her buttonhole. 'Flower sellers are swarming like flies on the embankments. These are from the south where, would you believe, it is warm already. Are you walking the perimeter? I'll join you. Anything's better than a stuffy room. What are you doing, Katya?'

Katya was hanging Vera's ring around her mother's neck. She'd removed one of her hair ribbons and threaded the ring on it.

They walked on, just another family enjoying the park; the hint of blue sky; the early taste of spring. As she peered into the ornamental lake at the budding reflections of trees, Katya felt her heartbeat even out. Her mother had thrown off her dark mood and was conversing in chirrups with her granddaughter. Irina had promised she would be 'The best grandmamma in the world', so long as she was allowed her veronal at night.

Tatiana was singing to herself, inordinately pleased with her violets, or perhaps with the little silver brooch that pinned them to her coat. A flea-market find? Katya couldn't imagine where the money had come from, but she said nothing. When Tatiana was happy, they all benefited.

'Isn't that Monsieur Morten?' Tatiana pointed towards a nearby path. 'Mama? Watch Katya blush.'

It was indeed Harry, marked out by his distinctive hair and the slight unevenness in his stride. Katya wasn't surprised; rue Goya led directly into the park. She could have run after him and given him back his cigarette case, which was at the bottom of her bag. But that would spark more teasing from Tatiana.

On the way home, they bought provisions, including herring from a fish stall. It would stink out their room for days but it was the cheapest food available. Sending the others ahead to get supper started, Katya called in at Dedushka's to return the tea she'd borrowed. Georgy invited her to make a fuss of the baby. His wife sat in a nursing chair, feeding plump little Masha. Maria Filatova looked worn out or perhaps the baby's suckling hurt. Vera had found breastfeeding exquisitely painful for the first weeks.

'You're not overdoing things?' Katya asked as Georgy went to fetch a nip of vodka for her. Kitchen work so soon after childbirth wasn't what the doctor ordered.

'This is my first baby,' Maria said with a wan smile. 'What is normal?'

Katya accepted a tiny, ridged glass from Georgy and tipped the liquor down her throat. '*Na Zdorovie!* Good health and long life.'

'To you as well,' Georgy returned. 'And to the gentleman in pursuit of you.'

'Motherhood is hard,' Maria complained, robbing Katya of the chance to ask Georgy which gentleman he was referring to. 'But I don't have to tell you that.'

'Careful what you say, Maria,' Georgy chided.

Katya corrected the misunderstanding. 'Anoushka isn't mine. She's my sister's girl. My other sister.'

'Course. I'm sorry.' Maria nodded. 'The sister who was taken by the Cheka.'

How did Maria know that? When she'd come here seeking work, Katya had outlined her situation to Georgy, but not a word had she breathed of Vera's fate. The only person in Paris, outside her family, who knew anything about Vera was Harry Morten. How came Maria to be so well-acquainted with Katya's life? Before she left, she remarked that she'd seen Aleksey Provolsky going into the doctor's that afternoon.

'Bad toothache, I believe. He underwent the only cure.' Georgy mimed the fast extraction of a molar. 'Did you know, the prince broke his jaw falling off a cavalry horse? His back teeth give him endless trouble.'

Returning home, Katya found that a letter had come for her. 'Hand delivered while we were out,' her mother said, 'and it smells of fish.'

'My fault,' Tatiana confessed. She was in their niche of a kitchen, stuffing herring with chopped onion and breadcrumbs. She didn't turn around, saying over the rapid bubble of potatoes in a pan, 'It was on the landing and I put it on top of our shopping. Who's it from?'

'I can't imagine.' The envelope did indeed smell of fish. Katya tore it open and found… nothing.

Confused, she checked the front.

Princess Ekaterina Vytenis, 6, rue Brazy, 8e.

'8e' meant 'huitième', the eighth. Katya found the address Harry Morten had scribbled down for her in Gothenburg. The writing was identical to that on her letter. He must have been cutting across the park on his way here. Georgy's comment about 'a gentleman in pursuit' now made sense, assuming Harry had asked for her address at the café. Not that Harry Morten was pursuing her, of course. He'd all but faded from her life recently. Even so, he'd gone to some trouble to leave her an empty envelope.

The next Sunday, Katya went to church and lit candles for her father, and for Vera and Mikhail. She thought she had the place to herself, as Divine Liturgy would not begin until later, but as she watched her candles burn, she became aware of breathing behind her. A woman, shrouded in shadow, knelt before an icon. Knelt on the hard floor.

A newcomer to their quarter? Katya thought she knew most people in rue Brazy and Daru, from her time in the café. But not this woman, whose figure was hidden under a cape, hair smothered by a headscarf. As the woman got up and went to the church door, her headscarf caught the morning light. Blood red.

Katya abandoned her candles and followed. Outside, the bright head-covering easily marked the woman out from other pedestrians on rue Daru. She was making for rue Brazy. Katya dashed across the road, heart thudding. She had no doubts. Absolutely none. 'Stop!' she called. 'I want to talk to you!'

The woman picked up speed but Katya was faster, reaching Dedushka's courtyard in time to see a flash of red vanish through Dr Shepkin's door.

She's been on my doorstep all this time. Katya stubbed her foot on the horseshoe doorstop but hardly felt the pain as she raced up the concrete stairs. 'Yana, you can't outrun me. Stop!'

The wretched creature must have been dragging every grain of speed from her legs because whenever Katya rounded a curve in the stairs, the pounding feet were always one flight ahead. Katya was groping for breath as she reached the stairs to the *sixième*, the maids' attic. Ahead of her, a door slammed.

Katya half-collapsed against it. A key turned. She slapped the panels with the flat of her hand. 'Yana, I know you're in there. How did you get here? Who brought you? You owe me answers, so open the door. Damn you, that's a command!'

Guarded breathing from the other side. Katya tried a different tack. 'I'm not angry, Yana. I won't go to the police, I promise. I only want to talk and to have our property back. Please?'

The scuff of feet against the base of the door. And then a ragged voice said, 'Leave me alone. Because I live the way I do, cleaning and skivvying for the doctor, does not give you the right to persecute me. Leave me be, Madame, please.'

It wasn't Yana. Not only did the voice have a warmer tone than Yana's, the plea had been delivered in fluent French. Yana had refused ever to learn a word of the language.

Mortified, Katya apologised profusely and retreated. This fixation with Yana Borisovna must stop. She must not jump into the air every time she saw a woman wearing a red scarf.

Katya accompanied her mother to church later that morning, for the service. They returned to an empty room. Tatiana, the baby and the perambulator were gone and were away long enough for Katya to start to worry. She was pinning on her hat when she heard Tatiana come up the stairs singing 'Oui, Oui Marie', a jaunty soldiers' song in the repertoire of a blind accordionist who played on the corner of rue de Courcelles, outside Kaminsky's jewellers.

'Someone's had a good time, anyway,' Katya muttered, removing hat pins.

Tatiana and Anoushka had been to the Tuileries Gardens, then for a 'lovely push' along the Seine to Avenue Matignon for a spot of window-shopping. 'I gawped at your famous Callot Soeurs,' Tatiana said with the hint of a giggle. 'Not much to see, is there?'

'Like a pomegranate, the beauty is all inside.'

'Ha-ha. It needs to be.' Tatiana seemed to be positively crackling with excitement, which, Katya suspected, had little to do with the new job they were starting tomorrow morning, at eight o'clock sharp.

Later, taking Anoushka out for a second airing, Katya discovered a lilac silk dress under the pram's mattress. Silk stockings too. Tatiana's, obviously. Bought at the same time as the little silver brooch? Katya put them back under the mattress, resolving to say nothing, but it left her troubled.

In Russia, on Christmas visits to their country manor, they used to go on rides in a troika, a three-horse sleigh. When the horses galloped in the same direction, the sleigh flew and it was like riding on the back of the wind. But if a horse tried to take its own line – disaster.

Please, let Tatiana not turn into that horse.

12 March

'Mademoiselle, look what you're doing!'

Alerted by the shrill warning, Katya looked over to where Tatiana was waiting at a table. Her sister was apparently mesmerised by activity over the road where men in overalls were struggling to get a massive cabinet through the door of a shop. The tea she was pouring had filled the cup and saucer and was gushing on to the tablecloth.

Katya put down her cake stand and rushed over. 'What's the matter with you, Tatya?' She grabbed the teapot. This was their third day at the English Tea Parlour, the first on which they'd been allowed to work unsupervised.

Tatiana looked down in astonishment, saying, '*Oh là, là, là, là!*' an exclamation she'd picked up from their employer, Monsieur Aristide. She attempted to blot the flood with a napkin until a grey-browed lady at the table pushed her chair back with a cry.

'Clumsy girl. You've scalded me. Are you entirely stupid?'

'I'm not at all stupid, Madame – unlike this ridiculous contraption they make me wear.' Tatiana pulled off the lace headband that was part of her uniform. It was supposed to lie a fraction above the eyebrows, but it required constant adjustment. Or glue. 'It keeps falling over my eyes.'

'I don't see why that should affect your ears. I warned you before the cup was full,' the lady accused. 'My skirt is ruined. Damn fool. Where is Aristide? You,' she meant Katya, 'fetch the proprietor.'

'He's busy icing his éclairs,' Tatiana chirped impudently.

'Let me deal with this. Tatiana, take over my table.' Katya added in a beseeching whisper, 'Don't wreck this, please.' She placed a clean napkin under the tablecloth to stop the stain spreading and began blotting the tea with another.

'*Non, non! Là, là, là.*' Monsieur Aristide waddled in, straining waistcoat buttons in his haste. 'You will drive the stain into the fibres. Did you call out, Madame la Marquise? A thousand pardons.'

He pressed his hand to his heart like an opera singer. Rotund, with a liquorice-curl moustache, there was much of the theatre about Monsieur Aristide. He took himself very seriously, however, and this parlour in the fashionable first was his world. Its decor replicated the drawing room of an English stately home and he dressed *à l'anglais* in a grey, cutaway coat, a waistcoat and striped trousers. To go out, he completed the look with a boater hat and cane. Generally blessed with an easy temper, a tide of tea and an angry customer – a marquise to boot – acted like vinegar in milk. He snatched the napkin from Katya's hand. 'Never, ever rub tea into a cloth, girl. Fetch salt.'

'I wasn't rubbing and Monsieur, you should never put salt on linen. It fixes the stain.'

'At once. *Mesdames*, I beg pardon for this grievous event. My dear, late wife always dealt with the waitresses and I am inclined to think it was what killed her. Allow me to prepare a new table.'

Katya returned with salt, which Monsieur Aristide poured liberally on to the stain. *On his head be it.* Their Moscow servant, Konstantin, had possessed many faults but had been gifted in the arts of laundry, and from him she'd learned that wine or tea on white linen required bicarbonate of soda. She was sent back for a fresh cloth and when she returned, the marquise was still carping about her skirt. Jeanne, one of the older waitresses, had warned Katya and Tatiana on day one to watch out for the marquise de Sainte-Vierge.

'Mean as flint, sharp as a vulture's beak.' A reference, Katya supposed, to a curvature in the marquise's neck, which forced her chin forward. The resemblance to a waiting vulture was heightened by a mauve-and-yellow striped turban, with a fierce-looking feather attached. Katya had felt sorry for the woman, attributing her sour expression to a painful spine.

Her sympathy drained as she heard, 'Somebody must pay. Not only is my skirt ruined, so are these.' The marquise hitched up her hem to reveal voluminous silk drawers and a rosette garter that would not have looked out of place in a bordello. Katya averted her gaze and unfortunately met Monsieur Aristide's horrified expression, which startled a snort of laughter from her. The marquise's companion, a matronly young woman, murmured, 'Must you, Tante Clotilde?'

Monsieur Aristide turned his discomfort on Katya. 'I suppose it was your inattention that led to this deplorable situation?'

'Monsieur, I am deeply sorry.' Katya hadn't the strength to argue. If anyone ever said that being a tearoom waitress was a lightweight job, she'd set them right. Three ten-hour days in a row so far. Sunday, her day off along with one moveable afternoon per week, felt a long time away. For their efforts, she and Tatiana would each take home enough to cover their rent. For food and everything else, they would rely on tips. Which was why Katya was taking the blame. Why Tatiana must swallow her pride, even if it stuck in her gullet. Eyes lowered, Katya helped lay the fresh cloth then stood to one side while her customers arranged themselves around the table.

The marquise clicked her fingers. 'Napkin.' Her black-bead eyes briefly fed on Katya, resenting her height, her unbowed posture. 'You realise, you have wrecked a Chanel skirt.'

The marquise's niece sighed. 'Why torment the girl? What can she do?'

'All very well, Agnès,' the marquise came back irritably, 'but the days have gone when one could pass a spoiled garment over to one's maid. None of the flighty pieces one employs these days have any skill. None that I can see.'

'Because you won't pay enough,' her niece replied. 'Skill costs.'

'Pah. The war spoiled the working classes. They all want to be something else now.'

'The war killed so many, they can be.'

It sounded like a well-trodden quarrel, in which Katya glimpsed the edge of an opportunity. As she presented lemon slices, she said something that sent her life in a new direction.

In later years she would say, '*Those words changed everything.*'

Chapter Eleven

'I will launder your skirt and charge you twenty francs, Madame.'

'What? You should pay me. Did you not hear me say that you've ruined a skirt from the atelier of Coco—?'

'Chanel, Madame. Yes. I understand what goes into a couture garment.'

'You do?' The marquise's gaze narrowed. 'Can you sew like Chanel?'

'She'd hardly be a tearoom waitress if she could, Tante Clotilde.' The niece was losing patience. 'Thank you.' A tight smile dismissed Katya. But Katya got her commission. Ungracious to the last, the marquise knocked her down to fifteen francs and told her to fetch the skirt later that day. 'One of my people will wrap it for you.'

'I'm getting my hands on a Chanel skirt,' Katya bragged as she and Tatiana left for home that evening. Katya mimicked the marquise. '*I shall have one of my people wrap it for you.*'

'Lucky you.' Tatiana was more interested in the building the removals men had spent all day filling. Its interior fittings suggested it would become an upmarket boutique. Further up the street, she stopped at a narrow-fronted hat shop, Modes Chanel. Nothing on display, though a row of stands, which the trade called 'sunflowers', suggested it would be worth a second look in the daylight. Tatiana sighed. 'Why are those women rich and we're not?'

'Which women?'

'The ones who come to drink tea. When are we getting Papa's money? And don't say "soon".'

'The bank is considering its next move.' Katya touched Tatiana's shoulder. 'If I got three or four commissions like this every week, I could stop worrying about money. Be pleased for me, Tatiana.'

'Because you're embarking on a career as a washerwoman? I shan't waste time buttering up horrible old women. I'm going straight to the top.'

'Top of what? The Eiffel Tower?'

Sniffing, Tatiana strode away and Katya called after her, 'Where did the new dress come from, and the stockings?'

'I found them under a gooseberry bush,' Tatiana trilled, and continued walking.

Katya let her go, hurt but not surprised. When it had been the three of them, Vera had been Tatiana's favourite, the patient one who always had a kind reply and never a snub up her sleeve. She reminded herself, *I have to remember what Tatiana saw, what she went through.*

The marquise's apartment was at the lower, more exclusive end, of Boulevard Malesherbes, a stone's throw from the church of the Madeleine. Katya rang a bell beside an imposing door and was admitted into a courtyard by a concierge. After a tedious wait, she was handed a badly wrapped parcel. The manservant who brought it didn't look at her, nor did he thank the concierge who stumped away muttering, 'Balourd.'

Not a word in Katya's glossary, but it sounded about right. As Tatiana had pointed out, being a laundress garnered little respect. Now all she had to do was lift strong tea from an expensive skirt.

*

The solution was, literally, borax. Sodium borate, used in every kind of cleaning. On her free afternoon the following day, Katya took a motorbus to Beaubourg in the fourth and bought a box of the fine white crystals and a sponge. Dissolved in warm water and dabbed on, it did the trick – if the change of colour of the water was anything to go by. The marquise had added her silk bloomers to the parcel, the ones that had sent Monsieur Aristide to the brink of a seizure. With Tatiana and her mother as her horrified audience, Katya washed them in a bowl of the solution. Soon, not a mark remained.

'What would your father have said?' Irina wept. 'His daughter, reduced to this.'

'Fifteen francs, Mama. Enough to buy tea and bread for a week.'

'I'd rather die than wash another woman's underwear,' Tatiana said through her teeth.

'Would you go to Dedushka's, see if our chicken is cooked?' Katya had bought a broiler hen from Les Halles, the teeming market next to Beaubourg, and Maria Filatova was stewing it for her with turnips and onions, having told Katya that if she roasted it, it would carve like an old boot. Katya wanted Tatiana to discover the connection between hard work and hot meals.

While her sister shuffled off to check their dinner, Katya hung the marquise's skirt and bloomers out to dry in their tiny back courtyard. The next day, she pressed her handiwork with a flat iron, studying how the skirt had been put together. Every seam was a work of art; the stitching was almost invisible, which was no surprise to Katya as she'd been trying on her mother's couture gowns for years. What intrigued her was that the fabric bounced back when pulled. Una McBride's outfit had been made of the same stuff. 'Bet it doesn't fray,' she muttered to herself.

The following evening, Katya stopped off on Boulevard Malesherbes and the same manservant held out his hands for the parcel. Katya kept hold of it. 'I will wait here for payment, thank you.'

Soon, it wasn't only the marquise bringing in garments for Katya to clean. Word of her talent spread among the marquise's friends. Among that lady's enemies too; the marquise seemed to have quite a collection of those. This unexpected success proved awkward for Katya. Catching her accepting a wine-stained blouse from a customer one day, Monsieur Aristide summoned her to his office.

'If you desire to run your own business, do so. But not here, Mademoiselle.'

After that, Katya collected in person. An address scribbled on a napkin, or a calling card handed over with the bill, usually escaped Monsieur's eye. As March winds pulled in their teeth and longer days arrived, Katya's second occupation took over her evenings and encroached on her time off. Tatiana was convinced the work was coming in only because Monsieur Aristide had let slip their identities.

'Your clients can boast that a Russian princess scrubs for them.'

'Let them, if it means I can occasionally put a chicken in the pot at home. At least I try.' The dig was intentional and came with feeling.

Tatiana had started turning up late for work in the mornings, lagging behind Katya so she could watch the shutters open on her favourite shops. On these occasions, Monsieur Aristide would pull out his English hunter watch and brandish it in Tatiana's direction.

Seeing her sister saunter in one afternoon, flagrantly late from her lunch break and wearing a pair of new, cream leather gloves, Katya followed her to the staff cloakroom.

'Are you trying to get sacked?'

Tatiana pulled her gloves off, a finger at a time. 'I never wanted this job.'

'Nor did I, but I work so that one day we can have a home we're proud of, and decent schooling for Anoushka when she's old enough.'

'And you think teapot duties and soaping collars at midnight will achieve it?'

'You have a better proposition?'

Tatiana seized Katya's hands, drawing her thumbs across the reddened knuckles. Borax solution was not kind to skin. 'I can tell you this much. My next position will not involve hot water, kettles, aprons or ridiculous headbands.'

'And what job is that, please?'

Tatiana replied with a shrug and a smile that left Katya exasperated and not a bit the wiser.

The first official day of spring, 21 March, landed on a Friday. Friday nights were the best of the week, as the Émigré Council always held a dinner at Dedushka's. Georgy Filatov would create one long table and the Russian community would come together. The chatter was in French, the songs were Russian. Musicians – some of them virtuoso – played and the tears ran. Talk was about the old days, families lost, battles fought. Guests would describe the aching boredom of life in the Imperial court, or the extinct joys of riding through forests, or skating on frozen rivers. Nobody alluded to their own or anyone else's current poverty.

Because they weren't needed at work until nine on Saturday morning, Katya and Tatiana could relax and enjoy the evening. This particular evening, however, Tatiana claimed a headache.

'But Mama looks forward to it so much.'

'I'm not stopping her from going. Please, Katya, take the baby and give me a few hours' quiet.'

Katya thought no more about it until Prince Provolsky, joining the party later that evening, mentioned that he'd seen a girl resembling Tatiana walking up Boulevard de Courcelles. 'No young woman should be out alone after dark.' He tickled Anoushka under the chin. 'Ah, this little person is getting fatter, I think.'

'Heavier, for sure.' Katya doubted Aleksey could have seen Tatiana. After all, where would her sister be going at this time of night? She changed the subject, teasing Aleksey by asking, 'How's your tooth?'

'Eh?' He frowned.

'I saw you go into the doctor's. Georgy Filatov thought you'd had one taken out.'

'What are you two talking about?' Aleksey's mother demanded coyly, and Katya never learned if Georgy had been correct or not. It was her cue to go and sit elsewhere. That their respective mothers were planning some kind of union for them was pretty obvious and had she never met Harry Morten, she might have gone along with it. Though Harry was no longer really in the picture, he would always be the man who had stopped her throwing herself from a train. Nobody could compete with that.

At one a.m., she bundled the sleeping Anoushka into a blanket and took her home… and found Tatiana in bed, steadily breathing. Had she not already discovered a dress and silk stockings under the pram mattress, Katya would have ignored Aleksey's intimations, but her trust had been fatally damaged. She found her sister's coat hanging on its hook. The sleeves and shoulders felt damp. A light drizzle had fallen during the evening. Tatiana's boot soles were moist too. Her sister had certainly been out.

*

Spring, like a shaggy bear, emerged from sleep and stirred up Katya's life. An hour into her morning shift on 25 March – the quarter day when the next three months' rent was due – she was clearing yet another table, separating her tip from the rest of the coins, when the doorbell tinkled. She turned, hoping to beat Tatiana to the first smile – and saw her sister striding out, flinging her lace headband behind her. Immobilised by her tray, Katya could only gape.

'This time she goes too far!' Monsieur Aristide stormed out from the rear of the shop. 'I told her, I have applicants ready to take over her job and she tells me I can… no,' he stroked his moustache, reinvigorating its curl, 'I will not repeat. Your sister most assuredly is not a lady.'

'She appreciates this work, truly—'

'I had my doubts about employing Russians. But I said to myself, "Aristide, is it every day princesses ask for work? They may lend your establishment a cachet even Ladurée or Angelina cannot match".' He made a sound, which from a less refined man would have been called a raspberry, and ordered Katya to carry on with her work. 'Your sister is not welcome here. As for you, I find no fault but from now on, I am looking. You understand?'

For the next three hours, Katya poured tea and served cake with agonised concentration. Thank heavens she had the rent money ready to pass over to Princess Provolskaya, who would knock for it this week. Without a second wage, life would be tight.

Hardly a week passed, but some basic commodity shot up in price. Her anxiety was noticed by her customers and when lunchtime came, she'd collected only a miserable few francs in tips. None of her personal customers had dropped in either. So, no laundry income tonight. *Could things get worse?*

Always a dangerous question. Within moments, the doorbell tinkled again. She looked across, forcing a smile that froze. Harry Morten stood in the doorway. He was looking for someone. His eyes found her and his expression was deadly.

Chapter Twelve

In her shock, Katya dropped a fifty-centime piece. Harry stopped its roll by stepping on it. He picked it up and handed it to her.

'I met your sister and she told me where to find you.'

'Did Tatiana say where she was going?'

His expression suggested he neither knew nor cared. 'I want an explanation.'

Monsieur Aristide was making one of his regular inspections of the mirrors behind the cake counter. They were kept to a crystal sheen, creating the effect of magical abundance. Katya saw herself in their reflection, rigid in her black-and-white uniform. Harry's anger filled every corner, a silent shout, if such a thing existed. Monsieur Aristide heard it, anyway. He came towards them.

'Harry, *please*,' she begged, 'don't get me sacked.' In her distress, she forgot her pledge never to be on first-name terms with him.

He answered through clenched teeth. 'I made a discovery this morning, not a pleasant one.'

'You did?' Had he heard about her washing business? Or something about Moscow, and her haste to leave the place?

'I passed a jeweller's shop not half an hour ago. On the corner of Daru and Courcelles. They buy items.'

'Kaminsky's. I know the shop—'

'Monsieur Morten, *bonjour, bonjour*! How long since we had the pleasure?' Monsieur Aristide was upon them, opening up his cutaway morning coat to display its lining. 'What do you make of this, heh?'

'It tells me you've found a good tailor.' Harry gave the patron's satin coat lining a terse moment's attention.

'You are not in the mood to spar?' Monsieur Aristide looked from Harry to Katya. 'Something offends? Permit me to show you to a table.'

'I'm not staying.'

Please. Katya begged with her eyes. Harry visibly took control of himself. 'All right. Assam, with lemon. I haven't much time.'

She served him and he caught her wrist before she got away. 'Do you get a lunch hour?'

'At one. Just half an hour.'

He checked his wrist watch. 'Be at my office at five past. I'm at Cour du Comte, off rue Duphot.'

'What number?'

'No number. You can't miss it: Morten et Compagnie. If I don't see you, I'll come back here and drag you out.'

Rue Duphot ran at an angle behind rue Cambon. On a map, the ground between would resemble a wedge of cheese. The street's main claim to interest was a glimpse of the Madeleine church. Beyond that, it offered a string of mid-range milliners and dress shops. As for Cour du Comte, 'the Count's courtyard', that was reached through a stone arch which, until now, Katya had always dismissed as a delivery entrance. As she walked into its shadows, she wished she'd changed out of her work dress and cardigan. She stumbled on a cobble, which was deeply grooved by generations of carriage wheels. The sense of stepping back in time was profound – until she caught sight of an imposing car, sapphire blue with polished chrome, its cabriolet roof pulled down. Her father would have drooled. But no time for that. Which door should she knock at? The buildings to her right were smartly painted while those to the left were shabby. Choosing the side that looked inhabited, she rang a doorbell that was answered almost at once.

A mature woman in a well-cut suit greeted her. 'Princess Vytenis? Please come this way.'

Katya followed her into a long room where racks of fabric sponged up the light from barred windows. She instantly began sneezing.

'Yes, sorry. We've been tidying up, bashing away four years' worth of cobwebs. While Monsieur Morten was away, trade was slow. Suddenly, it's like being on a cart, downhill with no brakes.' The woman tapped on a door between the racks and part-opened it. 'Monsieur? Your guest has arrived.' She indicated that Katya should walk in.

Harry sat at a desk so loaded with lever-arch files, only his head and shoulders were visible. He'd stripped off his jacket since Katya had last seen him. Silver bands above his elbows kept his shirtsleeves free of his work. He carried on writing while she absorbed a new reality. It was a long time since she'd imagined him to be a penniless wanderer. Instead, she had perceived him as a mercurial man-about-town, the kind who flits from one pleasure to another. But here he was, at work in a solid enterprise that bore his name. 'You sell cloth for a living?'

'Yes, a family company. Or it was. Now it's only me.' Harry screwed the top back on his pen. 'So. You came.'

'Of course. Will you explain to me why I have sunk so thoroughly in your estimation?'

Harry moved files aside and placed an object in the gap. A gold cigarette case. His cigarette case. And even though she recognised it, she pulled off her shoulder purse and jammed her hand inside. 'I don't understand,' she stammered as her search rendered a tin of peppermints, some cash, her address book and a stub of a pencil. 'I kept it in this bag. It fell out of your pocket in the taxi.'

'*Dis-donc.*' *You don't say.* Harry's lip curled, his mouth twisting. 'I spent days chasing down the driver. He swore he didn't have it and I believed him.' He waited coldly for her defence.

'I kept it but I was going to give it back to you.'

'When, exactly?'

'When I found the courage.'

'So how come I bought it back not two hours ago from Kaminsky's?'

'I don't know.' She battled on, in spite of his withering look. 'It wasn't me who took it there.'

'Sold it. It didn't take itself.'

Katya's mind raced through possibilities. Could her bag have been rifled in the tea-parlour cloakroom? Or at Dedushka's during dinner as she sang along with the balalaika players?

Who was she trying to delude? *Tatiana. The horse kicking free of its harness.* Tatiana had been looking in her bag while Katya was out borrowing tea and gripe water from Georgy Filatov. Katya clearly remembered her sister holding her address book up to the light, pronouncing her unfinished sketch to be 'Quite good'. Had Tatiana found the cigarette case then, or later?

'I didn't sell it.' A final stab at being believed.

Harry fished about in his drawer and presented her with a slip of paper. 'Kaminsky won't buy anything over a certain value without a signature. Read the name.'

It was her name. Her signature too, or a copy of it.

She said, 'Ask Monsieur Kaminsky what colour hair the seller had.'

Harry invited her to sit opposite him, then dialled the telephone on his desk. The minute of waiting as the operator put him through was excruciating. When the call was answered, Harry gave his surname. 'The gold cigarette case – the girl who brought it in, can you describe her? *Oui, oui. Longue et mince.*' Tall and slim. 'Eye and hair colour?' Harry glanced at Katya. 'I see. Thank you.' He put down the receiver. 'Green eyes, striking gold hair. You need to speak with your sister.'

She took the cigarette case and as she flipped up the lid and saw the initials 'CHM', a new shame flooded her. *Please, no.* 'Was this your brother's?'

Harry grunted assent; it had been Christian's.

She pressed a hand to her mouth and what started as a gentle sob took on a life of its own. 'It's how she was able to buy her new dress. And her brooch.' She sank her head into her hands, heard a thud and realised she'd knocked a number of files to the floor. 'Monsieur Morten, I'm so sorry.'

'To be fair, my desk needs tidying.' Harry was beside her. She was helped to her feet, a handkerchief smelling of cologne-mint pressed into her hand. She wiped her cheeks, and when she put the handkerchief down, Katya realised she was in Harry's arms. *How had she got there?*

'If I'd known it was your brother's, I'd have brought it to you at once. I was angry with you. Punishing you for...' *What?* She couldn't remember now.

'Shush.' The sound nestled in her hair. 'I know.'

Her pulse danced, her eyelids drifted shut. His lips were a hair's breadth away. All she needed to do was tilt her face... Harry wore a waistcoat with pockets and without considering the impact of her touch, she slipped the case into one of them. A shudder passed through him. She looked up. Emotions crowded his face, the restless nerve moved beside his eye. Then, as if he couldn't sustain her wide-eyed appraisal, he arched his neck and looked up at the ceiling.

The spell snapped and Katya backed out of his arms. 'I need to go. Monsieur Aristide watches the minute hand of the clock.'

'Do you need that job?'

'Of course.'

She made for the door, stopping as he said, 'I take it that my suggestion fell on stony ground.'

'Suggestion?'

'The note I left, suggesting you go to Callot Soeurs.'

'The empty envelope, you mean?'

He placed a couple of files back on the desk. One of them immediately fell off again, splaying like a shot bird. 'You say the most extraordinary things sometimes.'

'And you do the most extraordinary things. You left me an envelope with nothing inside. Several Saturdays ago? I saw you crossing the park.'

'The letter contained an introduction to Madame Amélie Veillon who assists Callot Soeurs' *directrice*. There was an opening for a new mannequin. One of their girls died suddenly. Flu, needless to say. I thought of you.'

'As a mannequin at Callot Soeurs?' She repeated it dumbly.

'It's not the best-paid work. Well, pretty awful actually.' Harry gave a rueful smile. 'It's always assumed the girls will make up their income...' he broke off. 'Not all of them, of course. And it's not as easy as it looks, but it has the advantage of late starts. You'd have leisure to develop your other passion.'

'Passion?' Her heart bumped. What had she given away?

'For design. You'd be at the heart of the industry, with time to study and learn.' He gave an exasperated headshake. 'Why didn't you respond? I did go to some little trouble.'

Katya repeated, 'The envelope had nothing in it. Tatiana found it.' *Tatiana, again.* 'Could she have opened it?'

'If she's nifty with a steam kettle and has no morals. You poor girl.'

Too distraught to say a proper goodbye, she left and arrived back at work fifteen minutes late. Monsieur Aristide was at the cake counter. He took out his pocket watch and shook his head. 'Go. Just go.'

She ran to him, grasping his arm. 'Please Monsieur, don't sack me. I beg you.'

He shook her off, batting the creases from his coat sleeve. 'Take the afternoon off. Jeanne will cover for you.' He nodded towards the other waitress who was busy taking an order. 'Go, go. From the look in your eyes, it would be most dangerous for you to be in charge of a hot teapot.'

Katya did not go home but pointed her feet towards Avenue Matignon. If, as before, Callot Soeurs' collection was shown at three, she had a little time in which to recover from the humiliation of what she'd seen in Harry Morten's face. *You poor girl.* She couldn't imagine ever looking him in the eye again.

This time, she entered the couture house without an indecisive two-step at the door. The same *vendeuse* again tried to direct her to the back of the salon, but Katya headed for the front row saying, 'I'd like a good view this time.' She added in a low voice, 'I heard you'd lost one of your mannequins. I'm so sorry.'

'Marie-Juliette. Such a desperate shame.'

'You have a new girl?'

'There are always girls eager to work here. Madame Veillon keeps a list. Will you excuse me?' Other customers were arriving.

Katya clasped her hands in her lap so nobody could suspect her of being here to copy. Which reminded her that though Una McBride had returned her sketches, she'd left them at the tearoom during one of Katya's lunch breaks and had not called back since. Una had enclosed a note:

'*Darling, let's meet soon.*'

But as Katya didn't know how to find Una, other than by hanging about at the Ritz, she had no idea if her designs had found favour or not.

The parade started. A striking olive-skinned girl with short, blue-black hair looked unfamiliar and Katya felt a splinter leave her heart. If that girl had taken the job Harry had meant for her, so be it. The important thing; she wasn't Tatiana.

The girl moved with a lazy grace, her fringed, black day dress making Katya think of a water snake among the reeds. The girl wasn't actually beautiful; her nose had a bump halfway down but everything about her commanded attention. Katya looked away to hide the envy she knew was written on her face. *That could have been me!* When she looked back, the dark-haired girl had been replaced by another wearing a green-fringed dress and a turban that added to her already impressive height. This girl's just-visible hair was coppery gold and sharply cropped. Katya could see the scissor bites. *Talk of snakes in the grass...*

Tatiana posed. Her gaze stopped at Katya and she jerked as if somebody had stuck a needle in her. She recovered herself, completed her choreography, and left. She didn't appear again.

Katya waited outside. At around five thirty, a troupe of girls emerged, all carrying box-bags with brass catches. Most of them turned towards the river – suggesting they lived on the Left Bank – while Tatiana and the girl with the blueberry-black hair turned right. Her sister was wearing a coat that tapered at the calf and a neat, small hat.

Katya followed, seething.

Halfway along Avenue Matignon, Tatiana flagged down a taxi. A moment later, both girls were inside it, driving away.

Katya sprinted back to the nearest métro which was Rond-Point, repeating '*pardon*' and '*excusez-moi*' as she ran down the steps. Catching a train moments before it moved off, she flumped into a seat and travelled to Étoile, where she changed to Line 2. She got off at Courcelles and ran all the way to rue Daru where she waited, panting hard, outside the cathedral gates. The whole journey had taken her under twenty minutes. Moments later, a taxi rounded the corner and the new short-haired Tatiana got out. A second head poked out of the passenger window – the dark girl had travelled with her.

Katya strode across the road and dug her fingers into Tatiana's coat sleeve. 'Very lovely. How did you pay for it?'

Tatiana jerked her arm away. 'Don't put tea parlour smears on it.'

Goaded, Katya yanked off her sister's hat, pins and all.

'Ow – my hair,' Tatiana raged. 'I can't work if my looks are spoiled.'

'Let's find some holy water to wash you in, shall we? I wonder if it would turn black. Thief. Traitor.' The dark-haired girl leaned out of the cab and demanded to know what was going on. 'Mind your own business!' Katya roared before bundling her sister through the cathedral door where habits of respect took over. She jammed the hat back on her sister's head, then took her to where the candles stood in their sand tray, dropped coins in the box and lit one. 'You stole my job. You opened my letter.'

'It was open already. The note fell out.'

'So? It was addressed to me. You stole from me, Tatya!'

Tatiana shrugged. 'You wouldn't have got the job.'

'Oh, really? Others seem to think I might.'

'I only got it after I'd been shown how to present myself. It wasn't just a case of buying a few new clothes, though I had to, of course. The other Friday, while you were at the dinner, I went up to the butte of Montmartre, to a ballet-teacher's flat.'

'The night you supposedly had a dreadful headache!'

'I paid her for two hours' coaching.' Tatiana spoke as if that justified everything. 'You see, we don't walk properly.'

'Speak for yourself. I have excellent deportment!'

'Exactly. See Princess Ekaterina walk the length of a cloister with the collected works of Pushkin on her head. Marvel at her ramrod back. Being a mannequin is about making clothes speak, while showing their detail back and front. It's about interpreting the spirit of the salon. Women must want the clothes you wear. All the gentlemen must want—'

'Hush!' Katya shot a glance left and right, appalled to think that a priest or one of the servers might be listening. Their audience, fortunately, was limited to sculpted saints and sacred icons. She added more money to the collection and lit a second candle which she thrust at Tatiana. 'I suppose when you ran out of the tea parlour, you were on your way to have your hair cut.'

'I was. And I'm not sorry.'

'It will break Mama's heart. Our hair was their joy, hers and Papa's.' Papa had teased his daughters about the time they spent brushing it. Teasing laced with pride. 'How much did it cost you to scalp yourself?'

'Nothing. The hairdresser kept what he cut off to sell to a wig maker. My coat and hat are on loan from Callot Soeurs.'

'And the dress you concealed in Anoushka's pram?'

'From Le Bon Marché.' Tatiana named the oldest department store in Paris, known for its accommodating prices. 'I had to have something for my try-out.' It was too dim in the church to see if Tatiana's cheeks registered a change of colour, but Katya fancied she heard a stumble. 'Honestly, Katya, you're going on as though I went to Worth or something.' Tatiana unbuttoned her coat as a mannequin would, dropping it off one shoulder to display the lilac dress. On her svelte form, it hung wonderfully. Its skirt was long enough to cover the tops of a pair of button-fronted boots. Katya ached with envy.

'Where did the money come from, Tatya?'

'From my tips.'

'Lying again. You sold a gold cigarette case to Kaminsky's, pretending to be me. Stolen from my bag.'

Tatiana laughed. '*Oh là, là, là.* A gentleman's case, with initials under the lid. Is my upright sister taking gifts?'

'It's Monsieur Morten's cigarette case. '

'He gave you an eighteen-carat gold ornament?'

'He dropped it. I was going to take it back to him. Oddly, it didn't cross my mind that there was an unprincipled cheat at home.' Katya spat the final words.

'You'd better not tell Monsieur Morten.' Urgency altered Tatiana's tone. 'He's highly regarded at Callot Soeurs. He supplies their suit cloth and all their winter-coat fabric.'

'He already *knows*, Tatiana. And so will our mother. I'll also mention that you've cut your hair.' In the silence, Katya thought she could hear her sister's heart pounding.

'Do it,' Tatiana whispered. 'I'm leaving home anyway. My friend Constanza has a flat in Batignolles.'

'I suppose it's her in the cab? You'd better call on Mama and break the news.'

'It's why I came, but she'll make such a beastly, dreadful fuss.'

Katya's anger finally gave way. 'She'll cry, Tatiana. Please, *please* change your mind. You can't have known this Constanza for more than—'

'I *do* know Constanza,' Tatiana pre-empted. 'We took our deportment class together. She's like you, strong. She'll look after me.'

Katya felt her last argument die. 'Go then, but tell me one last thing. Did you also sell a pair of Papa's cufflinks at Kaminsky's?'

'No. No and no. If I had anything of Papa's, I'd sleep with it under my pillow. All I'm guilty of is a burning desire to get out of that suffocating room, and make my own choices. You're so busy being the put-upon martyr, you don't see that our needs are exactly the same.'

'But I don't steal in order to meet mine! You took my chance at Callot Soeurs, nearly lost me my job and ruined my reputation with Monsieur Morten.'

Tatiana put her candle into the sand tray, crossed herself and made one last sally. 'Have you nothing on your conscience that you should confess, Saint Ekaterina?'

'What do you mean?'

Tatiana came so close, their noses all but touched. 'You dream out loud.'

'So do you. And Mama.'

'We don't beg Vera's forgiveness all night long.' Tatiana took Katya in a hard grip. 'Why do you need to be forgiven?'

'Because I failed her. Tatiana, I've spared you and mother the reality of Vera's prison. The slop pails, the gibbering creature in the cell opposite her... I risked my life to find our sister because there was the tiniest chance of freeing her. I wasted that chance. I blundered and I'll live with that until I die, but you need to know that the men who took Vera would never have let her out alive. She confessed to writing militant letters. People were shot or hanged for far less. I beg Vera's forgiveness in my dreams because in the end, I ran.'

Katya's heart was beating out of her chest. 'I found her, Tatiana, while you went to bed and slept. I brought our sister's baby home and only I know how I did it.'

Tatiana released her grip. 'I hear Vera whisper to me sometimes. I won't believe she's dead.'

'That's up to you.'

'Tell me you saw her die.'

Katya opened her mouth, daring herself to disclose the truth. What a relief it would be to unburden herself. But she had sworn never to reveal those final, appalling moments and so she tightened her lips again.

Tatiana walked away, her footsteps echoing across the floor. Katya walked in the opposite direction, towards the altar whose gilded screens blurred to liquid gold. 'I saved her child,' she whispered through her tears. 'Remember that, Tatiana, when you think you hate me.' Kneeling at the altar, she opened the shutters in her head.

*

Katya unbuttons her coat, places the lifeless weight against her heart. Baby Anoushka feels like a wax doll left outside overnight. The Cheka captain has stopped threatening Vera, because she's retreated to the back of her cell. He has no key, so he can't get in. By the same token, he could never have let her out. Maddened by his desire for alcohol, he thrusts his leather-clad arm through the bars. 'Give me that bottle, or I'll dance your sister on the end of a bayonet. You hear me?'

Vera does not hear. She is talking to her husband Mikhail whom only she can see. Talking so intently, the policeman doesn't hear the choking snuffle that breaks out inside Katya's coat. The snuffle is followed by a wriggle and a tiny, kitten cry. Anoushka has responded to the warmth of Katya's body. She is alive.

*

At home, Katya found her mother prostrate.

'My girl has gone. She walked in, claimed she had to leave us. Why? Fetch her back, Katya.'

Katya couldn't, having only Batignolles, a suburb somewhere to the north, as her starting point. 'She's hopped the cage.'

'To be a mannequin in a fashion house.'

'A good house.'

'Do you know how those girls pay their way? They find rich lovers.'

'Not Tatiana.' *Not yet, though soon, probably.*

Anoushka was standing up in her crib, her cheeks tight as drum skin from tears nobody had wiped away. Katya hoisted the child in her arms, stripping off soaking nappies. 'Don't cry, darling. Tatie-Tatya will soon be home. There, there. Tatie-Katya has you.'

Chapter Thirteen

April brought greenery to the boulevards and there was less need to feed the fire with coal, meaning Katya could put a little money aside. Easter was late, falling towards the end of April. The Saturday before, on an afternoon of darting swallows and blue skies, Katya took her half-day off and caught a bus to the fringes of Bois de Bologne where Agnès, duchesse de Brioude, owned a splendid townhouse. This was not Katya's first visit to the marquise de Sainte-Vierge's kind-hearted niece – some item from the duchesse's extensive wardrobe was given to Katya to clean or mend most weeks. Today, she was returning a handbag of oatmeal kid, which a friend of the duchesse planned to take to the holiday race-meeting at Longchamp. Somebody in the lady's household had put it in a damp drawer next to an old key. The rust mark this had left on it had foxed Katya for a while, but vinegar and salt had lifted it in the end. She unpacked the parcel in front of the duchesse's maid, who murmured, 'A miracle, how did you do it?'

'I prayed to Crispin, patron saint of leatherworkers.' Katya smiled. She never revealed her secrets.

'Madame will be ecstatic. She loves to surprise her friends with little acts of kindness. Wait while I show her.'

A little later, substantially richer, Katya walked away beneath chestnuts whose emerald leaves were tossed in sunshine. Give it a week or two and the trees would be in flower – those that had not been butchered during the war, at any rate. Her mother had described the sight and smell of the *grands boulevards* veiled in chestnut blossom, before desperate people had plundered the trees for firewood. Katya hoped she'd experience a Paris spring like it, one day. Still, it *was* spring, saw-tooth winds and dirty snow a memory. A thousand-franc note lay in her purse. She'd buy a toy for Anoushka and something to share with her mother; a visit to Parfums de Rosine, perhaps? But as she waited for her bus, she acknowledged the money wasn't hers to spend. Not until she'd repaid Harry Morten.

Harry's residence was No. 5, rue Goya. Katya had always avoided using the street to enter or exit the park, wary of bumping into him. So far, their every meeting had been blemished. Either they traded insults or kisses. *Near-kisses.* He had accused her of theft and fraud. She had insinuated that he was a coward and socially beneath her. He had implied that she was a piece of deluded jetsam, washed up on the receding tide of history. She had stood in his arms and wanted to stay there forever. *The next few minutes should be fun.*

Katya got off the motorbus on Malesherbes and checked her appearance in the reflective glass of a shopfront. Her suit, with its Moscow label and unfashionably long skirt, was a drab response to the season, but a white camellia in her buttonhole improved things. She'd braided her hair into a loose plait. These days, she could afford shampoo and bay oil and it shone again. As she walked along, humming, men tipped their hats. One treated her to a long backward glance and had she slowed her own step, no doubt he'd have turned and caught up with her. A second shopfront reflected her marching figure. *Would she pass for a modern working woman?* One of the new breed of typists or telephone girls who strode the pavements and rode the transport system?

Katya reached a set of black park gates, regal with gold spears and finials. Rue Goya lay the other side and was the most beautiful street she'd ever seen; a tunnel of flowering cherries whose scent transported her. On each side were cream stucco villas with ornate balconies and expressively arched windows, hinting at high ceilings and sweeping staircases. Perhaps even sheltered rear gardens. No. 5 had a path bordered with flowering shrubs, leading to a noble front door. It opened and Harry came out with Una McBride.

Katya and Harry's eyes met. Una strode towards her, smiling broadly. 'Hi there.'

Katya reluctantly looked away from Harry. Una was wearing a hip-length cardigan, similar to one Katya had bought for herself, and a swingy, chequered skirt with lace-up flat shoes. A combination known as '*Le look sportif*'.

Fitness was the mode. The spring fashion magazines featured pages of women cycling, golfing, dog-walking. Una's schoolboy hair was hidden under a sisal hat snug as a swimming cap and embroidered with bright flowers. Naïve shapes, a touch clumsy but charming.

Leaving the front-garden gate open for Harry, Una said cheerfully, 'I was thinking only this morning, "I wonder how that princess is doing?" And here you are.' She turned laughingly to Harry. 'When I was nursing, they called me a sorceress. I'd mention somebody and they'd turn up out of nowhere. Not at all welcome if it was matron or a visiting committee.' Una grasped Katya's arm, leaning in to kiss her cheeks. 'I'm going to say it. Your suit… *darling*… Nobody wears brown this side of Christmas except monks or bears. Did you never have springtime in Russia?'

'Oh, it's just something I threw on. I was hoping we'd meet.' Katya wasn't going to ask Una what she'd made of her sketches. Not in front of Harry who had yet to speak.

Perhaps Una *was* something of a sorceress because she immediately said, 'Those drawings, Oh Serene One. I've been meaning to stop by and chat. I loved them.'

'You did?'

'*He* did not.' Una inclined towards Harry. 'He vetoed them.'

'You showed them to him?'

'He forced me to and then,' Una made a throat-cutting motion, 'put his foot down. He really can put a foot down when he wants to.' She spread her arms like a preacher. 'Harry doesn't believe a girl has the right to make a living.'

'Rubbish.' Harry came through his gate at last. 'A girl can do as she likes, just not at my expense.' He offered Katya his hand to shake. 'In my opinion, Princess Vytenis, your work lacked signature. I'm not saying it wasn't promising, but you need to discover an original style.'

'I'll help you get started and promote you back home,' Una offered, 'so long as you call your boutique "Princess Katya".'

'My name is Ekaterina,' Katya said coldly. Harry's words had felt like a condemnation.

'And mine's Eunice Hildegarde Bigelow McBride. Imagine that over a shop door.'

Unseated by the American's determined good nature, Katya laughed. 'I wouldn't wish to trade on my title.'

'No? Leave that to me. Princesses go down a storm in the States.'

'Even Russian ones?'

'You bet. "Yurup" is all one to us.'

Nobody seemed sure what to say after that. Harry looked up, giving the impression of counting the petals on the cherry branches above. His hair had grown out since Katya had seen him last, a hint of bleaching to his wayward fringe. Perhaps, like her, he walked in the sunshine whenever he could. A blazer jacket and tapered trousers showed off his athletic shape. He carried a boater hat casually in his left hand. Lowering his chin, he caught her looking.

'Have you come to see me?'

'Yes, on a matter of business.'

He turned to Una. 'I promised you a ride in a car, so why don't you drive it yourself?' Something flashed. A key on a fob. Una caught it.

'You're making me break the bad news to Claudine all on my ownsome? Cruel man.'

'That's right. Claudine gets none of my Merton cottons until she becomes a better person.'

Una blew Katya a kiss. 'Make Harry show you the Merton samples, they're to-swoon-for. Let's meet soon.'

'But where can I find you?' Katya didn't know if it was an American thing, but '*We must get together soon*' ruffled her sense of propriety.

'At the Ritz Bar, of course. Toodle-pip.'

Harry led Katya up to a sitting room whose windows looked out into a pink blizzard of blossom. It felt like walking into the dawn. The whole apartment seemed impressively large, but it was the carpet that stole her eye. 'Aubusson,' she said, in pleasure. 'Woven at Creuse.'

'Do you know, or is it a guess?'

'Before he retired, my father was the curator of tapestries and carpets at Moscow's Imperial History Museum.'

Retired was a gloss. He had been sacked after the Bolsheviks took power.

'What did you want to see me about?' Harry was keeping a gap between them.

Katya fumbled the duchesse's banknote from her shoulder purse, releasing a shower of the almost-worthless coins that seemed to breed in her bag. She swooped on them and when she stood up again, Harry was holding the thousand-franc note out to her.

'You won't want to lose this.'

'Take it. It's why I came.'

'To pay me?'

'I – I realise I have a long way to go. Particularly since the business of the cigarette case.'

He continued to hold out the note. 'I've no need of it.'

No, she thought. Any lingering doubts of Harry Morten's wealth had fizzled away the moment she entered this room. In size and even decor, it was agonisingly like her old home. How wrong they'd all got him. 'I mean to pay you back, Monsieur Morten. Please tell me how much I owe in all.'

'Give me a moment while I fetch a team of accountants.' His mouth twitched. *A joke*. She couldn't join in. 'Fine. I'll fetch a pencil and pad from my office, though you realise, once a debt is written down, there's no escaping it.'

'Do I look as if I'm trying to escape?'

'You rarely look any other way. Every time I meet you, you're on one foot, poised to leap forwards or backwards. Make yourself comfortable.'

There was plenty of seating to choose from, from satinwood chairs and upholstered benches to buxom sofas. This room was furnished with guests in mind. A *salon* in the old-fashioned sense. A workroom too, with rolls of cloth propped against a wall. She was curious to see the cottons Una had mentioned, but saw nothing fitting the description of fabric 'to swoon for'. Choosing a chair next to a low table, she folded her hands and waited.

And waited. How long did it take a man to find a notepad and pencil? The table in front of her was a jumble of samples, and looking through, she came across swatches of vibrant printed cotton. Digging deeper, she uncovered something even more interesting. A certificate written in English, deeply scored from being folded. 'Harald D. Morten, Captain' jumped out at her. She couldn't resist reading each line out loud, though slowly as her English had never been strong. He'd been born in 1890 which made him six years older than herself. His permanent address, according to this, was Mill Yard, King Street in… she gave it a try. '*Manche…?*' The creases didn't help. There was mention of a regiment of the same name. '*Manch*-es-ter.'

'Manchester.' Harry came back into the room. 'You're looking at British Army form Z3. Interesting?'

She recovered herself. 'I love what I can't understand.'

'That's dangerous.' Harry sat opposite her. 'Sorry I took so long. The telephone rang while I was in my office. A *premier* from a tailoring establishment has realised halfway through his order book that he's taken too little of the grey barathea. As I warned at the time.' He picked up the document Katya had dropped in her embarrassment and refolded it. He might as well have said, '*See how abysmally wrong you were about me?*' But he never said more than was necessary.

'You were a soldier.'

'Four-and-a-half years, including time in hospital being repaired and two months' leave-of-absence to visit the Baltic coast. This certificate proves I have His Majesty's permission to be out on the street, a free man.'

'Which "majesty"?'

'His Britannic Majesty.'

'George the Fifth.'

'Correct.'

'He is the Tsar's cousin, did you know?' The mothers of King George and Tsar Nicholas had been Danish sister-princesses, which explained the uncanny similarity between the men – even their beards had been identical. Papa had modelled himself on both men, and she'd occasionally wondered if the Cheka's brutality towards him had been in part to do with his looks. She asked, 'Why did you serve in the English army, not the French?'

'The British army, if we're being precise. Because my mother was English and since Sweden, where my father comes from, stayed neutral, I had no other choice.'

There were two medals seemingly discarded among the fabric samples. One a silver cross, the other a disk imprinted with the profile of King George. Before she could pick up the nearest one, Harry closed his fingers around it.

'You – you won that?'

'It wasn't a race.'

'Of course.' In her nervousness, she tugged the ribbon holding her plait and it came loose in her hand. 'Your certificate says "January 1919" but we met two months earlier. That's when you were on leave?' Katya blushed, recalling her suspicions and her mother's accusations.

'I wasn't running away, that's for sure.' He gave a spectral smile. 'I've a piece of shrapnel in my knee the size of a lemon slice. When we met – or were "thrown together" – I was on official army business.'

'Are you allowed to tell me what?'

'I don't wish to, Princess.'

'Ekaterina, please.'

'I don't need to tell you, Princess, because we've already had the conversation. I was gathering sawdust, remember?'

'But that's not true.'

He shrugged. His intrusive tic reappeared and Katya was suddenly reminded of Armand de Sainte-Vierge, the marquise's son, who occasionally came with his mother to the English Tea Parlour. The young man wore a red-star medal denoting a war wound, though he had no visible injury.

Sometimes, Armand talked like a tap left running, while his mother patted his hand. Other times he'd stare blankly into his teacup. Harry Morten's fixed look, falling without warning, suggested a battle in constant progress. Katya sometimes likened her own thoughts to arrows shot backwards, landing in the same scarred patch of earth. Perhaps it was the same for him.

'Monsieur Morten, I want to apologise for what I've insinuated in the past, and what my mother said to you in the Ritz dining room.'

'About letting other men do the fighting?' He tossed the medal on to the table where it oscillated like a frantic butterfly.

'I leapt to judgement. As for Mama, she… well, she's a woman of her time.'

'We're all moulded by our time, but we don't have to be its prisoner.'

'I'm not sure.' Katya pulled the knots out of her crumpled hair ribbon, raking her fingers through her unravelling plait until there was nothing to do but shake it loose. 'The world will never go back to what it was, and that gives me a freedom I never dreamed I would have. But for women like my mother, change is frightening.'

'You wanted a tally of how much you owe me.' He flipped open the pad he'd brought in with him, his jaw tight as he wrote down a column of figures. 'Including the money I drew out for you in Gothenburg and half the cab fare—' he looked at her, inviting a protest.

'You'd have had to pay that anyway.'

'All right. I'll stand you that cab ride, as well as the milk and other essentials I bought for your niece.'

'I will pay for that.'

'Humour me. However, there's your bill at the Gustavus and the Ritz… and reimbursing me for having to buy back my own property from Kaminsky's…' He scribbled more figures, made a silent calculation, wrote something final, underlined it and ripped the page free.

'Oh.' She hoped her shock didn't show. A year's salary from the English Tea Parlour wouldn't pay this off. 'My family,' she steadied her voice, 'has expensive ways.' Silence built a wall between them. One of them must speak. 'I'll just have to work harder.'

'Pour more tea, or pour it faster?'

She told him about her side business, her titled customers. The ladies who relied on 'La Princesse Russe' to save their favourite garments. The curdled note in her voice made her cringe. 'If I keep getting commissions, assuming I make no mistakes, if our rent stays the same…' Katya kept talking, until her conviction gave out.

'You have an impressive client list,' Harry allowed. 'Is it a family enterprise? Does your sister help?'

'Tatiana no longer lives at home. Didn't you know?'

He shook his head. 'I saw her the last time I visited Madame Gerber but I didn't speak to her.' His mouth clamped, as if he feared what else he might say.

'Tatiana never liked getting her hands dirty.' Katya curled her fingers under, to hide her reddened knuckles. 'You despise me. Cleaning and skivvying for a few francs here and there. You think I'm doing the wrong thing.'

'It's not important what I think. What do you think?'

She shrugged. 'It's a means to an end. I intend to study couture, as soon as I can afford to. There are classes at several institutes.'

'How many hours a week do you put in now?'

'Ten, twenty.' Sometimes she worked all night when cornered by an impatient client.

'With your daytime work as well, you must be exhausted. What I'm saying,' he persisted in his slow, steady way, 'is that the market never rewards manual labour.' Harry let that sink in. 'It rewards scarcity. Sometimes it rewards ideas. You will never make more from this business than you do now, unless you find dedicated girls to work under you, who don't want to be paid much.'

'I'd be afraid, in case one of them ruined something irreplaceable.'

Harry went to the window. He took off his jacket and the afternoon sun turned his white shirt the colour of crab shell and thrust a short shadow behind him. On the train, his physique had intimidated Katya, but shorn of his winter clothing, she could see that he possessed grace. His shoulders were wide, his chest animated by the movement of his breath. He gave good advice, but she'd had ample proof that he was no soft touch.

She dropped his bill into her purse and put the thousand-franc note next to the form Z3. It was all she could do not to join Harry at the window and she wondered what he would do if she followed her desires, stroked his shoulders, the contours beneath the shirt. She stole a moment to admire the flower-print samples. 'If this is the look for spring, Merton must be a garden of paradise.'

'Not exactly, though it once was, I believe. It's a factory-ridden part of southwest London with a rather dirty river running through it. My cottons will do well with the couture houses who put out a "little season" during summer.'

'Una seemed to think so!' Katya was stalling. The door was in front of her, helpfully open. Nothing to stop her going through it.

He turned. Nodded. 'She's in league with Claudine Saumon. The large lady you met at Callot Soeurs?'

That Claudine. Booming voice. Balsam oil. Katya's eyes had stung for hours afterwards.

Harry went on, 'Una copies clothes from couture houses and supplies sketches, or sometimes the clothes themselves, to Claudine. Actually, Claudine's not above doing some copying herself, when she can be bothered to leave her office. It's said she has an eye like a camera. Her wholesale workroom runs off imitations for buyers who want couture at knockdown prices.'

'You're threatening to stop supplying Claudine?'

'I only supply her made-to-measure atelier, the respectable side of her business. If she blurs the line, I'll have her shut down and she knows it. Una is still young enough to believe she can get away with anything, but cheating in couture is like cheating at cards. You'll win a few hands but once people know, you're marked.'

'That's why you didn't like my sketches.'

'Let's call them "a tribute to Callot Soeurs".'

'I didn't do it on purpose.' Katya was almost at the door. 'I've so much to learn and I don't know where to start.'

'Wait here.' Harry cut past her before she could argue, returning within a minute. 'You're sure? If so,' he held out a card, 'here's an open door.'

Katya looked at the name on the card, her pulse taking off like a bird. *Claudine Saumon couture*. 'You think I should work for a woman you don't trust?'

'Claudine is…' Harry chose his words carefully, 'an acquired taste, but her atelier is good. Not the Rolls Royce of couture, nor a shaky Model T. Call it a sleek Pierce-Arrow.' He smiled. Katya wasn't sure why he was comparing couture with cars, but she didn't care.

'I could get work there?'

'One call from me will do it. Shall I?'

She nodded. Stupid, but her eyes filled and before she could stop herself, she stood on tiptoe and kissed him. On the mouth. Before he could react, or she could do any worse, she left.

Claudine Saumon worked from a building on rue Duphot, a short way from Cour du Comte and Harry's office. Assuming Harry would have made the promised telephone call in the days since she'd been to his flat, Katya walked into the lady's office feeling reasonably confident. She immediately started coughing. A cigarette burning in an ashtray on the desk was the most obvious irritant. But it was the oil lamp hanging from the ceiling, diffusing thick wafts of bronchial balsam that really hit the back of her throat.

She said hoarsely, 'Madame Saumon?'

The woman at the desk picked up the cigarette and dragged on it. 'Last time I looked. And you?'

Katya gave her name. Seeing no flicker of recognition in the eyes staring back at her, she decided on the spot to make no allusion to their previous meeting. 'I'm currently working at the English Tea Parlour but hoping to make a move into couture. A friend, Monsieur Morten, will have rung you on my behalf, I believe?' How was it, she wondered, when the rest of the world had struggled to keep flesh on bone for four years, the woman in front of her overflowed the sides of her chair? Madame Saumon's broad forearms took the weight of a colossal bosom. The Cheka had recruited similar bison-shouldered women—

No time to finish the thought. Claudine Saumon was informing her that Harry Morten had indeed rung and vouched for her so yes, she could have a job. 'Never hurts to have someone in the team who can sweet-talk a cloth supplier, eh?'

'I don't know about that, Madame.'

Claudine drew the last life out of her cigarette. 'Every girl I take on starts at the bottom. Princess or no.'

'I see.' Harry must have mentioned her title and Katya wished he hadn't. She wanted to start afresh.

Claudine outlined the working hours, wages and rules of conduct. 'Time-keeping, loyalty and cleanliness. As for chastity,' she sat back and her chair groaned alarmingly, 'what you do outside is your own business but for your information, I don't provide a clinic, a nurse, a dentist or a priest. You work. I pay you. End of story. All right?'

'I'd like to work in your couture section, Madame.'

'All new girls start in wholesale. That way, mistakes aren't so expensive.'

'But Monsieur Morten said—' Katya gave up as her interviewer tut-tutted.

'Harry Morten is a charming man. His brother was even more so. But one should not let a man have his way too often. Agreed?'

'Agreed, Madame.' She'd wanted a chance and here it was. Like asking for a prince and being handed a frog in a bucket. Sometimes all a frog needed was a kiss… 'Thank you, Madame Saumon.'

'Claudine or Madame will do. Let me see your hands.' Claudine turned them over. 'You've been made to wash up the tea things, ha? That ridiculous Aristide.'

'It's not him. I mend and clean clothes in my spare time.'

'That needs to stop. You can't sew fine fabrics with rough hands. It catches, and silk threads break. Buy a jar of paraffin wax, mix it with a little sugar and massage your hands three times a day.'

'Yes, Madame Sau… Claudine.' So, she'd accepted the job. 'I have to give in my notice at the tearoom, but as soon—'

Her hands were dropped and Claudine reached for a fresh packet of her workman's cigarettes. 'Tell Aristide to release you early, or I'll come and sit on one of his silly little chairs.'

Katya said a hurried 'good day' and left before the match was struck.

Arriving home, she found her mother frowning over a letter. Irina Vytenis looked up in relief. 'I was about to call on Princess Provolskaya to see if she understands this.'

'Who's it from, Mama?'

'The bank.'

'They've written? Let me see!'

'They say they require original certification.'

Without which, we cannot proceed.

'I thought you'd given them all our papers.'

'I did. I'm sure I did.' As Katya read the few lines, hopelessness washed over her. 'They're asking for Papa's certificate of deposit. The one he entrusted to me, that last morning.'

'Then take it to them.'

Katya flopped down on a chair. How many times had she explained that the document had disappeared with Yana and the musty, old carpetbag? She found herself eyeing her mother's veronal pills with a dangerous longing. Since making her promise in the park, Irina had dramatically cut back on her sleeping grains and there were enough left in that bottle for both of them. How good it must feel to fall into all-consuming sleep. Turning her back on temptation, Katya made them both a cup of strong, black tea. She didn't know what more she could take to the bank. Playing by the rules had failed. Perhaps prayer would help…

On 19 April, Easter Saturday, as darkness fell, Katya dressed Anoushka in her best bonnet and coat, and joined her mother, Princess Provolskaya and Aleksey in a candlelit parade around the cathedral. The vigil would last until the midnight bells rang to declare that Christ was risen from the dead. The ritual was crowded with memories of the previous Easter when, as a family of five, they'd linked arms and walked around Saint Basil's on Red Square. Vera, four months' pregnant, had fainted on the way home, a precursor of Anoushka's premature birth. She'd refused to rest. Vera, always able to discount pain in pursuit of what she saw as a true path. *Whereas I*, Katya thought, *hesitate and swerve. Or nearly step backwards into oblivion.* Anoushka, wearing her first pair of shoes, kicked in her arms. She was teething and fractious. Walking alongside as they began their fifth circuit, Aleksey said, 'Let me take her for a bit. Your sister Tatiana will join us?'

'I hope so.' Katya had sent Tatiana a note, care of Callot Soeurs, begging her to come. But when the midnight bells rang out and they filed into the cathedral, into a sea of candles, Tatiana had still not shown herself.

There were no seats or pews in the cathedral, and the worshippers circulated like heavy sediment. It was strangely peaceful, giving Katya an interval in which to express all the prayers, the hopes, she'd stored up. Aleksey interrupted her meditation, saying in her ear, 'I hear you have a new job.'

'In a couture house on rue Duphot.'

'Hm. Did you take those documents to your bank?'

'Yes, and now they're asking for something more. Give Anoushka back, you've done your stint.' She held out her arms, unwilling to discuss money on this holy occasion.

'Don't let them make you wait too long. French officials are lazy. They hide behind rules.'

'It's the same the world over.'

Katya was delighted when a voice behind her demanded, 'Hand over my fat little niece.'

'Tatiana! You came!' Katya offloaded the baby, inhaling a whiff of perfume and alcohol from her sister. 'Been to a party?'

'To a bar,' Tatiana whispered nonchalantly. 'I'm having fun these days. And you?'

'Every day is a fairy tale. Mama?' Katya waved to her mother, who stood alone, gazing into the face of a statue of the Holy Mother. 'Look who's arrived.'

Predictably, Irina took Tatiana's presence as proof of a homecoming. Her disappointment when it became clear that Tatiana had no such intention brought tears and a strong headache, which Irina insisted could only be cured one way: veranol and bed. Katya's heart sank, and it was hard not to blame Tatiana. After the final prayers had been said, sacred psalms sung, they left. Tatiana resisted coming further than the corner of rue Brazy.

'I'd come home more often if Mama would stop crying like this. Why should I feel guilty about living my life?'

'At least come in and take a sip of vodka with us?'

'No, it's too late. Constanza turns rabid if I wake her in the early hours.'

'Then give me an address, Tatya, so I don't have to send notes to your workplace.'

'I'll post it to you. Goodnight – or rather, good morning.'

Her sister hurried off towards rue de Courcelles, where a milky glow above the chimney pots revealed the imminence of dawn. Katya saw the outline of a car. An engine fired. Red tail lights flared. Katya tried not to feel jealous, like the stay-at-home drudge.

Her mother went on ahead, eager for her medicine, and Anoushka grew restless. Fearing she'd get no sleep at all, Katya put her niece in the pram and pushed her round the block. She was crossing rue Daru, heading for home, when a movement high up caught her attention. The moon was still bright enough to make out two people on a balcony five floors above Dedushka's Café. A room light was on behind them, and though Katya couldn't make out their faces, the silhouettes were of a man and woman. Dr Shepkin and the woman Katya had chased back from the church? The one who had reproached her with the words: 'Because I live the way I do, cleaning and skivvying—'

'*Live the way I do.*' Implying she did more than cook, mop floors and launder shirts?

Katya didn't like Vasily Shepkin, for all her mother and Princess Provolskaya acclaimed him as a secular saint. He might look fatherly with his downy, white beard but he had introduced veronal into their world. Once, while serving him coffee on a quiet morning in Dedushka's, Katya had asked him to *please* help her mother reduce her intake. Without glancing up from his newspaper, he'd answered, 'Princess Vytenis suffers from neurasthenia, a nervous disorder, and what she requires above all is sleep. Sleep and understanding.'

Katya had pointed out that there were times she feared her mother might not wake at all and he'd lifted his head to snap at her, 'Allow me to know best.'

Not a saint, not in her book. Katya wasn't even sure he was a proper doctor. Why would he hide himself away above a café, unless he lacked the proper licence to practice?

Later on Easter Sunday, after a fitful sleep, Katya wrapped the last of her laundry commissions. This one was for the marquise de Sainte-Vierge, and she put a note inside, thanking the marquise for her custom, explaining that she was shortly to become a couturier's apprentice. She could imagine the marquise's reaction. '*Damn fool!*' Perhaps she was, because she wasn't going to earn enough, not without a miracle.

The following morning brought one and it scared her.

It was inhumanly early and she was stumbling about, heating semolina for Anoushka who had woken with hungry cries. Once fed, the baby wanted to play and Katya carried her downstairs. 'How about a walk down to the river, to catch the sunrise? I can't think of anything I'd rather do at four-thirty in the morning.'

Dragging the pram from its niche, unbolting the front door, her eye caught something on the hall stand. A large letter with her name on it.

It yielded a document, creased and damp-spotted but without doubt, the lost certificate of deposit. The very item the bank wanted from her. There was her father's name and the signature of the bank's president. Last time she'd held this, Dr Zasyekin had been explaining its importance to her.

This could mean only one thing and she dashed out, shouting into the empty street, 'Yana? Yana Borisovna?'

No answer. She and Anoushka were the only souls awake on rue Brazy.

Katya had come to believe that Yana could not have reached Paris unaided. Wiley as their former maid undoubtedly was, Yana had known nothing of the world outside Moscow. Speaking only Russian, getting from Sweden to Paris would have been beyond her scope. Yet somebody had acquired Prince Vytenis's property and Katya's suspicions fell on Aleksey.

Who else knew how vital this document was? Or knew so much about her dealings with the bank? From the start, his behaviour had been odd. Take the way he'd appeared outside Montparnasse station within minutes of their arrival. And the fact that he'd known that they'd come from Moscow, though she'd said nothing during that first journey to suggest it. Of course, he or his mother could have gleaned information from Count and Countess Lasunskoy, but even so, he knew too much. And showed too much interest.

Could he have obtained items stolen by Yana? It was not impossible.

In the spirit of Machiavelli, of paying more attention to one's enemies than one's friends, Katya hunted him down in the café next morning, where he was having breakfast. She plonked herself on a seat at his table.

'Aleksey, I found the certificate. The proof the bank needs.' Faking amazement.

'Holy Mother!' His surprise seemed genuine too. 'Where?'

She showed him the envelope, though not the certificate itself. That was hidden safely at home. 'It appeared on the hall table. A miracle, no?' She watched his response.

'Remarkable, I agree. Will you take it to the bank?'

'Of course. I start my new job in a few days, so I have to go today or tomorrow. Will you come? Officials take more notice of men than women.' An impulsive invitation and not, she hoped, an error of judgement. She waited to see how eagerly he would take up the offer.

He shrugged, 'If you want,' and promised to pick her up the next morning, after his first shift. He gulped down the last of his tea, made a sandwich of a blini and mushrooms, picked up her hand and kissed it. 'I am happy for you, for all three of you.'

All three of us. Katya watched him leave. The day they'd arrived, he'd referred to them as 'three tall women'. It was how he'd recognised them, he'd claimed. Yet her Lasunskoy cousins had not known that Vera would be missing from their group. Katya had written to them of her father's death, but had not mentioned Vera's absence, unable to put the words on paper. Aleksey should have been expecting *four* tall women.

Next morning, as they drove to rue de la Paix, she studied him intently. He gave little away, whistling a tune as he cut in and out of the traffic. Only once did he turn to her, saying, 'Luck is with you, I feel it.' He made no other comment until he found a parking space near the Opéra, asking her only if she minded walking the short distance to the bank.

After a tiresome wait in the bank hall, they were admitted to the usual back office. Katya did her best to stay calm as the same official she'd come across previously tutted about the certificate's stained and crumpled appearance.

'But the content is readable, as is your president's signature.' Katya pointed. 'It is what you have asked for.'

The official rang for an underling. After a tense wait, a ledger was brought in and after a further delay, an entry was found that tallied with the details on the certificate. A bond had indeed been issued to Prince Ulian Vytenis for the sum of 500,000 francs in January 1914. The clerk shut the ledger. How had the prince come by such a large sum? It was essential to verify the origin of the funds.

'A transfer of cash derived from the sale of mining stock.' For over an hour the night before, Katya had extracted details of her father's financial arrangements from her mother, refusing to give Irina even a sniff of her sleeping grains until she had revealed everything she knew. 'My father sold his shares in a Russian–French mining company during his final visit to Paris. He deposited the proceeds with you, in return for this bond. You would have checked the source of the money at the time, surely?'

Aleksey gave his view that the late Prince Vytenis had been alert to political shifts in Russia, though sadly not immune to the madness. Touching Katya's arm, he said, 'His daughter has produced every document you've asked for, translated as requested, and has been patience incarnate. Her mother, Princess Vytenis, can present herself at any time to verify the claim.'

'Perhaps,' the official murmured.

'Perhaps?' Aleksey's composure deserted him. 'I fail to see what more you can require, Monsieur.'

The ledger was snapped shut. 'All seems to be in order.'

Aleksey pulled back. 'You mean – you accept this certificate as proof?'

'Indeed.'

'Monsieur, thank you.' Katya's smile reached almost to her ears. 'This means so much. So much.'

'All we now require,' the official made his comment to Aleksey, ignoring Katya, 'is a death certificate. Proof that Prince Ulian Vytenis is deceased, that his estate is the legal property of his surviving family.'

'He was murdered,' Katya burst out. 'Am I supposed to write to the thugs who bayonetted him, and ask if they'd be so kind as to sign a letter admitting it?'

The official vibrated his lips. 'Without a death certificate, I cannot advance this matter.'

Outside, Katya gave way. 'This is torture!'

Aleksey took her arm. 'I won't let you give up hope. Besides, you never had this money, so it's not as if you've lost anything. My mother held shares when she first came here. Month by month they dropped in value until they were worth nothing. That's pain. Shall we walk by the river? Why don't we go to Pont Alexandre, so you can see it on a fine day?'

'Take me to the Eiffel Tower.' Katya didn't want to see that either, but nor could she face going home.

'There's still barbed wire around it,' Aleksey warned.

'That will suit my mood perfectly.'

In the event, they weren't able to get close. The area around the tower's legs was fenced off and an armed guard followed them with his eyes as they walked. 'It's a radio mast,' Aleksey told her. 'In the war, it sent messages between London, America and St Petersburg.'

'Petrograd,' she corrected.

'Never that. Hey, shall we steal some onions?'

The land all around had been dug for allotments, and early onions and potatoes were poking through.

Katya managed a smile. 'Better not. Brrr.' A sharp wind was skimming off the river.

'Coffee then.' Aleksey put his arm around her. 'Where shall we go?'

She wondered why she felt uneasy in his company. He was tall and handsome enough to make most women blink. His reactions in the bank had been those of a friend, not a fortune hunter. She should trust what she saw, instead of always looking for the cracks. 'Rue de Rivoli. Angelina, for hot chocolate. Can you afford it?'

'For you, yes.' A smile lifted the corners of his eyes and then he was kissing her.

She let it take its course, thinking *this is nice*. Sweet. Stirring, even.

When he raised his head, he asked, 'Is there another man you care for, Katya?'

'Not really.'

'A little?'

She shrugged and he gave up, linking his arm with hers. 'I can wait for what I want.' As they walked towards Quai Branly, where he'd parked after driving from rue de la Paix, he asked, 'Who do you know in Moscow who you still trust?'

'Nobody.'

'There must be someone who could help arrange your father's proof of death.'

It felt profoundly unlikely but as they drew up in front of Angelina, an obvious name popped into her head. *Dr Zasyekin*. 'My father's friend, who sheltered us. You think I should write? I could, if he's still... safe.' She didn't want to say '*alive*'.

'Does he have influence? Has he gone over to the Bolsheviks?'

'He hadn't when I last saw him.'

'Then write to him,' Aleksey said. 'What is there to lose?'

That evening, Katya did as he suggested. She knew she would post the letter with little expectation of success, but this was her last shot, her last chance. Tomorrow she would begin her new job.

'My niece, Bibi Saumon, is in charge of the *petites mains*.'

Katya looked down at her tapering fingers: *little hands*. It sounded better than '*midinette*' a reference to the habit among Parisian seamstresses of rushing out to dine at midday. A term generally used disparagingly. Though it was not yet nine in the morning, the ashtray on Claudine's desk was a quarter full. Smothering a cough, Katya asked, 'May I get my bearings first?'

'If you want.' Claudine reached across her desk for the telephone receiver, her bosom acting like a snow-shovel, pushing papers to the far edge. Katya darted forward to rescue them. They were fashion drawings and she looked closer. Having spent many a lunchtime staring into first *arrondissement* boutiques, she knew at once that these were outright copies of the season's best sellers. One dress in particular was pure 'Worth'. Claudine yanked them out of her hand, then dialled a short number, using a pencil as her fingers were too fat for the holes in the rotary. 'Bibi? My office, now.' Claudine hung up, belatedly adding, 'Please.'

Minutes later, Katya was being introduced to a young woman with pale, reddish hair who was dressed in black, like her, though rather more smartly.

'My niece, Babette,' Claudine informed Katya. 'Known as Bibi. She manages the wholesale section and you'll report to her. Does that bother you? She's younger than you are.' Giving Katya no time to reply, Claudine went on, 'Bibi, this is the girl Monsieur Morten recommended. Be nice.'

Bibi Saumon looked Katya over. 'I've seen you before,' she said, shaking her head when Katya explained that she'd worked round the corner until a few days ago. 'No, at the Ritz.'

'I don't recall seeing you there.'

'I dined there with Harry Morten and you were at a table nearby. You wore pink, and we agreed that you must have been part of a touring theatre troop.'

Katya didn't believe Harry had agreed anything of the kind. His snubs had an erudition to them, and were the more effective for it. She said lightly, 'At least you noticed me, Mademoiselle. I'm sorry I can't return the compliment.'

Claudine laughed. 'That's put you in your place, Bibi. Such a curse, being insipid, neither blonde nor brunette. Oh, stop scowling and give Katya a tour of the establishment.'

As well as Claudine's office, the ground floor accommodated the made-to-measure atelier and the salon, where each season's collection was shown to clients. Second floor was the millinery workroom, which smelled of wet animal hair and resinous glue. Third floor was 'wholesale gowns and daywear', where Katya would work. The fourth floor was ruled over by a stocky, dark-haired tailor who paused long enough in his cutting to throw Katya a smile. The very top housed twenty resident girls. Claudine hired them from her home city of Lyon, Bibi explained tersely. 'Aunt waits until they've finished their apprenticeships in the silk factories, then entices them here. They're good workers and having them live in stops them getting poached by other houses. Where did you train?'

'I was taught by my governesses.'

Bibi Saumon turned slowly pink with disgust. A dash of freckles, like red lentils, coloured her nose. Her lashes were all but invisible and, like her aunt, she'd drawn on eyebrows with pencil. 'What are you doing here if your family is rich?'

'It isn't.' Katya hoped Claudine would have the sense to withhold the 'princess' part of her name. 'We fled here from Russia.'

'Oh, one of those. Bringing your begging bowl with you.'

Katya chose not to rise to the insult. 'I'm Parisian now, and,' she attempted a smile, 'a *petite main*.'

Bibi craned towards her. 'Until I say different, you are nothing, whatever my aunt thinks. Nothing.'

It was a daunting start and the following fortnight tested Katya. Her fellow seamstresses at first welcomed her, amused by the look on her face when she saw the treadle sewing machines lined up in the workroom. She'd supposed it would be all hand sewing. But no, she had to learn to wrestle with the beasts from day one.

Tentative friendships formed – until Bibi's hostility poisoned the air. One by one, her co-workers withdrew until only two remained willing to speak to her. These were Miryam and Fruma Kaminsky, sisters to the Kaminsky who owned the jeweller's shop on rue de Courcelles. Both women looked well past retirement age, and owned a wealth of experience. Between them, they taught Katya how to thread the machine and adjust the tension. The elder, Miryam, clicked her teeth whenever Katya was about to make an error. 'Not like that. Like *this*.' She treated her sister exactly the same, bickering in Yiddish, shielding Fruma from Bibi. Before Katya's arrival, Fruma Kaminsky had been the slowest worker in the wholesale atelier.

'I've saved you from that, then,' Katya said ruefully. Fruma stroked Katya's hair, murmuring '*Shaina maidel*'. Pretty girl.

One morning, admiring a dress ring on Fruma's middle finger, Katya admitted to frequently pausing to stare in her brother's shop window.

'Ah, so it is your nose print he wipes off his glass several times a week.'

'I never touch the glass! Once, I saw cufflinks I'm sure belonged to my father but somebody else got to them before I did.'

Fruma nodded. 'My brother Leon's prices are keen. Too keen. People come from a long way off to buy from him, then sell on at a better profit.'

Without the sisters, Katya wouldn't have kept going. Sitting in airless gloom while Paris burst into full flower was hard. The five-and-a-half-day week felt like double that. It didn't help that whenever Claudine waddled into their atelier, she would call across to Katya, 'I haven't forgotten about you, *chérie*. How is Monsieur Morten?'

That always made Bibi raise her head, and put a hard, vindictive light into her eyes.

In time, Katya's sewing machine ceased to be a fanged monster out for her blood. Dressmaking mysteries yielded to experience. By the third week of May, she was hand-finishing dresses she'd put together from scratch and not even Bibi could find faults, other than those the supervisor slyly created herself. Tearing a seam here, snipping a button off there. Katya found her rhythm and began to enjoy her work.

Not for long.

On 21 May, the day she turned twenty-four, Katya arrived for work early. Anoushka was going through a second bout of teething and had woken her while it was still dark. She had fed and bathed the baby, taken her for a sprint around the block in her pram, then tucked her into bed with Irina. After her brief lapse, Irina had reduced her veronal consumption again and Katya could leave each day without worrying what she'd find when she got home.

On this particular day, one of the Lyon girls approached Katya on the third-floor landing. Stopping in front of her, the girl dropped a deep curtsey. 'Good morning, Serene Highness.' Others who were tying on their aprons waited for Katya's response. Ignoring them, Katya went into the atelier, to the rack where the day's job-cards were put. She found hers, took her seat and prepared her machine. As she found the end of her cotton, Bibi came in and said, 'Leave that. Claudine wants you to have breakfast with her. If it's not too much trouble, Serene Highness.'

Silently, Katya obeyed. Doubtless, Claudine had given away her identity to rile Bibi, which she seemed to take pleasure in. What Katya did not yet understand was that Bibi's hatred went far deeper than class envy. Katya was keeping Bibi from something she passionately wanted. That 'something' worked across the street behind the stone walls of Cour du Comte.

Claudine always ate at her desk, and it was a perk to be invited to share a meal with her. Breakfast this morning was a basket of croissants, freshly baked. Croissants and brioche were both outlawed by the government to conserve flour, so Katya presumed that as well as running a black market in couture, Claudine had access to contraband food. 'This is very kind, Madame.' How had she earned the honour, she wondered?

Claudine reached for a croissant, grunting before falling back into her chair. 'Make coffee, will you? Nice and strong.'

As Katya lit the spirit stove and poured beans into a hand grinder, Claudine talked. 'You were the early bird today. Breakfast tryst with a lover?'

'With my niece. She's ten months old.' Katya set the coffee percolator to boil. Claudine was already on her second croissant. 'May I?'

'Mm-mm,' Claudine gave permission with her mouth full.

Katya bit off an end, savouring it. She sat down opposite Claudine as the percolator huffed and puffed. 'Did I do something wrong, coming in before the others?'

'Come early as you like, you won't beat me into work. I've called you in because as you left last night, I heard you chatting to the Kaminsky ladies. What about?'

Katya sensed danger, but she had too much respect for Claudine to fudge. 'Um, I wanted to know why our colour palette this season is so muted. It's the same in every fashion house,' she added hurriedly, 'but I'm intrigued to know why our wholesale line is all sludgy shades.'

Dresses, tunics and skirts were being churned out in plain silk. Whenever they were given cloth with a pattern, black and white dominated. Katya sometimes walked home with chequerboards on the backs of her eyelids. Yet Harry Morten had cloth in Garden-of-Eden colours. The Merton cottons. *Ah, now the breakfast, the croissants, made sense.*

The percolator began gurgling and Katya laid a tray, tea-parlour habits taking over.

'Sugar, milk *and* a napkin,' Claudine chuckled. 'That's more than Bibi ever does for me.'

'What is?' Bibi came in. Seeing the basket, her irritation turned to outrage. 'Why does she get croissants?'

'She's a princess and has ladylike habits as well as being most amusing. I'm minded to promote her.' The more Bibi scowled, the more twisted her aunt's smile grew.

'Do what you like,' Bibi snapped.

'I shall.' It fell as a warning. Claudine reached for her third croissant. She looked at Katya. 'There's some gorgeous cloth Harry Morten won't let me have. I asked an associate to prise some out of him, but she got nowhere.'

Una? Katya suspected as much.

'Get it for me,' Claudine finished, 'and you can have any job you like.'

Bibi cast an anguished glance at Katya. 'If Monsieur Morten had a new line, he'd have sent me a sample.'

'You think? She,' Claudine pointed the nub-end of her croissant at Katya, 'says different.'

Katya had said nothing of the sort. 'I'm surprised at the lack of colour this season, that's all.'

'Oh, not up to your regal expectations?' Bibi snapped. 'What do you know about Harry Morten's company?'

Claudine preened. 'She doesn't need to know about the company, she knows the man.'

Bibi's face went blank. Two people had come to the door. One was Roland Javier, the tailor. The other was elegant Pauline Frankel, who oversaw the couture side of the business. A meeting had evidently been scheduled and to Katya's relief, Claudine dismissed her. But not before ordering her to, 'Penetrate Morten's lair, get him to think again.' Claudine waved away Bibi's objections that it was not Katya's place to meet a supplier.

'A jumped-up *midinette*, Tante Claudine. Not even a half-decent one.'

'If anyone can sweet-talk Harry Morten, it's our princess, no? Knock him down.'

'Knock him—?' Katya blushed.

'To a fifteen-percent margin. I never pay more. Off you go.'

*

Harry was at his desk, shirtsleeves hitched up as before. When his assistant announced Katya as, 'A delegation from Maison Claudine,' he twitched, as if pepper had blown into his face. When he saw her, he sat back and put down his pen.

'Thank goodness it's you, not anyone by the name of 'Saumon'. Take a seat, Princess. Coffee, tea... cognac? Will I need it?'

'Tea, I think.' She'd not had the chance to drink her coffee with Claudine, and her mouth was dry. 'But I haven't long.' As she left, Bibi had hissed, 'An hour, no more' and she'd already used forty minutes. She pulled up a chair to Harry's desk and they stared at each other, checking for alterations.

'You've modernised,' he said at last. 'Looks good.'

A valuable perk of the wholesale atelier was that the staff were allowed to take home scraps and offcuts of cloth. This way, Katya had added to her own and Anoushka's wardrobes. She glanced down at her dress of black-and-grey check with its high-belted waist and oversized collar, as if she'd forgotten she had it on. 'Just something I made.'

'Thrown together. Of course. I like the daisies around the buttons. You embroider too?'

'Every night after Anoushka's asleep, I stitch away. I'm saving up for a sewing machine.'

Harry leaned forward. Professional evaluation. He need not know that instead of coming straight here, she'd taken a bus home and thrown off her work clothes in favour of this dress. His opinion mattered, and she wished it didn't. Wished she had more than fifteen minutes in which to extract a favour that would satisfy Claudine.

'Your own design?' He was studying her neckline. Or was it her neck? 'You look...' he waited for the word to come '...liberated. As if you could ride a bicycle into the country, have a picnic on the grass, then pedal home.'

The thought made her giddy. 'Mama says I look as if I've wandered out in my night things. According to her, clothes shouldn't show a woman's curves, they should create them.' Her underwear had adapted too. These days it was made from glove silk and barely there. *Did men notice that sort of thing?* She had a feeling Harry did.

'I like your hair,' he said. 'You've not cut it off, have you?'

'Certainly not!' S-shape waves clustered below her white straw hat, but the rest was bundled up inside.

'So.' He gave a one-sided smile. 'I'm presuming this isn't a social call?' He didn't let her answer, continuing, 'Oh, and thanks for the postcard.'

She'd sent one, letting him know she'd got a job at Claudine's. Harry's unblinking gaze called up their last time together, when she'd kissed him, then run. Time to strike the bell for business. 'Remember that pretty fabric I saw in your drawing room?'

He inclined his head.

'The Merton—'

'English cotton lawn. What of it?'

'Madame Claudine is a little upset that you won't give her the chance to buy it.'

'Nothing upsets Claudine, apart from the rationing of sugar and butter. She knows I'm reserving the cloth for select customers. More to the point, does it upset you?'

'Dreadfully.' Katya hammed up her answer, drawing a smile from him.

He got up to admit Mademoiselle Cooper bearing a laden tea tray. 'Coops, would you fetch me a bolt of the Merton Abbey cloth.'

'Which one?'

He gave Katya a thoughtful glance. 'Passion Flower.' He picked up the silver teapot, asking Katya, 'How do you take it?'

'Um, lemon please.' There was no jam on the tray. French people shuddered at the idea of it as a sweetener. Monsieur Aristide had looked ready to pass out when she'd described the samovar ritual to him. Accepting a cup, sipping the scalding liquid, she pressed Harry to explain more about his lawn cloth. 'Expensive to produce because of the war?'

'Not exactly. It's British cotton and perversely, there's a glut of the stuff because it couldn't be exported once war broke out. I bought thousands of metres and had it printed in the rainbow hues you like so much. That's the costly bit. Know how hard it is to acquire chemical dyes that give true, bright colour?'

'No, but I suppose it's why everything is monochrome this season?'

'And last season, and probably next. Colour is the nether side of impossible because the best synthetic dyes come from Germany.'

She put down her cup as an unpleasant suspicion crept through her. 'You trade with Germany? Is that why you were on our train?'

'Oh, was it *your* train?' His eyes burned with amusement. Sardonic amusement, the least comforting kind.

'Answer the question. Were you co-co—'

'…laborating with Germany? No. My father has been importing German dyes into Sweden for years. It's a neutral country,' he reminded her. 'He shipped what I needed to my London factory. The manager there could hardly believe his luck.' Harry drank his tea, not at all entertained by the emotions duelling in her eyes. 'You had me down as a Cheka agent, I recall. Have I sunk to being a turncoat?'

She leaned towards him. 'You claimed to have been collecting sawdust. I believed you.'

He looked at her steadily and she was the first to glance away. 'So, Claudine is frustrated and you're here to charm me into changing my mind?'

'We're fed up with those dismal silks.'

'The first months of peace are bound to be sober. Fashion mirrors politics. Admit it, the silk is good to work with. No fraying and a good hand. A crisp feel.'

'More than "crisp".' Katya made a face. 'Coarse.'

'Full of knots, you mean. "Noils" the trade calls them. The stuff you're using was spun to make the bags that held the powder that fired the guns. Thing about silk, when powder ignites inside a gun, it burns to nothing. No ash, no clogging, no hot fibres. The perfect fabric. But they made too much of it.'

'So you bought that too.'

A knock, and a youth of around fifteen came in. 'Monsieur? Mademoiselle Cooper sent this.' He was balancing a bolt of cotton under his arm. Harry made room for it on the desk.

Soon, Katya was looking at a flower print of misty greens, purples and blues. That was the reverse side. The right side glowed like a church window, amethyst, jade and ultramarine. Making a snick with a pair of scissors, Harry took the fabric between his hands and ripped off a length, sending cotton whiskers into the air. He folded what he'd torn off. 'Enough for a dress. Perfect shades for your hair and eyes.'

'I can't.' She got up. 'I can't take it.'

'Why not?'

Because it was more debt. More gratitude. And because Harry had shown a new side of himself, and she wasn't sure she liked it. 'I don't know who you are. I know you fought in the war, so you're not—'

'A member of the white-feather brigade? And?'

'You trade with Germany and they were Russia's enemy too. All right, your father does the trading but you profit.'

'I run the business I took over when I was younger than you are now. I left four years of my life in the mud of battle.' He turned a glassy stare not on a distant horizon, but on her. 'You watched your father die?' She answered with a terse nod. 'I watched comrades lose their lives too and I believe I have the right to claw back some shreds of the existence I once enjoyed. You? Do you want to salvage something – to be Princess Vytenis, dress designer?'

'I suppose.' Katya nodded more firmly. 'Yes, I do.' In a rush, she outlined her time at Claudine's, the good, the bad. 'I want to move out of wholesale gowns and into Madame Frankel's department.'

'So you should. How's Anoushka doing?'

'Growing milk teeth, mainly at night, and making a parcel of fuss about it.'

'And your mother, has she come through her shock?'

'Not really.' It was kind of him to call her mother's behaviour 'shock'. 'She still relies on opiates to sleep, though not nearly as much as before. Tatiana deserting us hasn't helped.' She explained her sister's move to a friend's apartment.

'I'm sorry for my part in that. The unintentional consequence of meddling. Will you come out with me one evening?'

The question burst like a paper bag behind her. 'For what?'

'Dinner and dancing afterwards. Left Bank, or perhaps Montmartre. Have you been up there? I'll take you to a cabaret.'

She shook her head. *Impossible.* 'Evenings are when I take care of Anoushka.'

'Can someone else look after the baby for a few hours? What about the Kaminsky sisters?' Katya had mentioned them as one of the positive aspects of working for Claudine. 'Don't they live with their brother above the shop?'

'You know everything.'

'Couture is a self-contained universe, we all know one another. They lost their nephew and sister-in-law to the influenza. I bet they'd love the chance to look after a baby.'

She shook her head. 'They're Jewish and—'

He interrupted, 'That matters?'

'Not to me. But Mother… Mama blames the Jews for Bolshevism and the revolution.'

'As opposed to nine-hundred years of repression by her own class?'

They locked eyes. Katya felt she ought to rise up and demand, 'How dare you?' but dry laughter came out instead. 'You have a point.'

'Challenge your mother. You'll be doing her a favour.'

Katya sighed and thought, *He doesn't have to mop up afterwards.* She said, 'I will ask Miryam and Fruma to mind Anoushka some time, but I can't come out with you.'

Because? Asked with a motion of his hands.

'I have nothing to wear.'

Harry went to a rack where his suit jacket hung alongside some black dresses. He held one up on its hanger for Katya to see. It had a wide skirt of black and gold stripes. Its bodice was a camisole top under a sheer black silk blouson that would protect the wearer's modesty. As her mouth dropped, Harry said casually, 'Your design, the one from your heart, not your eyes.'

'Where did you get gold cloth?'

'Una knows people in theatre design.'

'That was kind of her.'

'Not really. I gave something in exchange.' Harry gestured at the rack. 'Una's idea of heaven is to see a rail of frocks and be told to take her pick.'

'You make dresses too?'

'Not personally, and only to try out fabric or to show customers. Coops runs a small atelier, three old ladies who've been with us for years.'

Katya took the dress and held it at arm's length. Three weights of silk played with the light; taffeta for the skirt, crêpe de Chine for the camisole, organza for the over-blouse. She imagined slipping the whole thing over her head. 'It's lovely quality.'

'Only the best, Princess.'

'I'm really not sure I can accept it.'

'No matter. I'll hang it back up.'

'No. I will take it, but you must let me pay for the fabric and the labour.'

Harry sighed. 'Do I really have to write out another bill?'

'If you don't, I'll ask Una what it cost and pay you that.'

'Una has a new lover. She's busy.'

Katya detected an off-note in his voice. Not hurt, not anger. More disappointment. *He minds what Una does.*

He folded the dress away in a plain-lidded box, adding the length of cotton-lawn. 'I suspect you already know, Princess, that business success is ninety-nine percent digging rock and one percent finding gold. I'm interested to see what you do with 'Passion Flower'. And I'm looking forward to taking you out. I haven't danced since before war broke out.'

'I haven't danced in six years. I'll be clog-footed.'

'We'll dance close so nobody notices. What time shall I pick you up on Saturday?'

'This Saturday? But I haven't agreed.'

He smiled, tilting his head. He must know that when his eyes took on twilight softness, she weakened. It usually jolted her into saying something stupid. Or hostile.

Now was no exception. 'I don't want to, thanks.'

Harry took the box from her. She grabbed it back. 'You're saying that if I come out with you, I keep the dress?' She tried to sound outraged.

'I have no shame. Shall we say nine o'clock? We can eat first, or not.'

Katya gave in, then remembered that she'd failed entirely to promote Claudine's interests. 'How much cotton-lawn can Madame have? Oh, and she'll pay no more than fifteen percent over cost.'

'She'll pay the same as every other customer.'

'But she can have some?'

'Yes, with the usual provisos.'

'Not to use it for anything pirated from other designers—'

'You're learning the jargon.'

'Or you'll blacklist her with every merchant in Paris,' Katya finished, breathless because it had been easy after all. 'I'll be diplomatic.'

'Don't be, it's Claudine. Tell her that if I get a sniff of cheating, I'll have her abducted, driven in the boot of a car all the way to Toulon and put on a sardine boat for North Africa. One other condition.' With his fingernails, Harry flicked the box containing the dress and the cloth.

'Sorry, I forgot my manners. Thank you. I'm so grateful.'

He shook his head. She was being slow. 'What's the next rung of the ladder for you?'

'Um, to leave the wholesale side and work under Madame Frankel. After that, perhaps even under Monsieur Roland Javier, the tailor.'

'Because they'll teach you the secrets of *haute couture*. How long do you expect to struggle on under Bibi Saumon?'

'A few more weeks… months?'

He laughed. 'And end up crushed, like the others she's taken against? Use what I've given you. Don't hold back. I'll send the boy over to Claudine with samples and to write down her order. The order *you* secured.'

Katya needed to go. She'd outstayed her hour.

'One last thing.' Harry kissed her on the mouth, as she had done to him. But whereas hers had come and gone like a bird swooping on a crust, his lasted three or four heartbeats. His lips rested against her mouth. 'Nine o'clock, Saturday. I'll pick you up at home.'

'Not there. Outside Claudine's.'

Claudine inhaled on her cigarette while eying Katya. 'No discount?'

Katya stood with her hands behind her back. 'It's business, nothing personal.'

'I'm ecstatic to hear it. By the by, you can tell him that I never copy. I am an artist who allows other artists to inspire me. And that,' Claudine stubbed out her cigarette with force, 'makes me no different from Leonardo da Vinci.'

Having seen at this very desk sketches resembling the output of half the *haute-couture* houses in Paris, Katya knew Claudine was either lying or self-deluded. But why get into a fight? 'Quite so.'

'Hmm.' Claudine looked her up and down, noting the embroidered daisies on her button holes. There'd been no time for Katya to change back into her work things. She was holding the dress-length Harry had given her behind her back. Her bargaining chip. Her bottle of vodka.

Hand it back, Starova. It's forbidden for prisoners to have liquor.

'Are you all right?' Claudine demanded. 'My niece has been in twice, asking where you've got to. So if you've nothing more to tell me—'

'There is one more thing.' Katya fought the urge to cough. The balsam burner had gone out, a small mercy, but the ashtray had a day's worth of butts in it, though it wasn't yet midday. 'Another condition.'

Be my guest, Claudine gestured.

'Harry Morten thinks I should—'

'"Harry". Goodness me.'

'Monsieur Morten seems to believe... um...'

'Um?'

It was all very well for Harry to tell her to haggle a promotion. He didn't have to stand in front of a smoke-wreathed she-dragon whose eyes were creasing into slits. 'He suggested I ask you... that I put to you—'

'Spit it out, Katya. No offence, but I don't want yours to be the last face I see when I die. What fabulous strategy have you and Harry Morten cooked up?'

'He thinks I'm ready to move into Madame Frankel's atelier.'

'Uh-huh. Would he like to direct the running of my house?'

'I don't think so.'

'No. It's just you he's bothered about. Well, well. You're young and he's hot-blooded. Course he has plans for you. If I say no, you cannot move from my niece's section, then what?'

Katya shook out the fold of cloth and held it against herself for Claudine to see. Meagre electric lighting did little to bring out the beauty of 'Passion Flower' but Claudine's pouchy eyes sprang open. 'He implied that if my promotion was, um, expedited, his boy would come round to take your order this afternoon.'

'Give.'

Reluctantly, Katya handed over the cloth, trying not to flinch as nicotine-stained fingers inspected the weave. Claudine tugged it again, this time on the bias. 'Very nice. English?'

'Yes.' Katya tried to take it back but Madame had a firm grip. Claudine tucked it under her several chins so she could dial an internal line. 'Charlotte? Tell Madame Frankel I have something for her.' She rammed the receiver back on its hook and smiled beadily.

'The fabric's mine, Madame.'

'There'll be more of that, don't you fret. Harry Morten will treat you generously.'

'I'm not his *cocotte*, if that's what you're thinking.' Wary of Bibi's jealousy, Katya had left the box containing the new dress with Mademoiselle Cooper, intending to collect it on her way home. She had not compromised herself with Harry. *Yet*. But she knew she was drifting closer.

'A *cocotte* is a kept woman,' Claudine commented. 'If you were that, you'd not be working for me. Are you stepping out together?'

'Not really. He's taking me to Montmartre, to a cabaret. Nothing serious.'

'No.' Claudine pushed a cigarette between her lips. 'If he were serious, he wouldn't take you where the upper classes rub shoulders with prostitutes and pimps. He'd whisk you to the Ritz.'

Katya wondered if her mouth carried signs of being recently kissed.

Claudine grunted. 'Watch your step, *ma chérie*. Since the war ended, everyone in Montmartre dances from the hips down. Leads to trouble. Yes, Bibi, you can have her back now.'

Bibi Saumon stood in the doorway and her expression was not amiable. Katya asked Claudine for her cloth.

'Oh, *mon dieu*.' Bibi hurried over, snatched 'Passion Flower' from her aunt and bunched it against her face. 'I could eat it.'

'Kindly don't.' Claudine snatched it back.

'Careful!' Katya cried. 'It's mine!'

A low cough interrupted them. The *première*, Madame Frankel, had arrived with her customary absence of fuss. Somewhere in her thirties with sandy hair coiled in a perfect bun, Pauline Frankel's severe demeanour owed much to the thin-framed bifocal spectacles she wore. Miryam Kaminsky described her as one of the best couture technicians in Paris. Even Bibi Saumon treated Madame Frankel with respect.

Remaining in the doorway, Madame Frankel gave 'Passion Flower' a cool appraisal. 'Synthetic dyes. Whose?'

'Morten,' Claudine said.

'Really? A change of heart?'

'Heart, head or I-don't-know-what.' Claudine jabbed her cigarette towards Katya. 'This young lady possesses arts of persuasion. Madame Frankel, allow me to present to you your newest apprentice.'

Katya gasped. 'You mean… oh, Madame, thank you!'

Bibi croaked a protest, but Katya was too anxious to see how Madame Frankel was reacting to take any notice. Pauline Frankel looked at Katya over her spectacles and said in her low voice, 'You work with my friends, the Kaminskys, yes? You are—'

'Her Serene Highness, the princess,' Bibi said tightly. 'And, it seems, Harry Morten's latest fancy.'

'I'm Katya Vytenis, Madame.'

Pauline Frankel nodded. 'Made-to-measure is a very different discipline to wholesale, you realise? Everything you have learned at the sewing machine, you must unlearn if you're to be any use to me.'

'Don't consult me, will you?' Bibi crossed mutinous arms. 'My section is only eighty per cent of turnover, after all.'

'A horse is not a camel, Bibi,' Claudine informed her. Nobody knew what she meant, but they all understood that it was a taunt.

Madame Frankel's calm voice oiled the waters. 'You are quite correct, Bibi, your wholesale section supports mine, but couture makes wholesale desirable. We pull in the same harness.' She asked Katya, 'How hard are you willing to work?'

'Very hard, Madame. When may I start?'

'In the morning. For now, go home. Wash the clothes you have on.'

Katya looked down at the home-sewn dress she was so proud of. 'It is clean, Madame.'

Madame Frankel pointed at Claudine's ashtray. 'Why do you think I stand in the doorway? Nobody may enter my atelier smelling other than of clean flesh and soap. First thing tomorrow, nice and early.' With that, she left.

Katya made a last attempt to get her fabric back. Claudine held it above her head, straining the sleeves of her blouse to keep it from Katya.

'A wise woman knows when to retreat. I shall have this made into a summer blouse – for me.'

Accepting defeat, Katya gave what she hoped was a gracious nod. She had so much else to think about: a night out with Harry Morten; breaking the news to Fruma and Miryam that she was leaving their section.

And worse. Somebody was lying in wait.

Chapter Fourteen

As Katya reached the top of the stairs on her way back to her section, her hat was wrenched off, tearing out some of her hair. She pushed out at her assailant, who staggered backwards into a sand-filled fire bucket.

It was Bibi. Convinced this was no accidental encounter, Katya tried to walk past, but her skirt was grabbed, pulling her down. For a while, they fought like cats, but Katya was hampered because Bibi had hold of her hair, as if she meant to rip it from the scalp. Bibi got to her feet first and began to haul Katya along the corridor.

Katya shrieked. Her dress had ridden up, almost to her hips. She was close to vomiting from pain. The sound of feet close to her ear triggered memories. It was no longer Bibi Saumon assaulting her but leather-clad men, stinking of eau-de-cologne and blood.

Only an outraged voice ordering, 'Cease at once! What is this behaviour?' stopped her spinning into panic.

Bibi's grip relented. 'None of your business, Monsieur Javier. Go back to your tailor's bench.' The girl was hoarse from the effort of dragging Katya's weight.

'It is my business if somebody is being abused in this workplace. We heard you from the street.'

A small crowd had gathered. Katya could hear the anxious buzz of voices. Still helpless on the floor, she felt her skirt being tenderly pulled down. She was lifted to her feet. Her scalp felt as if a hundred wasps had stung her. Her knees sagged, and her nose found a landing place against a hard chest. Wool cloth, a button made of horn, flesh-warm cotton that smelled of cologne. She shuddered but told herself *it's not the same smell, nothing like it.*

'What the hell is going on?' Harry. Harry Morten.

'A brawl worthy of a dockyard.' Roland Javier.

Bibi said nothing. Katya later found out that she threw both men a look of furious defiance, stalked off and locked herself in her office.

Katya cried. Not only from pain, but from the shock of being overpowered. While Monsieur Javier went down to consult Claudine, Harry took her into a side room and sat her down.

She gripped his arm. 'Don't leave me.'

'I won't. It's all right. I've got you.'

'For a moment I thought they'd come back.'

'Who?'

'The Cheka. They dragged Vera away. At times, memories fly at me. They act out scenes in front of me. It's as if I'm being pulled in, to act with them.'

'You don't have to explain that to me.'

'Why – why are you here?'

Harry had come to deliver her dress. Had she meant to leave her box in Mademoiselle Cooper's office? He'd met Roland Javier outside and they'd got chatting. Usual stuff; yarn, warps and wefts. Her piercing scream had brought them upstairs.

Someone tapped at the door. Monsieur Javier leaned inside, 'Madame wants to see you in her office. Do you feel able?'

Katya put her hands to her head. *Hedge backwards*, and that was prob- ably being kind. 'I'll tidy myself up first. Bibi tried to pull my hair out.'

'If she tries again,' Harry said, 'let me know. You're not her slave and there are laws protecting you from mistreatment.'

In Claudine's office, after Katya and Bibi had each given their version of events, the proprietress raised a hand. 'You're both as bad as each other,' she said. 'Bibi, I don't care if we're related. Princess Vytenis, I don't care how ancient your name is, or how precious your golden locks. One more catfight and you're both out of the door. Now somebody please make me a cup of coffee and send out to Aristide's for cake.'

First thing the following morning, Pauline Frankel introduced Katya to her new colleagues in made-to-measure. Katya anxiously interpreted every glance, every 'hello'. Her altercation with Bibi was the drama of the hour and throughout that day and for the two following, there was an awkwardness. By day four, a thaw had set in. As première, Madame Frankel had put her under the direction of her *seconde*, Charlotte Brunet who, with her deep voice and whiskery upper lip, stimulated Katya's buried memories of a long-dead grandmother. Madame Frankel had said of Katya, 'She shows promise, but she has been working with sewing machines.'

'*Oh, la pauvre.*' Charlotte Brunet tutted sympathetically.

'She must learn the techniques of couture. I don't care how slow she is at first, so long as the finished result is perfect.'

'Glide like a swan, not paddle like a duck. *Oui, Madame.*'

Katya slipped into the current of the couture workroom. If not exactly a swan, nor was she a stubby-feathered duckling. Yes, she was slow, she made errors, but nobody harangued her. Perfection was the default standard in this atelier, and it was assumed that she aspired to it as fully as anyone. Before she knew it, it was Friday. Wages were handed out and somebody had written '*Well done*' on her envelope. Earlier, she'd slipped upstairs to see Miryam and Fruma, who were delighted at the thought of babysitting Anoushka. Katya confided to them that she was the happiest she'd been in many months.

Saturday arrived and with only hours to go until her date with Harry, Katya's anxiety flooded back. She still hadn't mentioned her plans to her mother, putting it off until they were sitting down to lunch on the day. 'I'm out tonight. Two of my colleagues will take care of Anoushka. At their house, so you can sleep, or play cards with Princess Provolskaya.'

Primed to do battle, she was astonished when her mother asked only what manner of women these colleagues were.

'Kind, grandmotherly. Dressmakers, and their brother keeps the jewellers on rue de Courcelles.' Katya waited for the cogs to whirr in her mother's brain.

Irina said, 'Jewish, I suppose?'

'I suppose so, Mama. Is that a problem?'

'No, if, as you say, they are kind. So long as I am not expected to receive them in my home.'

Katya swept a look over the sloping shoulders of their garret. Ignoring the implication of the look, Irina went on, 'Being displaced, we must be supremely careful with whom we associate.'

'Quite so and heaven forfend that your daughter should ever dance with a taxi driver.' At yesterday's Émigré Council dinner, after the tables were pushed back, she and Aleksey had performed a polka. People had commented what an elegant couple they made and his mother had come up and kissed them both.

'Aleksey is not a taxi driver,' Irina said. 'He is a prince who happens to drive a taxi. He is the son—'

'You wish you'd had. So you keep saying, Mama.'

'You don't like him?'

'Actually, I do. He is the brother I always wished I'd had.'

Shaking her head, Irina asked, 'Is it Aleksey you are seeing tonight? When I was young, two nights in a row would imply an engagement. His mother didn't mention anything, but I should not mind, so long as it is somewhere well-lit on this side of the river.'

'I'm not going out with Prince Provolsky. I'm...' *Lie, mislead or confess?* 'I'm going back to work. It's all about the fabric supplier. He's, um, being demanding and I volunteered to meet him to iron things out. I must be more diplomatic than I thought.'

Her mother frowned, as if so much was inexplicable in that little speech, she didn't know where to start. 'Your darling Papa was destined for diplomatic service, but he became fascinated by weaving and textiles. Whenever we attended a ball, I never had to drag him from the card room or the smoking room, but from the galleries where the tapestries hung.'

'So that's where I get my love of fashion.'

'That you get from me. Your Papa would have worn the same coat for thirty years, had I let him.'

'You don't mind being left tonight?'

'I wouldn't, if only Tatiana were here. Will you go to Dr Shepkin for me? I'm out of medicine.' Irina stared at the space her bed would occupy later, in sudden longing.

'Oh, Mama, I thought you'd learned how to sleep without the veronal. Don't tell me you've used another whole bottle?'

'I need it.' In the past, Irina had always become agitated at this time on a Saturday, fearful that the surgery would close, leaving her without a supply of tablets over Sunday. 'If I'm to be abandoned for a whole night…'

Katya gave in, though she made up her mind that this time she'd dole out one pill and hide the rest. A trip to the doctor's was an opportunity to give Anoushka a little airing.

Katya parked the pram in the courtyard and lifted out Anoushka. The doctor's door was wedged open as usual and she walked straight up, wondering how this climb would feel in high summer. On a floor above, somebody was clashing a mop and bucket while singing in Russian. Not a folk song, a piece from an opera. The voice was rich, if rather off the note. Katya carried on past the surgery door, thinking this might be her moment to apologise to the woman she'd chased upstairs previously. The singing stopped. Katya got the strong impression of a breath being held and she lost her nerve and retreated.

The surgery had once been a domestic sitting room. It was divided by a screen with a few chairs along one side with a table stacked with newspapers and well-thumbed magazines. On the other side of the screen was Dr Shepkin's consulting couch. Katya sat down and picked up a copy of *Vera*, the newspaper Aleksey Provolsky had urged her to read on the day they met. After a few lines, she threw it down again. Fervently anti-Bolshevik – which she had no objection to – it was claiming that the Imperial family was alive and well, its members spirited away to an 'unnamed Scandinavian country'. *Dreamers.* Her father had known men connected to the court, who had confirmed that without doubt, almost every member of the Russian royal family was dead.

From behind the screen Dr Shepkin was telling somebody to, 'Kindly stay still. I wouldn't be doing this if you took better care of yourself. Shut up and think of Mother Russia – ah-ah, no cursing. One day you might perform this service for me. Then I'll show you how a real man has a tooth out.'

Aleksey? Last night at dinner, chilled vodka had been passed around and Aleksey had winced as he knocked his back. She'd asked him, 'Not another bad tooth?'

He'd expanded on what Georgy Filatov had already told her. Riding into battle in the winter of 1916, he'd cracked his jaw when his horse had died under him after a shell exploded nearby. A broken jaw was only one of his injuries, he said. Vodka numbed the pain.

Katya didn't want to intrude on the struggle going on behind the screen, but Anoushka was pulling the face that meant she was about to fill her nappy. So when she heard a rattle that sounded like a tooth dropping on a metal tray, she called out, 'Dr Shepkin? I know you're busy, but can you put out some of my mother's usual medication?'

'Princess Vytenis?' Bristling brows and a shock of white hair appeared over the top of the screen. Sweat had gathered in the grooves scoring the doctor's forehead, suggesting it had been a well-bedded tooth. Katya was tempted to peer over and offer her condolences, except that Aleksey's fierce pride would be offended.

She offered to call back later.

'No need,' the doctor assured her. 'I always have a few bottles ready.' Shepkin ducked away, and there came the sounds of heavy-footed lumbering. He was untidy in his movements, and not for the first time, Katya compared him with Dr Zasyekin whose fingers had been so deft, whose manner had inspired trust. A few moments later, Shepkin stepped around the screen and handed her a roughly wrapped packet. He waved away her attempts to pay him. 'Another time.' There was blood on the front of his tunic, touches of it in his white beard.

At home, after she'd changed Anoushka, Katya removed a single tablet from the new bottle. Five grains of the barbiturate. A day's allowance. She hid the rest in her sewing box.

Time now to pack Anoushka's overnight things and go to the Kaminskys' flat above the jewellers.

With Anoushka safely settled with Miryam and Fruma, Katya arrived at Maison Claudine a few minutes after four, her evening clothes in a bag. The countdown to her evening out had begun. She wasn't expected at work, but putting in a few hours' unpaid labour went a little way to making up for lying to her mother, or so her conscience told her.

In line with most dressmaking businesses in Paris, Claudine's staff theoretically worked the *semaine Anglaise*, the 'English Week' of five full days, with a half-day on Saturday and all of Sunday free. In reality, a seven-day week was required to keep pace with orders. Even then, Claudine grumbled that she never made a profit. As Katya entered the ground-floor workroom, the butterflies that had been with her all day dissolved under an assault of familiar smells. Fabric, floor polish and chalk along with a hint of scorch from the ironing tables. Ten or so women sat around a long table. Charlotte Brunet's liver-spotted hand rested comfortably on a seamstress's shoulder. As Katya opened her work bag and took out the muslin collar she'd begun the previous day, Mademoiselle Brunet asked, 'Did you go to sleep and wake up thinking it was Monday?'

'I've come in to make up the time I missed due to… well, you know.'

The supervisor came over and ruffled her hair. 'All recovered now?'

'I think so. I'm going out later, so I thought I'd get ready here. You don't mind?'

One of the other girls chuckled knowingly. 'A white lie for your mother? Don't worry, we've all done it. Is your party dress in that bag? Show us.' When Katya revealed the black-and-gold dress, heads lifted in amazement.

'Who made it?' they all wanted to know. 'There's nothing like this in Claudine's collection.'

'It hangs a little like a Paquin.'

'I saw Denise Poiret wearing something similar. Paul Poiret's wife,' one girl told Katya. '*Soo* elegant. I've heard she hates the hobble skirts her husband keeps coming up with. I don't blame her. Do we want to fall over in the street, like our poor mothers? So, where's it from?'

'A friend.' Katya didn't dare admit the design was her own.

'High-quality silk… an old ball gown cut down?' Charlotte Brunet held the dress up to Katya. 'Good that you're tall and slim or the over-blouse would make you look like an Easter egg.'

'A Fabergé egg,' someone suggested cheekily. 'Who's your beau, Katya?'

Her colleagues cajoled but Charlotte Brunet cut them short. She glanced at the clock whose sturdy hands ruled their days. 'Put the dress somewhere safe and give me three hours of your time, Katya. Then you can get ready.'

The door opened. The happy atmosphere shattered. Charlotte Brunet adjusted her expression. 'Good afternoon, Mademoiselle Saumon. May I help you?'

Bibi's gaze arrowed to Katya who was hanging her dress by the door. She stared hard before turning back to Charlotte Brunet. 'I hope so.' Wholesale had run out of stiffening fabric. 'I put the order in days ago…' Bibi's eyes strayed back to the dress. 'Who is that for?'

Charlotte Brunet answered, 'It belongs to Katya. Stiffening fabric, you say?' She instructed a girl to fetch a roll from the store cupboard. 'Light or heavyweight, Mademoiselle Saumon? I said light or heavyweight?'

'Mm? Oh, both,' Bibi muttered.

Katya settled to her work and the clock's ticking melted into the air. They often sang as they worked, adapting popular songs to the in-and-out rhythm of their needles but this afternoon, it was round singing to the tune of 'Noël Nouvelet'. All was peaceful until Charlotte Brunet lifted her head, sniffing. 'Somebody left an iron on?'

No. The irons were all cool.

'It's definitely burnt cloth.'

Seized by a premonition, Katya glanced at her dress. It was half off its hanger. She hadn't left it like that. The door was slightly ajar, and she was sure it had been shut when they began singing. Her neighbour went to check. Lifted the dress off its peg. 'Oh, my heavens. It's ruined.'

They all agreed, after inspecting the ragged holes in the gauze over-blouse, that the lit end of a cigarette had been held to the fabric. Though nobody had seen Bibi Saumon lean in through the door to do it, they agreed it was the kind of thing she would do.

'I can't wear it now,' Katya said in despair. So nervous about the evening ahead, she'd failed to realise how much she was looking forward to Harry Morten's company. 'I can't go out.'

'Pah!' was Charlotte Brunet's response. 'I've seen worse disasters than this in my career. I've caused a few, too.' Laying the dress on the table, she cut away the damaged gauze, until it was just a black silk camisole top attached to a bold, striped skirt. 'Now try it on.'

'I've never gone out with bare shoulders in my life,' Katya said as she emerged from the changing cubicle. 'I'd need to wear a shawl.'

Cries of outrage. 'Time for shawls when you're fifty, *chérie*.'

Charlotte Brunet said pithily, 'One sees so many middle-aged women showing off shoulders as stringy as boiled mutton, you've no excuse to hide yours. But if you feel exposed, let's give you a stole.' She sent a girl to fetch something and the girl returned with a web of black silk net, scattered with flock roses. She'd also brought Katya a headpiece, curls of gold wire on a pearl-studded band.

'Perfect,' said Mademoiselle Brunet. She told Katya to go and do something with her hair and put on a little make-up.

The staff washroom was up on the third floor, and in the corridor where she'd been dragged by the hair, Katya was greeted by Bibi and two of Bibi's friends. They were in high spirits, but their laughter stopped instantly. Three to one.

One of the girls feigned dismay at the sight of Katya's bare shoulders. 'What's happened to your dress? One feels there should be so much more to it.'

'It lacks a top, that's what you're thinking, Dominique,' the other girl chimed in.

Bibi gave the dress a disparaging once-over. 'That's for wearing to a cabaret. Who are you going out with?'

'My grandmother,' Katya told her.

Noticing the headdress in Katya's hand, Bibi asked, 'Who gave you permission to take that?'

'Mademoiselle Brunet.' Katya calculated that Bibi would not take her battle to Madame Frankel's well-liked deputy. She was right. Bibi shrugged, then, drawing her friends in with a smirk, suggested that they could have yet more fun with their scissors.

'That skirt could do with shortening.'

Katya assessed her chances of getting down the stairs but likely, they'd come after her. An 'accidental' shove in the back and she'd be done for. *'My lioness.'* Her father's voice floated into her ear, a feather on the wind. She held Bibi's eye and said, 'Do me any more harm, I will repay you in kind. Even if it takes me ten years.'

They let her go.

As the washroom door swung behind her with no sound of following footsteps, Katya let out the breath she'd been holding. Fear had made her sweat, and she took off the dress so she could wash at the sink. She raised her arms, soaping and drying the pits. Since attending her first ball aged sixteen, she'd been in the habit of stripping her underarms with Persian wax. Vera had shown her how, though her sister's body hair had been floss-fine. Katya stared at herself, arms raised. Her breasts were more womanly these days, and firm, nipples the exact pink of her lips. She was about to spend the evening with a man, her body blushing at the prospect. They said it was a form of madness, wasn't it? These feelings... the ones well-born girls were not supposed to entertain. She ran her fingers over her breasts, astonished as the flesh hardened beneath her fingers. Trailed fingertips along her throat, over her lips which opened. Cupped her face, gently massaged her hair roots. How to do her hair tonight... she'd undo her braid, roll it into a bun, perhaps with a few curls escaping. Under the mirror lights her hair glowed like a cathedral screen.

What does Vera look like now? The mocking question came from nowhere, as though the mirror had spoken: *What of that ivory flesh, the platinum hair, the white bones...*

The door banging open was her deliverance. She tried to retrieve her dress as the lights went out. Somebody rammed her face into the sink. Her plait was yanked like a bell rope and she felt the cold kiss of steel against the back of her neck, heard the chunky bite of scissors.

Katya fumbled for the light cord and pulled it. The girl looking back at her in the mirror had wide eyes and hair springing either side of her neck like newly scythed corn. In the sink lay her amputated plait.

Chapter Fifteen

'Not cold, are you?' Harry had given Katya a travel rug to put over her knees. Though the car hood was down, as in Aleksey's cab there was no side glass.

'I'm fine.' She'd hardly said a word since he'd drawn up outside her workplace. Not even the car's showroom polish, its white wheels and gleaming spokes had wrenched more than a brief smile from her. She'd only just stopped shaking.

'If not cold, scared?' He sounded concerned.

'Speed doesn't scare me,' she assured him. 'I used to drive with my father and he'd race horse-drawn troikas. He'd have loved this car.'

'It's a Pierce-Arrow 66 and I love it too. Do your scarf up tight.'

Katya had wrapped the filmy stole over her head and shoulders, and Harry hadn't yet noticed anything different about her. *But when he did?* She often caught him looking at her hair.

'Where are we going?'

'Montmartre, though not to the butte.' He slipped on driver's gauntlets and fired the engine.

The Pierce-Arrow lived up to its name, flying along nearly deserted streets. The waxing moon was thin as rice paper in the twilight. Street lamps flickered because the power stations ran erratically at night. From Place de la Madeleine, Harry went up familiar Malesherbes, then across Place d'Europe, over the railway tracks feeding Gare Saint-Lazare. Follow them north and Katya knew they'd reach Batignolles where Tatiana lived. The promised address had never arrived. Katya sighed and Harry asked again if she was warm enough. 'Perfectly. It's a mild night.'

'Have you recovered from Bibi's attack?'

Katya's hand flew to her head. 'You know?'

'I was there. I picked you up off the floor.'

'Oh, that.' Bibi's first assault already felt like ancient history. Shock did strange things to time. This evening, she'd staggered down from the washroom, instinctively seeking out friends. While Charlotte Brunet had talked of calling the police, one of her couture colleagues had fetched curling tongs. Katya's shorn ends were now a halo of finger curls clustering under the gold-spiral headband. A style bang up to the minute, had it been her choice… Katya had left the severed plait in the washroom waste bin. Perhaps she should have kept it to sell to Tatiana's wig maker.

'I'm all right,' Katya lied and to get Harry off the subject, she asked if there would be dancing where they were going.

'Of course. I'm taking you to Boulevard de Clichy. You'll have heard of its most colourful landmark, the Moulin Rouge?'

'Yes. My friend Aleksey Provolsky goes sometimes. I overheard his mother telling him that it was a "den of naked trollops".'

Harry shot her a wry look. 'Not the cleverest way to persuade a young man to stay away from a place. The Moulin Rouge is where the cancan is danced.'

'But you are not taking me there?'

'No. I strive to be a gentleman.'

'Only strive?' A cutting remark, but her emotions were off-kilter. Long hair had always been part of her identity and she had a powerful suspicion that Harry was not going to look at her new style and say, 'Goodness, how very chic.' He would want to know why. She wouldn't tell him as Claudine had been clear: '*One more catfight and you're both out.*' Katya couldn't afford to lose her job if Harry took it on himself to fight her cause.

After twenty minutes or so, they swung into a broad thoroughfare. Shabby buildings, a hotchpotch of facades. After a while, Harry pointed to a pepper-pot structure with red wooden sails. 'Den of Trollops.'

'Was the Moulin Rouge ever a real mill?'

He explained that it was only a few years old, built after the last one burned down. 'I expect there was a mill on the site, once. For most of its existence, Montmartre was a village and it still has a rural feel. When we've got a day to spare, I'll show you rue Rustique and Place du Tertre where the painters gather.' A burst of speed, a whip of the breeze, then Harry pulled up outside a modern-looking building. He got out, discarded his coat and gauntlets on the driver's seat, opened the passenger door. Katya took his offered hand, sliding out with her knees pressed together as she'd been taught. *This was their cabaret?* Blacked-out windows trellised with decaying anti-blast tape. No lights, no name over the door. The only sound was the rumble of electric fans through the grating at the building's foot. The door was reinforced. 'Does it have a name?'

'It used to be "La Rose Rouge" but a few weeks ago it became "La Rose Noire".' Harry drew her attention to an art poster pasted to the door featuring five black bandsmen in tuxedos and bow ties. Four held brass instruments, one a banjo. There was sufficient moonlight for Katya to read, 'Bowler Hamilton and his…' she frowned. 'His Moo—'

'His Moochers. Don't ask me. They play a new kind of music, American jazz.'

She was about to tell him that he needn't explain, she'd already discovered jazz for herself, when a squeal of tyres made her jump. A car bounced to a halt against the kerb, the driver's door flying open. Giving no time for Katya to prepare herself, Aleksey Provolsky lurched from his cab, demanding to know what she was doing in this part of town.

'Does your mother know?'

Katya told him it was none of his business. *Please, not another confrontation.* She'd had enough ill-will tonight to last a lifetime.

'Who is this man?' Aleksey demanded, giving Harry an up-down look.

Harry answered him. 'You've left your handbrake off,' indicating the taxi, which was rolling gently backwards. Passengers could be heard howling inside.

Swearing through his teeth, Aleksey threw himself into the driver's seat and hauled up the handbrake in time to avoid a collision with the Pierce-Arrow.

'That would have cost him,' Harry murmured to Katya. 'Friend of yours?'

'Not any more,' Katya said curtly. 'Let's go in, please?'

'Run away?'

'Yes. Aleksey's being very Russian, and seems to think he's my elder brother.'

'I don't think "brother" covers it, from the way he looked at me. Am I trespassing on something?'

'No.'

Aleksey was back. 'I shall tell your mother you are out with a man, and no chaperone.'

'Do what you like.' The tang of liquor hung on his breath, and Katya had little doubt that he was looking for a fight. 'Go back to your passengers.' She could make out a man and woman in the back of the Renault, hatted, coated. 'You don't want to make them late for dinner.'

'I am taking them to the hill,' Aleksey informed her loftily, 'from where Russian artillery bombarded the city a hundred years ago. A glorious hill.'

'Sightseeing at this hour? Are they nocturnal, your passengers?'

Aleksey turned down his lip. 'Always you make a joke, Princess. Get into the front seat and I will take you home.' He seized Katya's arm, dragging the stole from her shoulders. As he took in the minimal cut of her bodice, flames rose in his eyes.

'You look like…' The word he chose belonged in the barracks and Katya couldn't find a response. But Harry could.

With the advantage of speed, he caught Aleksey Provolsky's arm, twisting it ruthlessly behind the prince's back. Aleksey gave a gurgle, then fell silent. Only his strenuous breathing as Harry marched him to his cab gave a hint of the pain.

'Go find a cup of coffee,' Katya heard Harry say as he shoved Aleksey onto the front seat. She hastily rearranged the stole over her hair and shoulders, and joined Harry in time to see him take the key from the ignition. Harry opened a rear door and tossed the key on to the male passenger's lap, saying, 'If you know how to drive, I suggest you do.'

Unimpressed, the man pulled a black, domed hat down over his brow and thumped on the glass partition, shouting in Russian for Aleksey to 'Get going!'

Katya glimpsed the woman beside him. She wore a dowdy hat, her face obscured by several layers of gauze veil.

'Whoever they are,' Harry said lightly as the cab's tail lights veered down the boulevard, 'I hope they've prayed to St Christopher.'

Humour evaporated. 'Nobody will ever speak to you like that again, Princess. Not in my hearing.'

'I take back what I said earlier. You do not 'strive' to be a gentleman, you are one. Aleksey doesn't understand the word.'

Inside the club, Harry bought tickets while Katya fiddled with her stole, unable to decide whether or not to remove it. The electrics snatched the decision from her, by abruptly dying. Katya heard the hat-check girl groan, 'Another damn blackout.'

In the darkness, Katya untied the stole. Now or never. Harry took her arm, using his cigarette lighter to find a baize door. A moment later, Katya was looking down a flight of stairs which disappeared into shadow. The last time she'd walked down into darkness, a nightmare had greeted her.

Harry registered her reluctance and took her arm, so they could go down together.

'Since I went looking for my sister Vera,' Katya explained messily, 'I've been left with a horror of dark places.'

'In the Lubyanka? Did you find her?'

'Dead. She was dead.'

Harry opened another baize-lined door and a moment later Katya was in a basement that was a sea of candlelight and saffron tablecloths. The air smelled of human heat, perfume and burned sugar. Waiters darted about, using cigarette lighters for illumination. Some moved in time to a tune being played on a grand piano. The pianist had to be working from memory, as his niche beside the stage wasn't bright enough for him to read a score. His whole body was engaged; his head thrown back. The rhythm was fast one moment, slow the next.

Katya said, 'It sounds like he's playing different tunes with his left and right hand.'

Harry didn't answer. He was looking at her. At her dress. 'Sorry?'

She repeated what she'd just said.

'Um, that is what he's doing. Playing ragtime. Princess, what have you—'

'Ragtime?'

'Ragged. Syncopated rhythm. What have you done to your dress?'

'The blouse part didn't suit me. I looked like an Easter egg.' Not so long ago, she had stared into the washroom mirror, stroking herself, imagining *his* hands. She'd imagined it again when she'd been moved by the sight of his gloved hands on the steering wheel. He touched her arm, moving upwards to her shoulders, neck, face. 'And your hair… I've picked up the wrong princess. Katya, what have you done?'

She turned away. 'Hadn't we better sit down? Nobody but a drunken sailor could dance to this music.'

When they had a table, Harry suggested they order quickly. 'Best strike while the ovens are still hot. Hungry?' There was a pucker between his brows, something unsaid.

Katya had been hungry, before Bibi got to her. Now she was awash with vertigo and terrible doubt. She felt very much like '*the wrong princess*'. An imposter in her own life. 'What sort of food do they do?'

'In theory, a scaled-down version of a pre-war menu. In reality, what they call "beef" can be something entirely different. Fish or chicken is a safer bet. Do you like rice? They do a decent Chicken Stroganoff.'

'I've eaten more of those here in France than in Russia. It ought to be beef, but I'll try it and I'm sure it will be lovely. Do I smell crème brûlée? It's my favourite dessert.'

Harry held the menu up to their table candle. 'Can't see it, but I'll ask. Shall we keep ourselves amused with bread and olives?' He signalled to a waiter. 'And to drink – the house cocktail? "Rose Noire" made from dark rum, cranberry juice and sugar syrup.'

'Is that why I can smell burned sugar?'

'Probably. They keep the syrup boiling behind the bar to overlay the whiff of damp basement. Or would you like champagne?'

'Isn't that very expensive? At the Ritz, with Una, some unfortunate stranger was given the bill. I offered to pay half but she said she had so many rich friends in Paris, one of them was bound to wander in during the evening.'

'I'm sure one did,' Harry agreed in a voice dry as grit, before signalling for a waiter to take their order. He asked for champagne, telling her when the waiter had left, 'You're honour-bound to drink as much as you can. As a Russian.'

'I am?'

'Millions of bottles went into Russian cellars before the revolution. Now, it's down to a few thousand. The champagne growers are desolate.'

'I can't believe any goes to Russia at all now. Bolsheviks don't drink French champagne.'

'My wine merchant says different. So unless it's being used to hose down the pavements, somebody over there is drinking it. Forgive me if I'm being boring,' Harry had not pulled his gaze from her for a long time, 'but you have done something dramatic with your hair.'

'A trim. You don't like it?' She touched the curls protruding from under the headband. 'I was assured it's the rage.'

'By whom, Una?'

'It's nothing to do with Una.' She lifted her chin. 'My hair, my choice.'

Harry inclined his head. Silence descended. A few couples had made their way to the dance floor and Katya used that as an excuse to twist around. Her ear was attuning to the music's odd beat. *Syncosomething?* 'You think me capricious,' she said, 'but I am not.'

'No. I don't believe you cut your hair on a whim.'

'I'm beginning to like this music. *Ragged Time.*'

'Ragtime.'

'I heard jazz for the first time in Brest, after we docked there.'

Harry nodded slowly. 'All the American soldiers, waiting to board ship and go home.'

'Mama came down with shingles and couldn't travel. In every café and bar, there were musicians in uniform playing strange, jerky tunes.'

'Black musicians?'

She nodded. 'The local girls were dancing with American soldiers. Dancing like that.' She gestured towards the exaggerated, sliding steps of the couples on the floor. Their arms were locked in a conventional waltz hold, their stomachs glued together. One pair must be professional, feet gobbling up the music. Every few spins, the lady threw in an extravagant dip, as if in worship of her partner. 'One time, I went out to buy fruit and wandered into a square. American soldiers were sprawled everywhere and they whistled at me. Black bandsmen were playing under a canopy, joyful music from the pit of their bellies and I knew Mama would have been horrified. I was about to turn back, when a solider ran up and begged me to dance. I didn't think I could get away, so I agreed.'

'Bored soldiers, waiting their turn to go home, can be hard to shake off. What devilment ensued?'

'A dance! I don't know. Foxy something.'

'Foxtrot. How shameless.'

She nodded, discerning a hint of jealousy behind the teasing. 'They all wanted a turn, and held me around the waist, laughing. I couldn't understand what they said, and they thought that was funny too. They gave me an apple drink which made me dizzy.'

'Strong Breton cider.'

'My hairpins came out and I thought how appalled Mama would be, how ashamed my father would have been, but I was not Ekaterina Ulianova, I was the part of her that flies away at night to dream. The American boys told me their names and I pretended I was called "Alyona" which means "light".'

'Where does this end?' A shadow had settled on Harry.

'A priest broke up the dancing, accusing us of spreading infection.'

'That's severe, even for a priest.'

She shrugged. 'Everyone was afraid of influenza. "Go home to your kitchens!" he shouted, meaning us girls. A clock chimed and I saw three hours had gone by. I ran back to where we were staying and found Tatiana at her wits' end and the baby yelling. My sister is right to be angry with me sometimes. I didn't leave Mama's bedside after that, keeping her spirit in her body, though she longed to give up. I would not let her because if I had lost her, it would have been one more—'

'One more what?'

Katya shook her head. She hadn't meant to step into confession.

'What is your Calvary, Princess? What do you carry on your shoulders?'

'Mistakes. Bad choices. Doesn't everyone have secrets? What is yours?'

Harry spread his hands. 'I'm an open book. Ask me anything.'

She thought about it. 'Why were you collecting sawdust when you should have been in France, with your regiment?'

'You are dogged on that subject.'

Champagne arrived, along with a basket of bread and a dish of olives. Harry was obliged to inspect the linen-white label before the waiter removed the wire *muselet* and released the cork. A sigh rose from the bottle's neck. The waiter decanted the champagne and presented it to Harry with a bow, saying, 'Fine acidity, a little dry to the palate. I need not explain that the grapes were picked early in the season?'

Harry nodded. 'Because the pickers thought the Germans were coming, and raced to get the harvest in.'

The waiter wrote down their dinner order, two Chicken Stroganoffs. When the man left, Harry made a toast to Katya. 'Your health, Princess.' They clinked glasses.

'Yours too, Monsieur Morten.' It was on her tongue to say that the time had come for first names, but just then, the lights came back on to a round of cheers. A moment later, the bandsmen filed out onto the stage. The trumpeter, who was the band leader, played a few solo bars and his Moochers swung in behind him. 'Come on.' Harry held out his hand. He was asking her to dance.

'What if our dinner comes?'

'It won't arrive quickly. The kitchen keeps us waiting to make us drink more.'

Popping a piece of bread topped with olives into her mouth, Katya took Harry's hand. 'That's encouraging dissipation.'

'It's not church. Let's see what those American boys taught you.'

Bowler Hamilton played a high trumpet riff, and a tune flowed out. 'Memphis Blues', Harry told her as he took her in a ballroom hold, one hand resting in the small of her back, the other under her shoulder blade. She followed his lead in a foxtrot. Slow, slow, quick, quick, quick. Unlike the soldiers, Harry did not pull her against him but allowed a tantalising gap between them. Yet the gap was closing. As his abdomen rested against hers, a melting sensation pushed through her. Harry's hand slipped lower.

The lights faltered, then went out again. People booed good-naturedly. A moment later, the maitre d' announced that all Montmartre was in darkness. 'A round of applause ladies and gentlemen, for our beloved Minister of Coal.'

Bowler Hamilton and his Moochers carried on playing, with a few wrong notes, and couples danced on, bumping into each other hilari-ously. Katya raised her face and Harry kissed her, tasting of champagne. They danced in candle glow, sitting down only when candelabra were brought to the stage so Bowler Hamilton and his Moochers could give them 'Castle House Rag'. Its tempo was way beyond the grasp of Katya's feet. *Dancing lessons*, she promised herself.

When the Moochers broke between acts, Harry said, 'I don't suppose we'll get fed very soon, if at all. The kitchen must be way behind. Why don't we look for dinner in the Latin Quarter? Do you need to be home any particular time?'

Yes, hours ago. 'Mama will hate to wake and find herself alone.' What was the betting her mother would have forgotten that Anoushka was with the Kaminskys? Then again, Katya had lost count of the times she'd desperately tried to wake her mother, to no avail. The primitive part of her wanted to be with Harry. He occasionally looked at her hair with an expression of regret, but she could forgive that. She was discovering that there was a powerful antidote to fear, guilt and nightmares and that was being with Harry Morten.

'I don't have to be home at all,' she whispered.

Chapter Sixteen

They found dinner in one of the eating places crowding ancient rue Mouffetard: Chez Tante Jacqui, where Harry was warmly embraced by the proprietress. Harry introduced Katya as 'Princess Vytenis', which rocked her because she'd determined during the drive that, as soon as they were seated, she'd call time on formality.

'Any friend of Harry's is our friend,' Tante Jacqui smiled.

'It's good to be back in rue Mouffe.' Harry looked around. 'Where's Albrikt?'

'In the kitchen. We lost our chef, perhaps you heard?' Jacqui explained for Katya's benefit, 'Albrikt is my husband, and a reluctant replacement chef but I tell him that the war has changed everything, including retirement plans.' She turned back to Harry. 'Your brother… he's back in Paris?' Her voice expressed a fearful possibility, which Harry immediately confirmed.

'Christian died helping to raise a plank-bridge over the Sambre Canal. He's buried in a cemetery close to Le Cateau.'

'That sweet boy. Your poor father.' Jacqui touched Harry's shoulder then changed the subject. 'We lost our power at five o'clock this evening and it came back an hour ago. Soup and omelettes only, I'm afraid.'

Harry said, 'Sounds good. We gave up hope of dinner on Montmartre. I suppose crème brûlée is out of the question?'

'Completely,' Jacqui laughed. 'Book another time and I will make sure of it.'

At their table, in a niche where candles in sconces showed up the masons' marks in the stone, Harry asked Katya if she could manage more champagne.

'Better not. Peppermint tea?'

Jacqui went off to make it and returned with a tray and a bowl, two tiny forks and two shots of vodka. *What's this?* Katya's look expressed. Harry whispered, 'It's how it's done.'

The bowl contained glistening black caviar. 'From Albrikt's emergency store cupboard,' Jacqui confided. 'Don't tell anyone.'

'Albrikt is an old friend of my father's,' Harry explained when he and Katya were alone. 'After he and Jacqui married, they settled with his family on the Swedish east coast. Albrikt used to ferry people across to Finland in his boat, which is how he and my father met. My father often travelled to Finland and Russia before the revolution.'

'How did your father come to marry an Englishwoman?'

A romantic story, Harry told her. 'My mother went to Sweden with a widowed aunt. For a holiday, castles and lakes. The story is she took a boat out on her own and got into difficulties on the water. My father, who was staying at the same hotel, saw what was happening and swam out to rescue her.'

'True story?'

'He certainly swam out to her boat. Whether she actually needed rescuing is an open question. After they married, my father settled in London and took over Mother's family business, which at the time was called Balcombe and Sons. It was failing, because there were no "and Sons" and the women of the family had no turn for commerce. He changed it to "Morten and Company" because – well, that's the sort of man he is. For a while he ran Mother's cloth business alongside his own family interests. In Sweden, the name Morten is synonymous with paper, inks and dyes. I'm from manufacturing stock on both sides. Not a drop of blue blood in me.'

'No white bone, then. What you call "blue blood" Russians call "white bone".'

He smiled. 'Mine are the colour of wood fibre and yarn. I'm not a spy, Princess, nor a covert revolutionary. When we met, I was on business.'

She decided then that she would not call him Harry until he had risked at least one 'Katya'. She asked, 'Was your mother involved in the business?'

'She owned shares but only stepped inside the factory at Christmas, for a glass of sherry with the staff. She liked being at home, looking after us. After she died, Father carried on for a while, teaching me and Christian the ropes. Then overnight, he inherited all the shares in the Swedish mills and made his choice. Gothenburg, not London. Paper, not textiles.'

'He helps you, though?'

'He keeps a cordial distance. When he signed the textile business over to me and my brother, his words were, "It's all yours. All the profit and any mistakes." Christian managed the English side while I ran the Paris arm. Now it's just me. It's what I was on my way to do…' Harry broke off, the motionless freeze entering his face.

He was silent so long, Katya gently prompted, 'On your way?'

'After I said goodbye to you and your family at Gothenburg station, I went to the telegraph office. There was a wire waiting for me. *Regret Lt. C. H. Morten killed in action.* It was like a shell going off in my face. When you jumped into my cab, I was on my way to tell Father.'

Katya put down her caviar fork, laid her hand on his. 'Oh…' she almost said 'love', changing it to 'dear'. 'There I was, full of my own need. You should have told me to go away.'

'Actually, you were a useful distraction.'

'That was all?'

He scavenged humour from somewhere. 'Do you suppose I often kiss unknown women in cabs? You stepped back into my life as it hit me that I'd never see my brother again. I couldn't bear the pain, I needed an escape. You've noticed, I can't easily talk about it.'

She finished her caviar without tasting it. Stupid to imagine that, as the bells rang and Harry had clasped her with drowning fervour, they'd been enacting a love scene. She'd helped him at his moment of despair, as he had her. 'You keep telling me you were collecting sawdust, but I think you said it to shock Mama.'

'True. It wasn't sawdust, it was wood pulp. There's a material called cellucotton which is many times more absorbent than cotton or linen and was used for binding wounds in field hospitals. "Nurses' miracle". Towards the back end of last year, supplies were running short, thanks to German submarines sinking our merchant shipping. Nobody was sure how long the war would drag on and there was a feeling there might be one last grand offensive with mass casualties. I went to Finland, to find a new source of the raw material.'

'Please tell me you were not trying to profit?'

Harry divided the last little hummock of caviar into two, piling it neatly on two pieces of bread, one of which he passed to Katya. 'It's a good thing I like you. If anybody else suggested that I was a war profiteer, I might get very angry. My expedition was sanctioned by the British government after my name was put forward by my godfather, a retired military surgeon. "Send that boy, he speaks all the right lingos." Whatever I may be, you cannot include "deserter".'

'Why let me believe that nonsense about sawdust?'

'You believed what chimed with your prejudices.'

'That's not fair. You saved me from jumping off the train. I might have gone to hell, if not for you. You were cruel, telling me I was an unfit guardian to Anoushka. Then you kissed me and helped me again. All the time, you said nothing about who you were or where you had been. You were playing a game with me.'

He owned the truth of it. 'I couldn't say. By travelling through Sweden on behalf of the British government, I was breaking Swedish neutrality. In the end, the whole exercise was pointless. The war finished, the wood pulp wasn't needed. I spent two months away from the front, while my brother stood in the line of fire.'

'That makes you feel guilty?'

'We were in the same unit.' Harry drew in breath. 'If I'd been alongside him, who knows? The worst part was, when I got to my father's house, he saw me walking up the path and said later that he knew it was bad news, only he wasn't sure which of his sons was lost. Christian and I look – *looked* – alike. Particularly in a fur hat; I hadn't thought to remove mine. I don't remember much after.'

'I wish you'd told me,' Katya said quietly. Harry's brother had died as generals and government ministers sat round tables thrashing out the terms of German surrender. 'I would have comforted you.'

'Yes. You know what it is to have someone you love ripped from you.'

She picked up a shot glass and tipped the vodka down. Heat slammed the back of her throat. 'Your turn.'

After he'd done the same, Harry asked, 'Who taught you to drink like that?'

'Nobody. We Russians never sip vodka.'

'Speaking of whom, what will your friend Aleksey make of your new hairstyle?'

'He will say I have made a pact with the Devil.'

'Then he'd be wrong. At heart, you're as upright as a flagpole.'

Their soup arrived. Mushroom, peppery and garlic-laden, served with rustic bread and soured cream. Dipping her spoon in, Katya rethreaded the conversational needle. 'And I think that at heart, you're not a smoker. You use cigarettes when you don't want to speak.'

'You're on to something. Christian insisted I took his monogrammed case on my journey, so I could smoke on the trains. There was a belief in the ranks that tobacco kept influenza at bay. It's why Claudine is always in a nimbus of fug. I've warned her, the fumes will get her before the flu, but she's morbidly afraid of dying. Did you show her your dress?' His eyes skimmed the straight-cut neckline, and her shoulders, which were almond-cream in the candle glow.

Katya shook her head. 'But one of my colleagues said it was like something Madame Denise Poiret would wear. I didn't admit it was my design. Didn't want them to think I was getting above myself.'

'Why not? Meek apology won't succeed in couture. You need a neck like a goose, a grasp of the feminine psyche, financial acumen and the drive that got Hannibal's elephants over the Alps. Are you still enjoying life at Claudine's?'

'When I don't have to see Madame's niece.' She hadn't meant to speak so bitterly. Or to touch her hair. Something changed in Harry's expression.

He said, 'If it ever gets too much, come to me. I will always—'

'Don't,' she flashed. 'Or I'll be too embarrassed to come home with you tonight.'

Harry had picked up the metal pot containing their peppermint tea, which they'd forgotten about. His grip wavered. 'Did you just say what I thought you said?'

She felt as shocked as he looked. 'I suppose I did. Unless you'd rather not.'

For a moment, Harry looked as if somebody had put a loaded gun to his temple. His smile came eventually, tentative and unsure. 'In that case…' he looked towards the kitchen and half rose, then sat down again with a small groan. 'Too late. Omelettes are on their way. Still, we've got all night. No?'

The Pierce-Arrow sputtered midway along Boulevard Malesherbes. Harry pulled over moments before the engine died. 'Damn. Our trip across the river threw me. I measure the fuel in this beast to the teaspoon.'

'How is it you get any at all?'

'I have an allowance, for the business.'

'Am I a business allowance?'

'No, but don't tell the ministry.'

They abandoned the car and he slipped his arm through hers. The only other souls around were two cats, yowling softly at each other in the middle of the road. The moon had gained vigour, bright in the western sky, making black cut-outs of the chimney pots. The power was still off on the *Rive Droite*. A breeze sang in their faces, and the air whispered of chestnut flowers. Traffic droned from the direction of the Madeleine where three roads met, but Malesherbes was so quiet they could hear a nightingale's song. Only the baleful 'ahooo' of a river barge and the glow of a baker's wood oven proved that not everyone was sleeping.

Rue Goya's gates were locked but Harry had a side-gate key. He shielded her on the way to his front door and Katya didn't have to ask why. He was preventing anybody observing her, should they be staring out of an upper window. If tonight ended where her blood was leading, she would see the morning as a new woman. No longer her father's immaculate daughter. This was the most headstrong, idiotic thing she had ever done.

She couldn't wait.

Chapter Seventeen

In Harry's apartment, at the drawing room door, he asked, 'Anything you'd like? I have a reasonably stocked kitchen.'

Katya couldn't think, so he suggested coffee.

'Go through.' He gave her his cigarette lighter, which had guided them through the dark. 'Light some candles.'

The lounge window shutters had been left open and she found her way around easily enough. Katya often found French homes cold but not this room, which had absorbed the day's heat. She went first to the window, letting her stole slide away. The cherry trees were indigo daubs, their flowering over, beauty blown and gone. Life was uncertain, she thought, and youth was wheat to the scythe. Harry's brother Christian had been twenty-five when he died. Her brother-in-law Mikhail a year older and Vera the same. It had come to her in the vaults of Jacqui's restaurant that she, Katya Vytenis, did not want to die without knowing what it felt like to be in a man's arms.

She cared about the consequences. Her mother's warnings about men's predatory ways raced forward, but it felt right to be here. She and Harry had held hands all the way home.

There were candlesticks on every surface and she lit them one after the other. The table which, on her last visit, had been a litter of cloth samples was clear but for a bowl of white hydrangea flowers. The small table had been moved to the side of a sofa and Katya got the impression that this was where Harry relaxed in the evening, perhaps with a book and a drink. The cushions held the indent of limbs. She sank deep into its sprung base and for a few seconds, critically inspected her legs. They were shapely from horse-riding and the tennis she'd played as a girl, during summer holidays in the country. This evening, she'd put on silk stockings held up with plain garters. From her table at the Rose Noire, she'd noticed women with their stockings rolled down, secured under the knee with flashy, ribbon garters. To make it easier to perform energetic dance steps, no doubt. Katya smoothed her skirt back over her legs, and buried her nose in the hydrangeas. Had Harry bought them, or had them delivered? Perhaps he had a maid. Of course he had a maid! He was a busy man, it was surely not his hand that applied beeswax to all this furniture. The light perfume from the curdy flower heads gave her a moment's reminiscence; her mother's writing paper, the bathroom floor when talcum powder was shaken over warm, pink feet. Vera on her wedding morning.

*

Vera backing away to the far end of her cell, where the Cheka captain cannot reach her…

Katya calls out to her, 'Anoushka's alive. Your daughter is breathing!' but Vera doesn't answer. She's too busy breaking the seal on the vodka bottle.

'Don't,' Katya warns. That bottle and the captain's craving is the only ace they hold. 'Vera, don't drink any. Don't spill it!'

'Take Anoushka and go,' Vera tells her. 'I'm done for, but my child deserves her life.'

The captain, face bloated with rage, threatens to put a bayonet through Katya and the baby. 'Both of them, Starova, while you watch.' His piercing falsetto sweeps Katya back to her father's last moments. She hadn't known before then that men scream, but they do. Vera, meanwhile, is tipping the bottle, releasing a colourless stream into the slop pail. She is pouring methodically, as if wasting the vodka is part of a plan. She gives Katya a plain look.

'You think I'm mad? Perhaps. I need to be with Mikhail and I can't wait any longer.'

*

Pulled back by the bump of Harry's foot opening the door, Katya knew she, too, had come to the limits of her waiting. She needed Harry's arms, his body. Not for a night. For life. Morning and night, her safeguard against terror. She wanted a blizzard of cherry blossom that never faded. And just as Vera had, she'd give anything, everything, in exchange.

'Sorry that took so long. I couldn't find matches to light the gas. My *bonne* enjoys setting puzzles for me.'

So, he had a maid.

Harry poured coffee into delicate cups, then sat down next to her. He hadn't worn his cap on the drive back and his hair was rumpled, like a farm boy who had spent a day on the hayricks. In the euphoric holding of hands, Katya had forgotten her butchered hair. She was reminded when Harry unpinned her headband so he could slide his fingers through her curls.

'You don't know how long I've waited to touch this... living gold.' He kissed her for long minutes, while their coffee grew cold.

She closed her eyes, her lips opening but he frustrated her by pushing curls off her ear and kissing the tender hollow where her pulse drummed. He kissed downward, the curve of her neck, her shoulder, beneath the straps of her dress, the top of her arm and the exquisitely sensitive skin beneath which made her writhe in delight. She settled against the cushions like a sleeper as Harry's hand moved down until she felt him pushing her skirt up over her thighs.

Never more glad than now that she'd jettisoned the underclothes of her youth and taken to wearing negligible nothings. She heard the catch of his breath as she slipped off her stockings, her knickers. She sighed as he caressed one thigh, then the other.

'You are as golden here as elsewhere.'

He teased her legs apart and Katya's own breath grew ragged, like the music that had dominated their evening together. She was moist and warm, silken, and knew that this was what her body had desired for weeks, months. Forget what the world said. When he touched her, she felt she could break free from her past.

He sat up and her eyes sprang open. He was unbuttoning his waistcoat, that was all, and his shirt. When he'd thrown them aside, he helped her pull down the bodice of her dress to reveal her breasts. The sensation of his lips on her nipples sent a wildness through Katya. She lifted her head, curling forward. The unruly fall of his hair tickled and she blew it aside, feeling Harry shiver at the sensation. She took his earlobe between her teeth, nibbling as she might on a costly delicacy. Harry shivered more deeply. She felt him stall and grow still. Not in the thrall of shock or distress, but as if he had been given a dreamed-of gift.

As he had, he told her. Night after night after night. In the train, on the ship to France, in Paris. 'You will not believe the persistence, or detail, of my dreams.'

'I won't blush.' She laughed against his mouth. 'I've grown out of blushing.'

'Never that. Stay as you are.' One hand found the nestled heat between her thighs.

Katya arched, parting her legs wantonly. She felt his arousal, and rocked her pelvis, to entice his fingers inside her. But as they entered her, she stiffened. Not in pain, but in involuntary fear of what might come next.

He said, 'I can't do this.'

She went rigid. 'Harry – why? What's wrong?'

He got off the sofa. Katya stared up at him, and quickly shoved her skirt down, scorched by her own vulnerability and the harsh look on his face.

'Why. What's wrong with me?'

'With you? You are beautiful. So much so I could cry. But you are you and I am me and I cannot take your virginity knowing I've got the advantage. Katya…' he stepped away, turning his back while she scrambled a semblance of dignity. Pulling up her dress, looking around for her stole, unable to remember where she'd put it.

'Katya, if you were anyone else, you know how this would end. This crucifies me. But I can't offer you what you yearn for.'

'How do you know what I yearn for?'

'It's in your face. Security. Certainty.'

She couldn't deny it. 'Tell me why you can't.' Her voice was as dense as her pain.

'I have obligations and commitments. You have your mother and Anoushka and you'll have Tatiana back one day.'

'This is about my family, my title?'

'Funny, that comes so quickly to your mind. I have qualms about your mother, who would certainly try to break us up. I have doubts about the clash of our pride, because I have just as much as you,

Princess. Don't look at me like that. In the morning, you'll thank me for showing you respect.'

Thank him, when she'd turned her back on all the rules of her upbringing? 'Is it because of how I've behaved? Letting you kiss me and... and the rest, as though we were married?'

'No. Oddly, I like you the more for it.'

'Do you still resent me for treating you like a peasant?'

'Peasant?' He laughed bitterly. 'I didn't realise I was so far down the rankings. I imagined it was, "The princess and the tradesman".' He walked across the room, bringing back her stole which he spread over her shoulders. 'I'll take you home.'

'To hell with you, Harry Morten. To think I was ready to dishonour myself, my name and yes, my rank.' Raising her hand, she dealt Harry the hardest blow in her power. Pain surged up her arm as his head rocked. He shot out a hand and for a split instant, she thought he was going to return in kind. But he was warding off a second strike. His eyes were translucent, irises dilated. They battled, their breathing the only sound. He spoke first.

'You'd like to borrow a coat? It'll be cold out. Wait here.' So killingly formal. She'd have welcomed a spitting lecture on her evil manners. But to be spoken to as a guest who had outstayed her welcome was more than she could bear.

As soon as he left the room, she lunged for her bag and sent a coffee cup flying. It landed on the priceless Aubusson carpet. She tried blotting it, but her handkerchief was too fine, so she fetched a newspaper from the arm of another sofa, pressing that into the wet patch. As she waited for the stain to come through, she noticed somebody had ringed an item on one of the pages. No time to be curious; she heard a door closing somewhere in the flat and abandoned her attempts to save the carpet. Grabbing her stole and bag, for the second time she ran out of Harry Morten's apartment.

She heard him calling her impatiently, imperiously. Because she hadn't a key to the side gate, she ducked behind a clipped box-bush in front of the house opposite. A moment later, she heard her name being called in the hoarse, controlled way people use when others are asleep nearby. At the sound of a metallic creak, she left her hiding place. Harry had gone through on to Malesherbes. If he believed she'd got over the gate, he'd assume she'd head towards Boulevard de Courcelles. She slipped out of rue Goya, taking the other direction.

At home, she crept upstairs, softly turning her door key so as not to disturb her mother. She needn't have worried. Irina was sleeping like a log dredged from the permafrost. That was when she realised she'd run home with Harry's newspaper clenched in her hand. The power was still off, so Katya lit candle stubs, enough to read by.

The paper was *The Times, London Edition*, dated from a few months back. An entry under 'Marriages' had been circled in pencil.

Morten : Lind
On 13 Nov, 1918 at Masthugg Church, Gothenburg, Harald Morten formerly of King Street, Manchester to Elsa Lind of Gothenburg, Sweden.

Katya read it over and over. In the end, she couldn't delude herself. Harry had rejected her for the simple reason that two days after the Armistice bells rang, he had married a woman named Elsa Lind.

Part Three

Chapter Eighteen

In his office, Harry unwrapped a parcel Mademoiselle Cooper brought in.

'By hand, one of Claudine's girls,' Coops told him. 'Shall I make coffee?'

'Please. Make it strong.' He needed it, not having been to bed at all. After she'd run from him, he'd spent an hour searching for Katya, giving up only when he reached rue Brazy and saw the glow of a light in her window. Back at home, he'd lain on the sofa, drifting off at an ungodly hour, only to wake when the electricity clicked back on and every lamp in the room came to life. He'd gone through the motions of washing and dressing, feeling like a delinquent who had taken a hammer to a church window. His only comfort was that had he made love to Katya he would now be feeling worse.

The parcel revealed its content and Harry reeled. A plait of corn-gold hair curled like a snake in a brown-paper nest. Katya had either gone mad or was taking ghoulish revenge. A closer look showed him that the braid had been sheared off. This wasn't a hairdresser's handiwork.

What made a woman do this? Katya had been so proud of her hair. His desire to touch and caress it, run it though his hands, had been drawn from her joy in it. Harry rewrapped the parcel as Coops came in with a tray.

'Do you know the girl who brought this?'

'Her name's Dominique. Surly young woman, speaks with a Lyonnais accent.' Coops poured his coffee. 'There was something not-quite-nice about her, and I did wonder from her smirk if the parcel contained horse droppings?'

'No. Just some material.' He drank his coffee at his desk, reliving the sight of Katya on the floor of the upstairs corridor at Claudine's, her hair and clothes wrenched awry while Bibi stood over her, flushed with triumph. Katya had said that she was happy at Claudine's as long as she was excused the company of the niece. Harry had always been repelled by something in Bibi Saumon, even when forced to entertain her for business purposes. Rumours went around: Bibi pushing a girl she didn't like down some steps; throwing a flat iron at a seamstress who had accidentally cut through a piece of expensive silk.

Locking the plait in a drawer, Harry put a call through to Claudine's couture workroom, hoping it wouldn't be famously reserved Pauline Frankel who answered. Charlotte Brunet picked up and she was highly forthcoming. Yes, she knew of the latest savagery unleashed on Princess Vytenis. Only Katya's pleading had stopped Mademoiselle Brunet from involving the police.

When he put the receiver down, Harry was no longer the easy-going Englishman with the half-smile. Even his mother wouldn't have recognised him.

Harry was not a vindictive type. The army had brought him into contact with men who were. Middle-rankers usually, out to stamp their authority by making others' lives miserable. He'd sworn never to be like them and so it was with a sense of crossing a Rubicon that he walked unannounced into Claudine's office, slammed a wad of unpaid invoices on her desk and informed her that he was calling in her debts.

'End of the week, Madame, or I will serve a summons.'

For once in their acquaintance, Claudine was struck dumb.

Meeting Pauline Frankel outside on the pavement, Harry invited the *première* to join him for coffee. At an inside table on rue Cambon, he asked her, 'What would it take for you to leave your present post?'

'A good offer, Monsieur Morten.'

'Do you aspire to run your own atelier?'

Pauline Frankel raised her eyebrows above her spectacles. 'Are you tempting me? Alas, I haven't the resources to set up on my own, nor anyone to back me. My husband is an invalid, I'm not sure if you're aware of that. I'm the breadwinner.'

He'd again asked what she would need and waited while she thought about it.

'Access to good cloth on three months' credit.'

'Can be done.'

'A five-year lease somewhere, the first six months rent-free.'

'Not impossible. Anything else?'

'Roland Javier to come with me.'

Harry smiled for the first time in many hours. 'Why don't we go and see him right away? I am happy to meet all your conditions, Madame Frankel, but with one of my own. You take Princess Vytenis with you and put her at the forefront of the business.'

'Is she ready for such a position?'

'A young woman who waded through blood to get her family out of Russia? I'd say so.'

*

Katya was late, timing her arrival to avoid the chattering women who always gathered outside the building before work started. She had come in at the lower end of rue Duphot to avoid passing Cour du Comte.

Married. He had never actually said he was single. So, presumably, he'd been after an *arrangement* as it was euphemistically called. *She* had created the love affair. For all that, she was filled with hate at this unimagined betrayal. At Claudine's, she strode into a scene of crisis. The office door was wide open and, for once, no vapours billowed out. Five people were bunched around Madame's desk, all talking. Bibi's was the most piercing voice.

'Breathe in, Tante Claudine, don't fight, the doctor's trying to help.'

Racking coughs interspersed with whooping gasps suggested the advice was not being taken. Katya recognised Pauline Frankel's back and Monsieur Javier's impeccably squared shoulders. A woman wearing a nurse's wimple said bracingly, 'Come along, the more we struggle, the harder it is for doctor.' Someone moved aside and Katya saw Claudine jammed into her seat with her head thrown back as she fought off a man with a stethoscope round his neck. He appeared to be trying to inject her with a hypodermic.

Seeing Katya, Pauline Frankel came over and whispered, 'She got in early, to go by the hill of cigarette butts on her desk. She'd made a start on some unpaid invoices, enough to give anyone a turn. I found her when I went to speak to her about what happened to you. That was appalling, Katya.' Madame Frankel glanced at Katya's head, but saw nothing more than a close-fitting cloche hat. 'I am so angry. But…' she looked helplessly back at Claudine. 'Blood in her phlegm.' The doctor was still attempting to position his hypodermic. 'How many times have I told her that she is in more danger from cigarettes than from the influenza?'

Roland Javier came and added a tail to Pauline Frankel's remark. 'An old shepherd in the Spanish mountains bought a dog so big and savage, it kept even starving wolves from his flock. But then the dog ate him. I am going to telephone the hospital and arrange for an ambulance. Claudine will push that needle into the doctor's arm.'

Pauline asked Katya to go to each of the workrooms and explain that Madame had been taken ill. 'Say "accidental choking" though I think we must prepare for a change of command.'

They glanced towards Bibi, then back at each other.

'We need to speak. Drop in to my office. *Mon dieu.*' Pauline hurried back to add her pleas to those of Bibi and the nurse. 'Madame Saumon, you *must* stop trying to punch the doctor.'

Katya went to spread the news. In Bibi's section, her announcement was heard in silence. The Kaminsky sisters, who had brought Anoushka back home yesterday outdoing each other for smiles, suddenly looked haunted.

By lunchtime, the change in command had taken effect. Dwarfed by her aunt's extra-wide chair, Bibi Saumon spread out her arms, outlining her new territory. Summoned as she emerged from a brief meeting with Madame Frankel, Katya walked in with a premonition. When she saw, as she was no doubt meant to, the 'Passion Flower' cotton thrown casually over Bibi's shoulder, Katya knew she wouldn't see the end of the working day as an employee here. She'd collect her personal possessions as soon as she quit this room.

'How is your aunt?' she asked.

Bibi shrugged. 'Well as can be expected, which is about the most useless phrase ever invented. Who does your hair, Princess Vytenis? You must give me the name.'

Katya lifted her chin. 'From the first, you've singled me out for ill treatment. For all that, I've become a good seamstress.' And thanks to that ten-minute conversation in the *première's* office, one with a future outside this place. Pauline Frankel wanted her to be part of a new business venture. No details as yet, but it was a lifebelt thrown at a critical moment. 'I can also draw and design, Mademoiselle Saumon.'

Bibi smiled. 'Every *midinette* thinks she can design, just as every carthorse thinks it can jump.'

'I doubt it. But my time here has run its course.'

Bibi looked nettled, the anticipated pleasure of a sacking denied her. 'If you quit of your own volition, I shan't have to give you a reference.'

'You won't need to. I have friends in the business.'

'You mean Pauline Frankel? A letter from her won't carry any weight, not after I've put the word out about you.'

'And what word would that be?' Katya had got to the door. Now she turned and gave 'Passion Flower' a thoughtful glance. Though it would smell of the last ten packets of cigarettes Claudine had smoked, she'd take it with her, one way or another.

'You imagine we haven't seen you peddling your wares at Harry Morten? I don't predict a happy ending there. He can afford to be choosy.'

'As he was when it came to you? Shall we be frank, Bibi? The pleasure you take in slandering me will be nothing compared to my joy when I've exposed you. I'm friends with Una McBride.'

Bibi sneered. 'Anyone who matters knows that woman's a gold-digger who fantasises about being the new Jeanne Paquin or sweeping up Coco Chanel's laurels. It's laughable, really.'

'Hilarious, particularly when she tells everybody they can get cheap Chanel copies by coming to you. It's the little secret she loves to spread around. Soon as I've collected my things, I'll walk to rue Cambon and call on Mademoiselle Chanel. She'll like to know that you've been churning out her models since Christmas. After that, I shall go to the House of Worth.'

The threat tumbled off Bibi. 'Nobody can prove a thing. So what if some of our lines are like other people's? They might be copying from us.'

For a while, Katya said nothing. She intended to repossess her fabric and make something glorious from it, to wear and be seen. Seen by Harry Morten, who might then grind his teeth over what he'd rejected. But how to take it without triggering a scuffle? She glanced up at the burner hanging above the desk and an idea rolled in. 'I wonder if someone tampered with the lamp oil to destroy your aunt's lungs? She was coughing up blood. How very comfortable you look in her chair, Bibi.'

Bibi looked at the lamp. 'You think I poisoned Tante Claudine?'

'I didn't mention you at all. But you know how people are. They'll say you have the most to gain from your aunt's ill health.'

Bibi instantly sat back, dispossessing herself of the desk and everything on it. 'I'm standing in while she's ill, that's all.'

Katya went closer to the desk, threading her fingers through her curls, inviting Bibi to feast on the rage that burst, like a boil, inside her. 'I don't forgive easily, it's a Russian vice. I will start a fire that will engulf you unless I get a glowing reference from you. Not that I need it, but it will amuse me to make you rack your brains to say something pleasant about another human being. Secondly, you will pay me to the end of the month.'

'I don't have to pay you anything.'

'But you'll do so as compensation for the damage you've done me. Three—'

'Three?'

'This is mine.' Katya swiped 'Passion Flower'.

Bibi pursued her to the door. 'You think you're powerful because Harry Morten took you for a spin in his car, but he's only a fabric merchant. There are twenty men in Paris who are bigger and better. He's not even French.'

'No,' Katya acknowledged, 'and you can have him. He's all right but his bones and his blood are the wrong colour. I am, after all, a Vytenis princess.'

*

Claudine recovered from her seizure but her lungs were so damaged, she was advised by her doctors to retire. Bibi consolidated her hold on the company. By the middle of June 1919 not only were the Kaminsky sisters looking for new positions, but Pauline Frankel had given her notice. Roland Javier was not far behind. On 19 June, Katya received an invitation for lunch, to discuss a business proposition. Pauline Frankel wrote, *I'm told there's a place on your street that offers good food, so shall we say twelve noon tomorrow, Friday 20 June? Monsieur Javier will join us.*

At Dedushka's, over pork-stuffed cabbage and rice, and a carafe of *pinard,* the rough, red wine that was as cheap as tap water, the three of them agreed to go into business together.

'We have the skills between us to create a select establishment,' Pauline Frankel said. 'Naturally, we cannot call ourselves "couture" until we conform to all the regulations, but everyone starts somewhere. You, Katya, can model the clothes and do some designing as well. Monsieur Morten says you have a flare for it.'

'Harry Morten spoke of me?'

'I must have creative control,' Roland Javier interrupted. 'Along with tailoring, I have a very clear eye for female fashion. While I will consider it an honour to mentor this young lady, she is not ready for a leading role.'

Here we go, Katya thought. *A door creaks open, then it slams.*

To her surprise, Pauline Frankel disagreed. 'Our agreement is to create a fashion house with a modern edge, don't you recall, Roland?'

'Edges can cut a person.'

'Semantics. Katya is a young, working woman who isn't watching the world change, she *is* the changing world. We need her vision.'

'We need a certain person's investment, I believe you mean,' Roland muttered.

Katya waited uneasily for Madame Frankel's response.

The *première's* composure did not slip. 'Dear Roland, let us congratulate ourselves on both being right. I suggest that Katya concentrates on *flou*. Nothing tailored as that is your specialisation.'

'*Flou?*' Katya asked. She was told it meant everything sinuous, floating, delicate and feminine.

'I am not alone in believing that you have a gift for the sensual.' A twinkle in Pauline's eye sent Katya's mind racing. 'Monsieur Morten is backing us because he believes in you. In me, and in Roland. He calls us "a virtuous triangle".'

Katya's cheeks tingled. When she and Harry had met at the Ritz after their long separation, he'd teased her with the remark, 'You've heard of a "virtuous circle"? Paris enjoys virtuous triangles.'

Oblivious of the emotions at play, Roland clicked his tongue. 'Very well, Katya may propose ideas for day and evening-wear, but surely we must find some premises? Soon it will be July, we are too late already to launch an autumn–winter line.'

Pauline was more optimistic. They might yet pull something out of the hat. Priority, meanwhile, was indeed securing premises as well as finding skilled staff. 'As for money, Monsieur Morten has not only offered start-up capital but also three months' credit on any fabrics we buy from him.'

'Why is Monsieur Morten being so helpful?' Katya blurted out.

'Because,' she was told, 'he sees a business opportunity. Naturally, he will expect to be paid back eventually, with profit.'

'When did he make these offers, Madame?'

Pauline named the date.

The day after Katya had hit him and stormed out of his apartment. 'You're certain he's serious? I mean, people make promises, then have second thoughts.'

'I think not,' Pauline replied. 'He is a man of business, an entrepreneur, and we are three fine people united by a love of adventure. He would be a fool to say no.'

Katya rolled her eyes. 'Believe me, Monsieur Morten is perfectly able to say no.'

After a few days, and sleepless nights, Katya decided she couldn't go through with the venture, though it broke her heart. Imagine facing Harry Morten, investor, across a table. What if the whole thing failed and she ended up owing him even more money?

She drafted formal letters to her new colleagues, explaining her fears, then screwed them up, unsent. Harry must have been thinking of their failed lovemaking when he offered to fund the business. *A sop, most likely, to his conscience.* If she backed out, he really might withdraw the offer, leaving her business partners high and dry.

No getting away from it, she had to speak to Harry. Except she hadn't the courage to make the first move.

Katya sought out Una McBride at the Ritz, intending to ask the American to act as her intermediary. She didn't get as far as mentioning Harry's name, however. Having shrieked in amazement at Katya's new hairstyle, '*Belle gamine!*', Una bubbled out the news that Harry had gone away.

'To Sweden, leaving a "to-do" list for Coops as thick as an English omelette. And you know what?' Una waved to catch the eye of a waiter. 'He took a Sèvres dinner service with him and that means only one thing. Setting up home. And he says my poor cats are sly.'

'He's already married, Una. A lady named Elsa Lind. It happened last November.'

Una stared. 'No! The crafty... Now he'll be away for weeks, just as Claudine's atelier has put its trotters in the air. I've a ream of clients demanding their special dresses and nobody to make them.' She snatched Katya's arm. 'Hey, you wouldn't–'

'Not if they're copies.'

'They're not copies.'

'I won't make "tributes" either.'

'Oh, shoot.' Una sighed. 'So, there's a Madame Harald Morten tucked away in Gothenburg?'

'Seems so.'

Una sniffed and ordered champagne. 'On the van der Boor account,' she instructed the waiter. 'I've a new friend,' she confided. 'Dutch businessman and art collector. My heart is American, my tastes Parisian but when it comes to painting, I'm truly international. I think

Harry could be gone awhile. He means to head on to Finland, pursuing this thing… can't remember the name… something to do with wood?'

'Cellucotton.'

'Get you, *Webster's Dictionary*. Beats me how wood fibre can become something anyone would want to wear, but I can vouch that it soaks up a lot of blood. We nurses loved it. Do you badly need to see him?'

'Harry? No.' Katya said it so sharply, Una's eyes stretched.

'My goodness, that bad?'

Katya sagged. 'Will you be honest with me, Una? Did you and Harry ever—'

'Dance the tango? No.' A moment later, Una was raising a glass of Veuve Clicquot paid for by an unsuspecting Dutchman. Sighing, 'Delicious,' she tackled Katya on her 'Desertion of Claudine', as she phrased it. 'Leaving smack in the middle of the summer rush, Roland Javier and Pauline Frankel too. Poor Claudine. I heard she set herself on fire.'

Katya corrected her. 'No fire, just too much smoke. And I didn't desert, I resigned when Bibi took over.'

Una made a grim face. 'That Jezebel. She's back-pedalling on the orders I've put in, even though I made a down payment. I've had clients in tears on my shoulder. Darling, you wouldn't reconsider?'

Katya explained that she had an opportunity to join forces with other refugees from Claudine's in a new fashion house, but there was an obstacle and she'd value Una's opinion.

'Which refugees?' Una insisted. Her mouth dropped when Katya named names. 'Oh. My. Stars. If I can tell my ladies I've jumped ship for Pauline Frankel and Roland Javier, they'll forgive everything.'

Freeing her arm from Una's terrier grip, Katya admitted she hadn't a clue which way to leap. 'Harry Morten has offered to fund us.'

'And that is a problem?'

'To me, yes.'

'Okay. How many people live in Paris?'

Katya had no idea. 'Half a million, perhaps?'

'Then let me tell you, 499,999 of them will never be in your shoes. Throw up this chance, it won't come to you again.'

Katya hung her head. This wasn't making her feel any better.

'What's the business called?' Una demanded, then scratched the question. 'Obviously, Roland Javier will want to call it after himself. I adore that man but if he were a twin, he'd still want to blow out all the candles on the cake. Good luck keeping him in check. Not,' she added hastily, 'that that should put you off. You'll buy your fabrics from Harry, of course?'

Katya nodded.

Una sat back, nursing her glass. 'Now I get it. You've already talked to Harry. Things got a little steamy, and that's when he confessed to being married. Why you want to sit in a corner and cry.' Una said nothing for a while. Then, 'Life's a game played with a loaded dice. The secret is to make sure it's loaded in your favour. So, Harry's married. Doesn't make his money no good. When we've emptied this bottle, we're going to rue Cambon to stand before the House of Chanel. She got into business thanks to a modest loan from her lover.'

'Harry isn't my…' Katya broke off as Una began laughing at her.

In spite of having no work to go to, Katya was out of bed early the next day as usual. She'd take Anoushka out for an airing and find a bread queue to join.

'Princess Vytenis?' Maria Filatova came to the café door as Katya wheeled the pram past. She held something out. 'A letter, they put it in the wrong door. From Moscow, by the look of it. Happy news, I hope?'

The hammering of Katya's pulse proved that anything Russian still had the power to frighten her. Only when she reached the park and sat down on a bench did she study the letter. Russian stamps, poor-quality unbleached paper. Her address written in both Cyrillic and Roman characters. A moment later, her shaking fingers were holding a letter signed and stamped from within the Russian Ministry of Internal Affairs, testifying to the death of Prince Ulian Vytenis 'in the course of his arrest'.

Her cry scared a pair of pigeons into flight. *A lie!* But as minutes passed, Katya admitted that she could hardly expect the Bolshevik authorities to state the truth. This was what she'd asked for, never believing she'd get it. Dr Zasyekin must have gone to such trouble, possibly to personal risk, to induce the authorities to write.

A search inside the envelope yielded a brief message:

I pray this will help. E.Z.

She kissed the note. 'Thank you, my dear Emil Zasyekin.' Would the bank finally be satisfied? If so, she was holding the key not just to their survival, but to her dream. *She* might fund the couture venture. No need to take anything from Harry. She got home so fast, the pram wheels smelled of warm rubber. She abandoned it in the hall and ran up six flights, Anoushka clamped to her chest. Bursting into their room, she cried, 'Wake up. Mama, wake up!'

Irina's eyelids peeled back a little way. 'Mm?'

'Get dressed! Dr Zasyekin has sent proof of Papa's death. We have to go to the bank.'

Irina sat up and examined the letter. 'It's in Cyrillic. They won't look at it.'

Katya groaned. She'd forgotten that detail. 'I'll call on Aleksey. No, why should I need to? I'll translate the letter myself.'

At Dedushka's, she borrowed the typewriter Maria used for the menu cards. The work took her only a few minutes. Now all she had to do was take it to the notary and have it authenticated. Putting the cover back on the typewriter, she walked through the café – and saw Aleksey coming in. They hadn't spoken since he'd insulted her in front of Harry. Passing each other on the street, she'd kept her eyes fixed ahead, aware of him glowering in her direction.

Yet once again, he surprised her.

He bowed, his hand on his heart. 'You will forgive my outburst the other evening? As your friend guessed, I had drunk too much.'

'Far too much. You could have had an accident.'

He made a dismissive noise. 'You'd be surprised, it makes me a better driver. But not a better friend. I hope I did not spoil your evening?'

'Not at all.' Harry had managed to do that admirably on his own. With her help, of course.

'And the gentleman with the cold eyes… you are stepping out with him?'

'No, that's quite over.'

Aleksey nodded, as if he'd expected her to say so, and invited her to join him for a very early lunch. She accepted and over a plate of roast Jerusalem artichokes with bacon, she told him her latest news. Showed him the letter.

'I only wrote to Dr Zasyekin at your prompting, Aleksey. So thank you.'

He mimed a bomb exploding. 'This time next month, you will be rich. No longer to share a plate of common food with the likes of me.'

'Rubbish. I shall never forget my friends in Little Moscow.' Lunch over, she walked to the notary's office, taking her mother with her.

On Thursday, 26 June, she presented these latest documents at the Franco-Russe bank. The official, whose furrowed brow and thinning hair had become far too familiar, read the translation and studied the original letter at length. Katya waited for the brush-off, but he looked at her earnestly.

'I will peruse these in more detail and communicate my findings. Please be patient a little longer.'

For two weeks, Katya lit candles and prayed fervently. And when not praying, she worked on ideas for a line of free-flowing dresses that would impress her new partners. On Friday, 11 July, unable to bear the suspense, she returned to the bank. As she walked up rue de la Paix and with the bank's ornate frontage in sight, a taxi drew away. Aleksey's. Was he ever going to get his rattling exhaust pipe fixed? She wondered if he'd driven here to meet her, yet she hadn't told him that she was planning to make this trip today. Only her mother knew of it.

Ah. Irina and Princess Provolskaya were spending quite a bit of time together these days, playing cards or companionably knitting clothes for Anoushka and the other babies of the district. Ludmilla Provolskaya had recently taken Irina to the doctor's, worried that Princess Vytenis might be suffering from a return of shingles as she was once again complaining of muscle pain and sleeplessness. This little service had struck a wrong note in Katya's mind. Such officious kindness, just as the Vytenis family luck was about to change...

In the bank, Katya was ushered into the familiar office whose occupant got to his feet, looking surprised to see her. 'I trust you are better, Madame? I've already told your friend of my decision regarding your funds.'

The polite smile froze on Katya's face. 'Friend?'

'Prince Provolsky gave me to understand that you were indisposed but anxious for news, so I have explained our decision to him.'

Katya bit her tongue, asking only, 'What did you tell him?'

'That the Franco-Russe bank is pleased to accept the proofs of identity supplied and will make funds available as expeditiously as possible.'

'You mean—?'

'You will have your money, as soon as my clerks have done the paperwork.'

The miracle had happened. Life would never be the same again. She nodded and hurried away, unable to hold back her tears.

Chapter Nineteen

The sun beat down from a peacock sky. It was Monday, 14 July and Paris was in a wild, carnival mood for Bastille Day. The first unshadowed *Quatorze Juillet* in four years. It was full of emotional resonance for the Vytenis family too, as Vera's wedding had taken place on that day. In a kinder world, she and Mikhail would have been celebrating five years together.

Katya and Irina wheeled Anoushka through Parc Monceau and watched the revelries with wistful, foreign eyes. Katya couldn't stop herself glancing about for Harry – to avoid him, she told herself. She had little expectation of seeing him, having heard no rumour of his return.

Aleksey and his mother joined them, all smiles, putting Katya instantly on her guard. She'd had no chance to speak to him since seeing him drive away from rue de la Paix and still didn't know what to make of his appearance at the bank. *Show nothing*, she warned herself. *Smile.* Accepting Aleksey's invitation to stroll to the lake while their mothers cooed over Anoushka, she waited for him to mention the visit. When he failed to, she went straight to the point.

'Why were you at my bank on Friday, saying I'd sent you?'

He touched her arm. 'But you asked me to go.'

'When?'

'When we stood beside the Eiffel Tower, you said, "Banks never listen to women". You needed my help, you made it my task.'

'I didn't ask you to invent illness for me.'

Aleksey frowned. 'I told that official you were anxious for news, and joked that it might put you into a fever. Is it my fault the fool misheard? What are you accusing me of, Katya?'

He looked so hurt, suddenly she wasn't sure. 'Nothing.'

He took her hand. 'You have your money now. Will it change things between us? Yes, money does that. Emil Markov is your fairy godfather, but I hope there is still room for me.'

'Emil who?'

Aleksey's mouth tightened. 'Emil Markov Zasyekin. Is that not the doctor's correct name? It was my advice to write to him, for proof of your father's death. You said so.'

'I've only ever called him "Dr Zasyekin". Aleksey – have you been digging?

'What has become of you, Katya? Do the people you mix with now fill your head with suspicion? Your mother referred to the doctor by his full name when she took tea in our apartment. I am sorry that riches have stepped into our friendship, Princess Vytenis.' He bowed in a soldierly way and strode back to his mother. He must have said something brusque because Princess Provolskaya looked anxiously towards Katya, then relinquished Anoushka's hand, walking away with her son towards the gates.

At home, Katya explained to her mother what had passed. 'I just don't trust them, Mama. This money is ours, but others will be jealous.'

'Princess Provolskaya has been so good to us. She doesn't want money for herself,' Irina protested.

'So, she has asked?'

'A donation to Émigré Council funds, that is all.'

And that, Katya told herself, *is just the beginning.* Miserly? Perhaps. But the fortune lying in the Franco-Russe bank was something she'd guard like a lioness. 'This windfall must keep us for the rest of our lives, Mama. Anoushka's too, and she might live into her seventies.'

'We can't spend anything?'

'A little. A new outfit, a hat or two. We'll definitely move somewhere nicer. With your permission, I will invest in a business to bring in an income. Money must make money, else it trickles away.'

'We'll consult Dr Shepkin before making any decisions,' her mother said. 'He has advised me not to leave all my money in one bank, in case of... what did he call it? A financial crash.'

'Dr Shepkin knows about our money?'

'He is my very good friend and a sensible man. I am obliged to seek him out, as you keep hiding my sleeping tablets.'

Katya privately vowed to find them a new home as fast as she could, away from the Russian quarter, from Shepkin and his ready pills. Meanwhile, she met again with Roland and Pauline and announced that she was now in a position to fund the venture. Or rather, her mother was willing to become the principal investor in the as-yet-nameless fashion company.

In consequence, messages couched in terse telegraphese winged between Paris and Gothenburg:

'From P. Frankel to H. Morten: Must respectfully inform investment no longer needed stop Explain on your return stop.'

'From H. Morten to Mme Frankel: Deposed am I stop Identity of rival of great interest stop.'

With the implication that Harry was not going to back away quietly, Katya steeled herself for the day of explanation. There grew in her a pressing desire to sit down with a sketchbook and lose herself in creativity. After all, soon she would have to persuade Roland Javier that he was not the only creative force in their partnership.

Parc Monceau made the perfect outdoor studio. As the street cleaners tidied up the holiday debris and the discarded bunting, Katya sat on a bench, a pad on her knee. With Anoushka parked in a shady spot nearby, she scribbled, agonised and, finally, lost herself.

On 20 July 1919, Katya's mother became a director and principal investor in Vytenis-Javier-Frankel et Cie, shortened to VJF. Katya signed the forms as her mother's legal proxy. With hard work, she might one day become wealthy and Harry Morten might add one more name to his roster of five.

After they'd all shaken hands, Roland Javier sought assurance that Princess Irina Vytenis would be 'only a sleeping partner'. He blinked as Katya burst into slightly hysterical laughter.

On 22 July, the three directors met again at a café on Boulevard Malesherbes. This time, the Kaminsky sisters were invited. Both would be working for VJF and Miryam had been offered the task of recruiting sewing staff.

That lunchtime, Katya was the last to arrive, having minutes before signed papers for a five-room apartment on rue Rembrandt, an avenue off Parc Monceau. It was expensive, it would make her a near-neighbour of Harry's, but it was a lovely flat and they could move in immediately. They would occupy the *étage noble*, the floor one up from street level; from their balcony they would watch the seasons turning through fringes of acacia trees. She'd stopped at a post office to scribble a card to Tatiana at Callot Soeurs, alerting her sister to their new address, adding an invitation to Anoushka's birthday tea that coming Saturday.

Ordering a café crème for herself, she took a pen from her smart, new attaché case and joined a discussion that was well underway. '"VJF" sounds like a military vehicle,' Pauline was saying. 'We need a proper name. Something feminine but serious. Pretty, but dignified.'

Katya had an idea. 'Why not "Marie-Madeleine"? I thought of it as I walked past the Madeleine church and today is the feast day of Mary Magdalene.' She looked from one to the other. 'What have I said?'

Roland made an apologetic sweep of the hands. 'When it comes to business, it is best to avoid church, politics and former lovers.'

'I don't understand.'

Pauline gently explained, 'We're all Jewish. Apart from you, of course. So perhaps, no references to the Catholic sainthood?'

'Oh, I see. I meant no disrespect. Incidentally, I have no former lovers.'

'We have none either,' Miryam Kaminsky offered sadly.

'What a boring bunch we are,' said Pauline. 'Roland?'

His turn to blush; it was the first and last time Katya was ever to see that phenomenon. 'We should use a name we already have,' he said.

'"Maison Vytenis"?' Katya suggested mischievously, remembering Una's comment about this man and names.

Roland shook his head. '*No, no,* too hard for the French tongue. Nor "Frankel"—'

'Which sounds too German,' Pauline agreed dryly. 'What name comes to mind? Hm. Memorable yet stylish, heroic, yet imbued with a touch of the exotic?'

Roland Javier was not tormented by doubts, but he possessed humour. 'I cannot think,' he responded, 'unless you agree that "Javier"—'

'But why did we not think of it before? It is perfect. How clever of you.'

"Maison Javier". The decision was unanimous.

Pauline brought them down to earth. 'Finding seamstresses is becoming our greatest challenge. You will try to recruit older women, Miryam?'

'We've begun. Our Aunt Rose has signed up.'

'Wonderful. I am agreeing terms on our premises. But first, let's look at what our designers have come up with for our autumn line.'

Knots tightened in Katya's throat, and she was relieved when Roland offered to show his ideas first. Their coffee grew cold as they passed around a portfolio of sketches. He'd served up skirts and fisherman's smocks, the latter for wearing on blue-sky days, with bullet-shaped coats when chilly weather arrived. His winter-weight *tailleurs* – suits – were semi-fitted, giving room for arms to swing and legs to stride.

'Emancipation begins at the dressing table,' he said. 'Men returned from war do not wear any longer the stiff collar, the frock coat. Women will never go back to the old ways either, if we give them wearable elegance.'

He'd chosen plain weaves and light yarns for his suits, cavalry twills for the coats. English cloth, traditional for the male market, less so for womenswear. 'Supplied by our friend.'

Your friend, Katya silently corrected. 'Monsieur Morten may not be back for some time,' she warned, hoping that was true. 'Should we not approach alternate suppliers?'

'But I saw him yesterday.' Pauline Frankel pulled a face. 'I'm sure it was him unless he has a brother who drives his car.'

Katya explained that Harry's only brother had died.

'Then it was him. There was a lady passenger with him, fair-haired. But never mind that – you have something to show us, Katya?'

'I'm not sure. I don't think I'm ready.'

Pauline laughed. 'But we are, and you are clutching that attaché case as if it contains family jewels. Are we to see what our genii of the *flou* has conjured up?'

For the next ten minutes, Katya hardly breathed. Working not only in daylight but into the recesses of the night, she had finally arrived at twelve basic shapes. To be made in supple fabric, textured with embroidery. Una, when Katya showed them to her at the Ritz Bar, had been impressed.

'Chanel meets Callot Soeurs with a shake of Russian orthodoxy. Embroidery is good, it never looks frivolous.' Una had raised her glass. 'To you and Monsieur Javier. May the gods bless your union.'

Miryam and Fruma made encouraging noises as Katya's sketches did the round. Roland kept an unnerving silence. Pauline said, 'You've given us skirts longer than the current mode. Is that deliberate?'

Katya nodded. 'Nobody seems sure which way hems will go. I think some designers will cut them short and lose their more conservative clients.'

'Think, or know?' Roland came to life.

'*Think*, as I don't own a crystal ball. Most of our customers will have lived through times when to show an ankle was indecent. They don't want to be at the vanguard of fashion. For what it's worth, I think hems will drop once the shadows of war recede and normal life returns.'

'You're saying hems have risen from shock, like eyebrows?' Pauline laughed.

Roland nodded slowly. 'I like what you have given.'

'You do?'

He smiled at Katya's amazed blankness. 'Simple and elegant, the waist set close to the hip—'

'I've been watching waists,' Katya eagerly interrupted. 'They're sinking. I predict there won't be a waistline at all in a year or two.'

'Then let us rejoice and order more cake. In heaven, there are no waistlines.' Roland indicated one of Katya's sketches that he'd returned to several times. 'This will work perfectly with my coats. A coat should give the impression of hiding a lovely dress, while a dress should enjoy the protection of a coat. A perfect marriage. For your evening wear, I would like to see a little more flourish… but… I am content to work with you to the next stage.'

Katya released the stricture on her breath. 'I want to make my daywear from linen, the evening wear from silk, bias-cut—'

He waved her hopes away. 'You will never get linen. The Belgian flax fields turned from blue flowers to lakes of blood and will take years to regrow.'

Pauline suggested a silk-wool mix. 'Poplin drapes well, takes embroidery and Harry Morten has it in fine colours. You've done well,' she smiled at Katya. 'Many girls your age would have over-elaborated in a desire to impress, but you understand that simplicity is the soul of style. You are happy?'

'I'm ecstatic!'

Miryam Kaminsky congratulated her. 'From *midinette* to couturier.'

'Apprentice couturier,' Roland corrected.

Fruma Kaminsky patted Katya's hand. 'You design with seam-stresses in mind, which is good.'

Pauline took a diary from her bag. 'Let us gather again the day after tomorrow when I hope to show you our new premises. How about we meet on rue Cambon, at the English Tea Parlour at four o'clock?' She turned to Katya. 'Do you know where I mean?'

Katya did, of course, better than any of them.

She'd had to bring Anoushka as her mother had gone to bed with inflamed sinuses. As she parked the pram outside the English Tea Parlour, Katya felt that life resembled a cheap biscuit tin. Push down one side, the other pops up, however often you turn it. Yesterday, they'd moved into their dream apartment, only for Irina to start sneezing. Apparently, Katya had chosen the wrong park with the wrong sort of trees.

Her stress was partly alleviated when Monsieur Aristide rushed up to greet her and Anoushka, exclaiming, '*Là, là, là, là,* how well you are looking, not at all the sad-eyed girl who came to me for work. And you have a baby!' He bowed her to the table where the others were waiting.

Katya was aware of being scrutinised by other customers. She was wearing Harry's 'Passion Flower' fabric. Having washed it in borax to remove the smell of Claudine's cigarettes, she'd made it into a body-skimming tunic. It had trumpet sleeves with a mauve collar that picked up the amethyst tones in the print. Her skirt was the same mauve and instead of a hat, she carried a lilac silk parasol. She'd had her hair trimmed, to tidy the ends, and cluster-curls fell to the midpoint of her neck. Among those watching was her former patroness, the duchesse de Brioude, to whom she nodded courteously.

The marquise de Sainte-Vierge was with her niece, eyes glinting at Katya's ensemble.

Agnès de Brioude regarded it wistfully. Would her mourning ever relent, Katya wondered? Madame de Brioude's husband had been one of the highest-ranking officers to be killed at Verdun. A little boy of three or four sat between the women, solemn as a child would be when squeezed into a jacket, shirt and bow tie on a hot summer's day. Anoushka, by contrast, was all in white, except for a bonnet made from a 'Passion Flower' offcut. As she went by, Katya heard Agnès de Brioude sigh, 'What a little cherub!'

Passing another table of ladies whom she had waited on many times, Katya overheard something that stripped the smile from her face.

'… with Harry Morten. Yes, a liaison. And, it would seem, a result.'

As Roland rose to pull out a seat for her, she hissed, 'They think Anoushka is mine. Apparently, they even know who the father is. She's my sister's child. Can't they see she's a year old?'

Pauline advised her to ignore them.

'They're staring at me.'

'They're looking at your beautiful outfit. What a clever idea, matching the little one's bonnet to your tunic.'

Everyone took turns in making a fuss of the baby, even Roland, who crooned in Spanish and seemed not to mind when Anoushka attempted to peel away his meticulously groomed moustache. Tea was brought and a cake stand bearing the latest house speciality, sponge *babas* saturated in coffee-rum syrup. For Anoushka, a coconut madeleine arrived in a wooden dish. Sitting on Roland's knee, she picked up her cake in both hands, smearing raspberry jam over her face.

'Stop smiling, Monsieur, or the gossips will imagine she's yours,' Pauline teased.

'How could I ever father a child with blue eyes? This little one is brought here by the stork from the land of flaxen hair. From Russia or…' Roland timed his silence as Katya waited, a forkful of cake halfway to her lips, 'Sweden?'

'Her father was as Russian as I am.' Choking on her cake, Katya said between gasps, 'Anoushka is my niece, and no bastard. Nor have I ever – *ever* – had, well, you know, with Harry Morten. Never.'

Roland asked her pardon. 'It is a shame, though, to deny the chance to make more such beautiful babies.' He moved the conversation on to work, and produced his portfolio with such a flourish, it was as if he wanted the whole room to see. They realised that was exactly his plan when he said in a stage whisper, 'Nobody must set eyes on our *exquisite* autumn–winter collection but we five, understand?'

'Not until the day we launch,' Pauline agreed, loudly. 'Until that day, total secrecy. Does everyone swear to it?'

They all solemnly swore.

Roland had taken Katya's drawings away and synthesised them with his own.

Katya gave a smile as wide as one of Anoushka's when she saw how he had added to her ideas. 'I can't help being proud of myself.'

'With good reason,' he said generously, before making a noise of dismay. 'Ah, perhaps the combination of baby and madeleine was not so inspired.'

Anoushka was wiping jam onto his jacket. Fruma Kaminsky took the baby into her arms.

'Look at her, jam in her ears.' Fruma dipped her napkin into a finger bowl.

Katya offered to take the jacket to the back to clean it up. 'A knife blade and a drop of eau de cologne will do the trick.'

In the kitchen, the steam rising from the water boilers caught the back of Katya's throat. A woman in a waitress's uniform was tying one of the parlour's white cake boxes with coloured twine. She turned in surprise as Katya explained her presence.

'It really is you, Princess Vytenis? I thought it was but I didn't like to presume. You look so very stylish these days.'

'Jeanne?' Katya suddenly recognised the homely features beneath the wilting headband. 'How are you?'

As Katya scraped off jam and dabbed lily-of-the-valley cologne on the lapels of the jacket, they raked up old times. Jeanne was glad to hear that Katya had left Claudine's. 'She never paid for the cakes we sent round. Not until Monsieur Aristide threatened to mount a barricade outside her premises. She's retired through ill health, I hear?'

'Her niece has taken over.'

'Mm. Just in time to go bankrupt. Suppliers are calling in debt, and they aren't as patient as Monsieur Aristide.' Jeanne wrote an address on the white box. 'Actually, these are for Bibi Saumon.' She put a finger to her lips. 'Croissants. Monsieur bakes a few when he forgets it's not allowed. That girl will grow as fat as her aunt.'

'I'll be sorry if Claudine's goes out of business.'

Katya was making a last rub at the jacket when Jeanne ventured a hesitant comment. 'I hate tittle tattle, but…'

'Go on?'

'Your sister comes here sometimes.'

'She's allowed to, if she can afford it.'

'I mean, with a gentleman. The marquise de Sainte-Vierge's son.'

'Armand?' Katya had no difficulty bringing his face to mind. Pale-cheeked, dark hair obediently greased across his brow. Nervous hands and a damaged stare. 'He used to wear an injury medal… They come here alone?'

'No, sorry, it's the marquise's *elder* son, Gérard, she comes in with. An hour before closing, when his mother is certain not to catch them. If I can judge if a girl is in love, then your sister is that girl.'

Katya stiffened. It shouldn't be so surprising. 'And this Gérard?'

'Oh, he likes her. She's beautiful. But he won't marry her as he's already engaged. I've heard his mother speaking of it – some well-connected girl who's been promised to him for years. French aristocrats marry French aristocrats. Don't be offended, but they do not wed their *irregulières*. I wouldn't like your sister to…' Jeanne left the rest hanging.

'No,' Katya agreed. 'Thank you for telling me.' As she returned to the tea room, she pledged to seek out her sister. She'd use Anoushka's birthday party as her excuse. Not, she thought wearily, that Tatiana would listen.

The marquise and the duchesse, on their way out, had paused to speak with Roland and Pauline. As Katya took Anoushka back into her arms, she smiled at the little boy who held his mother's hand tightly. He must now be the duc de Brioude. Poor mite. There were beads of sweat on his small forehead, and Katya's fingers itched to whip off his jacket. The duchesse turned to her.

'Princess Vytenis, how are you? We couldn't help noticing fashion plates being handed around, but Monsieur Javier will tell us nothing. Except that you intend to display a collection in October?'

Two months' time? They'd better get sewing, then. 'Um, right. Yes. Absolutely. I do hope you will honour us with your presence.'

'I always go to my château that month, but not until the second week.'

Katya took the gracious hint. 'We're launching on the first of the month,' she said firmly. 'Later than other houses, but that cannot be helped.'

'What are you called?' the marquise demanded. She was wearing one of her scary turbans and Katya tried to imagine her as Tatiana's potential mother-in-law. She couldn't. Jeanne was right. Tatiana was heading for a crash.

'Our name, Madame? We are "Maison Javier".'

'*Janvier*?' the marquise snorted, having misheard. 'You're calling yourselves after the most miserable month of the year? Won't work. Damn stupid.'

Her niece quickly stemmed the insult. 'Why not, Tante Clotilde? January is the year's beginning, it looks back and forward. I rather like it.'

'*Janvier*?' Pauline tried it out. 'Mm.'

'I like it too,' said Katya, with a sidelong glance at a most-offended tailor.

'But it will look as if I cannot spell my own name,' Roland objected.

'I still like it,' said Pauline. 'Katya has cleaned your coat, Monsieur, and it's time to go.'

The pram was hot as an oven from being left out on the pavement. Roland volunteered to wheel it if Katya intended to carry Anoushka. 'I feel it is the only time in my life I will do this.'

Pauline took them into rue Duphot, stopping at the entrance of Cour du Comte. She led them into the cool of the courtyard and gestured to the low buildings to her left. 'Our new premises.'

'This is Monsieur Morten's place.' Roland looked about. 'I have not heard he is moving.'

'Nor is he, but he doesn't use this side of the yard.' Pauline took a key from her bag, telling them that in the eighteenth and nineteenth centuries, Cour du Comte had been a fashionable *manège*. 'Ladies of the *ton* would come to learn how to ride side-saddle in their flowing habits, and other not-so-respectable ladies would learn how to outdo them for skill. Being elegant has always been a competition.' She pointed. 'Monsieur Morten's offices occupy the former grooms' quarters.' The building she was about to unlock was the old stables. 'They were last used by a lampshade manufacturer which went out of business early in the war. I've negotiated a year's lease which we can extend to five. I know...' Pauline interpreted Roland's frown, 'it needs a layer of paint.'

'And more! There are weeds in the gutter, the windows need new glass. There are no skylights. I must have overhead light, I cannot work in darkness.' He was growing agitated.

'If you can acquire glass, you will be a hero across Paris. The windows need cleaning, is all,' Pauline chided. 'Where else will we find such generous space in the heart of the couture district?'

'The rent?' Katya shared Roland's unease, though from a different cause.

'Reasonable, first six months free. Best of all, our landlord is—'

'Harry Morten.' Katya had not seen this coming.

'He offered me terms before he left,' Pauline said. 'His second-in-command, Mademoiselle Cooper, did the rest.'

'But now he's back, he could have changed his mind?' *Please let him have changed his mind.*

Giving the key to Miryam Kaminsky and asking her to go on ahead, Pauline took Katya aside. 'I know you and Monsieur Morten have a friendship, but what I don't know is if it will affect the atmosphere between us all. If you cannot work in his vicinity – say so.'

Had it been Una asking, Katya would have said a great deal but this was poised Madame Frankel, so she sighed, 'It's fine.'

Pauline looked less than convinced and was about to say more, when the snarl of an engine drew their eyes towards the courtyard arch. A car rolled in, roof folded back, sapphire-blue flanks dusty from a journey. Harry sat at the wheel wearing a cap and goggles. Beside him, a woman, her hat secured by a fluttering veil. Katya had an impression of a fine bosom. A man in the back of the car was holding on to bolts of cloth. Harry's apprentice, she supposed. She couldn't see awfully well through a blur of tears.

Leaving the pram in a block of shade, with Anoushka in her arms, Katya hurried to join the others inside the old stables. With luck, Harry would take his passengers straight into his office. *Please let him not think this the moment to discuss business. Please, please not take this moment to introduce his new wife.*

The interior was woolly with cobwebs but Katya immediately saw Pauline's point: strip away the grime, and the building would make a perfect atelier. It was dark only because the electricity had been turned off, and the windows needed sluicing. There were even skylights, green with a war's worth of fallen leaves.

'Spacious, isn't it?' Pauline had followed her in and she looked at them all in turn. 'Are we agreed, this is to be the home of *Janvier*?'

Roland objected. 'We must be "Javier", or something quite different.'

'But you accept this building?' Pauline persisted.

'Yes, yes, if you wish it.'

Pauline called for an immediate vote on the signing of the lease. Five hands rose, Katya's the first to rise. Her personal feelings must not be allowed to obstruct business. 'And the name?' Pauline queried. 'I don't think we can do better than "Maison Javier". Another vote?'

Again, five hands went up. As they walked out into the heat, Roland shook his head. 'You tricked me, Madame. While I am fretting about the name, you slide a building past my nose.'

'A means to an end. We're now committed to launch on the 1 October.'

A call of 'Hello?' hooked their attention. Harry, in shirt sleeves, emerged from his side of the courtyard. He was followed by a queenly blonde woman in billowing white. With pale silk stockings and ivory shoes, a spray of jasmine in her hat, she seemed to Katya to be parading her new-bride status. Who else but Elsa, formerly Lind, now Morten? She approached with a sweet smile, saying to all of them at once, 'I am telling Harry he must put flowers on his desk. How can he work in a room without flowers, poor darling?'

'And I've been telling Elsa that I've managed for years.' Harry shook hands with each of them before saying formally, 'Allow me the pleasure of presenting Madame Harald Morten.'

When it was her turn to take Elsa's hand, Katya dropped the contact before it was strictly polite to do so.

Harry's smile grew lemon-sharp. He leaned towards her. 'I like what you've done with my 'Passion Flower'. And the parasol... good touch. Hello, Horror.' From her high position in Katya's arms, Anoushka was attempting to grab a lock of his hair. 'You're not catching me this time.' He turned to Elsa. 'She may be blonde and blue-eyed, but she has a surprising talent for inflicting pain.'

Of course he meant Anoushka, but Katya detected more when he added, 'I am sorry to be deprived of the pleasure of funding VJF. May I know who outranked me?'

As the others looked at her, Katya had no choice but to admit, 'My mother.'

Harry nodded. 'Thus ensuring all traces of sawdust are kept away from the business.'

'It made sense—' Katya began, only to be interrupted by Elsa Morten who, clearly bored by the drift of the conversation, begged to be allowed to hold the baby.

Katya had never handed Anoushka over with more reluctance. It would have been much easier if Harry's wife had possessed a hard-riven face and a mean eye. But far from it. The worst she could say was that Elsa wasn't the young girl she appeared from a distance. She was older than Harry, by several years if the lines at the edges of her eyes were anything to go by. Eyes the same green-grey as Harry's.

Anoushka began to grizzle. Too much cake and jam, Katya explained as she took her from Elsa. 'Oh, dear.' Dampness under the padded bottom. 'We need a sink.' Harry was talking to Pauline, offering to smarten up the old stables before they moved in, but he seemed to know instinctively that Katya wanted him.

'Why don't we all go inside? Will you lead the way, Elsa?'

'Of course, darling. I will put these flowers in water for you.' Elsa Morten had found a clump of white daisies sprouting from a channel between the cobbles. Katya thought she'd rarely seen anyone so unaffectedly happy and hated herself for wishing the woman back in Sweden.

Inside, Mademoiselle Cooper showed Katya to a small bathroom, and laid towels across the washstand for Anoushka to lie on. Elsa came in as Katya was pinning on a clean nappy.

'Such a good little pumpkin,' Elsa said in her up-and-down pattern. She met Katya's eyes in the washstand mirror and her smile clouded. 'Harry has told me that this is your sister's baby, your sister who is dead?'

Katya fiddled with the safety pin. 'She was called Vera.'

'She died giving birth?'

'No. When Anoushka was three months old.'

'An accident?'

'No.' Katya didn't want to snub Harry's wife, but this was like being rubbed down with a cheese grater. 'We lost her to the political situation in Russia.'

'Ah, I understand.' Elsa added haltingly, 'You will call me superstitious but I hate to hear of mothers dying. You see,' she touched her stomach, 'I too am expecting a baby.'

It was a well-aimed bullet.

'You think it too soon after our wedding for me to be in the family way?'

'It's not my business to think anything, Madame Morten.' Katya dressed Anoushka, tying the baby's bonnet strings. Had Elsa trapped Harry? Young men were in short supply throughout Europe and unmarried women had to seize their chances. It hovered on Katya's tongue to reveal that a few weeks before, Harry had almost taken her virginity. *We wanted each other, so much.* She swallowed the nastiness down. Elsa was no enemy, just a happy woman expecting Harry's child. *And you never strove to please*, Katya reminded herself. Hadn't she relentlessly played the princess, letting him carry bags and slighting him? Desired him, only to hiss and put up her tail like a Bengal cat. 'It's wonderful news for you both.'

A beaming smile greeted that. 'At first, I feared Harry would not be pleased. Such a difficult situation – you know of his brother's death? But life is precious, war makes us realise how precious. As we drove here, dear, darling Harry turned to me and said, "Elsa, I am happy that another little Morten will soon enter the world." Isn't that kind?'

'Kind? Yes. Very.'

Elsa touched Katya's arm, 'At first, I thought Harry a cold sort of man. He *was* cold. But now, I like him very much.'

Like him? Katya thought that if she didn't get away from Elsa's wholesome, full-milk smile, she'd be sick. Or cry again. She picked up Anoushka, grabbed the nappy bag and almost let the washroom door bang in Elsa's face. *Like him.*

That's all the woman could summon up, having married the man that she—

That I – Katya tried to stop herself but the thought had taken root. *You've taken the man I love, and you 'like' him.* This blow was no less crucifying for the fact that it was all her own fault. And Harry's too, of course. He had allowed her to fall for him. Helping her, taking her out, kissing her. At least half his fault.

Did she love him more than hate him?

The door to Harry's office was wedged open with rolls of linen that looked like the ones from the back of the Pierce-Arrow. Everyone was clustered around the table where the object of interest was a gadget with a turning handle, not unlike the implement their Moscow cook had used to mince pork and beef. Except this one possessed a pair of toothed wheels, which Roland Javier was examining with a mechanic's zeal.

'How have we ever gone on without a pinking machine?' Miryam Kaminsky wondered out loud.

Katya watched the machine cut a strip of cloth in a zigzag pattern. It made a noise like a clockwork mouse racing across floorboards, but she was unimpressed. Then again, the world's biggest diamond on a velvet cushion would have earned the same half-glance. She targeted everything at Harry, who stood with his back to her, demonstrating how to adjust the tension of the wheels. In the dimness, his hair showed streaks of salt-and-pepper, as if he'd aged since she'd last seen him.

Elsa gave a conspiratorial giggle. 'Harry? I've told her about the baby. Was I wrong? I want to tell everyone.'

'It's your news to tell or keep as you wish,' was the response. 'In time, you won't have to mention it. You'll have an obvious bump.'

'Oh, tut-tut. You shouldn't say such indelicate things.'

'Then don't bring the subject up, Elsa.'

Katya stood bolted to the spot. She was looking at Harry instructing Roland not to turn the handle quite so fast, yet the dry reprimand given to Elsa had come from behind her. Katya turned and there was Harry. Insolently attractive Harry. Something implacable in the way he returned her gaze.

He asked her, 'Did Coops give you what you needed?'

'I – yes.' She looked back to the broad-shouldered man at the table. Then back at Harry. 'Who is that?'

'How remiss of me, Princess Vytenis. It's—'

Elsa Morten squealed, 'Princess? Madame, I beg your pardon, I had no idea. You will think me so forward.'

'Not at all,' Katya answered. 'Please, no formalities, it's not necessary.'

Harry flicked up an eyebrow. 'Really? You have changed. Will you allow me to present the senior Harald Morten to you?' He called, 'Father?' and the man at the table turned. A future Harry, grey at the temples, his face grooved with frown lines. The men were almost identical in stature. Harald Morten senior came over and shook Katya's hand. He said something in Swedish.

'My father has little French,' Harry explained. 'Father, speak Russian if you want this lady to understand you.'

His father gave Katya an inspection, then did as his son recommended. 'So – you are the difficult woman Harry has been complaining about. The princess who is now a seamstress but still will not allow him to kiss the hem of her gown. Is it you that makes him so discontented and jumpy?' Harald Morten imitated his son's facial tic.

Katya didn't know what to say, giving Harry time to observe laconically, 'I've told you, Father, the twitch arrived after I was exposed to continuous gunfire for thirteen days. It came of its own accord and I hope it will go in the same fashion. It could have been worse. One of my men took to singing "Auld Lang Syne" over and over in high falsetto. When they took him away, he was still singing.'

Katya found her voice. 'Monsieur Morten, I – I like your son's twitch. Oh, and I'm a fashion designer, not a seamstress.' Who had let Harry kiss far more than the hem of her gown, but she wasn't going to mention that. She'd probably scuppered any chance of a polite relationship with Harry's father but what did it matter?

To her surprise, Harald Morten senior smiled broadly. 'A designer? Don't tell my wife…' he threw a glance at Elsa, 'or she'll monopolise you.'

Katya followed his gaze. 'Elsa is your wife?'

'Naturally she is. Do you imagine me travelling from Sweden in her company if she were not?'

'Not – not Harry's wife?' Her mouth had grown a donkey's tongue. 'I thought…'

The announcement in the newspaper had been brief. *In Gothenburg, Harald Morten to Elsa Lind.*

Harry's father tossed a comment in Swedish to his son who didn't answer. Harry-the-younger was desperately trying not to laugh.

Chapter Twenty

Harry came into the courtyard as Katya was tucking Anoushka into her pram, which had cooled considerably from being left in the shade. He asked her if she was heading home. 'Shall we go together across the park?'

Without looking up, she told him that she'd moved. Getting home no longer required a detour through Parc Monceau.

'What a shame. Don't you miss the caress of dappled shadows?'

She flicked up her parasol, making a screen between them. 'I take Anoushka there every day to see the ducklings on the lake.'

'I haven't seen the ducklings yet.'

'Madame Harald Morten seems a very charming lady.'

'She's a pearl and makes my father happy.'

He was still laughing at her. As she pushed the pram under the stone arch, he fell into step. He'd put on a light waistcoat over his shirt, and wore the straw boater she'd seen before. The effect was casually Parisian. In fact, they probably looked like fashionable young parents, promenading with their baby.

'Am I allowed to know where you're living?'

Harry threw her a look of surprised approval when she told him. He knew rue Rembrandt, of course. 'Am I to take it that your money finally came through? It's why you're able to fund your business yourself.'

'That's right. It all happened so fast.' She leaned forward to straighten Anoushka's bonnet. The baby was deeply asleep, eyes screwed shut. 'At last, we're living somewhere Mama is proud to call home. Or she will when she's settled. And I no longer have to worry about paying the bills.'

'You're a good daughter.'

'I'm not. I am assuredly not.'

'I wish you'd tell me why.'

Instead, Katya asked him about Sweden. He told her about his overdue filial visit to his father's home, and meeting Elsa's exuberant family. About travelling on to Finland to secure a cargo of wood pulp and of the linen cloth he'd bought during a side trip to Denmark.

'Linen is in desperate short supply here,' she couldn't resist mentioning.

'Yes. Want some?'

'Yes. No. Perhaps…'

By now, they'd walked as far as Boulevard de la Madeleine, crossing the wide street in front of the church where Harry pulled her back to avoid an erratically driven van. As they waited, he said, 'My father wants to work with me again. He's already found a warehouse near the Gothenburg docks where we'll store the raw wood pulp.'

'For cellucotton?'

'You have a good memory! We don't call it that as it's a trademarked name. Elsa wants to call ours "swansdown". I'm unconvinced, but my father is in love, appearances to the contrary, so I'll probably be outvoted.'

She felt his sidelong glance, his spiky amusement. 'You will be very rich,' she said. 'You'll spend more time in Sweden, making swansdown from sawdust.'

He laughed. 'My father's keen to build an empire for the coming child, who of course will be a son.' Something lay behind the amusement. Not bitterness... regret? 'If I spend more time anywhere, it'll be Manchester or London. I have a manager running that side of things, but the business is getting more complicated. I'm likely to be shuttling back and forth, growing intimate with the Golden Arrow sleeper car. It may be years before I'm settled.'

I have lost him, Katya acknowledged.

They spoke little for most of the length of Boulevard Malesherbes, but when Katya bid Harry goodbye and turned into rue Monceau, her route home, he continued at her side.

He suggested taking a turn around the park and she seized the opportunity for a few more minutes of his company. They took the perimeter path, a stroll that could easily be extended to an hour. The late-afternoon heat was cloying, offering no inducement to hurry.

Fearful of another silence, Katya probed Harry about his English business and he told her that his factory was in the cloth-weaving heart of Manchester, next door to his family home. 'Which since the war has been a nurses' hostel and may never be reopened as a house. My parents kept a staff of eight.' Then there was his fabric printworks in south London. 'A headache these days, without Christian,' he admitted, his gaze shooting skywards. 'Are we in for thunder?' The air was getting stickier as day crossed into evening, blunt-headed clouds rolling in.

Katya indicated a bench overhung with chains of yellow laburnum. 'Shall we sit a moment?' The air in the park smelled bruised, stale. Flies everywhere, strident birdsong warning of imminent change. There would never be a pain like that of losing Vera but Harry's rejection of her at the moment of her surrender still tore at her. If he left Paris, as it seemed that he might, she would never gain closure to these feelings. She took a steadying breath. 'Will you answer a question?'

'I'll try.'

'Have you ever…' she cleared her throat. 'Ever known the air so stifling?'

'Often, in August,' he answered, giving her a searching glance. 'It usually ends with thunder. Here's a question for you. Do you like ice cream?'

'Very much!'

They'd passed an ice-cream cart earlier. Harry strode back to it, returning with vanilla cornets which were already beginning to melt. He sat beside her and she spread one of Anoushka's clean napkins across her knee and his. Tiny black bugs immediately landed on it.

'Ice cream was one of the things I fantasised about in the trenches.' Harry wiped a smear from the side of his mouth. He'd loosened his tie and perspiration nestled in the hollow of his throat. In the strange, ripening light, the smattering of hair on his upper lip gleamed. 'It's odd,' he said, 'what gets you. Coffee of course and buttered toast. Cold, fresh water. And any music that wasn't brass bands or bad accordion playing.'

'What was that song your soldier sang? The one whose mind was shattered?'

'"Auld Lang Syne". I can't hear it now without shuddering.'

'Your father should not have made fun of you. You were very patient with him.'

'As you are with your mother. Do you really like my twitch?' He didn't let her answer, but wiped a speck of ice cream from her chin with his knuckle. Katya made no move to stop him. Not that she could, one hand holding her cornet, the other her parasol, which was keeping bugs off Anoushka as she slept. It would be easy to shift so their knees touched, but that wouldn't get her question asked. She finished her ice cream and tipped cologne on her handkerchief to wipe her fingers. Harry finished his and she wiped his fingers for him.

'Last time anyone did that for me, I was in short trousers.'

'Why did you pull away from me the night you took me home? Because you think I am proud and haughty?'

'You *are* proud and haughty. It's the carapace you retreat behind. Like now.' She looked away and Harry flicked her arm, making her turn back. 'I don't respond to the princess who grants me the honour of a smile now and then. I don't much like her.'

'I *am* a princess, I can't help that.'

'I prefer Katya. I like it when she melts.'

Everything was melting, including the mask Harry often wore in her company. His tic returned. 'Damn thing,' he cursed. 'It comes on when I've got more than two things to think about at once.'

'Say it. Say the truth. Why did you reject me?'

Harry frowned down at his hands; a long way off thunder-drums played. His prediction of a storm was dead on. 'I knew we would end up in bed,' he said finally. 'It's what I wanted.' He sandwiched her fingers with his palms. 'There's a moment for lovers to stop – after which you might as well try and reverse a train that's driven off a bridge. I was almost beyond recall, and you were so ready, your hair a living treasure spread out behind you.' He stroked her curls, and his hard mask made a momentary return. 'I knew it would be the first time for you and it didn't seem fair.'

'On me?'

'You were struggling to look after a family and would rightly expect marriage. I wasn't going to offer it.'

She recoiled. In his flat, she'd admitted to herself that she wanted him for ever. That meant marriage but she hadn't said it out loud. *So how did he know?* 'Is there someone you'd consider marrying? A French or English girl, perhaps?'

'There is nobody else and that's the truth.'

'Then why not me?' It took an act of will to hold his gaze.

Harry smacked a bug on his wrist. 'I won't marry until I find a woman who is totally open and honest with me. It's why I pulled away, Princess. You're not free to give yourself because of all you carry. You're like a waiter loaded up with everybody else's dirty crockery, staggering under it, unable to put it down. None of the women I've known in the past have sought to corner me. In most cases, we've parted as friends but I knew it wouldn't be like that with you. You're all-or-nothing so I chose… nothing.'

Grumbling behind the clouds warned that the storm was closing on them. Moments later, fat raindrops fell. Katya folded her parasol and got up off the bench, gripping the pram's steel push-bar. Not since her last moments with Vera had she known such visceral emotion. The idea of Harry and other women laughing, dancing, making love, made her want to retch. 'I'm going home.'

The pram wheels left skewed tracks in the gravel as Katya hurried away. Pauline Frankel had better cancel the Cour du Comte property because proximity to Harry was unthinkable. 'Clumsy fool!' she muttered as she bumped the pram against the edge of the path, waking Anoushka who sat up, grinning in a way Katya would have found endearing at any other time. Harry caught up with them.

'I suppose one of those accommodating lovers was Una?' she hissed, before he could say anything.

'Never. Una was my brother's girl.'

'That's why you help her, picking up her bills, supplying cloth for the stuff she copies?' Her sharpness snuffed out Anoushka's smile. The baby began kicking.

Harry continued to walk alongside. 'I don't supply Una's cloth. I pick up her tab only when I take her out… though she's not above putting her bar bill on my account if she thinks I won't notice. Most of our conversations involve me warning her to keep to the right side of the law.'

'And the other half?'

'We talk about Christian, who loved her.'

'But you've had affairs since Gothenburg?'

'Do you want a list? I've never claimed to be celibate. When I met you, I was a man of twenty-eight who wasn't sure he'd make it to twenty-nine. You were hanging on to life by your fingernails. We were birds crashing in flight, which doesn't make it any easier.'

The rain came heavily then, raising dust-devils from the path. Her outfit drew in moisture like tissue paper. Harry's shirtsleeves cleaved to his arms. In under a minute, water was running down their faces, their hair flattened. A cold wind barrelled in from nowhere, scouring the boughs, flinging leaves at their feet.

'Go home!' Katya shouted, 'But go the other way. I lied earlier. I don't like your twitch.'

Harry looked down into her angry face. 'And I don't like your boyish haircut but I know it wasn't your doing. Even so, you let me believe you'd hacked it off for fun. You didn't trust me with the truth.'

'And you rejected me. Just go!'

He did so, striding back the way they'd come. Katya continued on, refusing to look back and when she was sure he couldn't see her, she began to run, pram wheels spraying dirty water up her stockings. Rain was bouncing off the pram's hood, Anoushka's blanket was drenched. Katya's feet were sliding about inside her shoes and twice, she nearly turned her ankle. If she could locate the acacia trees by the gates to her road, she'd know how far she had to go. But the friendly park trees had been possessed by demons and were bending and yawing in the wind. A vein of lightning shone behind the cloud. Thunder followed, shaking the ground and Anoushka began to howl. Gibbering that they'd be all right, they'd be home in a blink, Katya raced as fast as the pram's small wheels allowed until they hit a pothole. The sudden stop skinned her knuckles. Her skirt was binding to her legs and she had to wring it out before she could move. Someone was pelting up behind her, shouting her name.

Katya pushed on until the handlebar was grabbed, the pram pulled to a stop.

'For God's sake, woman!'

She told Harry to leave her alone. 'Get your hands away.'

But he wouldn't. He pulled Anoushka out from under her blanket. The baby went rigid as the rain struck her.

'What the hell are you doing?' Katya roared. 'Give her—'

But Harry was pulling Katya, dragging her. She made a grab at the pram.

'Leave it! Run.'

One of Katya's shoes came off as she pounded to keep up with him. It was either that or fall on her face. Harry had Anoushka under his arm like a parcel, heading for an open area of grass. She folded at the waist as lightning forked overhead, a blinding flash followed by a bang and a hissing sound, like a pan boiling over on a gas stove. They looked back down the path, their nostrils filled with the smell of burning. The perambulator was a black skeleton in a ball of flame.

Katya clutched Harry, Anoushka between them. Rainwater fused them, they melded like wet clay. 'Oh God. You saved her, Harry!'

'You called me "Harry". I think that's the first time, Princess.'

'Katya. Call me Katya.'

He did, three times, then kissed her until their cheeks slid apart. Over the storm's rage, Harry ordered, 'Take my hand!'

Part Four

Chapter Twenty-One

The previous day Anoushka had turned one and today, 2 August, was her party. Katya was polishing a circular table, bringing it to a lustre with beeswax. The table and twelve chairs – in fact, nearly all the furniture in the apartment – had come from an auction house in Porte de Clichy. Harry had taken her there after Katya had said how odd it felt eating off a café table in an echoing dining room.

She'd walked with him through the showroom, awed by so much fine furniture. All at knockdown prices. The round table had caught her eye, its beautiful grain matted with dust. A set of Louis-Quinze chairs, their S-curve legs sticking up in the air, exposing canvas bottoms, had pleaded, 'Liberate us!' That same afternoon, she'd bid for the contents of a small manor house, the dealer explaining that it had been so badly damaged in the German offensive at Epernay, its owners had abandoned it. Why his warehouse was so full, he said. The countryside had fled to town, where living space was smaller.

Katya's purchases had arrived the next day on horse-drawn drays. Their rue Rembrandt apartment was now overlaid with an unknown family's existence. A dining-room dresser groaned with silver. Rustic pots, pans and utensils filled the kitchen. They'd even acquired a suite of eighteenth-century portraits, which Katya had hung in this room. She finished off the table and put down a bowl of pink roses.

It was to be a lunch party for friends and family. Harry was coming, as Anoushka's saviour. Definitely not because he had kissed her in the rain, calling her 'Katya' over and over.

Una was invited, and Fruma and Miryam Kaminsky with their brother Leon. Pauline and Roland had regretfully declined, being busy interviewing seamstresses. Georgy and Maria Filatov and their baby were the sole invitees from rue Brazy. When her mother had spoken of asking the Provolskys and, of course, 'Our dear Dr Shepkin', Katya had promised she'd write, then conveniently 'forgotten'. Of her three former neighbours, she wasn't sure who she distrusted most. *Besides, Harry and Aleksey in the same room?*

Inevitably, Irina had been unimpressed by the guest list. 'Are you including our char lady, perhaps? What about the park-keepers and the boy who sweeps the leaves?'

'I have invited friends, Mama.'

'No, you have invited social inferiors to plague me.'

'This is Paris, a melting pot.'

'I shall die before I am melted. You have asked Tatiana?'

'Of course.' Two days before, Katya had waited for her sister to emerge from Callot Soeurs. A long wait, as the autumn–winter collection was being launched and the avenue was packed with cars and taxis. At last, Tatiana had come out, striking in black and tawny-brown. To Katya's relief, she'd been alone.

'You look pale, Tatya,' she'd observed after they'd kissed cheeks. 'Don't you get out into the sunshine?'

'Have you any idea how driven we are in the run-up to a collection? Hours of fittings, not a chance to loll about outdoors. Besides,' Tatiana spoke as though Katya ought to have known, 'the last thing our *chef de cabine* wants is a parade of sunburned necks and arms.'

Katya assumed the *chef de cabine* managed the mannequins in some capacity, but as Tatiana always managed to make her appear ignorant, she dropped the subject. Her revenge was to ask, 'How is Gérard de Sainte-Vierge?'

Tatiana flushed like a carnation. 'Why mention him?'

'Because I know you're having an affair. Did you set your sights on him when we were working at the tea parlour?'

'If you must know, Gérard came here with his mother to watch an afternoon parade.' Tatiana's voice dipped mockingly, though without losing its defensive note. 'Our eyes met across the velvet carpet. I suppose you're jealous?'

'No – I'm afraid. I can't bear to see you throw yourself away on a man who doesn't care about you.'

'What would you know?'

It was tempting to repeat Jeanne's warnings but Tatiana's eyes radiated pain. Fear too. So, Katya changed the subject. 'You haven't forgotten that Anoushka turns one tomorrow? Please come to her party.' Katya waited for a look of love, or guilt. What came was a sullen accusation.

'A few days ago, I called at rue Brazy, and found our room stripped out and empty. Not even Princess Provolskaya knew where you'd flitted to, but she told me you'd come into money. *We* had come into money. Were you ever going to tell me?'

'Of course. I sent you our new address and it's not my fault if you don't respond. Will you not come back to live with us? There's a room for you.'

'A cupboard at the back, I suppose.'

'A large bedroom facing west. So you won't get woken by the morning sun.'

Tatiana visibly struggled to find fresh cause for offence, but in the end she said grudgingly, 'I'll visit when things have calmed down here. I like your dress.'

Katya was wearing one of her own designs in dark tangerine with a double row of black buttons giving it the look of a hussar's tunic. Tatiana's approval seemed genuine, but a moment later she was checking her watch.

'My lift's due and it would be best if you went.'

'Because…?'

'Gérard is picking me up and I can't see you near him without imagining you washing his mother's drawers.'

Katya almost laughed. 'Dear me. Does the image pop into your head over dinner? At the breakfast table?'

'Oh, be quiet!' Tatiana was staring towards the end of the street, searching the cars, presumably for one she recognised. 'I don't pontificate on you going to bed with Harry Morten.' She met Katya's gasp with a supercilious laugh. 'Everyone knows. Couture is a deeply incestuous world.'

'I'm not sharing a bed with him or anyone else.'

'No? Then do so, because it's stupid to have the rumours without the pleasure. Please go, Katya. I'm asleep on my feet, not at my best. I'm not sure what I'm doing on Saturday afternoon, so give Anoushka a loving kiss from me.'

'No. If you won't come, no excuses.'

'You are impossible.' Tatiana walked away, then swung round and her voice carried to the street corner. 'I'm free to do as I like now, d'you see?'

'Yes, I do, but tell me, please, because I cannot understand. Why do you hate me so much?'

'I don't hate you, but I won't be ruled by you. D'you know, these days, I find myself sympathising with Yana? You tried to control her every breath and thought. She got away and so have I. I will never walk back into prison.'

The reference to prison was too much. Had Tatiana ever touched the bars of a cell? Seen the crawling lice, smelled the degradation? *Witnessed a sister surrender to its horror?* Wanting to hurt as she was hurt, Katya hurried after Tatiana, crying, 'Your Gérard is engaged to another woman. His mother arranged it and it's a done deal.' She clicked her fingers. 'That's how much he cares for you.'

Why do I say things in anger? Katya asked herself as she rifled in the dresser drawer for place mats. She found a stack of them, chased silver with cork bases. *Because it feels good at the time, but the damage is irreparable.* As Katya had thrust in the knife, Tatiana had swayed as though about to faint. She'd pulled herself together, but the change in her face was not something Katya would forget quickly.

Her mother came into the dining room, and as if Katya had spoken the name 'Tatiana' out loud asked, 'You are laying a place for my darling?'

'I am.' *Though I don't count on her using it.*

Irina gaped at the portraits, which Katya had hung in the time since her mother had left the breakfast table. 'Who on earth are they?'

'Our new great-great-grandparents.'

'Those horrible wigs. Rouged to the eyelids. They look so smug.'

'Don't they? They couldn't guess that they'd end up on our walls. You know the party starts at twelve, Mama? Have you decided what to wear?' Katya had taken her mother shopping, at last persuading Irina to buy dresses in the modern style.

'The blue spot, I think.' Irina straightened the place mat Katya had just laid. 'You need to put some more out. Princess Provolskaya and her son have accepted, and Dr Shepkin.'

'But they haven't been – I mean, I forgot…' Katya let out a sigh. 'You asked them, I suppose?'

'I too have friends, Katya.'

Katya counted on her fingers. 'That makes us thirteen at the table. Not very auspicious. Perhaps I *will* invite our char-lady.'

'I suppose somewhere in Moscow,' Irina said dolefully, 'our family tableware is being used by strangers. What a world this is, where heirlooms are flung from one hand to another.' Irina then remembered why she'd come in: to pass over a note from Harry. He'd sent it by hand, along with two pom-pom bouquets of freesias. The kind of gesture her mother appreciated – from any other man. Irina put her flowers to her nose and said, 'Very fragrant,' as if that were a black mark against them.

'You'll be polite to Monsieur Morten?' Katya urged. 'But for him, we would be burying Anoushka, not celebrating her birthday.'

Irina said stiffly, 'Naturally I feel gratitude, but do not ask me to forget that we know nothing of him.'

'I know a great deal.'

'Then you should not.'

Harry had written to explain that he might arrive a few minutes late.

Dragooned into taking Father and Elsa to Barbizon. E. desperate to picnic by the river and imagine herself an artist's muse. I shall leave them there and be with you by twelve-fifteen latest.
Yours, H.

Mine. Do I dare believe that? Katya put the note in the dresser, alongside an envelope containing a repayment of the full debt to Harry. She'd present it as soon as she seized a moment alone with him.

'We owe that awful man *how much?*' Irina had demanded when Katya had explained that now they had the means, they must pay Harry back.

Katya had outlined everything Harry had advanced from the hour of Yana's desertion in Gothenburg. 'Without him, we'd have been hamstrung.'

'But it was his idea that we stay in that fussy hotel in Gothenburg, and yours to stay at the Ritz. Why, child, if we couldn't afford it?'

'Because every time I found us modest lodgings, you and Tatiana threw your hairbrushes on the floor and blamed me for betraying the family pride.'

'So it was our fault?'

'In a way. You loaded everything on to my shoulders. You turned me into Papa, the strong one who took the lead, while knocking down my every decision. I admit, the Ritz was a mistake but now we can afford to pay Harr – Monsieur Morten – we must.'

'A gentleman would not ask.'

Katya had resorted to sarcasm to get her way. 'I'm sure he's woefully inferior, Mama, but you still let him carry our bags.'

'It's what a gentleman does.'

'So you admit he's a gentleman. In that case, repaying him is a matter of honour.'

Her mother had muttered ominously about consulting Dr Shepkin.

'Over my dead body!'

'But if that man is pressing us for money—'

'He is *not*.' Katya prayed for patience. No point saying that Harry had repeatedly refused to take anything from her. Nor describing yet again the horror of the burning pram. Her mother was capable of accusing Harry of conjuring up the lightning himself.

The ormolu clock on the dresser read ten-past nine. Plenty of time to wash crockery, shine silver, arrange flowers and then get herself ready. She'd commissioned Monsieur Aristide to cater for the party and bake the cake. The food would arrive at eleven.

The arrival of the post threw everything out. Just the one letter, addressed to herself. At the bottom, Katya saw Leon Kaminsky's name and immediately thought, *they're crying off*. But it wasn't so. Leon began by saying how much he, Miryam and Fruma were looking forward to celebrating with them later, then came to the point.

You asked me to tip you off should I come across anything bearing your family crest. I have seen something in a colleague's window which I believe you will want to examine.

An Avenue de Clichy address was given, not too far from where she'd bought her furniture. Katya calculated she had time to get there and back before the party food arrived. 'I'm going out,' she called to her mother, seizing her parasol and purse before Irina could object.

The jeweller's window needed a good clean. Wares were displayed higgledy-piggledy; rings, gold chains, watches, necklaces and bracelets thrown together on trays. Yet again, the fingerprints of wealth being offloaded. Where, among this glut, was the thing she needed to see? *There*. A single row of pearls on a black-velvet bust. Matched stones with a teardrop pendant displaying a white stag with flaming antlers. *The Vytenis Hart.*

The man behind the counter asked twice how he might help before Katya could find words.

'The – the pearls in your window. With the teardrop? How much?' Katya quickly abandoned any idea of claiming them as her property. She had no receipt of purchase, no provenance.

The man fetched them and named a price far lower than Katya had expected. He gave a shrug of the lips. 'They're old-fashioned. And the crest, see? What use is that unless it belongs to your family?' He laughed at the very idea and Katya threw in a choking laugh of her own.

'Are you considering these for yourself, Madame?'

Katya nodded and offered a down payment. She'd come back with the rest in a few days, she said, confident her mother would agree to pay for the return of Vytenis property. 'I don't suppose you recall who brought them in?'

'A woman,' the man told her. 'It was only a few days ago.'

Katya's pulse boomed. 'Did you take any details?'

'No.' The jeweller hefted his chin towards the clutter in the window. 'If I did that every time, I'd never get anything else done.' He reached under his counter, saying, 'They came in a presentation box. Bear with me, I'll see if I can find it.'

'Was she Russian? Short and plump?'

The jeweller looked up, troubled by Katya's vehemence. 'I hope I'm not going to regret this transaction, Madame?'

'No, no. I promise I'm not trying to get you into trouble. Just, I think these pearls may have belonged to…' she swallowed, 'to a friend. What did she look like, this woman?'

'Thirty or forty, maybe more. Hard to pin down her age. One of those faces, you know?'

'Was she nervous?'

'Not exactly. Reserved. Worn down, perhaps.'

That could describe Yana. 'What colour hair? Sandy, laced through with premature grey?'

The jeweller shook his head. 'She wore a headscarf. Ah, here we are.' He found a leather case imprinted with the Vytenis Hart. 'How's that for service?' Putting the pearls inside, he attached a label and wrote 'Sold'. 'Into the safe, Madame, to await your return.'

Katya thanked him. 'This woman—'

'Definitely a note of Russian in her accent.'

That clinched it. Yana was in Paris, no doubt of it, selling off piecemeal everything she'd stolen.

Katya glanced at the clock on the wall behind the counter. A quick errand had turned into an hour's trip. She needed to run.

By 12.30 p.m., twelve adults and two babies had taken their places at the table. One empty place. Tatiana had not come.

Masha, the Filatov's baby, was nestled in her mother's lap but Anoushka had graduated from laps to her first high chair and was banging her spoon against its tray. When her grandmother took the spoon from her, she began to cry. Una gave her gold-beaded cloche hat to the baby who immediately began bashing it against the tray.

'Oh well, a hat needs to be worn in, don't you find, Prince Provolsky?' Una's eye had lit upon Aleksey as he'd arrived with his mother. She'd nudged Katya, loudly whispering, 'Oh my stars. Is that a Cossack?'

'No, and please don't say so in his hearing.'

'Introduce me.'

'He isn't wealthy, Una. Wouldn't you prefer to sit beside Harry?'

'Certainly not. When you told me – erroneously, as I now know – that Harry was married, I examined my heart. I adore him, but he is not Christian. Nobody ever will be. Put me by your Cossack, so I can keep the peace. You'd better,' Una warned. 'Did you not notice the look he gave Harry just now? Sabres at dawn.'

So Katya put Una beside Aleksey who appeared instantly riveted by her voice, warm as a toffee desert. His mother was less thrilled. As Katya handed around the *hors d'oeuvres*, Princess Provolskaya launched an investigation into Una's background.

'American, really?' she said in response to Una's patchy account of her upbringing.

'Guilty as charged,' Una grinned. 'I came over in '17 on a convoy, as a nurse, with the US Army.'

Wasn't she somewhat young to have served in the war, the princess suggested?

Not a whit intimidated, Una adopted her elbows-on-table conversational style. 'You bet I was too young. I put three years on my age when I filled in the forms. If I'm truthful – and why not be? – I've just turned nineteen.'

Harry grew slightly pale on hearing this. Katya wondered if his brother had known he was courting a girl hardly old enough to leave home. Catching her eye, reading her thoughts, Harry shook his head.

Princess Provolskaya hadn't finished with Una. 'Are you staying long in Paris?'

'Sure I'm staying,' Una replied. 'The man I mean to marry lives here.'

'He does? Who is your intended?'

'Oh, we've not met. But we will and we'll live happily ever after with a château in the Loire, a place on Fire Island – that's in my home state, New York – five children and a pair of English setters.'

'Not a pair of jaguars?' Harry asked.

'Darling, the countess took them back to Romania.' Una imitated the cats' plangent yowl and Anoushka stared at her in comic astonishment.

Everyone laughed except Irina who tried, and failed, to release Una's expensive hat from her granddaughter's astonishing grip.

Katya rescued it by distracting Anoushka with a silver napkin ring. Meanwhile, Una asked Princess Provolskaya who made her clothes.

'I dress myself,' Princess Provolskaya answered crisply, her gaze connecting with that of Katya's mother. *Vulgar*, the two women agreed in a glance. Katya shrugged irritably. The jobs she'd had since coming to Paris had nearly cured her of snobbery, but not everyone around the table felt the same. Case in point, Dr Shepkin addressing Princess Provolskaya and Katya's mother as 'Serene Highness' and Aleksey as 'Excellency'. Treating the Filatovs with roguish bonhomie while his nose drew a line over the Kaminskys. Katya made a point of liberally filling her friends' plates with fish mousse and dill mayonnaise. Monsieur Aristide had provided enough for twenty, and everyone had come with a hearty appetite. Except for Harry, who seemed on edge.

'Are we to expect Tatiana Ulianova?' Princess Provolskaya looked at the empty chair, smiling just a little gloatingly at Katya.

'Not if Callot Soeurs is showing the collection,' Una got in first. 'She'll be in the *cabine*, fighting for breath and shrieking because someone's stolen her stockings.'

'I feel sure she'll come,' Katya said. 'Mother, may I help you to some more mousse?'

'She should be here for her niece's party,' Aleksey said, a frown indicating the depth of his disapproval. 'Family first.'

'You heard Princess Vytenis say that she expects her,' Harry remarked pointedly.

'I do not require you to explain Princess Vytenis's comments to me,' Aleksey shot back.

'Family first, you are so right, Excellency.' Dr Shepkin nodded warmly in Aleksey's direction. Katya was reminded of the time she'd overheard him pulling out another man's tooth. There had been no ingratiating 'Excellency' then. Dentistry, like death, was a great leveller.

Una silenced them all with, '*He who maun to Cupar maun to Cupar.* That means, "Some people will damn themselves however you try to help them.". My former husband recited it whenever I behaved wilfully.'

'You have a former husband?' Irina asked with chill incredulity.

'Wed at sixteen. Tommy McBride was on shore leave from a merchant ship, we married then divorced in the shortest time possible. I've kept his name, a dash of Scotch is never wasted.' Una raised her glass; she'd drunk quite a lot. 'To little Anoushka, happy birthday, may she never marry a dream only to find herself shackled to a jackwagon.'

Harry murmured, 'It's customary to wish long life and happiness.'

Katya decided there and then that despite their rocky start, she and Una would be lifelong friends. Anyone able to render a roomful of people speechless must not be squandered. But what was a 'jackwagon'?

When Katya got up to clear plates, Una stood up to help, as did Fruma. When, a few minutes later, they came back from the kitchen with platters of cold meat and salad, it was to hear Aleksey interrogating Harry.

'You are a businessman, I understand?'

'You understand correctly. Textiles.'

'How sensible,' Princess Provolskaya chimed in. Perhaps the danger of her son and Harry locking horns had dawned on her, too. 'After food, people need clothes.'

'Is trade good?' Aleksey emphasised 'trade' which made Katya itch to ask him how things were going for cab drivers.

Harry answered imperturbably, 'Demand is immense, supply is the harder part. I'm lucky to have my own fabric mills in England.'

'How is it a foreigner runs a business in Paris? How did you obtain your license?'

'Three generations of meeting the right people.'

'Oh, "the right people".' Aleksey held out his glass for refilling, which worried Katya. Una drunk was Una-times-five. Aleksey drunk was a different matter, as she was only too aware. Fruma came unintentionally to the rescue by knocking her wine glass over as she reached for a bowl of potatoes.

She was mortified. 'Such a beautiful cloth. It must have been in your family for generations.'

'Three days, actually,' Katya smiled. 'I'll fetch something to sop it up. Let Harry refill your glass.' Everyone looked at her. 'I mean, Monsieur Morten.'

'With pleasure, Princess,' Harry said solemnly.

Things settled down as they made their way through salt beef and cold chicken, five kinds of salad and buttered potatoes. By the time

Katya brought out a blackcurrant tart, the party seemed to have found its feet. Anoushka bounced in her seat, anticipating her pudding, gummily chanting a rendition of her name: 'Nou-Nou-Nou.'

Katya cut a tiny slice of blackcurrant tart, but as she passed it over, Irina whisked it out of reach saying, 'She cannot have any.'

Anoushka showed off her new, baby teeth by howling at the top of her lungs.

Katya insisted that a mouthful wouldn't hurt.

'It is a well-known fact that blackcurrant curdles babies' stomachs,' Irina countered. 'If the child cannot behave, take her away.'

The baby's misery was ear-splitting, and Katya reflected that her mother had been a far kinder grandmamma while she'd been sedated on veronal. The wretched medicine had had its uses after all. She searched for Anoushka's sipping cup, which was full of diluted juice, eventually finding it on the dresser. 'There, there,' she cooed, pressing it into the baby's hands.

'Take her to her room,' Irina commanded. 'She has to learn a lesson, that she cannot have everything she wants.'

'It's her birthday. Must she learn lessons today?'

'I have spoken, Katya. And really, now that we have the money, can we not hire a nursemaid?'

Silence fell like frost. Princess Provolskaya and Aleksey exchanged looks. Harry closed his eyes briefly. Maria Filatova, who so far had said little, eagerly launched into a description of her own 'nursery girl'. 'I could not do without her. I certainly wouldn't get any sleep, thanks to this little night owl.' She looked adoringly down at the baby on her knee, adding that Princess Irina Vytenis was right, blackcurrant made Masha sick even though she was still on the breast. 'I ate pie made from the bottled fruit and the results, I cannot tell you! You ordered me, Dr Shepkin, to eat no sharp fruits until Masha is weaned. You said, "If it goes into your mouth, it comes out in the breast".'

Georgy poked his wife's arm. 'Shush.'

Dr Shepkin said coldly that he'd said no such thing.

'But you did.' Then, catching her husband's expression, Maria bit her lip. 'Or somebody said it.'

Anoushka upended her cup. The lid came off, splurging berry cordial down her snowy smock.

'Bad girl!' her grandmother admonished. 'Bad, bad creature.'

Katya carried the dripping baby to the little box-bedroom and stripped her. Fruma hurried after her, offering help.

'This party is a nightmare. I'm so sorry, Fruma.'

'People should leave their personalities at home, and Madame Filatova should tie a knot in her tongue. "What comes through the breast", my poor brother will never recover!'

Katya took Anoushka's Sunday smock from its hanger, asking Fruma to please dress the baby. 'You have my permission to take her back to the party. If Mama objects, simply pretend to be deaf. I'll put this spoiled muslin in to soak.'

'If anyone can get stains out, it's you,' Fruma smiled.

'Don't mention that in front of Mama…' Katya broke off at the sound of raised voices. 'Now what? Perhaps it will distract them if I bring out the cake.'

Returning to the dining room, she was astonished to hear, 'Take it back, or you'll be sorry.'

It was Una issuing the threat. Not the Una Katya knew. No more sweet, melting toffee, her voice rang with cold fury. She was on her feet, jutting a red-stained cake slice towards Aleksey. For a horrible instant, Katya thought there'd been a stabbing, until she remembered the slice had been used on the currant tart. Even so, Una looked ready to use it on the prince. Fortunately, she spotted Katya.

'Do you know what this *blaireau* said?'

Blaireau – badger, moron, Katya silently translated.

Harry spoke. 'Leave it, Una. This isn't the place.'

'Why did he say it, then? That Harry is a dowry-hunter. A gold-digger, after the Vytenis's money.'

'Because he doesn't know me.' Harry took the cake slice out of Una's hand. 'I should go. As for him,' he indicated Aleksey, 'I invite him to repeat those accusations when there are no ladies or babies present. He picked his time well.'

Aleksey got unsteadily to his feet, a bar of angry red across his nose. 'You are the coward, Morten. I know your story. You hide away in neutral countries. A war profiteer.' The prince lifted his chin, as though still wearing the high stock collar of a cavalryman. 'They say your warehouses are crammed with *bleu-clair* fabric which should have gone to make uniforms.'

'That does it!' Una grabbed the bread knife.

Harry put up a hand. 'Put it down, Una, I can answer for myself. I have never traded in military-surplus cloth which, in this war-weary age, has as much value as military-surplus mud. Provolsky is welcome to visit my warehouse any time and see for himself.'

'A prince,' Aleksey said, his voice creaming with disdain, 'does not care to visit such places.'

'Be damned Harry, he's asked for it.' Una raised her fists.

Princess Provolskaya scrambled to her son's side. 'Put those down, young woman.'

'Oh, sure, if Mommy says so.'

'Una,' Katya got between them, 'you're making things worse.' Harry looked in control but from the line of his mouth, and the flickering rictus, one more prod and he'd go off like a landmine. Her mother, meanwhile, had assumed her blank look, warning of hysterics on the horizon. Katya asked everyone to please sit down, then addressed Aleksey. 'Prince Provolsky, I can testify that Harry Morten's warehouse contains silk, cotton and wool from England. Oh, and some nice Danish linen.'

'Linen?' Una's interest kindled. Katya waved her to be quiet.

'He is not a war profiteer.'

Something nasty flashed in Aleksey's eye. 'You have been duped, Katya, and I will fight this man in single combat, cut out his gizzards, and drop them at your feet.'

'I'd really rather you didn't,' Katya said. 'Anyway, you're a hundred years too late for duelling, you'd be arrested for a public offence.'

'You come to his aid because he is a coward.' Aleksey thumped the table. Glassware jumped.

Something finally broke for Harry, who fixed Aleksey with an unflinching stare. 'If it's to be fists, let's go to the park.'

Una went and put her arms around Harry, looking all around the table. 'If Harry won't defend himself from the slur of cowardice, I will.' She cleared her throat, as if addressing a crowd. 'August 1, 1914—'

'Stop it, Una,' Harry growled.

'No. I'm saving you from yourself. I know your history because your brother told me everything. Five years ago, you left Paris for a recruiting office in the north of England. That same month, you were sent back to France in uniform, where you served continuously with the Manchester Regiment until you were injured by a shell and dispatched to a hospital near Arras, where I helped patch you up. They tossed you back into the fray for another two years and four months.' Una turned to face Aleksey. 'Any idea what that's like, Prince Provolsky?'

'You know nothing of war.' Aleksey folded his arms. 'A *nurse*.'

'I know plenty. Guns going night and day, so close we shoved rags in our ears so not to go deaf. Injuries the like of which I will not mention here. I may only be a nurse, but what I saw took me into hell.'

'My son fought valiantly,' Princess Provolskaya said, her cheeks flushing, 'and has the scars to prove it.'

'So where do these accusations come from, one soldier to another?' Una demanded.

'From Princess Irina Vytenis, who knows what this man, Morten, truly is.' Princess Provolskaya pointed to Irina who woke from her vapid state long enough to insist that she'd repeated only what Katya had told her.

Katya shook her head in Harry's direction. He returned a sardonic smile.

'We met him on a train,' Irina spelled out, as though that were a crime in itself. 'What was he doing so far from the front?'

Harry shrugged. *You work it out.*

Una was right, Katya resolved. If Harry wouldn't speak up for himself, they must do it for him. She went to the dresser, removed the envelope of money and put it down in front of Harry. She addressed everyone around the table. 'When my family and I were stranded in Sweden, Monsieur Morten came to our aid. Without him we'd have been sent back to Russia, into the arms of the Cheka. Mama?' She looked at her mother. 'He saved us and now it's time to repay him.'

Irina gave a flick of the hand. 'I did not ask him to save me and there is a line to be drawn. One must always know where to draw a line.' She turned to Princess Provolskaya. 'In Russia, there were many social climbers, no? Industrialists, foreigners, adventuresses. One had to draw—'

'A line. We get it.' That was Una.

Katya looked helplessly at Harry but he'd retreated behind the mask. He weighed the envelope in his palm and the action unleashed Aleksey's scorn.

'A gentleman would never take money from a lady.'

Una stepped in. 'Hey there, Prince, your Mommy says you have scars. Anyone can *say* they have scars. Show them.'

She must have expected Aleksey to decline, but to everyone's astonishment, he got to his feet. He bowed to the ladies, begging pardon for the affront he was about to offer and unbuttoned his jacket.

Katya objected. 'This is not necessary!'

'Honey, don't stop him,' Una countered and when Aleksey Provolsky turned his naked back to them all, she sighed, 'My blazing stars, what a torso. Pity he's a schmuck.' The scarring on Aleksey's back snaked from the base of a shoulder blade and disappeared into his waistband. Una made an efficient summing-up. 'Shrapnel fragment wounds, debrided of damaged and infected tissue. What's that on your shoulder?' She took a closer look. 'A tattoo. The Imperial Eagle? Now we know which team you're on. Cover up, soldier. Your turn, Harry.'

'Absolutely not.' Harry thanked Katya for her hospitality. 'Oh, and I nearly forgot.' He took a parcel from his pocket, wrapped in pink tissue. 'For Anoushka. A wooden train. Don't let her eat it.'

Aleksey, who was putting his waistcoat back on, laughed. 'No scars and now he has been paid, he slinks away.' Though in fact, the envelope of money lay on the table for them all to see.

Despite her frustration, Katya had felt an intense admiration for Aleksey upon seeing those wounds. So badly hurt, and never a word of self-pity. Now, he'd squandered her sympathy in an instant. She said, 'Monsieur Morten not only spent time in hospital, he was also awarded medals.'

'The War Medal,' Harry said dismissively. 'For turning up early. If I'd known how long the blasted business would last, I wouldn't have done.'

Obstinate man. 'I saw two,' Katya insisted. 'A round one and a cross.'

Una backed her up. 'He got the M.C., the Military Cross for gallantry while engaged against the enemy. Why won't you speak of it, Harry? Christian was so proud of you.'

Katya nodded. 'That's what I saw in your apartment.'

'You have been to this man's apartment?' Irina looked appalled.

'Show these good people your battle scars,' Una commanded. 'So they know.'

'I don't care enough.' Harry sketched a bow to Irina. 'I will take my leave, Princess Vytenis.'

'If you won't show yours, Harry Morten, I'll show them mine.' Unmoved by the flurry of disapproval that whipped around the table and Harry's sharp, 'No!', Una undid the front buttons of her dress, revealing a baby-blue slip with an insert of spotted tulle. Torn between a crazy desire to laugh and the conviction that this must be the most catastrophic child's birthday party ever, Katya watched to see if Una meant to keep going. She should not have doubted. Una stepped out of her dress, revealing that her slip ended in wide-legged knickers and that her stockings were gartered daringly below the knee.

'Ala-kazam!' Una displayed a small half-moon scar on her kneecap. 'Want to see the rest?' She nudged the strap of her slip off her shoulder.

'Aleksey!' Princess Provolskaya gave her son a hard nudge. Shocked he might be, but he couldn't drag his eyes from Una's lithe shape. His mother held out the dress Una had discarded. 'Put this back on, young woman! Your behaviour surpasses comprehension.'

'Not to me,' Harry said. 'Una loves to shock. Goodbye everyone.'

Katya got to the door first. He might not care what these people thought of him, but it was life and death to her. Una said he had scars and didn't he walk with a slight limp? Katya would go as far as necessary to get him to prove it.

Lacking Una's aplomb, she wrestled with her first two buttons.

The mask slid away. Harry faltered. 'What are you doing? Katya! You're embarrassing your mother.'

'And you as well?' She released button number three.

'Any more, and I will throw you out of this house!' Irina cried urgently.

'Harry? Will you save me from homelessness?' Katya undid button number four. She would never recover socially but she would not tolerate slander against Harry. *She* might abuse him, reject him, but nobody else had the right. Button five was the last.

'All right. You win.' A spark in Harry's eyes promised some form of retaliation. For now, he was the sportsman who knew he was beaten. He made short work of stripping. He was built differently from Aleksey; he was stockier, broader shouldered. As he showed his back, there were murmurings of dismay.

'You like it, my map of the Balkans?' Scars clustered across his mid-back, attesting to the surgeon's knife.

'Damned shrapnel,' Una said. 'Caught when a shell exploded thirty feet away. Satisfied, Prince?'

Aleksey Provolsky muttered something. The men's eyes met. They nodded. Honour satisfied.

'Might we all get dressed?' Princess Provolskaya suggested.

'And cut the cake?' Fruma Kaminsky pleaded. She still held Anoushka in her arms. 'The little one is falling asleep.'

Katya made herself decent, then went to Harry who was doing up his shirt buttons. 'I had no idea it was so bad.'

'Had we woken up together in morning light, you'd have seen the mess I am. But we never will.' He shook her hands away when she tried to help him with his collar, then glanced at Katya's mother. 'You can't leave her, or Anoushka, and to be in a household where I'm considered good only for bag carrying is not the life I want.'

She gripped his arms. 'You have to understand Mama. She's—'

'A child of her time. Unfortunately, her time is overlapping with mine. She's not the only one who draws lines, Katya. In time you'll start believing her.'

'Never.' Behind her, Fruma and Miryam were fussing over the cake, asking if any gentleman had a match for the candle. 'I won't,' she insisted.

'Yet I've heard you voice the same opinion,' Harry said bleakly. 'You are, after all, a Vytenis princess.'

'I don't care about that any longer.'

'I'm not so sure. Tell me the secret you brought to Paris. What happened back in Russia?'

'Please Harry, it's time to make wishes for Anoushka.'

He kissed her hand. 'Goodbye, Katya.'

It would have been a chilling exit, but the door was flung open before he got to it. Two people stumbled in. A man supporting a girl clad in a dress of black and tawny-brown.

Irina let out a cry, 'Tatya! My darling. What is wrong with you?'

Katya saw Tatiana pass a hand across her face, then sag, her knees buckling. Her companion tried to hold her, but she crumpled at his feet. He stepped back, realising only then that the room was full of people. He cleared his throat. He was rakishly thin, with haughty features and an aquiline nose. Katya had no trouble guessing that she was finally meeting Gérard de Sainte-Vierge.

He told them that Tatiana had collapsed at work as she arrived for the afternoon parade, complaining of a fever. 'I took her to her family doctor on rue Brazy, but he wasn't helpful.'

Dr Shepkin flushed and muttered, 'I don't know what the fellow means.'

'I'm sorry for Tatiana,' Sainte-Vierge continued, 'but my responsibility ends here. I pray she gets well.'

Then he was gone.

Dislike set aside, Harry and Prince Provolsky carried Tatiana to the drawing room, laying her on a sofa. Everyone followed, the cake forgotten.

'She was pale and tired when I saw her the other day,' Katya fretted. 'Look how pink her forehead is. Doctor?'

'Her breathing isn't good.' Harry stood aside to let Dr Shepkin through.

The doctor felt for a pulse, then put his ear to Tatiana's chest. Opened one of her closed eyelids and uttered the dreaded two words:

'Spanish flu.'

Chapter Twenty-Two

The Filatovs went first. Maria cried, 'My baby!' and her husband bustled her out. Seeing how wretched Leon Kaminsky looked, having lost his wife and son to the epidemic, Katya suggested he leave. 'Fruma, will you take Anoushka with you? I'll come for her later.'

Princess Provolskaya backed away when Katya came near, explaining breathlessly, 'If it were myself alone, I would stay, but Aleksey has been less exposed. Besides, I have my piano pupils. What if I were to pass the disease to one of them?'

'Of course you must leave.' As doors closed behind them, Katya went to the kitchen to fill a bowl with cool water. Her mother joined her, pleading, 'Tell me what to do.'

Katya gave her the bowl and a cloth. 'Bathe her forehead and Mama, no tears. Tatiana needs to know she's in capable hands.'

In the dining room, where she went looking for napkins to use as compresses, she found Una getting back into her dress.

Una said, 'It feels tawdry now even if it was fun at the time. Hey, don't despair. The flu's on its last legs, honestly. Most people are surviving now, and your sister's young and strong.'

'And heartbroken. Or she will be.'

'The *parfit gentil* knight who hoiked her over the threshold? Not worth a bean. Did you have it already?'

For a second, Katya thought Una meant heartbreak. 'The flu? No, we all escaped till now.'

'You are probably vulnerable then. Your mother ought to do the nursing, as she's more likely to have built up resistance.'

Katya shook her head. 'Mama never knows what to do. I must stay.'

'No, honey, I'll stay.' Una shook down the hem of her dress. 'I went down in the first sweep, when it wasn't too severe. Harry too – half his unit had it before they knew what it was.' She followed Katya to the drawing room where they found Dr Shepkin explaining that he could do nothing for the patient without his medical bag.

Harry offered to fetch it for him. 'My car's outside, or if you think Tatiana would be better off in hospital, I'll drive her.'

'If her mother wishes it.'

'No, no.' Irina insisted she had utmost faith in her dear doctor.

'Then I need my thermometer and stethoscope.' Shepkin took brusque leave, muttering that he would allow 'the young American girl' to take care of Tatiana in the meantime.

'He was in a hurry to go,' Una observed as the door closed behind him, adding, 'I don't need a thermometer to tell us your sister's on fire. Any ice in the kitchen?'

Their lunch had arrived on layers of crushed ice. At Una's direction, Katya knotted tea towels to make ice-pillows. Returning to the lounge, she found her mother crying at the foot of the sofa. Una and Harry were bent over Tatiana. Harry looked up. 'Your sister's trying to tell us something. Can you make out what?'

Katya laid an ice pack on Tatiana's brow. 'Darling, we're going to get you well.'

'Leave.' Her sister was muttering. 'Must leave Moscow.'

'Shh,' Katya soothed. 'You're in Paris now. Safe in Paris.'

'Find Vera. Must get Vera!' Tatiana's distress brought her mother to her side.

'My darling angel, don't distress yourself. Let us look after you.'

'She's delirious, Mama,' Katya said.

Tatiana began thrashing, throwing off the ice pack.

'Let me.' Una placed ice each side of Tatiana's throat. 'We need to bring your temperature down, you hear?'

Tatiana rocked her head. 'I will see Vera. Soon.'

Irina wept uncontrollably. 'Not another child, please God, not another!'

'Mama,' Katya raised her mother to her feet. 'Go and lie down. You're overwrought.'

'I can't leave my child!'

'You can. Una's a trained nurse. Sleep, so you can be useful later. But no veronal,' Katya said sternly, 'in case we need to wake you.'

Tatiana was still rambling when Katya knelt beside her again.

'She says the doctor's woman sent her away. Any idea?' Harry asked.

Katya frowned. 'The doctor has a cleaning woman. I spoke to her once, through a locked door. She wouldn't be authorised to turn a patient away.'

'Of course not,' Una agreed.

Glancing towards the door, Harry muttered, 'Shepkin ought to have taken my offer of a lift. You'd have thought a doctor would understand urgency.'

Tatiana was mumbling again about the doctor's woman. 'Sent me away.'

'Who is this woman?' Una demanded. 'She needs to be shot.'

Katya frowned. 'Some months ago, I came home late from the Easter vigil at Saint Alexander Nevsky and saw the doctor with a woman. They were on the balcony, at the top of the building. I couldn't see their faces, but I thought at the time she was more than just the domestic help.'

'In the shadows at dead of night,' Harry said.

Katya nodded. 'When I first saw her, it was in church and she was on her knees, praying. Wearing a red scarf. I thought she was Yana.' Jamming her fists to her temples, Katya exclaimed in frustration.

'Leave it for now,' Harry advised.

'Vera,' Tatiana was saying. 'I will see Vera soon. Turned me away.'

'Who turned you away?' Harry gently asked. But Tatiana's eyes were closing again. 'It could have been on Shepkin's orders,' he said. 'If Tatiana got to his surgery before he set out to come here, he might have refused to treat her. Did that scoundrel sit at your table, and look at Tatiana's empty chair all through the meal?'

Una disagreed. 'Your timing's off, Harry. Her boyfriend said she collapsed as she arrived for the parade at Callot Soeurs. It begins at three, more or less, and the girls get there with an hour to spare. That means we were all here, eating, when she was taken ill, Shepkin included. I didn't take to the man, but even so—' she broke off. Tatiana was muttering again. 'What are you telling us, darling? More about this Vera-person?'

Katya held her breath. What came next brought a chilling spectre into the room.

Tatiana rasped, 'Vera is alive.'

Chapter Twenty-Three

Had he ever seen Katya this tormented, Harry asked himself? He watched her back away from the couch. He went to her and took her wrist. 'Breathe, before you pass out. Katya?' Beneath his fingers, her pulse was hectic. 'From what you've told me in the past, it isn't possible that your sister Vera is alive. Tatiana's rambling. Why are you so afraid?'

She stared at him blankly.

He went on, 'You're afraid she might be? Or of something somebody knows?'

The life sprang back into her. 'Get away from me, Harry.'

'Not until you've told me. What really became of Vera?'

'What is this?' Irina swayed in the doorway, a glass of water in her hand. She lanced hatred at Harry. 'How dare you speak Vera's name? She is dead.'

'Your daughter Tatiana says different.'

'Harry, don't,' Katya warned. No sweetness in her voice now, no loving concern. She looked ready to strike at the next person who spoke.

Irina came in and stopped in front of Katya. 'You went to the Lubyanka, you saw her body.' She pulled out Vera's ring from inside her clothing. 'You took this from her. You told me so and it broke my heart.'

'Any aspirin in the house?' Una was trying to bring normality back to the proceedings. 'Peppermint tea, feverfew? We want to tone down Tatiana's fever, not ramp it up.'

In a single, extreme effort, Tatiana rose to a sitting position on the couch. She pointed at her sister. 'Katya ran away and left Vera to die. Vera was alive and Katya abandoned her. Katya saved herself.'

Harry found Katya in the kitchen, in front of an open cupboard, rifling through the shelves. She was repeating, 'Feverfew. We have it, from when Mama was ill. Here – no. That's camomile. Feverfew. Where is it, where is it?'

He set the kettle to boil and waited. He'd learned how to slow his pulse in the trenches, saving the energy-surge for the moment the whistles blew. Had his princess, his Katya, left a sister to her fate in the Lubyanka? The irony was not lost on him that he'd spent months fighting off slurs of cowardice from her family, only to want to protect her from the same. 'What have you to say for yourself?'

Her hand pounced on a packet wedged behind a jar of dried peas. She said in triumph, 'Knew we had it. Would you—' Noticing steam rising from the kettle's spout, she frowned, then said, as if reciting lines, 'Tatiana will recover. The epidemic has almost worn itself out. She'll be sick awhile, but she will be all right.' She slowed, like a gramophone record running down. 'I cannot believe what that man did.'

'You mean the gallant Dr Shepkin?'

'No, Gérard de Sainte-Vierge.' She spoke as if he ought to have known. 'Tatiana's lover. Times like this, I wish I had a brother. Sainte-Vierge deserves to be publicly whipped.'

'Katya, stop stalling.'

She stared at him, her eyes enormous blue daubs. He put his arms around her, his lips to her forehead. 'You told me, clearly as you're standing here: Vera is dead, her little girl is motherless. Is that not true? If you left Vera in Moscow, it's because you had to, right?'

She pulled open a drawer, and he didn't see why until there was a knife in her hand. An instant later, he was wrestling the blade from her knowing she'd been about to take it to her wrist. 'What the hell, Katya?'

'Push me, Harry, I will do it! You don't know what you're meddling with.'

'I know you're hiding something. Your reaction is screaming "guilt".' He slammed the knife back in the drawer. 'Stop the histrionics and tell me. Is Vera alive or dead?'

'Leave my home. Just go, Harry.' She shoved him towards the door. 'Go, or I swear I will kill myself. You said once that you couldn't bear knowing that your brother was dead. I didn't make you talk about him, did I? And yet you plague me for "truth". I let you kiss me, to help you bury the feelings. Return the favour by leaving me alone or my blood will be on your hands.'

Bewildered, enraged, he left her. In the drawing room, he told Una he was going to chase up the doctor. He asked Irina for directions to the surgery, saying before he left, 'Go help your daughter.'

'I am helping.'

'Not that daughter. The other one, who also needs you.'

On rue Brazy, Harry stopped outside Dedushka's Café. He'd come for Shepkin but would be equally content to confront the doctor's mystery woman. He didn't care a fig for other people's covert relationships.

What he wanted was to know who had planted wild and dangerous information into Tatiana Vytenis's fevered mind.

Through the café window, he saw Shepkin. The doctor was seated opposite a stranger to Harry, a craggy-featured man. A carafe of red wine sat on the table between them. There was something familiar about the domed hat the stranger wore high on his head. The passenger inside Aleksey Provolsky's cab had worn a hat very much like it, the night Harry had taken Katya to the Rose Noire. There had been a woman passenger in the cab too, he recalled. Heavily veiled.

Harry walked into the café, unseen by the men who were deep in conversation in Russian. It gave them both a fright when he said, also in Russian, 'Can't find your bag, doctor?' Resting his knuckles on the table, he put his face between the two of them. 'If you don't get yourself to rue Rembrandt and take care of that girl, I'll make sure you're kicked out of your profession!'

He walked out, not bothering to see what Shepkin did, reckoning Tatiana Vytenis was safer in Una's care anyway. How about a house call of his own? It was unlikely he'd encounter 'the doctor's woman' in public, given that she'd taken such pains to remain incognito for weeks or even months. One glance would tell him whether the woman was the runaway maid, Yana, or yet another stranger. Whoever she was, she might know something of the secret corroding Katya's heart.

Irina had advised him that the doctor's door was always wedged open. And so it was. He glanced at the plaque screwed to the wall. Just Shepkin's name, no title, no letters. Harry had gleaned that this was an unregulated practice, for a community finding its feet. An impression that solidified as he went upstairs between walls of dimpled paintwork. On the third floor he came across a door marked WAITING ROOM/CLINIC in French and Russian. As he grasped the handle, he heard people talking inside and he stayed where he was. A woman was speaking:

'... stay here until we're sure.' An older woman, a familiar voice – used to giving orders. 'I will not lose you, Alyosha, and I cannot afford to fall sick either. Not when I have two pupils about to take their entry to the *conservatoire*.'

Princess Provolskaya. She was a piano teacher, wasn't she?

A second voice: 'Mother, I need to work. I'm not sick.'

So, 'Alyosha' was Aleksey, the same way that he'd been 'Harry-kins' to his mother, until he'd threatened to run away if she didn't stop. Prince Provolsky shouldn't be thinking of driving after all the wine he'd downed at lunch. Harry checked his watch. It was a few minutes to four.

Aleksey was still speaking: 'It is highly unlikely we could contract anything from a few seconds' exposure.' When he added irritably, 'And don't call me Alyosha,' Harry almost laughed out loud.

'What a stupid, selfish thing to do,' his mother then declared, 'bringing a sick girl into a room full of people. Babies too. My opinion of Ekaterina Vytenis has tumbled today.'

'How was she to know that her sister would be delivered like a pile of washing?'

Princess Provolskaya made a noise of disdain. 'If you ask me, money has flown to those women's heads. Did you look at the furniture? What do three skinny creatures want with a sofa that could seat six? And those absurd portraits – think what the money could do for our cause.'

'We won't speak of it now,' her son slurred. 'The others will take care of everything.'

'*The others…*' The wine-quaffers? In the café, while waiting for his moment to interrupt, Harry had overheard Shepkin's craggy companion say, 'I have sown the seeds, Shepkin. We act now, today, while the women are weak from shock. Checkmate them, before the pieces shift on the board.'

Chess? A cruel game if you hadn't been taught the rules. Harry heard an approaching step. A moment later a woman was asking, 'Can I help you, Monsieur?'

French, but the voice held the trace of a Russian accent.

'I'm not sure, Madame.' He turned and knew instantly that he was not looking at Katya's missing maid-servant. This woman was in her late forties, a duster knotted around her head, a crossover apron cancelling out her shape. She carried a bulging laundry sack, which must have been heavy as she was bowed sideways by it. Yes, a candidate to be the 'doctor's woman' with her intelligent, if inscrutable, stare. Was she the one he'd glimpsed in Prince Provolsky's taxi? Hard to say…

Harry fired off a question he hoped would throw her. 'Does someone called Yana live here?'

'Who wants to know?'

'Princess Ekaterina Vytenis. Yana worked for her family and stole valuables during a journey from Moscow, leaving them without money. The princess wants to speak with her.'

'I should imagine so. This Yana, you believe she is in this part of Paris?'

'It's possible.'

The woman spread her arms. 'You understand, many people come and go in this building.'

'Of course, but this is a tight-knit community. You see everything.'

'Not so. I don't go about much. Always too busy with my chores.' The canvas sack slipped from her grasp, landing with a thump that suggested it was filled with more than sheets and shirts. She covered the moment by asking, 'You wish to see Dr Shepkin?'

'No. It's you I've come to see. A patient was brought in earlier today with suspected influenza. Tatiana Vytenis?' His eyes bored into hers, hunting for a reaction.

'Means nothing to me.'

You're good, he thought. *You know how to lie.* 'Unfortunately, she was sent away. Did the doctor hold his surgery this morning?'

'Of course.' The woman raised her eyebrows, setting the time limit on her patience. 'There is a surgery every morning except Sunday, but on this occasion we closed early as Dr Shepkin had a social engagement.'

'"We" closed early?'

A fractional pause. 'Dr Shepkin finished early and I shut the door behind him. I have no authority in this place, I simply do as I'm told.'

'So you did not turn Tatiana Vytenis away when she was brought here?'

'I have already said, the name—'

'Means nothing to you.' Harry looked up at the ceiling, gathering his thoughts while allowing the woman's anxiety to ripen. She was guarding something. He mused out loud, 'If I were to go to the café downstairs, somebody there might confirm that a girl was brought in with suspected influenza. It's the sort of thing that's hard to keep quiet, it scares people.' He swung his gaze back to the woman, catching her change of expression.

She gave a strained smile that showed too much of her teeth. 'Now I recall, a young lady was brought in, as you say. Only "suspected influenza", mind. You said "Vytenis"… that is what confused me.

The name Tatiana Ulianova was given. Poor creature was rambling and refused to let the doctor help her. I advised the gentleman with her to take her home, or to a hospital.'

'What time was this?'

'About two thirty this afternoon, perhaps a little later.'

When Dr Shepkin had been tucking into his lunch in Katya's dining room. Una had been right. Yet Harry had just heard this woman say that Tatiana 'refused to let the doctor help her'. Curious.

'What exactly do you want, Monsieur?'

'To know how a doctor can be in two places at once. And to find whoever told Tatiana Vytenis that the sister everyone believed to be dead is still alive.' Harry felt instinctively that the mother and son behind the waiting-room door were listening to every word. 'Did you do that cruel thing, Madame?'

'I may have. Call it "making conversation". Tatiana has a sister – another sister – who talks in her sleep. She also sings when she thinks nobody is listening.'

Harry went cold. 'Go on.'

'No more to say.' The woman shrugged.

Before he could ask more, the surgery door was flung open, sending him sprawling. Breaking his fall on the laundry bag was like crashing into bricks. He saw why as he got painfully to his feet. Inside, among a bundle of used sheets, was another bag. A grubby yellow one that stank of mothballs. Harry pointed to it. 'That belongs to Katya Vytenis, Madame. Perhaps you'll explain why you have it?'

Behind him, a voice growled, 'Shut up and turn around.'

Harry did so.

'Cornered.' Aleksey Provolsky gave a winner's smile.

The corridor was narrow, ill-lit and Harry's hands had taken the brunt of his fall. On the plus side, the prince was easily a bottle of wine drunker than he was. And Aleksey's mother was showing every sign that she'd fling herself between them if things got nasty. Harry tacitly invited his opponent forward, saying, 'You and your mother have an unhealthy interest in the Vytenis family money.'

Aleksey Provolsky's answer was a straight-arm punch, catching Harry low in the stomach. Harry doubled over. A second blow followed, a brutal elbow jab to the side of his neck. As he retched, Harry was aware of feet hammering up the stairs behind him. A moment later, a man was demanding in furious Russian, 'What the hell, what the hell?'

Harry tried to turn round to face this new threat, but Princess Provolskaya had grasped his collar, pulling him off balance. She cried urgently, 'Doctor! This man has been asking questions about the Vytenis girls.'

'Find my medical bag,' came the reply, rough and deep. 'Bring it to me and I will do what needs to be done. As for our curious friend—'

Pain splashed behind Harry's eyes as a heavy object smashed against the back of his skull. After that, it was a dive into black soup where his thoughts dissolved.

Chapter Twenty-Four

It was almost quarter to five and Katya had been ringing Harry's doorbell for twenty minutes. His shutters were pinned back, but they always were, so she had no way of telling if Harry was ignoring her or was elsewhere. She'd left Una with Tatiana, but Katya knew she couldn't trespass on the other woman's kindness for much longer. Her dress was sticking to her. Thunderbugs and midges couldn't keep away from her. The day would close with another storm if the massing clouds were anything to go by.

All Katya knew was that finding Harry, humbling herself, even running into the jagged wall of his anger, was better than losing him. He had to understand that the vow she'd made to her father had pushed her to a savage choice. The second, secret vow, made to Vera, was a closed book. 'After all,' she argued as she leaned her finger on Harry's bell one last time, 'he could have let me throw myself on the rail track and find peace, but he didn't. So now he has to put up with the consequences.'

He wasn't at home, and though she could have walked to Cour du Comte and looked for him there, she had to go home and relieve Una.

*

As she let herself in at rue Rembrandt, Una poked her head out of a bedroom door. They'd carried Tatiana into Katya's own room and made her comfortable. 'Oh, honey, your face says it all. No Harry?'

Katya shook her head bleakly. There was some comfort awaiting her in her own bedroom, however. Her sister's cheeks carried a healthier tinge. 'Did the doctor ever come?'

'About forty minutes ago, but your mother dealt with him. I stayed behind this door, afraid I might say something ill-suited to a humble former nurse. He brought aspirin and the good news is, our patient's temperature is down to 101 degrees. Tatiana will pull through. I was able to tell your mother so before she went out.'

Katya was laying the back of her hand on Tatiana's forehead as Una's words caught up with her. 'Mama's gone out?'

'Uh-huh. With the doctor some place. She left a note on the dining table. Are you happy to take over now? I'm meant to be having dinner out and I need to go home and change. If Tatiana's temperature spikes—'

'Sorry. Wait, please.' Katya rushed into the dining room. Irina had used the envelope containing Harry's money on which to write her note. The money was gone. Sick with dread, Katya read what her mother had written:

Katya, our dear friend the doctor has brought such wonderful news that I can hardly write. I fear I am dreaming. Our beloved Vera is <u>alive</u>…

That last word was underlined three times.

…and in France. I am fetching her home.

No. No, that was not possible. Katya read on, noticing how her mother's writing deteriorated the nearer it came to the end.

Our dear, dear friend is taking me to collect her, and I am ready to pay all the money in the world for one kiss from Vera.

All the money. Sirens wailed in Katya's head.

The people who escorted her from Russia have done so at their own expense and, of course, must be repaid immediately.

'Oh, sweet mother of God.' Katya ran to her mother's room and from under the bed pulled out a suitcase where they kept their cash, identity papers and, crucially, the passbook her mother took to the Franco-Russe bank whenever she wanted to withdraw money. Ten thousand francs, cash flow for Maison Javier, had gone and so had the passbook.

She stumbled into her own room. 'Una, my mother's been duped.'

Una put a finger to her lips. 'Hospital rules, please. What's up?'

Katya outlined the situation. 'Did Mama say anything to you before she went?'

'Nothing I could understand – she was talking about bringing home her daughter. I thought she meant you. She was rabbiting that the doctor was waiting in a taxi…' Una raised her brows. 'You don't think Dr Shepkin's taking advantage of her state of mind and getting payment before treating Tatiana?'

'I fear it's worse than that. They've taken money from here and they could be on their way to get the rest. Una, what shall I do? If only Harry were here.'

'I second that. It's not only bag-carrying Harry's good at.'

'I have to get to the bank... will it still be open?' Katya could hardly read the clock, her mind in ten different places. Una told her it was 5.10 p.m. That meant her mother and the doctor had had almost an hour's advantage.

'If it's any help,' Una said, 'she took what looked like an empty knitting bag.'

'For stowing cash, what else?' A moan from Tatiana took Katya to the bedside. She lifted a limp hand to her lips. 'Darling Tatya, I'm sorry it took the flu to bring you back, but I'm glad you're home. Una will take care of you a while longer.'

'Una has a date,' came from the other side of the bed.

Katya sent a pleading look. 'I wouldn't ask, but we could end up bankrupt. Roland Javier and Pauline Frankel are hiring seamstresses on the expectation of my investment.'

'Well, since it's them. But you owe me a magnum of my favourite brut rosé.'

'Two magnums.'

'And a dress, honey. First pick. Go find your mother.'

Katya arrived at the bank to find it firmly closed. She immediately set off for the only other place she could think of: Dr Shepkin's practice on rue Brazy.

Chapter Twenty-Five

In the trenches, Harry had discovered pocket-sized *ouvre-boites*. Tiny can openers, invented by a Frenchman, sharp enough to de-gut any ration tin, or even to rip into a shell casing. It felt to Harry that the tool was currently at work on his skull. His face was mashed into a none-too-clean sofa. *God rot Shepkin.* As he thought it, he heard the man's voice above him.

'You are awake, I thank God. Does it hurt?'

Harry swore. 'What d'you think? Help me turn over.'

Hands slid under his ribs, giving him enough leverage to swing his legs around and sit against the sofa back. As his focus sharpened, he saw Dr Shepkin standing awkwardly in front of him, his stance that of a bear unsure whether to attack or flee. Harry glanced slowly about, taking in furniture, books. A plant in a glazed pot. 'Your private room?'

Shepkin nodded. 'You had a fall.'

'I was hit,' Harry closed his eyes, marshalling fuzzy memories, 'by you.' He touched the back of his head, and his fingers came back bloodied. 'Why?'

'Assuredly, I did not hit you.' Sweat had gathered in the doctor's jowl creases and his attempt at a reassuring tone did not come off. 'I save life, not take it.' He leaned forward to inspect Harry's pupils. 'You feel sick? Dizzy?'

'Not sick – yes, dizzy.'

'Are you able to bend the neck?'

'Is that a philosophical question?'

'A medical one.'

Harry tried it. It felt as though rocks were loose inside his head. As the doctor probed his wound, Harry smelled alcohol on his breath. Seeing red-wine stains in the white beard, he pulled back, saying, 'That's enough.'

'Nasty,' the doctor concurred. 'Will you go to hospital?'

'No, but you can clean it for me.' As Shepkin went to fetch the means to do so, Harry reassembled the moments before he was struck. He'd been questioning the woman in the apron. Something about Vera Vytenis. Alive or dead? And then… wham! Illegal blows had floored him. Harry fancied he heard his brother Christian laughing in his ear: *Slowing up in your old age, Harald!*

The doctor came back with lint strips and a bowl of water that smelled strongly surgical.

'This will sting, my friend,' Shepkin warned.

'I'm not your damn friend.' It did, though. Like a hatful of bees. 'You neglected your duty to Tatiana Vytenis. Drinking, instead of returning to help her.'

'I, drinking? You are mistaken.'

'You and a fellow in a hat, in Dedushka's.'

'I took wine with the patron, Georgy Filatov, while advising him on keeping his child safe from the danger of infection.'

'I know what Filatov looks like. You were with a man I once saw in Aleksey Provolsky's cab.'

'You mean, his Serene Highness Prince Provolsky's cab? My dear Monsieur, your unfortunate accident has caused you to hallucinate.

There – the wound is as clean as I can make it.' The doctor dropped a bloody pledget of lint into the bowl. 'May I fetch you a glass of tea? Water? You must drink, you will be dehydrated.'

'What's your cleaning woman's name?' Harry accepted tap water from the doctor. His thoughts were blowing in pinwheels, like dead leaves in an alley.

'Her name is her private affair. I address her as "Madame".'

'Never as "Mon amie"?'

'Sometimes. For she has become a good friend.'

A conspiracy of friends. The phrase came to Harry uninvited. 'I was asking questions,' he said. 'Your nameless cleaning woman was fending me off. Aleksey Provolsky then piled in, to shut me up.'

'Dear me, this is sounding like a French farce!'

'Then you came up from below and coshed me.'

'I, run upstairs? Now you are certainly hallucinating, Monsieur.'

'Princess Provolskaya called out, "Doctor!" You asked for your medical bag. Where were you going?' A door slammed at street level as Harry got unsteadily to his feet. When his shoe banged against something hard, he bent painfully, picking up a rusty horseshoe. It was the one from the street door and there was a smudge of blood on one edge. Heavy enough to have killed him. So why hadn't Shepkin finished him off while he could?

Because Shepkin hadn't hit him.

The door flew open and a woman in a dark orange dress burst in. Ignoring Harry, she propelled Dr Shepkin across the room.

'What have you done with my mother?'

'Princess Vytenis, you are—' The doctor tried to say 'throttling me' but as that was precisely what Katya was doing, he couldn't get the words out.

Harry pulled Katya off and got her to turn around. 'What makes you think your mother's here?'

'Him – Shepkin!' She spat in the doctor's direction. 'He lured Mama from home with a false promise. Doctor? He doesn't care for the sick. He left Tatiana to her fate. He's a phoney.'

Shepkin growled, 'I did not need to go back, she was well taken care of.'

'But you did go back!' Katya insisted. 'While I was out, you persuaded Mama to go with you to the bank. You had a taxi waiting.' She stalled, her fury stilling. '*Whose* taxi?'

Shepkin curled his lip. 'Why are you not at home, at your sister's bedside?'

Katya coloured, a raw nerve touched. 'Una's there. Tatiana's temperature is falling, she seems to be out of danger.' At last, she acknowledged Harry. 'I slipped out to find you.' Her voice cracked on 'you'. 'When I got back, this coward had tricked Mama, who thinks Vera's waiting for her somewhere nearby.'

'Your mother believes Vera is alive?'

'Of course, because she needs to.' Katya rounded on Shepkin again. 'What kind of man dupes a grieving mother into believing that her daughter is happy and well, in France, when such a thing is impossible? Fraud. Monster.'

'I am no such thing,' Shepkin insisted.

Harry looked at his watch, only to find its face had shattered as he fell. But there was a clock in the room and that read 6.10 p.m. He'd been out cold for over two hours! Long enough for Dr Shepkin to have slugged him, collected his medical bag, made his way to rue Rembrandt and lured Irina Vytenis to the bank. Easy if he'd had the help of an obliging, princely cab driver. And hadn't Princess Provolskaya shouted

'Doctor!' a moment before the blow fell? But something didn't add up. The last voice he'd heard before he dropped unconscious troubled him. *Two places at once.* Harry pressed his palms to his temples. His head was thudding.

Katya's eyes grew round, 'What's happened to you?'

'That.' Harry pointed to the horseshoe. He let her examine his scalp, glad that her fingers were gentler than the doctor's. 'Awful, isn't it? I met the mystery cleaning woman, by the way.'

'Oh? You recognised her?'

'It wasn't Yana, if that's what you mean. It was some female who didn't like my questions. A respectable, self-effacing type who simply does...' *as her doctor tells her.*

'Does what?' Katya wanted to know.

'Wait.' Harry threw all the emotional jumble from his mind. He mentally reviewed the skeleton facts, and there it was. 'It's obvious, really—' he began to say when a fretful voice stole in on them.

'Doctor? Will you look at the little one?' Maria Filatova had crept up behind them, baby Masha in her arms. 'She is so restless. I'm afraid she's going down with the flu. Oh—' Maria recognised Katya and made a sharp suck of breath.

'I'm not contagious,' Katya said. 'No more than the doctor or Monsieur Morten at any rate.'

'No. Of course.' Maria blushed. 'And I'm sorry for what I said at lunch. Georgy was furious with me.'

Katya shook her head. Either she couldn't remember or it didn't matter.

But Harry remembered. 'The doctor advised you against eating sharp fruit while nursing, Madame Filatova. Isn't that right? Which doctor gave that advice?'

'It was—'

At an urgent grunt from Dr Shepkin, Maria closed her mouth.

Observing that the baby looked perfectly well, but better to be safe than sorry, Shepkin ushered the woman to his consulting room.

'How silent the house is now.' Harry took Katya's arm. For once, it was he who needed her support. When they reached the stairs, he said, 'They'll have been living under the eaves. An iron bed frame and a washstand, the usual luxuries. Shall we go up?'

Katya nodded, allowing Harry to use her arm as his strength seeped back. She said, 'Once, I followed a woman to the top of this house, thinking she was Yana. The poor thing accused me of persecuting her. She wouldn't open the door.'

'And another time, you saw a couple standing out on the balcony, in the moonlight. I say that people who hide in darkness deserve to be dragged into the light. Shall we?'

The attic-room door stood open and it was stifling inside. Harry flung open the window and shutters. If he'd wanted to, he could have stepped out on to the narrowest of balconies. Katya came to stand beside him, saying, 'She's gone, I'd say.'

'I agree.'

A single wardrobe stood empty. The nightstand was clear and nothing hung from the numerous wall hooks. The double bed was made, the quilt pulled up over the pillows. Harry traced the outline of a bag on the bed. *A yellow bag hastily filled?* He peered into the washstand and pulled a face. '*They've* gone. She was living here with a man, but not Dr Shepkin. Look.'

In the bowl, caught in greasy soap foam, were the trimmings of grey-black stubble.

'Dr Shepkin's beard is like thistledown,' Katya said slowly.

'And still attached to his face, as I remember.' Harry knuckled his temples again. 'I'll bet a year's profits that Shepkin never slept up here. He didn't entice your mother from home either. I'll even do him the courtesy of saying that he probably didn't hit me over the head with a horseshoe. The voice I heard before I was struck wasn't Shepkin's. Know what I think? There are—'

Katya hushed him. Someone was coming upstairs. Her voice dropped to a whisper. 'You're saying that another man, pretending to be Shepkin, tricked Mama into going with him to the bank? No. In her letter, she called him "Our dear friend the doctor". Who else but Shepkin?'

'What are you pair doing?'

Harry instinctively stepped in front of Katya. There was no way out of this room, with Aleksey Provolsky's frame now filling the doorway. Harry's ribs throbbed in memory of that punch. The climb had brought a flush to Aleksey's cheeks, or was the lunchtime wine still in his system? Dark, up-tilted eyes glittered, passing across Harry to Katya. *Doesn't care that I could have died in front of him. Ruthless to the edge of his smile.*

Katya saw no danger, however. She put her hands on her hips. 'You took Mama to the bank in your taxi,' she accused. 'You conspired with Shepkin. The least you can do is tell me where she is.'

Aleksey curled his lip. 'You think I'd harm a woman who is going to donate to our cause? It will be the best thing she has ever done in her life.'

'What cause?'

'The Tsar and his family. A group of us, here and abroad, plan to reinstate him on his throne.'

Katya uttered the most disdainful laugh Harry had ever heard from her. 'What are you, children? The Tsar's dead. So is his family.'

'That's a dirty lie!' Aleksey Provolsky beat his fist against his palm. 'They were smuggled to safety.'

'Don't you know anything?' Katya oozed scorn. 'The Bolsheviks don't let their prisoners go. I thought your cause was about singing old songs and writing nostalgic pieces for a newspaper. You really imagine… No.' She stepped forward and poked Aleksey. 'You're not so stupid. Your *cause* is about getting yourself a shiny new taxi. And a new piano for your mother. A better apartment? Dreamers and thieves. Where is my mother?'

Aleksey glanced towards the empty wardrobe, and his expression altered. 'She was supposed to be coming here and that's the truth. I took them to the bank, then drove away and picked up a fare. I have just come back, this minute.'

'Who are "they"?' Harry demanded. 'You said you took "them" to the bank.'

Aleksey brushed away the question.

Katya sank down on the bed and a scrap of paper dropped off the quilt. Harry got to it first. It had been ripped from a larger piece and was buff-coloured, of a grainy quality. Three words were written on it, with some numbers. Times, by the look of it.

'What does it say?' Aleksey demanded.

'It says "Gare de Lyon".'

'The station?' Katya sought Harry's eyes. 'Trains leave from there for the south, don't they?'

Harry nodded. 'For the Riviera and Italy, the Alps and Switzerland. It says, "Platform 19" and "6.50 p.m.". I'm guessing that's a departure time.'

Harry checked to see how the prince was taking this news. Badly; it was clear that this had not been part of Aleksey's plan. His handsome face sagged. Harry jerked his chin towards the washstand. 'My guess is, the man who was living here was the Russian I overheard talking with Dr Shepkin in the café downstairs. You drove him to rue Rembrandt to collect Katya's mother and take her to the bank, yes?'

Aleksey gave an infinitesimal nod. Yes.

'Let's imagine he's making his way to Gare de Lyon, richer by many, many thousands of francs, having abandoned Katya's mother somewhere on the way. Meanwhile, the woman he shared this room with is on her way to join him, having stayed long enough to tidy up. Only a woman would make a bed she's never going to sleep in again. They'll meet on the 6.50 train from platform 19: the man and his mistress.' Harry tore the note into fragments, dropping them into the washstand. 'You, Provolsky, and your mother, have been outplayed by a pair of swindlers who evidently don't support your cause. Who are they?'

But the prince was gone, taking the stairs two at a time. Katya ran out and leaned over the banister to yell, 'Aleksey Provolsky, if you were a proper man, you would help us find my mother!'

Help *us*, Harry noted. He could assume, then, that her demands earlier in the day to '*Get out*' and leave her alone, were cancelled. Far below, the street door slammed. Harry flinched at the sound. 'I wonder if he's got enough fuel in his cab to get to the eleventh.'

'You think he's going to Gare de Lyon?'

'Chasing the money. He might have offered us a lift. Why do I have this kismet feeling that this day has not done with us, Princess? You should be more careful whom you associate with.'

Katya's chin regained its arrogant tilt. 'And you should go home and rest your head, Monsieur Morten. I'll go to the station in case my mother is there. She wouldn't get on a train with a stranger. Would she?'

'She's your mother. You tell me.'

'She would, if she thought she was travelling to find Vera. Oh, please let her be safe. There's no time to stop her boarding a train that's leaving in only a few minutes.'

'Actually, it leaves at 7.20 p.m.,' Harry told her. 'I lied. Blame my poor, weak head. We don't even have to hurry.'

Chapter Twenty-Six

It was a short journey; Monceau to Villiers, Saint-Lazare to Gare de Lyon. Emerging from the métro, Katya looked towards the station's bulbous clock tower: 6.55 p.m.

The station concourse was heaving, families returning from countryside jaunts. Everyone seemed to be armed with picnic baskets, boxes of fruit and vegetables, the plunder of rustic gardens. A woman almost knocked down Katya with a wicker basket of chickens whose beaks pecked indignantly under the lid.

She held Harry's hand, fearful of being separated from him. 'Are you sure the paper said platform 19? I can't see it.' He didn't answer. He'd been quiet on the journey. Perhaps her company irked him, and he was helping her from habit and kindness, which would cease once they'd found her mother. *If* they found her mother. She stopped a porter who shook his head and said, 'There is no platform 19.'

Harry sprang back to life. Gave a short, cold smile. 'That doesn't surprise me. What's the betting we find an abandoned mistress here somewhere?'

'It's Mama I'm frightened about. I can bear losing the money. It's… well, it's money.' She'd just have to work harder. 'But my poor mother thinks she's getting Vera back. What will this do to her?'

'Make her more sensible?' Harry apologised immediately. 'Below the belt, sorry. While you're looking for your mother, keep an eye out for a lady with a brown duster on her head, and the kind of apron women wear when they've given up on life.'

'You're describing the doctor's woman? She won't be wearing that now,' Katya said with certainty. 'Even domestic drudges change into their Sunday best for travelling.'

'So, we need to look for a desperate-looking female in respectable apparel searching for a ghostly platform and a vanished lover. I could almost feel sorry for her.'

'Don't,' Katya hit back. 'Imagine if somebody came to you when you were at your most vulnerable, and swore they'd seen your brother Christian alive in a hospital. And they'd take you to him, if you'd just pay them for their trouble.'

'All right.' He squeezed her hand. They threaded through the crowd. Soon, Katya's eyes ached from the strain of searching. Which was why, as they approached the departures board, she blinked and glanced away, then looked again before yanking Harry's arm and hissing, 'There. Staring up. Fawn suit, black hat. Coat over her arm.'

'You're sure?'

'Look by her feet. That bag... I'd know it anywhere.'

'So would I,' Harry muttered. 'Come on.'

They moved fast, and while Katya grabbed the yellow holdall, Harry took the woman in a polite, insistent grip and bore her to a less-crowded corner. Their captive made no struggle, perhaps because her face was thickly veiled, obscuring her vision. Or she thought he was a policeman and was coming quietly.

When Harry sat her down on a bench and asked if she was here alone, emotions tumbled from her, tears and hiccoughs bursting out from behind her veils. 'He left me a note,' she managed to say, 'to meet him at platform 19. There is no—'

'Platform 19, we know,' Harry agreed. 'Would you please uncover your face?' When the woman refused, he tried a different tack. 'The man, your friend… where is he?'

'I don't know! And there is no 7.20 train to Annecy,' the woman sobbed.

'You've been betrayed,' Katya said, almost angry to find herself moved. She looped the yellow bag tighter over her arm. 'Serves you right if he's left you. Now tell me, where is my mother?'

'With him. He is going to Ann-eh-cee.'

'Annecy,' Harry pronounced it correctly. *Ainsi.* 'That's near the Swiss border.' He added thoughtfully, 'Lots of Russians have made their home in Switzerland. He is Russian, your friend?'

This prompted a new outburst of weeping. 'Help me find him. What can I do here, all alone?'

Katya's feelings tipped beyond anger. 'Did you ever consider what this would do to us? Using my family's grief to fill your pockets!'

Harry pulled the weeping woman's attention back to himself. 'We know there's a conspiracy to steal from Princess Irina Vytenis, and the plan was put into action today. You are in serious trouble, so help us. We need to know she's safe.'

The woman put her hands over her face, screwing her veil into pleats. She couldn't say – nobody told her anything, unless it was lies. She had been used, cleaning and cooking. 'For months I hardly saw daylight! I travelled so far with him. I nursed him in sickness. Why has he done this, after all we have been to each other?'

'The perennial question, Madame. How can one human abuse the other who loves them?'

Katya, meanwhile, was rootling through the yellow bag, her fingers sliding over clothes, finding the edge of a book, and what felt like a number of small, velvet boxes. She said accusingly, 'The last person to have this bag was my maid, Yana. How do you come to have it?'

'She sold it to us,' the woman sobbed, 'after we found her in Gothenburg. We fled Moscow when we heard the Cheka was coming for us and found Yana begging at the station, living on what she could forage. Stupid girl! A fortune stashed in a bag she didn't know what to do with. She couldn't go back to Russia and didn't know how to get to France. So she sold us everything, your jewels, your books—'

'And my father's bank-deposit certificate. Wait. It was you who left it for me to find!'

The woman admitted it.

'And Yana?'

'We brought her with us to Paris because she knew where you would be staying, and could lead us to you. She sold your life to us... and then left us after we fell out. I haven't seen her for many weeks. Why, after all, should you have so much and we so little?'

'We...' Katya echoed, then leaned forward and ripped the veils from the woman's hat. The earth tipped. 'You,' she breathed. 'No. Not you.'

'Katya?' Harry tapped her arm. 'Trouble's arrived.'

Aleksey Provolsky was descending on them, eyes wild, hair damp with perspiration. With a cry of, 'Give me that,' the prince yanked the bag off Katya's arm so he could empty it of blouses, stockings, underwear, jewellery cases. Coins rolled across the concourse. A Russian Bible flopped open, spitting out a beaded prayer rope that Katya pounced on. It was Vera's, with a hundred knots and jade beads, given by Mikhail on the morning of their wedding. A signet ring was threaded on it, engraved with the Vytenis Hart. Katya's blood curdled with anger as she stared into the woman's tear-stained face. 'Anyone but you,' she said. 'Anyone.'

Aleksey's rage was drawing a crowd, men in uniform descending on the scene. After helping Katya pick up everything of value from the floor, Harry whisked her away, taking her to Le Train Bleu, a restaurant inside the station. Though far from quiet, it was a gilded haven after the emotional tornado Katya had experienced outside. A waiter showed them to a banquette seat and she sank down, empty of everything but questions.

After giving their order, Harry said, 'I take it you know her?'

Katya nodded. 'Olga Kirillova. She was cook and housekeeper to Emil Zasyekin, my father's oldest friend. I don't understand.'

'Two doctors, Katya. It's what I was trying to say before, in the attic room. There were two doctors in the house on rue Brazy. Shepkin, bumbling medic, and another individual. The one who tricked your mother…'

'Emil Zasyekin isn't in Paris. He's in Moscow. I know because he wrote to me. He's a good man who protected us from the Cheka. He was the best of doctors.'

'Maybe he was,' Harry said grimly. 'But your mother left with somebody she trusted without question. A doctor. A dear, dear friend. Would she say that about Shepkin?'

'Yes,' Katya insisted.

'All right,' Harry accepted. 'But you heard that woman – Olga, did you say? – tell us that she'd accompanied her lover from Moscow. Black beard-hairs in the washbowl. What colour hair does Zasyekin have?'

'Black,' Katya whispered. 'Always a full beard until he caught the flu, and had to have it shaved off.'

'Your family doctor, Katya. In Paris, living under Shepkin's roof. Co-conspirators, though I suspect he's scampered off with the money all on his own.'

'I won't believe it until I see him with my own eyes, Harry.'

'Very well.' While talking, Harry had been casting glances to his right. He now told her to do the same. 'But don't make it obvious.'

Katya glanced towards a table where a large family was devouring platters of cake and bread and butter. Such an animated group, it was a moment before Katya noticed the static, middle-aged couple sitting just across from her. The woman's dress, blue with a white spot, told her that at least one of her nightmares was over.

Chapter Twenty-Seven

Katya scrambled up, almost taking the tablecloth with her.

'Mama!'

Irina stared rigidly ahead. Hands gloved in cream net were folded around a quilted knitting bag. She didn't react when Katya waved fingers in front of her eyes. 'She's in a trance.'

Harry moved a cup and saucer and picked up Irina's wrist to try her pulse. At the unfamiliar touch, Princess Vytenis blinked and said in a whispery monotone, 'Vera was to meet me today but it was a cruel lie and so I have killed him.'

'Killed…?' Steeling herself, Katya finally looked into a face that belonged to a far-off life. Emil Zasyekin's hair had grown back and his skull no longer resembled a blackbird's egg. He was thinner, his throat sinews more starkly defined. Hollow cheeks were coated in stubble. Katya recalled the mess in the washbowl; trimming a beard with scissors had left a scab on the bulb of his chin. 'Doctor Zasyekin? It's Ekaterina Ulianova.'

Emil Zasyekin stared blankly into nowhere, unresponsive even when Katya pinched his arm.

Harry leaned past her and tried his pulse before saying in a compressed voice, 'Your mother isn't lying, he's gone. Is it him?'

'Yes. Papa's oldest friend. The "*dear, dear*" friend who delivered Anoushka.' This man, who had taken such care of Vera and of the premature baby that was not expected to survive. All the time, a predator. 'I showed him Papa's bank document in Moscow. Asked his advice. He must have decided then to take the money from us.' He'd followed her to Paris, bringing Olga Kirillova with him. Housekeeper, skivvy and lover. Hadn't Olga said in her kitchen, long ago, 'One never knows... traitors everywhere. Sometimes, it is the most unexpected people.' Had she been smiling inside as she spoke?

Katya let out a gasp of disgust as one of Dr Zasyekin's hands, resting on the black, domed hat on his knee, slipped and brushed her thigh.

'Get your mother up,' Harry said quietly.

Irina rose with Katya's help, overturning her teacup with the corner of her knitting bag. Katya gave the party further up the banquette an anxious glance, but they were cheerfully arguing over the last cake on the plate.

'I killed him,' Irina repeated. 'I told him my husband was in heaven and saw every treacherous act. I told him Ulian was at his shoulder. Zasyekin tried to silence me. And then that waiter, see him?' Irina pointed to a man in a black tuxedo, serving nearby, a white apron around his middle. His hair was grey, but his neatly trimmed beard held vestiges of red. 'Russian like us,' Irina sighed. 'Zasyekin did not see him until he leaned across us to refill our coffee cups and said, in Russian, "Welcome to Paris. Are you here to meet friends?" How the colour drained from Zasyekin's face! He opened his mouth to speak but the life went from him. I am not sorry he is dead. It was wicked of him to promise me Vera.'

'I know, Mama. And you do know that was a lie?'

Irina nodded. 'A lie to get our money.'

Speaking of which... Katya dived a hand inside the knitting bag. It was empty and she gave a small cry. Harry reached down beside the doctor's feet, locating a medical bag. When he saw what was inside, he gave a soft whistle. 'I've often wondered what a thieves' haul looks like.' He gave it to Katya, told her to go. 'I'll call a waiter over in a minute. Don't look back.'

Chapter Twenty-Eight

'Vagal Inhibition,' Una hypothesised later that evening when Katya described Dr Zasyekin's misfortune. She was giving Tatiana a bed bath, wringing out a flannel in scented water, easing towels under her patient without waking her. 'Severe shock affecting a major nerve leading to the brain. I saw it happen once. A young soldier – a boy, really – needed to have his arm amputated. An orderly brought up the gruesome device, like a mini guillotine, fast and clean. Poor kid took one look at it and died. I saw him… just die. People assume it's the heart but it's the nerve linking the heart to the brain.'

Katya tried to imagine Dr Zasyekin reacting in the same fatal manner. 'Could it have been enough of a shock, believing that my father was standing over him?'

Una nodded. 'If the existence of unquiet souls was part of his credo, I don't see why not. The fact is, he died. He wasn't a young man, you say?'

'Papa's age.'

'And he'd been drinking wine, and running up and down stairs in the heat?'

'Yes, and Mother said that in the restaurant, he was taking aspirin for toothache, popping them in his mouth like salted nuts, washing them down with coffee. He'd be anxious, too, because he'd struck Harry hard enough to kill him. And he was cheating his co-conspirators, trying to get away before they caught up with him.'

'In that case, I wish he'd died sooner. And I wish I'd garrotted Aleksey Provolsky with one of my garters when I had the chance. You know, Katya, I believe your Aleksey's a little bit mad. His mother and Dr Shepsky too.'

'Shepkin.'

'As for Zasy-whatever-he's-called, reassure your mother that he'd have turned up his toes sooner rather than later.'

'I think Mama would rather think of his death as divine retribution.'

'Is she all right?'

'Not really, but I won't let her have any more veronal. I believe Shepkin was prescribing it to make her gullible and easy to manage.'

'That suggests intent.'

'"A conspiracy of friends" Harry calls it. Zasyekin and his house-keeper came to Paris, to rue Daru, because Yana had told them we would eventually arrive there, looking for our cousins. They recruited Dr Shepkin and along with the Provolskys, schemed to bleed us of our money. Every bit of neighbourly help, every little miracle that fell our way, was part of a plot.'

'But to pounce today, on Anoushka's birthday, and with Tatiana so ill. How callous is that?'

'Oh, I think Tatiana's illness spurred them into action. They knew Mama well enough to believe that if Tatya died, she might lose her reason. I would then be in charge of the money, and I am not quite so easy to gull. Harry guessed the truth – there were two doctors. One operating the clinic, the other hiding at the top of the house. I'm sure Zasyekin advised Shepkin now and again. Like his mistress, he only ever slipped out at night but Zasyekin made one mistake. He bumped into Maria Filatova at the surgery and because she was so distressed about her baby being sick, he advised her never to eat—'

'Blackcurrants while breast-feeding,' Una finished. 'Know what? I'll take that advice to my grave. Hey, it explains why Tatiana got turned away from the surgery. Shepkin had already left, and maybe Olga called Zasyekin down: influenza, an emergency. Would the woman have known it was Tatiana who'd been brought to their door?'

Katya considered it. 'Perhaps not at first. When we stayed with them in Moscow, Tatiana spent most of the time asleep. Or weeping, her face swollen and red. But Zasyekin would recognise the name "Tatiana Ulianova" and he'd have known that she'd instantly identify him.'

'So he told his woman to turn her away.' Una made a face. 'Evil beast. At some level, I'd say that Tatiana recognised Olga Kirillova, but couldn't make sense of it. Something made Olga tell her that Vera was alive. What, though?'

'Because the news would have more power coming from Tatiana's lips, for Mama at any rate.' Katya shuddered. 'To think, for a moment at the station, I felt sorry for Olga Kirillova.'

A conspiracy of friends. Two doctors, masterminding the strategy while feeding sleeping grains to Irina. Aleksey, finding a translator for Katya's documents – or had he simply done the work himself? Katya had a feeling that if she ever tracked down the old translator, Tolbanov, he would look at her in bewilderment. 'Documents? What documents?'

Aleksey, trailing her to the bank, looking over her shoulder while trying to seduce her. And what about Princess Provolskaya, conveniently offering them a room two floors above her own?

The blood shunted from Katya's head.

'Now what?' Una demanded.

'My cousins, the Lasunskoys. Did they really die of influenza?'

Una looked Katya straight in the eye. 'Leave that question right there, honey, or you'll lose your mind. Now where are you off to?'

Another realisation had just hit Katya broadside. 'I have to check on something.'

'But your sister will wake soon, and she's been asking for you. Her temperature's come right down, and we do not want to send it up again.'

'Tell her I love her.' Katya backed out of the room. 'Tell her this is about the rest of our lives.'

As another approaching storm laid streaks across the sky, Katya left home for what she hoped was the last time that day. The letter which she'd believed Dr Zasyekin had obtained for her had looked genuine. But if not and the bank ever discovered… all their money might be forfeit. She ran out of the house, not stopping until she reached rue Daru. By then, her lungs were fit to burst.

On rue Brazy, the café door stood open, evening service coming to an end as it was gone 9.00 p.m. Four diners sat near the window, hunched around plates of stuffed eggs and pickled cucumber. Aleksey and a subdued Olga Kirillova faced the window while Princess Provolskaya and Dr Shepkin had their backs to it. Aleksey glanced up, but there was no flicker of recognition for Katya. The sun had set, leaving rue Brazy in semi-darkness and Katya had changed her orange dress for a shapeless brown one. In flat shoes, a felt cloche hiding her hair, she was nobody. Even Maria Filatova, jigging a grizzling Masha on her hip at the café door, gave her only the merest smile.

The horseshoe was back in its usual place. The sight momentarily checked Katya. Emil Zasyekin had wanted the unlucky stranger –

Harry – silent, so in total contradiction of the oath he had sworn on qualifying as a doctor, he had struck him. A different place on the skull, and Harry might not have survived. Contemplating the stairs, Katya forced breath into her protesting lungs which were burning by the time she reached the top level. The attic room was a more pleasant temperature now as she and Harry hadn't closed the windows earlier. Even so, how could anyone have endured life shut up, day and night, in this tiny space?

Because the bear will put its paw in a bee's nest for honey. With a grimace of disgust, Katya fished the scraps of torn paper from the washstand. Now she looked closer, the buff-coloured paper was familiar.

The answer wasn't in this bare room, however, and after a brief rest, she went back down to the ground level where she saw Maria Filatova standing at the entrance to the courtyard, crooning to her baby. Maria's presence made Katya's next move risky. Dare she confide in the woman? She'd always believed that Georgy and Maria's kindness had been founded on true liking... but now she wasn't sure. She couldn't ignore the fact that the letter that had triggered the release of their money had been handed to her by Maria. '*Someone posted it through our door. I hope it is good news from Moscow.*'

Very good. Too good.

She looked across to the wash house whose door stood open. The instant Maria's back was turned, she dashed inside. The room smelled of starch and of cold ashes. Surfaces were uncluttered but for a wicker basket full of sheets, awaiting the tub. 'Men never appreciate capable women,' Katya murmured. Olga Kirillova must have thought she was leaving all this behind.

The newspapers on the hearth were back-numbers of Aleksey's journal, *Vera*, 'Faith'. The paper stock was the same weight and colour as the scraps in her hand. Rifling through, she found blank sheets, suggesting that Aleksey had brought paper home from the newspaper office for his own use. One of the sheets had been written on: it was a letter signed by the Russian Minister of Internal Affairs, testifying to the death of Prince Ulian Vytenis 'while resisting arrest'.

It was the same letter she'd presented to the bank. Except, if her memory served her, that one had recorded Ulian Vytenis dying 'in the course of his arrest'.

There were several other versions, along with pages covered in an official-looking signature. Practice attempts that began tentatively, and eventually showed a confident flourish. *Dr Zasyekin's handiwork?* All she could know for certain was that when she'd imagined him mediating for her with the Russian authorities, he had been here in Paris. 'They should have burned this lot,' she muttered out loud. 'But I suppose they didn't expect me to come poking around.'

'On the contrary, I expected it.'

The voice at the doorway made Katya leap. 'Aleksey! So you did see me.'

'Don't fret, I haven't told the others.' He glanced at the forged letter in her hand. 'Admiring my craftsmanship?'

She let out a heavy breath. 'We were marked out, weren't we? My sister, mother and me, from the moment we stepped off the train at Montparnasse.' Though her voice remained steady, her heart hammered. Aleksey was like a two-sided playing card. One side charming, the other cold-blooded.

He gave a half-smile. 'I would have burned it all, but Olga Kirillova, she keeps every bit of paper.' He put a hand to his mouth, whispering coyly, '"For the smallest room". You can imagine, I am not happy to have my journal used that way.'

'Naturally.' She needed to get out, but instinct told her it was not the moment to challenge Aleksey. 'You're cleverer than I.' She pretended to re-read the forged letter, as though in admiration. 'Did you keep copies in case your plan to rob us went awry, so you might use them to blackmail us? "Pay up, or we show them to the bank."' She spoke as if the whole thing were rather a joke. 'Am I right?'

'Who am I to contradict a lady?' Aleksey stepped right inside the room. 'You know, it would have been so much easier if I hadn't fallen in love with you. Outside the railway station, the moment I set eyes on you. Why would you not take what was offered?'

'I never asked for it, Aleksey.'

He shrugged. 'What I am now, where and how I live, I never asked for that either. And I would have shared the money with you, Katya. You would never have wanted for anything.'

Katya refrained from commenting on this generous assurance. 'And your "cause" of reinstating the Tsar? Or was that a ruse to impress me?'

Fervour put a glint in Aleksey's eyes. 'We who have vowed to serve Tsar Nicholas will bring him back in triumph to his throne.'

So he was a little bit mad. Una had been right. Moving slowly, humming as Olga Kirillova might once have done as she worked, Katya heaped all the paper – the blanks, the news-sheets and the practice forgeries – into the stove. There were matches on the hearth. She struck one, her skin creeping in anticipation of his hand on her collar, astonished when Aleksey made no move. The paper caught reluctantly... it was agonising... then it exploded in a puff of flame. Katya stood up, giving Aleksey a machine-like smile. He was watching her, not the flames.

How beautiful he was, the corruption all inside. 'I think,' she said slowly around the knot in her throat, 'you are a loyal soldier. Loyal to a dream. Consumed by it.'

'I am consumed with love, Ekaterina Ulianova.' He stepped right up to her, his breath against her face.

She stammered some nonsense. Anything to douse the need that radiated from him. 'That – that time I overheard Dr Shepkin pulling out a man's tooth? It wasn't yours, it was Dr Zasyekin's wasn't it?'

'He was the one with the rotten mouth, not I.'

Katya glanced towards the stove where flames licked busily. Had Zasyekin and Shepkin known each other in Russia? Possibly, as the chances of them bumping into each other again in "Little Moscow" were fairly high. She remembered clearly, as though Emil Zasyekin had said it only this morning:

'*Of ten university friends who used to meet to smoke cigars and set the world to rights, only he and two others survived. Of them, one had "gone over" to the Bolsheviks and the other, a chemistry teacher, had fled to Paris.*'

Shepkin, a chemist masquerading as a doctor? The flames were sinking now, the papers reduced to smoking leaves. Nothing to be salvaged, which gave her back a little confidence. 'Had I looked over the screen and discovered Zasyekin in the chair, what might he and Dr Shepkin have done with me?'

'Nothing.' Aleksey caressed her shoulder. 'I would never have let them hurt you.'

'Glad to hear it. Goodness, is that Maria's baby?' The crying sounded colicky, which explained why Maria was haunting the courtyard. Pacing, sparing her customers the unhappy wailing. Katya called out, 'Maria!' and when that brought no answer, she picked up the basket of sheets and hurled it towards the open door.

'Nobody is coming to rescue you, Katya.' Aleksey pushed her to the wall to kiss her, his breathing gaining a disturbing rhythm. Katya forgot her resolve to humour him. She kicked, letting out a scream.

'What is going on?' Outrage from the doorway. 'Aleksey, are you with some girl? Who is the shameful creature?'

Aleksey responded with a loosening of grip, and Katya took advantage. Ducking her head, she darted past the bristling figure in the doorway. Kept running. Aleksey's mother would never know that 'some girl' had been her unless her son told her. She rather suspected he wouldn't. How things would have ended had Princess Provolskaya not intruded, Katya would never know. As Una had said, there were some questions best not asked.

Deep within the satin-black night, thunder rumbled. Katya flopped down on a bench in Parc Monceau, worn out and light-headed. It should have surprised her, finding the park gates unlocked but nothing had the power to astonish her any more. She ought to go home and relieve poor Una but she needed to clear her mind first. A lifetime had unfolded in the space of a day. *Thank heavens no baby ever remembers her first birthday.*

'Sit here much longer, we'll have to clamber over the railings.'

She jumped. 'Harry? How did you know I was here?'

'I didn't.' He'd been to her house, he explained, and was on his way home. He too had noticed the open gates and speculated that the pest-men might be on duty, trapping vermin in the dark. He sat down next to her. 'I wanted you to know that your duplicitous 'Dr Z' is on his way to Quai de la Rapée.' When she asked, 'Where?' he said grimly, 'The morgue. The police will hold an enquiry into the cause of death, but don't worry.' He'd not mentioned Irina's name, or hers. 'I was simply a concerned fellow diner, raising the alarm when I saw a man appearing to have a seizure.'

'But the waiters—'

'Were rushed off their feet. Not even the friendly Russian one could describe the lady with Zasyekin, because she didn't speak. So many women in Paris, and your mother could be any of them.'

'Thank you.'

'Don't mention it.'

Katya felt him preparing to go and she grabbed his arm, pulled him down beside her. 'I have to say it. I have to shout it. Plaster it on billboards, that you have been nothing but good to me and my family. You have taken my ill nature, my mother's high-handedness and my sister's deceit, and though you have been often angry, you have never abandoned me.'

She couldn't see his expression – he was all in shadow. Thunder rumbled, and the first drops of rain landed on the crown of her hat.

He said, 'Gratitude is like being force-fed sugar syrup. I want nothing from you, Princess.'

It was a razor blade to the heart. Strange, how humiliation had once been something to avoid at all costs, to fight against. Right now, she'd have drunk a magnum of it to have Harry turn and smile at her. She pulled off her hat and let her hair fall about her neck in soft waves. She had about twenty seconds before the rain ruined the effect. Seizing his hands, she kissed his fingers. He looked at her then, and saw the way her damp curls picked up the distant glimmer of a street light. She felt the change of tension in him, the movement of his hand from her lips to her hair.

'Let's go before we get another drenching.'

No, let's not. Katya leaned towards him and put her mouth on his. She was kissing a man who was worn out by her and would not yield. She slipped her tongue under his top lip and teased the super-sensitive flesh. He pulled his mouth away and she thought *it's over*, until he groaned her name, and knitted his fingers into her hair. After that, there were no boundaries to lips and fingers as the rain sought to drown them. They cleaved together, poured from the same vat. Only when a thunder clash offered a gruff, last warning did they split apart. Harry took Katya's hand. He ran, she raced. Laughing because it was to his flat they were heading.

Over rue Goya, the storm brought in cannons for its finale. Rain flailed against the windows of Harry's apartment but neither he nor Katya heeded it. They lay in his bed, a loose knot of limbs. He was sprawled on his side, his injured head raised with pillows, and she was curled like a comma against his chest. With sated lips, he caressed the nape of her neck. 'If I was too fast, too urgent, forgive me. Blame the storm.'

'I blame you, Monsieur Morten, for leaving it so long. We could have been well-trodden lovers by now, already getting bored.'

He ran his fingers down her spine, to nestle where nobody had ever touched her before. 'We have no excuse to get bored.'

'You want to prove that?' Katya drew up her legs and pressed herself against Harry, smiling privately at the quick, male intake of breath. She was learning her power, breaking rules, taking risks and loving every moment. 'You said in the park that you wanted nothing from me.'

'Nothing from the princess. I want everything from Katya.'

Later, as he dug out an umbrella and prepared to walk her home, he said, 'Everything, including the truth you have run away from for so long.'

As they walked the wet pavements, breathing in night air that tasted of laundered nectar, Katya finally told him. She told him how they'd taken refuge with her father's old university friend Dr Zasyekin. He had welcomed them, though his housekeeper had urged Katya not to stay too long.

'The doctor warned me that the Lubyanka never gives up its prisoners, and he was right. But when he knew I was going there anyway, he gave me something to take as a bribe.'

'Vodka?' Harry repeated incredulously when she told him. 'I'd have thought a sack of rubles would have been more effective.'

'No.' Katya explained how impossible good vodka had been to find, how men were willing to drink the most toxic brews to sate their cravings. 'It was like giving me a bar of gold. I do think he wanted me to get Vera out. He really was fond of her.'

'An investment. To be paid back later a thousandfold.'

'Perhaps.' The word was lost under the noise of rainwater gurgling along the gutters. She could make out the wet crowns of the trees on rue Rembrandt, shining under the street lights, and she slowed her step, thinking guiltily of Tatiana and Una. But even the desire to get home and see her sister was secondary to this moment. If she paused in her story now, she'd never return to it. She came to a halt. 'I went, Harry, to the Lubyanka. I couldn't see Vera with permission, so I found my own way. How nobody caught me, I'll never know.' She described her descent into the depths and being challenged by the man who had overseen the killing of her father. She recounted her first sight of Vera, the shock of her sister's rapid deterioration. 'I promise on my soul, Harry, if I could have torn the bars apart, I would have.'

'Just tell me what happened.'

*

'Go,' Vera commands her.

Her sister has the vodka bottle. She steps back, mocking the Cheka captain who doesn't have keys to her cell. He forces his arm between the bars in an effort to reach her.

Vera breaks the seal on the bottle and tilts it, which Katya knows is tantamount to suicide. She pleads, 'Vera, give him the bottle.' When he tastes vodka, his anger will die. There's a chance he will then intervene on Vera's behalf.

Rubbish, of course he will not, but giving him what he craves will buy her a few minutes in which to think of something else. If only she had a key...

Vera's laughter jolts her back to reality. Her sister is pouring the liquor into the metal pail in the corner of her cell. She is mocking the captain, who is screaming profanities but cannot touch her. Not yet, anyway.

A cackle makes Katya turn. The louse-ridden prisoner in the cell opposite beckons her over. Katya reels at the stench rising off the scabrous body.

The prisoner hisses, 'That girl's dead meat. She won't be getting out of here, she's confessed.' Unblinking eyes fasten on Katya's breast, where the baby's head is just visible between her coat lapels. 'Is it dead?'

'No, she's alive.'

'Then go. I've seen what they do to babies here.'

The Cheka captain turns, sees Katya and bawls, 'No fraternising. Get back here.' He means to come and grab her but his arm is stuck between the bars. His leather coat is so thick, he's wedged tight. Vera has wasted the last drops of vodka and she's stopped laughing. The Lubyanka grants a moment's silence and Katya uses it to tell her sister that Anoushka is alive.

'Take her and go,' Vera orders her. 'I'm done for, but my child deserves her life. I don't care if they kill me or send me to a labour camp, if it takes me closer to Mikhail.'

'Vera, you can't put Mikhail before your child. And what of us? We love you so much. You are the best of us and I won't leave you. I'll get you out somehow.'

The Cheka captain is struggling to free himself, swearing obscenely.

Vera's voice seems to come from far away. 'Katya, you're deluding yourself. I want to die. Get my child out of this place or I will never forgive you. I will curse you. You want that?'

Through streaming tears, Katya sees the graven intent on Vera's face. She knows this is the end. 'If I go, say you'll forgive me,' she sobs.

'On one condition… you say nothing of this. You tell no one that I ended up soiled and degraded. I will always be the beautiful princess that all the princes wanted. Swear it, Katya.'

Katya swears. The next sound is the shattering of a bottle on a stone floor and that puts fire into her feet. Katya runs out of that place, saving herself and the one who can be saved. A choice that will push her to the point of despair on a train in Sweden—

*

'That's when you threw yourself into my life. The life I was about to give up,' she told Harry. They were not yet at her door, but in a minute, they would walk inside together and everything would change once more. He took her hands, so tightly, and she closed her eyes. He drove a silent message into her flesh, into her soul. *Now I understand, Katya.*

August was turning into a month of storms. The five people sharing a pan of vibrant, red borscht in Dedushka's Café had lost count how many times the sky had turned black and thunder, like remembered guns, had sent people running for cover. They reached across each other for rye bread and the vodka bottle as rain lashed the windows. The café was empty of customers, so they didn't bother keeping their voices down.

Georgy Filatov used his cuff to wipe a splatter off a map he'd opened out on the table. It showed the city of Nice on the Cote d'Azur. 'There is the Orthodox cathedral, see?' He tapped with his finger. 'Dedicated to Saint Nicholas in honour of our beloved Tsar. There are houses to rent, large and cheap. I will easily find a better place than this, and plenty of hungry people to eat my food. There are almost as many Russians in Nice as in Paris.'

'And the climate is so much better. Sunshine most of the year,' Olga Kirillova agreed with nervous enthusiasm. 'You have made the right decision, my friend. Paris has become an unhappy place for us all.'

'Ah, but you are on your way back to contentment, no? Show us that ring again,' Georgy teased.

Olga obliged. It was only a second-hand one from the dealer at Porte de Clichy where she'd sold the Vytenis pearl necklace, but it was a nice ruby and weighed on her finger with the promise of permanence. After Zasyekin's sudden death, she and Dr Shepkin had talked all night, and all the following night too. She'd had to be the strong one because he had folded, afraid of being blamed for Emil's death. Afraid of the authorities knocking on the door. She'd had to remind him that this was France, not Russia. There was no Cheka sharpening their bayonets. No firing squad in Parc Monceau.

Out of the blue, Shepkin had proposed marriage and she had accepted. *Why not?* Men and women were not created to be alone.

They too were leaving Paris. Olga planned to set up Shepkin in an apothecary's shop. No more doctoring; that was too dangerous. She still had a few pieces of jewellery to sell as not everything had been in that wretched yellow bag. She'd had the foresight to stitch some choice items into the hem of her coat the day she left to follow Emil Zasyekin.

'When exactly do you leave?' Princess Provolskaya asked her.

'At the end of the month, Madame. Have you considered following us?'

'Dear me, no.' The princess squeezed her son's arm in a way that made Aleksey flinch. 'I am sure Nice is delightful but it is not Paris. Here, I have more pupils than I can teach. As for Aleksey, the problem with a sunny town is that people like to walk.' Princess Provolskaya laughed skittishly, then stopped just as suddenly. Anxiety had haunted her face from the moment she'd learned of Zasyekin's betrayal.

'Will his excellency continue in the motor business?' Dr Shepkin asked with a deferential tilt towards Aleksey.

'I drive a damn taxi.' Aleksey turned a shot glass around in his long fingers. The vodka bottle was moving by degrees closer to his elbow.

'Naturally, my son is always looking around for better opportunities.' Princess Provolskaya deftly turned the subject by asking Georgy if he had found it easy to persuade Maria to leave rue Brazy.

'The easiest thing I've ever done! When I told my wife that the air of the south would be healthier for Masha, she practically packed her suitcase on the spot! You should come, Princess. What "better opportunities" does Prince Provolsky foresee here?'

Aleksey looked up. 'Paris will always lure in my compatriots. Wherever there are Russians, there are people eager to loosen their purse strings in support of a noble cause. I will stay here until I have seen the restoration of our beloved Tsar.'

'He is dead,' said Olga Kirillova quietly. 'He and his family.'

Aleksey rammed his fist down on the table. 'You are an ignorant fool, hold your tongue!'

'Children shout when they are contradicted,' Olga retorted.

Aleksey pushed back his chair, reached for the vodka bottle and marched out into the pelting dark.

His mother went after him. She could be heard faintly calling his name.

Now it was just the three of them, they let out a communal breath.

'Thunder always brings arguments. Eat up, Shepkin, and you, Madame,' Georgy urged.

When they'd finished, Olga took the empty pan with their bowls to the kitchen, putting everything into the sink so Maria wouldn't have to scrub dried-on borscht in the morning. She would be glad to get away from this place. Their bags were packed, hers and Shepkin's. They weren't waiting to the end of the month, nor were they going to Nice, but to Cherbourg on the northern seaboard. From there, to America. Tickets, passports and money were in her handbag, which never left her side. Olga Kirillova had learned that betrayal could strike at any time, from the most unexpected quarters. For the rest of her days, she intended to remain in control of her means of survival.

Chapter Twenty-Nine

The start of a new season, 1 October 1919

Pauline Frankel had known how hard it would be to staff their atelier and get out a first collection within a matter of weeks. She knew because she'd done it before for Claudine. Recruitment had been patchy, the expansion of Chanel sucking labour into the five floors on rue Cambon. Other couturiers were growing too, to meet a surge in demand for Paris fashion from across the world. War, financial turmoil and influenza had subdued trade for five years. Then something had shaken the bottle and the cork had flown out.

So what if Maison Javier had only ten customers? Ten customers this side of Christmas would grow to twenty by New Year. Double that every few months…

They were using Harry's apartment for their opening show. In his spare bedroom, Katya, Tatiana and Una were being dressed by Pauline Frankel and Miryam Kaminsky. Anoushka, wearing a miniature copy of one of Katya's dresses, was having her flaxen curls teased into bubbles by Fruma. Anoushka's appearance at the end of the first segment would have all the mothers and grandmothers scribbling numbers on their programmes, unless they had hearts of flint.

In the sitting room, waiters dashed in and out with champagne and canapés from the Ritz. That was Harry's contribution, along with a string quartet who were playing a plangent air by a Czech composer.

'No saccharine champagne-bar pieces,' Harry had advised. 'Let your audience know they're in for something serious.'

Charlotte Brunet, who had jumped ship from Claudine's and was acting as their mistress of ceremonies, came in to tell them that all the invitees had arrived. 'Except for Monsieur Morten's father, but Monsieur Harry says not to wait for him as he is often late.'

Katya smiled. Harald Morten senior had been late to the hôtel de ville where she and Harry had married. What had begun as a sticky relationship had mellowed – she and her father-in-law enjoyed speaking Russian together. He liked engaging her on politics, she liked to shock him by advocating women's rights. She turned her wedding ring on her finger. It had become a bit loose recently. Finishing the collection to her colleagues' perfectionist standards had got between her and many a meal. Lucky that she and Harry worked next door to each other, or they'd only have met in bed and at breakfast. They'd had a working honeymoon.

'Are we ready?' She watched Miryam tie a white cardboard disk to Tatiana's wrist. It stated 'No. 1'. Coats, hats and day dresses would be shown first, numbered one to twelve. Their audience would note down any items they wanted to see more of.

What if nobody wanted to see more of anything?

Oh, come on. Elsa Morten had already tried to buy the entire collection. The duchesse de Brioude had promised at least one commission. Una, dear shameless Una, had coerced every wealthy American in Paris to be here, as well as the wives of two of her former lovers. Who, naturally, did not know they were wives of her former lovers. Katya had banked on an audience of twenty but from the buzz, it sounded as if the room held twice that number.

Tatiana went out in a camel coat trimmed with russet satin and a matching cloche that almost covered her eyes. She looked as fragile as a Siamese cat. She was over her illness but her heart had not mended, and she was often red-eyed in the mornings. She hadn't gone back to Callot Soeurs, too hurt by the friends who had not visited while she was bedridden. It had been Katya's hand she had held during the declining days of her fever. It would be too much to say that they never argued now, but since Katya had confessed the story of her visits to the Lubyanka, Tatiana had stopped being the angry child. 'Vera brought on her own death. I see that. You did all you could to spare us from knowing it. You have all the courage in this family.'

Irina had listened to the climax of Katya's story, then wept, 'She really was alive when you left her?'

'Yes, Mama.'

'Then she can be saved!'

Katya had looked helplessly at Harry who had taken Irina's hands and said, 'One day, when the Russian state allows it, we will find out the fate of your eldest daughter.'

'Thank you. You are good.' From that moment, Irina had adored Harry uncritically.

While Tatiana strutted and posed on the makeshift walkway between the chairs, Katya and Una waited in the hall, listening intently. All they heard was their mistress of ceremonies crisply reciting the salient points of the outfit being shown.

'Too much silence,' Katya whispered.

'It's awe.'

'Or… just silence.'

'Awe,' Una insisted. Tatiana was returning. 'How was it?' Una hissed.

Tatiana raised an eyebrow. Her haughty professional persona would not break until she was back in the changing room. Katya checked that 'No. 2' was still attached to her wrist. She re-set the angle of her hat in the mirror. Then, tucking her tongue behind her teeth, assuming the faint smile she'd practiced, she entered the improvised salon. The shock of walking into a room packed with bodies, chairs, hats and rustling programmes stopped her dead. Tatiana had taught her and Una how to walk, but Katya couldn't think how to kick off. She stood, one hip forward, one leg back, thinking, *I look like a woman at a bus stop desperate to get to the lavatory.*

She saw her mother, eyebrows raised to heaven. Roland Javier, standing behind the last row of chairs, scooping his arms like a conductor who has forgotten his baton. Elsa Morten nodded encouragingly, her bright, unaware smile putting an edge on Katya's panic. And then she saw Harry, lounging at the window. Outside, cherry branches filtered the low sun, casting broken light on his hair. He gave his half-smile, a shift in stillness, and Katya's heart performed a skid inside her chest. *My husband.* He tilted his head, assessing her outfit because he never saw clothes without judging the cloth, the drape. A current passed between them and her frugal smile became a beam of pleasure. What was she worried about? She was showing her designs, fruit of her collaboration with Roland Javier. She was a working woman and a desired wife. And here, within these walls, she was Katya. Only once a week, on Sunday in church, did Princess Vytenis come out of the shadows, free of the secrets that had chained her. The daughter who had fulfilled her vow, to the best of her ability.

She walked forward, undoing the buttons of her coat, pushing one edge behind her hip to reveal the dress beneath. A smatter of spontaneous applause broke out, and she laughed, and said, 'Why, thank you.'

Five hours later, visitors gone, she and Harry demolished a bottle of champagne and itemised the day.

'Applause lasted over two minutes,' Harry said.

'Roland reckoned two minutes twenty-four seconds.'

'He would count the seconds. And twenty-three appointments for fittings.'

'Of course, Anoushka was the star.'

'You did well, my love.'

'*We* did well. Without you I'd have none of this. Everyone gushed praise over your apartment.'

'Our apartment. You're sure you don't want a bigger one? Or a house, so we can employ a live-in maid?'

'Why should I want a maid? I want to be alone with you.'

'Only,' he said, 'I saw somebody the other day, begging at Étoile métro. She was moved on before I had a chance…'

'What are you telling me?' Katya was loosening his shirt, not really interested in any poor indigent. In a moment she'd have all his attention on herself. This was their favourite time to make love.

'I think it was Yana.'

'No!'

'We should find her and offer her shelter. A job, in short.'

Katya sat up. 'You want to bring that woman into our home?'

'Happy people know how to forgive. You are happy?'

'Harry, I cannot forgive her. It wasn't simply theft. But for your intervention, Anoushka might have died from lack of food.'

'I'm not defending what Yana did, but terrible circumstances make people do terrible things. Have you forgotten, you brought her from Russia because you needed her? Now she needs you.'

'It's no use appealing to my softer side. I haven't one and I can't change.'

'Everyone can change. I once knew a princess who was so proud, she thought her handsome—ouch.'

A cushion fight ensued that only stopped when Katya's necklace snapped and they had to scramble to stop pearls rolling under the skirting boards. The pearls were Katya's precious link with her father. Harry had had the necklace restrung, adding a hundred more stones to make a waist-length strand.

When they were at rest again, Harry threaded his fingers through her hair and brought her face close to his. He kissed her lips, her throat. 'New perfume?'

'Poiret's "Aladin". I tried it for free, once. Yesterday, I treated myself to a bottle.' She made a sound of capitulation. 'All right. Tomorrow, we will search for Yana Borisovna.'

As the moon rose above the city and birds roosted in the park trees, Katya and Harry promised each other that in this age of swirling change, their love would remain a binding vow. Durable, infinite and a blessing to those whose lives were interlaced with theirs.

*

Three thousand kilometres away, a prisoner shuffling back from the camp factory gazed up at the star-dredged sky. Brushed by their light, the prison roofs glowed with a pencil-lead sheen. While the guard prodded another exhausted woman, urging her to move faster, Vera Starova stepped away from her group. She raised her palms to the infinite blackness and imagined herself clasping the brightest star in the sky. Her lips formed a kiss as she wished it goodnight.

A Letter From Natalie

I want to say a huge thank you for choosing to read *The Secret Vow*. If you enjoyed it and want to keep up-to-date with my latest releases, just sign up at the following link. Your email address will never be shared with anyone else and you can unsubscribe at any time:

www.bookouture.com/natalie-meg-evans

I first visited Paris aged fourteen, an intense introduction to what is still to me the most inspirational city in the world. My mother and I were shown around by a native Parisian whose love-affair with the city began before the Great War. It is his Paris that I have attempted to re-create. I hope you experienced a similar sense of discovery as Katya did in her story.

Writing *The Secret Vow*, I've stepped back a generation from my usual settings in the 1930s–40s. Anyone who has read *The Dress Thief* and *The Milliner's Secret* will have noticed some established characters jumping in: Una McBride (Una Kilpin by the time she sashays through *The Dress Thief*) and Roland Javier, the lovable if self-important couturier, along with his loyal *première* Pauline Frankel. One of the joys of sliding back in time is discovering these characters as their younger selves. I never write Una's lines without a smile, but when I did the maths and realised that in 1919 she could only have been 18 years old, there was no way she could be the stylish society woman she is in *The Dress Thief*. I loved creating the outrageous caterpillar from which the butterfly-Una would eventually emerge.

But the story is, of course, Katya and Harry's and I hope their romance left you as uplifted as I felt by the end.

If you have enjoyed *The Secret Vow*, please let me know or write a review if you'd like to. I love to hear from readers and am always happy to tell you what I'm up to next!

Until next time,
Natalie Meg Evans
Suffolk, 2018

 @natmegevans

 NatalieMegEvans

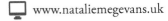 www.nataliemegevans.uk

Printed in Great Britain
by Amazon

43838991R00232